The Price Of Love
A Tale

by

Arnold Bennett

The price of love
A tale
by Arnold Bennett

ISBN: 978-93-64280-96-9

Published by

DOUBLE 9 BOOKS

2/13-B, Ansari Road
Daryaganj, New Delhi – 110002
info@double9books.com
www.double9books.com
Tel. 011-40042856

ABOUT THE AUTHOR

Arnold Bennett (1867-1931) was a prominent English author and journalist known for his novels, plays, and essays. Born in Hanley, Staffordshire, Bennett grew up in a working-class family and began his career as an office clerk before pursuing writing full-time. His early experiences and observations of industrial life in the Potteries greatly influenced his literary work. Bennett's work is marked by its **realism, social commentary,** and focus on the **individual's struggle** within societal constraints. He was also a prominent **essayist**, contributing to discussions on a wide range of topics, from literature and culture to politics and social issues. During World War I, Bennett served as a **war correspondent**, providing firsthand accounts of the **Western Front** in works such as "Over There: War Scenes on the Western Front" (1915). His observations of the war and his role as a **war journalist** allowed him to offer a unique perspective on the conflict, contributing significantly to his public profile. Despite his success, Bennett faced criticism for his perceived lack of innovation and the conventional nature of some of his works. However, his contributions to English literature, particularly his skillful portrayal of social and personal dynamics, have cemented his place as an important figure in early 20th-century literature. Arnold Bennett's legacy endures through his comprehensive and empathetic explorations of human life and his significant contributions to literature and journalism.

CONTENTS

CHAPTER I
MONEY IN THE HOUSE

I

In the evening dimness of old Mrs. Maldon's sitting-room stood the youthful virgin, Rachel Louisa Fleckring. The prominent fact about her appearance was that she wore an apron. Not one of those white, waist-tied aprons, with or without bibs, worn proudly, uncompromisingly, by a previous generation of unaspiring housewives and housegirls! But an immense blue pinafore-apron, covering the whole front of the figure except the head, hands, and toes. Its virtues were that it fully protected the most fragile frock against all the perils of the kitchen; and that it could be slipped on or off in one second, without any manipulation of tapes, pins, or buttons and buttonholes—for it had no fastenings of any sort and merely yawned behind. In one second the drudge could be transformed into the elegant infanta of boudoirs, and *vice versa*. To suit the coquetry of the age the pinafore was enriched with certain flouncings, which, however, only intensified its unshapen ugliness.

On a plain, middle-aged woman such a pinafore would have been intolerable to the sensitive eye. But on Rachel it simply had a piquant and perverse air, because she was young, with the incomparable, the unique charm of comely adolescence; it simply excited the imagination to conceive the exquisite treasures of contour and tint and texture which it veiled. Do not infer that Rachel was a coquette. Although comely, she was homely—a "downright" girl, scorning and hating all manner of pretentiousness. She had a fine best dress, and when she put it on everybody knew that it was her best; a stranger would have known. Whereas of a coquette none but her intimate companions can say whether she is wearing best or second-best on a given high occasion. Rachel used the pinafore-apron only with her best dress, and her reason for doing so was the sound, sensible reason that it was the usual and proper thing to do.

She opened a drawer of the new Sheraton sideboard, and took from it a metal tube that imitated brass, about a foot long and an inch in diameter, covered with black lettering. This tube, when she had removed its top, showed a number of thin wax tapers in various colours. She chose one, lit it neatly at the red fire, and then, standing on a footstool in the middle of the room, stretched all her body and limbs upward in order to reach the gas. If the tap had been half an inch higher or herself half an inch shorter, she would have had to stand on a chair instead of a footstool; and the chair would have had to be brought out of the kitchen and carried back again. But Heaven had watched over this detail. The gas-fitting consisted of a flexible pipe, resembling a thick black cord, and swinging at the end of it a specimen of that wonderful and blessed contrivance, the inverted incandescent mantle within a porcelain globe: the whole recently adopted by Mrs. Maldon as the dangerous final word of modern invention. It was safer to ignite the gas from the orifice at the top of the globe; but even so there was always a mild disconcerting explosion, followed by a few moments' uncertainty as to whether or not the gas had "lighted properly."

When the deed was accomplished and the room suddenly bright with soft illumination, Mrs. Maldon murmured—

"That's better!"

She was sitting in her arm-chair by the glitteringly set table, which, instead of being in the centre of the floor under the gas, had a place near the bow-window—advantageous in the murky daytime of the Five Towns, and inconvenient at night. The table might well have been shifted at night to a better position in regard to the gas. But it never was. Somehow for Mrs. Maldon the carpet was solid concrete, and the legs of the table immovably embedded therein.

Rachel, gentle-footed, kicked the footstool away to its lair under the table, and simultaneously extinguished the taper, which she dropped with a scarce audible click into a vase on the mantelpiece. Then she put the cover on the tube with another faintest click, restored the tube to its drawer with a rather louder click, and finally, with a click still louder, pushed the drawer home. All these slight sounds were familiar to Mrs. Maldon; they were part of her regular night life, part of an unconsciously loved ritual, and they contributed in their degree to her placid happiness.

"Now the blinds, my dear!" said she.

The exhortation was ill-considered, and Rachel controlled a gesture of amicable impatience. For she had not paused after closing the drawer; she was already on her way across the room to the window when Mrs. Maldon said, "Now the blinds, my dear!" The fact was that Mrs. Maldon measured the time between the lighting of gas and the drawing down of blinds by tenths of a second—such was her fear lest in that sinister interval the whole prying town might magically gather in the street outside and peer into the secrets of her inculpable existence.

II

When the blinds and curtains had been arranged for privacy, Mrs. Maldon sighed securely and picked up her crocheting. Rachel rested her hands on the table, which was laid for a supper for four, and asked in a firm, frank voice whether there was anything else.

"Because, if not," Rachel added, "I'll just take off my pinafore and wash my hands."

Mrs. Maldon looked up benevolently and nodded in quick agreement. It was such apparently trifling gestures, eager and generous, that endeared the old lady to Rachel, giving her the priceless sensation of being esteemed and beloved. Her gaze lingered on her aged employer with affection and with profound respect. Mrs. Maldon made a striking, tall, slim figure, sitting erect in tight black, with the right side of her long, prominent nose in the full gaslight and the other heavily shadowed. Her hair was absolutely black at over seventy; her eyes were black and glowing, and she could read and do coarse crocheting without spectacles. All her skin, especially round about the eyes, was yellowish brown and very deeply wrinkled indeed; a decrepit, senile skin, which seemed to contradict the youth of her pose and her glance. The cast of her features was benign. She had passed through desolating and violent experiences, and then through a long, long period of withdrawn tranquillity; and from end to end of her life she had consistently thought the best of all men, refusing to recognize evil and assuming the existence of good. Every one of the millions of her kind thoughts had helped to mould the expression of her countenance. The expression was definite now, fixed, intensely characteristic after so many decades, and wherever it was seen it gave pleasure and by its enchantment created goodness and goodwill— even out of their opposites. Such was the life-work of Mrs. Maldon.

Her eyes embraced the whole room. They did not, as the phrase is, "beam" approval; for the act of beaming involves a sort of ecstasy, and Mrs. Maldon was too dignified for ecstasy. But they displayed a mild and proud contentment as she said—

"I'm sure it's all very nice."

It was. The table crowded with porcelain, crystal, silver, and flowers, and every object upon it casting a familiar curved shadow on the whiteness of the damask toward the window! The fresh crimson and blues of the everlasting Turkey carpet (Turkey carpet being the *ne plus ultra* of carpetry in the Five Towns, when that carpet was bought, just as sealskin was the *ne plus ultra* of all furs)! The silken-polished sideboard, strange to the company, but worthy of it, and exhibiting a due sense of its high destiny! The sombre bookcase and corner cupboard, darkly glittering! The Chesterfield sofa, broad, accepting, acquiescent! The flashing brass fender and copper scuttle! The comfortably reddish walls, with their pictures—like limpets on the face of precipices! The new-whitened ceiling! In the midst the incandescent lamp that hung like the moon in heaven!... And then the young, sturdy girl, standing over the old woman and breathing out the very breath of life, vitalizing everything, rejuvenating the old woman!

Mrs. Maldon's sitting-room had a considerable renown among her acquaintance, not only for its peculiar charm, which combined and reconciled the tastes of two very different generations, but also for its radiant cleanness. There are many clean houses in the Five Towns, using the adjective in the relative sense in which the Five Towns is forced by chimneys to use it. But Mrs. Maldon's sitting-room (save for the white window-curtains, which had to accept the common grey fate of white window-curtains in the district) was clean in the country-side sense, almost in the Dutch sense. The challenge of its cleanness gleamed on every polished surface, victorious in the unending battle against the horrible contagion of foul industries. Mrs. Maldon's friends would assert that the state of that sitting-room "passed" them, or "fair passed" them, and she would receive their ever-amazed compliments with modesty. But behind her benevolent depreciation she would be blandly saying to herself: "Yes, I'm scarcely surprised it passes you—seeing the way you housewives let things go on here." The word "here" would be faintly emphasized in her mind, as no native would have emphasized it.

Rachel shared the general estimate of the sitting-room. She appreciated its charm, and admitted to herself that her first vision of it, rather less than a month before, had indeed given her a new and startling ideal of cleanliness. On that occasion it had been evident, from Mrs. Maldon's physical exhaustion, that the housemistress had made an enormous personal effort to *dazzle* and inspire her new "lady companion," which effort, though detected and perhaps scorned by Rachel, had nevertheless succeeded in its aim. With a certain presence of mind Rachel had feigned to remark nothing miraculous in the condition of the room. Appropriating the new ideal instantly, she had on the first morning of her service "turned out" the room before breakfast, well knowing that it must have been turned out on the previous day. Dumbfounded for a few moments, Mrs. Maldon had at length said, in her sweet and cordial benevolence, "I'm glad to see we think alike about cleanliness." And Rachel had replied with an air at once deferential, sweet, and yet casual, "Oh, of course, Mrs. Maldon!" Then they measured one another in a silent exchange. Mrs. Maldon was aware that she had by chance discovered a pearl—yes, a treasure beyond pearls. And Rachel, too, divined the high value of her employer, and felt within the stirrings of a passionate loyalty to her.

III

And yet, during the three weeks and a half of their joint existence, Rachel's estimate of Mrs. Maldon had undergone certain subtle modifications.

At first, somewhat overawed, Rachel had seen in her employer the Mrs. Maldon of the town's legend, which legend had travelled to Rachel as far as Knype, whence she sprang. That is to say, one of the great ladies of Bursley, ranking in the popular regard with Mrs. Clayton-Vernon, the leader of society, Mrs. Sutton, the philanthropist, and Mrs. Hamps, the powerful religious bully. She had been impressed by her height (Rachel herself being no lamp-post), her carriage, her superlative dignity, her benevolence of thought, and above all by her aristocratic Southern accent. After eight-and-forty years of the Five Towns, Mrs. Maldon had still kept most of that Southern accent—so intimidating to the rough, broad talkers of the district, who take revenge by mocking it among themselves, but for whom it will always possess the thrilling prestige of high life.

And then day by day Rachel had discovered that great ladies are, after all, human creatures, strangely resembling other human creatures. And Mrs. Maldon slowly became for her an old woman of seventy-two, with unquestionably wondrous hair, but failing in strength and in faculties; and it grew merely pathetic to Rachel that Mrs. Maldon should force herself always to sit straight upright. As for Mrs. Maldon's charitableness, Rachel could not deny that she refused to think evil, and yet it was plain that at bottom Mrs. Maldon was not much deceived about people: in which apparent inconsistency there hid a slight disturbing suggestion of falseness that mysteriously fretted the downright Rachel.

Again, beneath Mrs. Maldon's modesty concerning the merits of her sitting-room Rachael soon fancied that she could detect traces of an ingenuous and possibly senile "house-pride," which did more than fret the lady companion; it faintly offended her. That one should be proud of a possession or of an achievement was admissible, but that one should fail to conceal the pride absolutely was to Rachel, with her Five Towns character, a sign of weakness, a sign of the soft South. Lastly, Mrs. Maldon had, it transpired, her "ways"; for example, in the matter of blinds and in the matter of tapers. She would actually insist on the gas being lighted with a taper; a paper spill, which was just as good and better, seemed to ruffle her benign placidity: and she was funnily economical with matches. Rachel had never seen a taper before, and could not conceive where the old lady managed to buy the things.

In short, with admiration almost undiminished, and with a rapidly growing love and loyalty, Rachel had arrived at the point of feeling glad that she, a mature, capable, sagacious, and strong woman, was there to watch over the last years of the waning and somewhat peculiar old lady.

Mrs. Maldon did not see the situation from quite the same angle. She did not, for example, consider herself to be in the least peculiar, but, on the contrary, a very normal woman. She had always used tapers; she could remember the period when every one used tapers. In her view tapers were far more genteel and less dangerous than the untidy, flaring spill, which she abhorred as a vulgarity. As for matches, frankly it would not have occurred to her to waste a match when fire was available. In the matter of her sharp insistence on drawn blinds at night, domestic privacy seemed to be one of the fundamental decencies of life—simply that! And as for house-pride, she considered that she locked away her fervent feeling for her parlour in a manner marvellous and complete.

No one could or ever would guess the depth of her attachment to that sitting-room, nor the extent to which it engrossed her emotional life. And yet she had only occupied the house for fourteen years out of the forty-five years of her widowhood, and the furniture had at intervals been renewed (for Mrs. Maldon would on no account permit herself to be old-fashioned).

Indeed, she had had five different sitting-rooms in five different houses since her husband's death. No matter. They were all the same sitting-room, all rendered identical by the mysterious force of her dreamy meditations on the past. And, moreover, sundry important articles had remained constant to preserve unbroken the chain that linked her to her youth. The table which Rachel had so nicely laid was the table at which Mrs. Maldon had taken her first meal as mistress of a house. Her husband had carved mutton at it, and grumbled about the consistency of toast; her children had spilt jam on its cloth. And when on Sunday nights she wound up the bracket-clock on the mantelpiece, she could see and hear a handsome young man in a long frock-coat and a large shirt-front and a very thin black tie winding it up too—her husband—on Sunday nights. And she could simultaneously see another handsome young man winding it up—her son.

Her pictures were admired.

"Your son painted this water-colour, did he not, Mrs. Maldon?"

"Yes, my son Athelstan."

"How gifted he must have been!"

"Yes, the best judges say he showed very remarkable promise. It's fading, I fear. I ought to cover it up, but somehow I can't fancy covering it up—"

The hand that had so remarkably promised had lain mouldering for a quarter of a century. Mrs. Maldon sometimes saw it, fleshless, on a cage-like skeleton in the dark grave. The next moment she would see herself tending its chilblains.

And if she was not peculiar, neither was she waning. No! Seventy-two—but not truly old! How could she be truly old when she could see, hear, walk a mile without stopping, eat anything whatever, and dress herself unaided? And that hair of hers! Often she was still a young wife, or a young widow. She was not preparing for death; she had prepared for death in the seventies. She expected to live on in calm satisfaction through indefinite decades. She savoured life pleasantly, for its daily security was impregnable. She had forgotten grief.

When she looked up at Rachel and benevolently nodded to her, she saw a girl of line character, absolutely trustworthy, very devoted, very industrious, very capable, intelligent, cheerful—in fact, a splendid girl, a girl to be enthusiastic about! But such a mere girl! A girl with so much to learn! So pathetically young and inexperienced and positive and sure of herself! The looseness of her limbs, the unconscious abrupt freedom of her gestures, the waviness of her auburn hair, the candour of her glance, the warmth of her indignation against injustice and dishonesty, the capricious and sensitive flowings of blood to her smooth cheeks, the ridiculous wise compressings of her lips, the rise and fall of her rich and innocent bosom — these phenomena touched Mrs. Maldon and occasionally made her want to cry.

Thought she: "*I* was never so young as that at twenty-two! At twenty-two I had had Mary!" The possibility that in spite of having had Mary (who would now have been fifty, but for death) she had as a fact been approximately as young as that at twenty-two did not ever present itself to the waning and peculiar old lady. She was glad that she, a mature and profoundly experienced woman, in full possession of all her faculties, was there to watch over the development of the lovable, affectionate, and impulsive child.

IV

"Oh! Here's the paper, Mrs. Maldon," said Rachel, as, turning away to leave the room, she caught sight of the extra special edition of the *Signal*, which lay a pale green on the dark green of the Chesterfield.

Mrs. Maldon answered placidly —

"When did you bring it in? I never heard the boy come. But my hearing's not quite what it used to be, that's true. Open it for me, my dear. I can't stretch my arms as I used to."

She was one of the few women in the Five Towns who deigned to read a newspaper regularly, and one of the still fewer who would lead the miscellaneous conversation of drawing-rooms away from domestic chatter and discussions of individualities, to political and municipal topics and even toward general ideas. She seldom did more than mention a topic and then express a hope for the best, or explain that this phenomenon was "such a pity," or that phenomenon "such a good thing," or that about another phenomenon "one really didn't know what to think." But these remarks sufficed to class her apart among her sex as "a very up-to-date old lady, with a broad outlook upon the world," and to inspire sundry other ladies with a fearful respect for her masculine intellect and judgment. She was aware of her superiority, and had a certain kind disdain for the increasing number of women who took in a daily picture-paper, and who, having dawdled over its illustrations after breakfast, spoke of what they had seen in the "newspaper." She would not allow that a picture-paper was a newspaper.

Rachel stood in the empty space under the gas. Her arms were stretched out and slightly upward as she held the *Signal* wide open and glanced at the newspaper, frowning. The light fell full on her coppery hair. Her balanced body, though masked in front by the perpendicular fall of the apron as she bent somewhat forward, was nevertheless the image of potential vivacity and energy; it seemed almost to vibrate with its own consciousness of physical pride.

Left alone, Rachel would never have opened a newspaper, at any rate for the news. Until she knew Mrs. Maldon she had never seen a woman read a newspaper for aught except the advertisements relating to situations, houses, and pleasures. But, much more than she imagined, she was greatly under the influence of Mrs. Maldon. Mrs. Maldon made a nightly solemnity of the newspaper, and Rachel naturally soon persuaded herself that it was a fine and a superior thing to read the newspaper—a proof of unusual intelligence. Moreover, just as she felt bound to show Mrs. Maldon that her notion of cleanliness was as advanced as anybody's, so she felt bound to indicate, by an appearance of casualness, that for her to read the paper was the most customary thing in the world. Of course she read the paper! And that she should calmly look at it herself before handing it to her mistress proved that she had already established a very secure position in the house.

She said, her eyes following the lines, and her feet moving in the direction of Mrs. Maldon— "Those burglaries are still going on ... Hillport now!"

"Oh, dear, dear!" murmured Mrs. Maldon, as Rachel spread the newspaper lightly over the tea-tray and its contents. "Oh, dear, dear! I do hope the police will catch some one soon. I'm sure they're doing their best, but really—!"

Rachel bent with confident intimacy over the old lady's shoulder, and they read the burglary column together, Rachel interrupting herself for an instant to pick up Mrs. Maldon's ball of black wool which had slipped to the floor. The *Signal* reporter had omitted none of the classic *clichés* proper to the subject, and such words and phrases as "jemmy," "effected an entrance," "the servant, now thoroughly alarmed," "stealthy footsteps," "escaped with their booty," seriously disquieted both of the women—caused a sudden sensation of sinking in the region of the heart. Yet neither would put the secret fear into speech, for each by instinct felt that a fear once uttered is strengthened and made more real. Living solitary and unprotected by male sinews, in a house which, though it did not stand alone, was somewhat withdrawn from the town, they knew themselves the ideal prey of conventional burglars with masks, dark lanterns, revolvers, and jemmies. They were grouped together like some symbolic sculpture, and with all their fortitude and common sense they still in unconscious attitude expressed the helpless and resigned fatalism of their sex before certain menaces of bodily danger, the thrilled, expectant submission of women in a city about to be sacked.

Nothing could save them if the peril entered the house. But they would not say aloud: "Suppose they came *here*! How terrible!" They would not even whisper the slightest apprehension. They just briefly discussed the matter with a fine air of indifferent aloofness, remaining calm while the brick walls and the social system which defended that bright and delicate parlour from the dark, savage universe without seemed to crack and shiver.

Mrs. Maldon, suddenly noticing that one blind was half an inch short of the bottom of the window, rose nervously and pulled it down farther.

"Why didn't you ask me to do that?" said Rachel, thinking what a fidgety person the old lady was.

Mrs. Maldon replied— "It's all right, my dear. Did you fasten the window on the upstairs landing?"

"As if burglars would try to get in by an upstairs window—and on the street!" thought Rachel, pityingly impatient. "However, it's her house, and I'm paid to do what I'm told," she added to herself, very sensibly. Then she said, aloud, in a soothing tone—

"No, I didn't. But I will do it."

She moved towards the door, and at the same moment a knock on the front door sent a vibration through the whole house. Nearly all knocks on the front door shook the house; and further, burglars do not generally knock as a preliminary to effecting an entrance. Nevertheless, both women started—and were ashamed of starting.

"Surely he's rather early!" said Mrs. Maldon with an exaggerated tranquillity.

And Rachel, with a similar lack of conviction in her calm gait, went audaciously forth into the dark lobby.

V

On the glass panels of the front door the street lamp threw a faint, distorted shadow of a bowler hat, two rather protruding ears, and a pair of long, outspreading whiskers whose ends merged into broad shoulders. Any one familiar with the streets of Bursley would have instantly divined that Councillor Thomas Batchgrew stood between the gas-lamp and the front door. And even Rachel, whose acquaintance with Bursley was still slight, at once recognized the outlines of the figure. She had seen Councillor Batchgrew one day conversing with Mrs. Maldon in Moorthorne Road, and she knew that he bore to Mrs. Maldon the vague but imposing relation of "trustee."

There are many—indeed perhaps too many—remarkable men in the Five Towns. Thomas Batchgrew was one of them. He had begun life as a small plumber in Bursley market-place, living behind and above the shop, and begetting a considerable family, which exercised itself in the back yard among empty and full turpentine-cans. The original premises survived, as a branch establishment, and Batchgrew's latest-married grandson condescended to reside on the first floor, and to keep a motor-car and a tri-car in the back yard, now roofed over (in a manner not strictly conforming to the building by-laws of the borough). All Batchgrew's sons and daughters were married, and several of his grandchildren also. And all his children, and more than one of the grandchildren, kept motor-cars. Not a month passed but some Batchgrew, or some Batchgrew's husband or child, bought a motor-car, or sold one, or exchanged a small one for a larger one, or had an accident, or was gloriously fined in some distant part of the country for illegal driving. Nearly all of them had spacious detached houses, with gardens and gardeners, and patent slow-combustion grates, and porcelain bathrooms comprising every appliance for luxurious splashing. And, with the exception of one son who had been assisted to Valparaiso in order that he might there seek death in the tankard without outraging the family, they were all teetotallers—because the old man, "old Jack," was a teetotaller. The family pyramid was based firm on the old man. The numerous relatives held closely together like an alien oligarchical caste in a conquered country. If they ever did quarrel, it must have been in private.

The principal seat of business—electrical apparatus, heating apparatus, and decorating and plumbing on a grandiose scale—in Hanbridge, had over its immense windows the sign: "John Batchgrew & Sons." The sign might well have read: "John Batchgrew & Sons, Daughters, Daughters-in-law,

Sons-in-law, Grandchildren, and Great-grandchildren." The Batchgrew partners were always tendering for, and often winning, some big contract or other for heating and lighting and embellishing a public building or a mansion or a manufactory. (They by no means confined their activities to the Five Towns, having an address in London—and another in Valparaiso.) And small private customers were ever complaining of the inaccuracy of their accounts for small jobs. People who, in the age of Queen Victoria's earlier widowhood, had sent for Batchgrew to repair a burst spout, still by force of habit sent for Batchgrew to repair a burst spout, and still had to "call at Batchgrew's" about mistakes in the bills, which mistakes, after much argument and asseveration, were occasionally put right. In spite of their prodigious expenditures, and of a certain failure on the part of the public to understand "where all the money came from," the financial soundness of the Batchgrews was never questioned. In discussing the Batchgrews no bank-manager and no lawyer had ever by an intonation or a movement of the eyelid hinted that earthquakes had occurred before in the history of the world and might occur again.

And yet old Batchgrew—admittedly the cleverest of the lot, save possibly the Valparaiso soaker—could not be said to attend assiduously to business. He scarcely averaged two hours a day on the premises at Hanbridge. Indeed the staff there had a sense of the unusual, inciting to unusual energy and devotion, when word went round: "Guv'nor's in the office with Mr. John." The Councillor was always extremely busy with something other than his main enterprise. It was now reported, for example, that he was clearing vast sums out of picture-palaces in Wigan and Warrington. Also he was a religionist, being Chairman of the local Church of England Village Mission Fund. And he was a politician, powerful in municipal affairs. And he was a reformer, who believed that by abolishing beer he could abolish the poverty of the poor—and acted accordingly. And lastly he liked to enjoy himself.

Everybody knew by sight his flying white whiskers and protruding ears. And he himself was well aware of the steady advertising value of those whiskers—of always being recognizable half a mile off. He met everybody unflinchingly, for he felt that he was invulnerable at all points and sure of a magnificent obituary. He was invariably treated with marked deference and respect. But he was not an honest man. He knew it. All his family knew it. In business everybody knew it except a few nincompoops. Scarcely any one trusted him. The peculiar fashion in which, when he was not present, people "old Jacked" him—this alone was enough to condemn a man of his years. Lastly, everybody knew that most of the Batchgrew family was of a piece with its head.

VI

Now Rachel had formed a prejudice against old Batchgrew. She had formed it, immutably, in a single second of time. One glance at him in the street—and she had tried and condemned him, according to the summary justice of youth. She was in that stage of plenary and unhesitating wisdom when one not only can, but one must, divide the whole human race sharply into two categories, the sheep and the goats; and she had sentenced old Batchgrew to a place on the extreme left. It happened that she knew nothing against him. But she did not require evidence. She simply did "not like *that man*" —(she italicized the end of the phrase bitingly to herself)—and there was no appeal against the verdict. Angels could not have successfully interceded for him in the courts of her mind. He never guessed, in his aged self-sufficiency, that his case was hopeless with Rachel, nor even that the child had dared to have any opinion about him at all.

She was about to slip off the pinafore-apron and drop it on to the oak chest that stood in the lobby. But she thought with defiance: "Why should I take my pinafore off for him? I won't. He shan't see my nice frock. Let him see my pinafore. I am an independent woman, earning my own living, and why should I be ashamed of my pinafore? My pinafore is good enough for him!" She also thought: "Let him wait!" and went off into the kitchen to get the modern appliance of the match for lighting the gas in the lobby. When she had lighted the gas she opened the front door with audacious but nervous deliberation, and the famous character impatiently walked straight in. He wore prominent loose black kid gloves and a thin black overcoat.

Looking coolly at her, he said—

"So you're the new lady companion, young miss! Well, I've heard rare accounts on ye—rare accounts on ye! Missis is in, I reckon?"

His voice was extremely low, rich, and heavy. It descended on the silence like a thick lubricating oil that only reluctantly abandons the curves in which it falls.

And Rachel answered, faintly, tremulously— "Yes."

No longer was she the independent woman, censorious and scornful, but a silly, timid little thing. Though she condemned herself savagely for school-girlishness, she could do nothing to arrest the swift change in her.

The fact was, she was abashed, partly by the legendary importance of the renowned Batchgrew, but more by his physical presence. His mere presence was always disturbing; for when he supervened into an environment he had always the air of an animal on a voyage of profitable discovery. His nose was an adventurous, sniffing nose, a true nose, which exercised the original and proper functions of a nose noisily. His limbs were restless, his boots like hoofs. His eyes were as restless as his limbs, and seemed ever to be seeking for something upon which they could definitely alight, and not finding it. He performed eructations with the disarming naturalness of a baby. He was tall but not stout, and yet he filled the lobby; he was the sole fact in the lobby, and it was as though Rachel had to crush herself against the wall in order to make room for him.

His glance at Rachel now became inquisitive, calculating, It seemed to be saying: "One day I may be able to make use of this piece of goods." But there was a certain careless good-humour in it, too. What he saw was a naïve young maid, with agreeable features, and a fine, fresh complexion, and rather reddish hair. (He did not approve of the colour of the hair.) He found pleasure in regarding her, and in the perception that he had abashed her. Yes, he liked to see her timid and downcast before him. He was an old man, but like most old men—such as statesmen—who have lived constantly at the full pressure of following their noses, he was also a young man. He creaked, but he was not gravely impaired.

"Is it Mr. Batchgrew?" Rachel softly murmured the unnecessary question, with one hand on the knob ready to open the sitting-room door.

He had flopped his stiff, flat-topped felt hat on the oak chest, and was taking off his overcoat. He paused and, lifting his chin—and his incredible white whiskers with it—gazed at Rachel almost steadily for a couple of seconds.

"It is," he said, as it were challengingly—"it is, young miss."

Then he finished removing his overcoat and thrust it roughly down on the hat.

Rachel blushed as she modestly turned the knob and pushed the door so that he might pass in front of her.

"Here's Mr. Batchgrew, Mrs. Maldon," she announced, feebly endeavouring to raise and clear her voice.

"Bless us!" The astonished exclamation of Mrs. Maldon was heard.

And Councillor Batchgrew, with his crimson shiny face, and the vermilion rims round his unsteady eyes, and his elephant ears, and the absurd streaming of his white whiskers, and his multitudinous noisiness, and his black kid gloves, strode half theatrically past her, sniffing.

To Rachel he was an object odious, almost obscene. In truth, she had little mercy on old men in general, who as a class struck her as fussy, ridiculous, and repulsive. And beyond all the old men she had ever seen, she disliked Councillor Batchgrew. And about Councillor Batchgrew what she most detested was, perhaps strangely, his loose, wrinkled black kid gloves. They were ordinary, harmless black kid gloves, but she counted them against him as a supreme offence.

"Conceited, self-conscious, horrid old brute!" she thought, discreetly drawing the door to, and then going into the kitchen. "He's interested in nothing and nobody but himself." She felt protective towards Mrs. Maldon, that simpleton who apparently could not see through a John Batchgrew!... So Mrs. Maldon had been giving him good accounts of the new lady companion, had she!

VII

"Well, Lizzie Maldon," said Councillor Batchgrew as he crossed the sitting-room, "how d'ye find yourself?... Sings!" he went on, taking Mrs. Maldon's hand with a certain negligence and at the same time fixing an unfriendly eye on the gas.

Mrs. Maldon had risen to welcome him with the punctilious warmth due to an old gentleman, a trustee, and a notability. She told him as to her own health and inquired about his. But he ignored her smooth utterances, in the ardour of following his nose.

"Sings worse than ever! Very unhealthy too! Haven't I told ye and told ye? You ought to let me put electricity in for you. It isn't as if it wasn't your own house.... Pay ye! Pay ye over and over again!"

He sat down in a chair by the table, drew off his loose black gloves, and after letting them hover irresolutely over the encumbered table, deposited them for safety in the china slop-basin.

"I dare say you're quite right," said Mrs. Maldon with grave urbanity. "But really gas suits me very well. And you know the gas-manager complains so much about the competition of electricity. Truly it does seem unfair, doesn't it, as they both belong to the town! If I gave up gas for electricity I don't think I could look the poor man in the face at church. And all these changes cost money! How is dear Enid?"

Mr. Batchgrew had now stretched out his legs and crossed one over the other; and he was twisting his thumbs on his diaphragm.

"Enid? Oh! Enid! Well, I did hear she's able to nurse the child at last." He spoke of his grand-daughter-in-law as of one among a multiplicity of women about whose condition vague rumours reached him at intervals.

Mrs. Maldon breathed fervently—"I'm so thankful! What a blessing that is, isn't it?"

"As for costing money, Elizabeth," Mr. Batchgrew proceeded, "you'll be all right now for money." He paused, sat up straight with puffings, and leaned sideways against the table. Then he said, half fiercely— "I've settled up th' Brougham Street mortgage."

"You don't say so!" Mrs. Maldon was startled.

"I do!"

"When?"

"To-day."

"Well—"

"That's what I stepped in for."

Mrs. Maldon feebly murmured, with obvious emotion—

"You can't imagine what a relief it is to me!" Tears shone in her dark, mild eyes.

"Look ye!" exclaimed the trustee curtly.

He drew from his breast pocket a bank envelope of linen, and then, glancing at the table, pushed cups and saucers abruptly away to make a clear space on the white cloth. The newspaper slipped rustling to the floor on the side near the window. Already his gloves were abominable in the slop-basin, and now with a single gesture he had destroyed the symmetry of the set table. Mrs. Maldon with surpassing patience smiled sweetly, and assured herself that Mr. Batchgrew could not help it. He was a coarse male creature at large in a room highly feminized. It was his habit thus to pass through orderly interiors, distributing havoc, like a rough soldier. You might almost hear a sword clanking in the scabbard.

"Ten, twenty, thirty, forty, fifty, sixty," he began in his heavily rolling voice to count out one by one a bundle of notes which he had taken from the envelope. He generously licked his thick, curved-back thumb for the separating of the notes, and made each note sharply click, in the manner of a bank cashier, to prove to himself that it was not two notes stuck together. "... Five-seventy, five-eighty, five-ninety, six hundred. These are all tens. Now the fives: Five, ten, fifteen, twenty, twenty-five." He counted up to three hundred and sixty-five. "That's nine-sixty-five altogether. The odd sixty-five's arrear of interest. I'm investing nine hundred again to-morrow, and th' interest on th' new investment is to start from th' first o' this month. So instead of being out o'pocket, you'll be in pocket, missis."

The notes lay in two irregular filmy heaps on the table.

Having carefully returned the empty envelope to his pocket, Mr. Batchgrew sat back, triumphant, and his eye met the delighted yet disturbed eye of Mrs. Maldon, and then wavered and dodged.

Mr. Batchgrew with all his romantic qualities, lacked any perception of the noble and beautiful in life, and it could be positively asserted that his estimate of Mrs. Maldon was chiefly disdainful. But of Mrs. Maldon's secret opinion about John Batchgrew nothing could be affirmed with certainty. Nobody knew it or ever would know it. I doubt whether Mrs. Maldon had whispered it even to herself. In youth he had been the very intimate friend of her husband. Which fact would scarcely tally with Mrs. Maldon's memory of her husband as the most upright and perspicacious of men—unless on the assumption that John Batchgrew's real characteristics had not properly revealed themselves until after his crony's death; this assumption was perhaps admissible. Mrs. Maldon invariably spoke of John Batchgrew with respect and admiration. She probably had perfect confidence in him as a trustee, and such confidence was justified, for the Councillor knew as well as anybody in what fields rectitude was a remunerative virtue, and in what fields it was not.

Indeed, as a trustee his sense of honour and of duty was so nice that in order to save his ward from loss in connection with a depreciating mortgage security, he had invented, as a Town Councillor, the "Improvement" known as the "Brougham Street Scheme." If this was not said outright, it was hinted. At any rate, the idea was fairly current that had not Councillor Batchgrew been interested in Brougham Street property, the Brougham Street Scheme, involving the compulsory purchase of some of that property at the handsome price naturally expected from the munificence of corporations, would never have come into being.

Mrs. Maldon knew of the existence of the idea, which had been obscurely referred to by a licensed victualler (inimically prejudiced against the teetotaller in Mr. Batchgrew) at a Council meeting reported in the *Signal*. And it was precisely this knowledge which had imparted to her glance the peculiar disturbed quality that had caused Mr. Batchgrew to waver and dodge.

The occasion demanded the exercise of unflinching common sense, and Mrs. Maldon was equal to it. She very wisely decided that she ought not to concern herself, and could not concern herself, with an aspect of the matter which concerned her trustee alone. And therefore she gave her heart entirely up to an intense gladness at the integral recovery of the mortgage money.

For despite her faith in the efficiency of her trustee, Mrs. Maldon would worry about finance; she would yield to an exquisitely painful dread lest "anything should happen"—happen, that is, to prevent her from dying in the comfortable and dignified state in which she had lived. Her income was not large—a little under three hundred pounds a year—but with care it sufficed for her own wants, and for gifts, subscriptions, and an occasional carriage. There would have been a small margin but for the constant rise in prices. As it was, there was no permanent margin. And to have cut off a single annual subscription, or lessened a single customary gift, would have mortally wounded her pride. The gradual declension of property values in Brougham Street had been a danger that each year grew more menacing. The moment had long ago come when the whole rents of the mortgaged cottages would not cover her interest. The promise of the Corporation Improvement Scheme had only partially reassured her; it seemed too good to be true. She could not believe without seeing. She now saw, suddenly, blindingly. And her relief, beneath that stately deportment of hers, was pathetic in its simple intensity. It would have moved John Batchgrew, had he been in any degree susceptible to the thrill of pathos.

"I doubt if I've seen so much money all at once before," said Mrs. Maldon, smiling weakly.

"Happen not!" said Mr. Batchgrew, proud, with insincere casualness, and he added in exactly the same tone: "I'm leaving it with ye to-night."

Mrs. Maldon was aghast, but she feigned sprightliness as she exclaimed—

"You're not leaving all this money here to-night?"

"I am," said the trustee. "That's what I came for. Evans's were three hours late in completing, and the bank was closed. I have but just got it. I'm not going home." (He lived eight miles off, near Axe.) "I've got to go to a Church meeting at Red Cow, and I'm sleeping there. John's Ernest is calling here for me presently. I don't fancy driving over them moors with near a thousand pun in my pocket—and colliers out on strike—not at my age, missis! If you don't know what Red Cow is, I reckon I do. It's your money. Put it in a drawer and say nowt, and I'll fetch it to-morrow. What'll happen to it, think ye, seeing as it hasn't got legs?" He spoke with the authority of a trustee. And Mrs. Maldon felt that her reputation for sensible equanimity was worth preserving. So she said bravely—

"I suppose it will be all right."

"Of course!" snapped the trustee patronizingly.

"But I must tell Rachel."

"Rachel? Rachel? Oh! *Her*! Why tell any one?" Mr. Batchgrew sniffed very actively.

"Oh! I shouldn't be easy if I didn't tell Rachel," insisted Mrs. Maldon with firmness.

Before the trustee could protest anew she had rung the bell.

VIII

It was another and an apronless Rachel that entered the room, a Rachel transformed, magnificent in light green frock with elaborate lacy ruchings and ornamentations, and the waist at the new fashionable height. Her ruddy face and hands were fresh from water, her hair very glossy and very neat: she was in high array. This festival attire Mrs. Maldon now fully beheld for the first time. It, indeed, honoured herself, for she had ordained a festive evening: but at the same time she was surprised and troubled by it. As for Mr. Batchgrew, he entirely ignored the vision. Stretched out in one long inclined plane from the back of his chair down to the brass fender, he contemplated the fire, while picking his teeth with a certain impatience, and still sniffing actively. The girl resented this disregard. But, though she remained hostile to the grotesque old man with his fussy noises, the mantle of Mrs. Maldon's moral protection was now over Councillor Batchgrew, and Rachel's mistrustful scorn of him had lost some of its pleasing force.

"Rachel—"

Mrs. Maldon gave a hesitating cough.

"Yes, Mrs. Maldon?" said Rachel questioningly deferential, and smiling faintly into Mrs. Maldon's apprehensive eyes. Against the background of the aged pair she seemed dramatically young, lithe, living, and wistful. She was nervous, but she thought with strong superiority: "What are those old folks planning together? Why do they ring for me?"

At length Mrs. Maldon proceeded—"I think I ought to tell you, dear, Mr. Batchgrew is obliged to leave this money in my charge to-night."

"What money?" asked Rachel.

Mr. Batchgrew put in sharply, drawing up his legs— "This!... Here, young miss! Step this way, if ye please. I'll count it. Ten, twenty, thirty—" With new lickings and clickings he counted the notes all over again. "There!" When he had finished his pride had become positively naïve.

"Oh, my word!" murmured Rachel, awed and astounded.

"It is rather a lot, isn't it?" said Mrs. Maldon, with a timid laugh.

At once fascinated and repelled, the two women looked at the money as at a magic. It represented to Mrs. Maldon a future free from financial embarrassment; it represented to Rachel more than she could earn in half a century at her wage of eighteen pounds a year, an unimaginable source of endless gratifications; and yet the mere fact that it was to stay in the house all night changed it for them into something dire and formidable, so that it inspired both of them—the ancient dame and the young girl—with naught but a mystic dread. Mr. Batchgrew eyed the affrighted creatures with satisfaction, appearing to take a perverse pleasure in thus imposing upon them the horrid incubus.

"I was only thinking of burglars;" said Mrs. Maldon apologetically. "There've been so many burglaries lately—" She ceased, uncertain of her voice. The forced lightness of her tone was almost tragic.

"There won't be any more," said Mr. Batchgrew condescendingly.

"Why?" demanded Mrs. Maldon with an eager smile of hope. "Have they caught them, then? Has Superintendent Snow—"

"They have their hands on them. To-morrow there'll be some arrests," Mr. Batchgrew answered, exuding authority. For he was not merely a Town Councillor, he was brother-in-law to the Superintendent of the Borough

Police. "Caught 'em long ago if th' county police had been a bit more reliable!"

"Oh!" Mrs. Maldon breathed happily. "I knew it couldn't be Mr. Snow's fault. I felt sure of that. I'm so glad."

And Rachel also was conscious of gladness. In fact, it suddenly seemed plain to both women that no burglar, certain of arrest on the morrow, would dare to invade the house of a lady whose trustee had married the sister of the Superintendent of Police. The house was invisibly protected.

"And we mustn't forget we shall have a man sleeping here to-night," said Rachel confidently.

"Of course! Of course! I was quite overlooking that!" exclaimed Mrs. Maldon.

Mr. Batchgrew threw a curt and suspicious question— "What man?"

"My nephew Julian—I should say my grand-nephew." Mrs. Maldon's proud tone rebuked the strange tone of Mr. Batchgrew. "It is his birthday. He and Louis are having supper with me. And Julian is staying the night."

"Well, if you take my advice, missis, ye'll say nowt to nobody. Lock the brass up in a drawer in that wardrobe of yours, and keep a still tongue in your head."

"Perhaps you're right," Mrs. Maldon agreed—"as a matter of general principle, I mean. And it might make Julian uneasy."

"Take it and lock it up," Mr. Batchgrew repeated.

"I don't know about my wardrobe—" Mrs. Maldon began.

"Anywhere!" Mr. Batchgrew stopped her.

"Only," said Rachel with careful gentleness, "please don't forget where you *have* put it."

But her precaution of manner was futile. Twice within a minute she had employed the word "forget." Twice was too often. Mrs. Maldon's memory was most capriciously uncertain. Its lapses astonished sometimes even herself. And naturally she was sensitive on the point. She nourished the fiction, and she expected others to nourish it, that her memory was quite equal to younger memories. Indeed, she would admit every symptom of old age save an unreliable memory.

Composing a dignified smile, she said with reproving blandness—

"I am not in the habit of forgetting where I put valuables, Rachel."

And her prominently veined fingers, clasping the notes as a preliminary to hiding them away, seemed in their nervous primness to be saying to Rachael: "I have deep confidence in you, and I think that to-night I have shown it. But oblige me by not presuming. I am Mrs. Maldon and you are Rachel. After all, I have not yet known you for a month."

IX

A very loud rasping noise, like a vicious menace, sounded from the street, shivering instantaneously the delicate placidity of Mrs. Maldon's home. Mrs. Maldon gave a start.

"That'll be John's Ernest with the car," said Mr. Batchgrew, amused; and he began to get up from the chair. As soon as he was on his feet his nose grew active again. "You've nothing to be afraid of, missis," he added in a tone roughly reassuring and good-natured.

"Oh no! Of course not!" concurred Mrs. Maldon, further enforcing intrepidity on herself. "Of course not! I only just mentioned burglars because they're so much in the paper." And she stooped to pick up the *Signal* and folded it carefully, as if to prove that her mind was utterly collected.

Councillor Batchgrew, leaning over the table, peered into various vessels in search of his gloves. At length he took them finickingly from the white slop-basin as though fishing them out of a puddle. He began to put them on, and then, half-way through the process, abruptly shook hands with Mrs. Maldon.

"Then you'll call in the morning?" she asked.

"Aye! Ye may count on me. I'll relieve ye on [of] it afore ten o'clock. It'll be on my way to Hanbridge, ye see."

Mrs. Maldon ceremoniously accompanied her trustee as far as the sitting-room door, where she recommended him to the careful attention of Rachel. No woman in the Five Towns could take leave of a guest with more impressive dignity than old Mrs. Maldon, whose fine Southern accent always gave a finish to her farewells. In the lobby Mr. Batchgrew kept Rachel waiting with his overcoat in her outstretched hands while he completed the business of his gloves. As, close behind him, she coaxed his stiff arms into the overcoat, she suddenly felt that after all he was nothing but a decrepit survival; and his offensiveness seemed somehow to have been increased—perhaps by the singular episode of the gloves and the slop-basin. She opened the front door, and without a word to her he departed down the steps.

Two lamps like lighthouses glared fiercely along the roadway, dulling the municipal gas and giving to each loose stone on the macadam a long shadow. In the gloom behind the lamps the low form of an open automobile showed, and a dim, cloaked figure beside it. A boyish voice said with playful bullying sharpness, above the growling, irregular pulsation of the engine— "Here, grandad, you've got to put this on."

"Have I?" demanded uncertainly the thick, heavy voice of the old man.

"Yes, you have—on the top of your other coat. If I don't look after you I shall get myself into a row!... Here, let me put your fist in the armhole. It's your blooming glove that stops it.... There! Now, up with you, grandad!... All right! I've got you. I sha'n't drop you."

A door snapped to; then another. The car shot violently forward, with shrieks and a huge buzzing noise, and leaped up the slope of the street. Rachel, still in the porch, could see Mr. Batchgrew's head wagging rather helplessly from side to side, just above the red speck of the tail-lamp. Then the whole vision was swiftly blotted out, and the warning shrieks of the invisible car grew fainter on the way to Red Cow. It pleased Rachel to think of the old man being casually bullied and shaken by John's Ernest.

She leaned forward and gazed down the street, not up it. When she turned into the house Mrs. Maldon was descending the stairs, which, being in a line with the lobby, ended opposite the front door. Judging by the fixity of the old lady's features, Rachel decided that she was not yet quite pardoned for the slight she had put upon the memory of her employer. So she smiled pleasantly.

"Don't close the front door, dear," said Mrs. Maldon stiffly. "There's some one there."

Rachel looked round. She had actually, in sheer absent-mindedness or negligence or deafness, been shutting the door in the face of the telegraph-boy!

"Oh, dear! I do hope—!" Mrs. Maldon muttered as she hastily tugged at the envelope.

Having read the message, she passed it on to Rachel, and at the same time forgivingly responded to her smile. The excitement of the telegram had sufficed to dissipate Mrs. Maldon's trifling resentment.

Rachel read—

"Train hour late. Julian."

The telegraph boy was dismissed: "No answer, thank you."

X

During the next half-hour excitement within the dwelling gradually increased. It grew out of nothing—out of Mrs. Maldon's admirable calm in receiving the message of the telegram—until it affected like an atmospheric disturbance the ground floor—the sitting-room where Mrs. Maldon was spending nervous force in the effort to preserve an absolutely tranquil mind, the kitchen where Rachel was "putting back" the supper, the lobby towards which Rachel's eye and Mrs. Maiden's ear were strained to catch any sign of an arrival, and the unlighted, unused room behind the sitting-room which seemed to absorb and even intensify the changing moods of the house.

The fact was that Mrs. Maldon, in her relief at finding that Julian was not killed or maimed for life in a railway accident, had begun by treating a delay of one hour in all her arrangements for the evening as a trifle. But she had soon felt that, though a trifle, it was really very upsetting and annoying. It gave birth to irrational yet real forebodings as to the non-success of her little party. It meant that the little party had "started badly." And then her other grand-nephew, Louis Fores, did not arrive. He had been invited for supper at seven, and should have appeared at five minutes to seven at the latest. But at five minutes to seven he had not come; nor at seven, nor at five minutes past—he who had barely a quarter of a mile to walk! There was surely a fate against the party! And Rachel strangely persisted in not leaving the kitchen! Even after Mrs. Maldon had heard her fumbling for an interminable time with the difficult window on the first-floor landing, she went back to the kitchen instead of presenting herself to her expectant mistress.

At last Rachel entered the sitting-room, faintly humming an air. Mrs. Maldon thought that she looked self-conscious. But Mrs. Maldon also was self-conscious, and somehow could not bring her lips to utter the name of Louis Fores to Rachel. For the old lady had divined a connection of cause and effect between Louis Fores and the apparition of Rachel's superlative frock. And she did not like the connection; it troubled her, and offended the extreme nicety of her social code.

There was a constrained silence, which was broken by the lobby clock striking the first quarter after seven. This harsh announcement on the part of the inhuman clock seemed to render the situation intolerable. Fifteen minutes past seven, and Louis not come, and not a word of comment thereon! Mrs. Maldon had to admit privately that she was in a high state of agitation.

Then Rachel, bending delicately to sweep the hearth with the brass-handled brush proper to it, remarked with an obvious affectation of nonchalance—

"Your other guest's late too."

If Mrs. Maldon had not been able to speak his name, neither could Rachel! Mrs. Maldon read with painful certainty all the girl's symptoms.

"Yes, indeed!" said Mrs. Maldon.

"It's like as if what must be!" Rachel murmured, employing a local phrase which Mrs. Maldon had ever contemned as meaningless and ungrammatical.

"Fortunately it doesn't matter, as Julian is late too," said Mrs. Maldon insincerely, for it was mattering very much. "But still—I wonder—"

Rachel broke out upon her hesitation in a very startling manner—

"I'll just see if he's coming."

And she abruptly quitted the room, almost slamming the door.

Mrs. Maldon was dumbfounded. Scared and attentive, she listened in a maze for the sound of the front door. She heard it open. But was it possible that she heard also the creak of the gate? She sprang to the bow window with surprising activity, and pulled aside a blind, one inch.... There was Rachel tripping hatless and in her best frock down the street! Inconceivable vision, affecting Mrs. Maldon with palpitation! A girl so excellent, so lovable, so trustworthy, to be guilty of the wanton caprice of a minx! Supposing Louis were to see her, to catch her in the brazen act of looking for him! Mrs. Maldon was grieved; and her gentle sorrow for Rachel's incalculable lapse was so dignified, affectionate, and jealous for the good repute of human nature that it mysteriously ennobled instead of degrading the young creature.

XI

Going down Bycars Lane amid the soft wandering airs of the September night, Rachel had the delicious and exciting sensation of being unyoked, of being at liberty for a space to obey the strong, free common sense of youth instead of conforming to the outworn and tiresome code of another age. Mrs. Maldon's was certainly a house that put a strain on the nerves. It did not occur to Rachel that she was doing aught but a very natural and proper thing. The non-appearance of Louis Fores was causing disquiet, and her simple aim was to shorten the period of anxiety. Nor did it occur to her that she was impulsive. Something had to be done, and she had done something. Not much longer could she have borne the suspense. All that day she had lived forward towards supper-time, when Louis Fores would appear. Over and over again she had lived right through the moment of opening the front door for him at a little before seven o'clock. The moments between seven o'clock and a quarter past had been a crescendo of torment, intolerable at last. His lateness was inexplicable, and he was so close to that not to look for him would have been ridiculous.

She was apprehensive, and yet she was obscurely happy in her fears. The large, inviting, dangerous universe was about her—she had escaped from the confining shelter of the house. And the night was about her. It was not necessary for her to wear three coats, like the gross Batchgrew, in order to protect herself from the night! She could go forth into it with no precaution. She was young. Her vigorous and confident body might challenge perils.

When she had proceeded a hundred yards she stopped and turned to look back at the cluster of houses collectively called Bycars.

The distinctive bow-window of Mrs. Maldon's shone yellow. Within the sacred room was still the old lady, sitting expectant, and trying to interest herself in the paper. Strange thought!

Bycars Lane led in a north-easterly direction over the broad hill whose ridge separates the lane from the moorlands honeycombed with coal and iron mines. Above the ridge showed the fire and vapour of the first mining villages, on the way to Red Cow, proof that not all colliers were yet on strike. And above that pyrotechny hung the moon. The municipal park, of which Bycars Lane was the north-western boundary, lay in mysterious and forbidden groves behind its spiked red wall and locked gates, and beyond it a bright tram-car was leaping down from lamp to lamp of Moorthorne Road towards the town. Between the masses of the ragged hedge on the north side of the lane there was the thin gleam of Bycars Pool, lost in a vague, unoccupied region of shawdrucks and dirty pasture—the rendezvous of skaters when the frost held, Louis Fores had told her, and she had heard from another source that he skated divinely. She could believe it, too.

She resumed her way more slowly. She had only stopped because, though burned with the desire to see him, she yet had an instinct to postpone the encounter. She was almost minded to return. But she went on. The town was really very near. The illuminated clock of the Town Hall had dominion over it; the golden shimmer above the roofs to the left indicated the electrical splendour of the new Cinema in Moorthorne Road next to the new Primitive Methodist Chapel. He had told her about that, too. In two minutes, in less than two minutes, she was among houses again, and approaching the corner of Friendly Street. He would come from the Moorthorne Road end of Friendly Street. She would peep round the corner of Friendly Street to see if he was coming....

But before she reached the corner, her escapade suddenly presented itself to her as childish madness, silly, inexcusable; and she thought self-reproachfully, "How impulsive I am!" and sharply turned back towards Mrs. Maldon's house, which seemed to be about ten miles off.

A moment later she heard hurried footfalls behind her on the narrow brick pavement, and, after one furtive glance over her shoulder, she quickened her pace. Louis Fores in all his elegance was pursuing her! Nothing had happened to him. He was not ill; he was merely a little late! After all, she would sit by his side at the supper-table! She had a spasm of shame that was excruciating. But at the same time she was wildly glad. And already this inebriating illusion of an ingenuous girl concerning a common male was helping to shape monstrous events.

CHAPTER II
LOUIS' DISCOVERY

I

Louis Fores was late at his grand-aunt's because he had by a certain preoccupation, during a period of about an hour, been rendered oblivious of the passage of time. The real origin of the affair went back nearly sixty years, to an indecorous episode in the history of the Maldon family.

At that date—before Mrs. Maldon had even met Austin Maldon, her future husband—Austin's elder brother Athelstan, who was well established as an earthenware broker in London, had a conjugal misfortune, which reached its climax in the Matrimonial Court, and left the injured and stately Athelstan with an incomplete household, a spoiled home, and the sole care of two children, a boy and a girl. These children were, almost of necessity, clumsily brought up. The girl married the half-brother of a Lieutenant-General Fores, and Louis Fores was their son. The boy married an American girl, and had issue, Julian Maldon and some daughters.

At the age of eighteen, Louis Fores, amiable, personable, and an orphan, was looking for a career. He had lived in the London suburb of Barnes, and under the influence of a father whose career had chiefly been to be the stepbrother of Lieutenant-General Fores. He was in full possession of the conventionally snobbish ideals of the suburb, reinforced by more than a tincture of the stupendous and unsurpassed snobbishness of the British Army. He had no money, and therefore the liberal professions and the higher division of the Civil Service were closed to him. He had the choice of two activities: he might tout for wine, motor-cars, or mineral-waters on commission (like his father), or he might enter a bank; his friends were agreed that nothing else was conceivable. He chose the living grave. It is not easy to enter the living grave, but, august influences aiding, he entered it with *éclat* at a salary of seventy pounds a year, and it closed over him. He would have been secure till his second death had he not defiled the bier. The day of judgment occurred, the grave opened, and he was thrown out with ignominy, but ignominy unpublished. The august influences, by simple cash, and for their own sakes, had saved him from exposure and a jury.

In order to get rid of him his protectors spoke well of him, emphasizing his many good qualities, and he was deported to the Five Towns (properly enough, since his grandfather had come thence) and there joined the staff of Batchgrew & Sons, thanks to the kind intervention of Mrs. Maldon. At the end of a year John Batchgrew told him to go, and told Mrs. Maldon that her grand-nephew had a fault. Mrs. Maldon was very sorry. At this juncture Louis Fores, without intending to do so, would certainly have turned Mrs. Maldon's last years into a tragedy, had he not in the very nick of time inherited about a thousand pounds. He was rehabilitated. He "had money" now. He had a fortune; he had ten thousand pounds; he had any sum you like, according to the caprice of rumour. He lived on his means for a little time, frequenting the Municipal School of Art at the Wedgwood Institution at Bursley, and then old Batchgrew had casually suggested to Mrs. Maldon that there ought to be an opening for him with Jim Horrocleave, who was understood to be succeeding with his patent special processes for earthenware manufacture. Mr. Horrocleave, a man with a chin, would not accept him for a partner, having no desire to share profits with anybody; but on the faith of his artistic tendency and Mrs. Maldon's correct yet highly misleading catalogue of his virtues, he took him at a salary, in return for which Louis was to be the confidential employee who could and would do anything, including design.

And now Louis was the step-nephew of a Lieutenant-General, a man of private means and of talent, and a trusted employee with a fine wage—all under one skin! He shone in Bursley, and no wonder! He was very active at Horrocleave's. He not only designed shapes for vases, and talked intimately with Jim Horrocleave about fresh projects, but he controlled the petty cash. The expenditure of petty cash grew, as was natural in a growing business. Mr. Horrocleave soon got accustomed to that, and apparently gave it no thought, signing cheques instantly upon request. But on the very day of Mrs. Maldon's party, after signing a cheque and before handing it to Louis, he had somewhat lengthily consulted his private cash-book, and, as he handed over the cheque, had said: "Let's have a squint at the petty-cash book to-morrow morning, Louis." He said it gruffly, but he was a gruff man. He left early. He might have meant anything or nothing. Louis could not decide which; or rather, from five o'clock to seven he had come to alternating decisions every five minutes.

II

It was just about at the time when Louis ought to have been removing his paper cuff-shields in order to start for Mrs. Maldon's that he discovered the full extent of his debt to the petty-cash box. He sat alone at a rough and dirty desk in the inner room of the works "office," surrounded by dust-covered sample vases and other vessels of all shapes, sizes, and tints—specimens of Horrocleave's "Art Lustre Ware," a melancholy array of ingenious ugliness that nevertheless filled with pride its creators. He looked through a dirt-obscured window and with unseeing gaze surveyed a muddy, littered quadrangle whose twilight was reddened by gleams from the engine-house. In this yard lay flat a sign that had been blown down from the façade of the manufactory six months before: "Horrocleave. Art Lustre Ware." Within the room was another sign, itself fashioned in lustre-ware: "Horrocleave. Art Lustre Ware." And the envelopes and paper and bill-heads on the desk all bore the same legend: "Horrocleave. Art Lustre Ware."

He owed seventy-three pounds to the petty-cash box, and he was startled and shocked. He was startled because for weeks past he had refrained from adding up the columns of the cash-book—partly from idleness and partly from a desire to remain in ignorance of his own doings. He had hoped for the best. He had faintly hoped that the deficit would not exceed ten pounds, or twelve; he had been prepared for a deficit of twenty-five, or even thirty. But seventy-three really shocked. Nay, it staggered. It meant that in addition to his salary, some thirty shillings a week had been mysteriously trickling through the incurable hole in his pocket. Not to mention other debts! He well knew that to Shillitoe alone (his admirable tailor) he owed eighteen pounds.

It may be asked how a young bachelor, with private means and a fine salary, living in a district where prices are low and social conventions not costly, could have come to such a pass. The answer is that Louis had no private means, and that his salary was not fine. The thousand pounds had gradually vanished, as a thousand pounds will, in the refinements of material existence and in the pursuit of happiness. His bank-account had long been in abeyance. His salary was three pounds a week. Many a member of the liberal professions—many a solicitor, for example—brings up a family on three pounds a week in the provinces. But for a Lieutenant-General's nephew, who had once had a thousand pounds in one lump, three pounds a week was inadequate. As a fact, Louis conceived himself "Art Director" of Horrocleave's, and sincerely thought that as such he was ill-paid. Herein was one of his private excuses for eccentricity with the petty cash. It may also be asked what Louis had to show for his superb expenditure. The answer is, nothing.

With the seventy-three pounds desolatingly clear in his mind, he quitted his desk in order to reconnoitre the outer and larger portion of the counting-house. He went as far as the archway, and saw black smoke being blown downwards from heaven into Friendly Street. A policeman was placidly regarding the smoke as he strolled by. And Louis, though absolutely sure that the officer would not carry out his plain duty of summoning Horrocleave's for committing a smoke-nuisance, did not care for the spectacle of the policeman. He returned to the inner office, and locked the door. The "staff" and the "hands" had all gone, save one or two piece-workers in the painting-shop across the yard.

The night watchman, fresh from bed, was moving fussily about the yard. He nodded with respect to Louis through the grimy window. Louis lit the gas, and spread a newspaper in front of the window by way of blind. And then he began a series of acts on the petty-cash book. The office clock indicated twenty past six. He knew that time was short, but he had a natural gift for the invention and execution of these acts, and he calculated that under half an hour would suffice for them. But when he next looked at the clock, the acts being accomplished, one hour had elapsed; it had seemed to him more like a quarter of an hour. Yet as blotting-paper cannot safely be employed in such delicate calligraphic feats as those of Louis', even an hour was not excessive for what he had done. An operator clumsier, less cool, less cursory, more cautious than himself might well have spent half a night over the job. He locked up the book, washed his hands and face with remarkable celerity in a filthy lavatory basin, brushed his hair, removed his cuff-shields, changed his coat, and fled at speed, leaving the key of the office with the watchman.

III

"I suppose the old lady was getting anxious?" said he brightly (but in a low tone so that the old lady should not hear), as he shook hands with Rachel in the lobby. He had recognized her in front of him up the lane—had, in fact, nearly overtaken her; and she was standing at the open door when he mounted the steps. She had had just time to prove to Mrs. Maldon, by a "He's coming" thrown through the sitting-room doorway, that she had not waited for Louis Fores and walked up with him.

"Yes," Rachel replied in the same tone, most deceitfully leaving him under the false impression that it was the old lady's anxiety that had sent her out. She had, then, emerged scathless in reputation from the indiscreet adventure!

The house was animated by the arrival of Louis; at once it seemed to live more keenly when he had crossed the threshold. And Louis found pleasure in the house—in the welcoming aspect of its interior, in Rachel's evident excited gladness at seeing him, in her honest and agreeable features, and in her sheer girlishness. A few minutes earlier he had been in the sordid and dreadful office. Now he was in another and a cleaner, prettier world. He yielded instantly and fully to its invitation, for he had the singular faculty of being able to cast off care like a garment. He felt sympathetic towards women, and eager to employ for their contentment all the charm which he knew he possessed. He gave himself, generously, in every gesture and intonation.

"Office, auntie, office!" he exclaimed, elegantly entering the parlour. "Sack-cloth! Ashes! Hallo! where's Julian? Is he late too?"

When he had received the news about Julian Maldon he asked to see the telegram, and searched out its place of origin, and drew forth a pocket time-table, and remarked in a wise way that he hoped Julian would "make the connection" at Derby. Lastly he predicted the precise minute at which Julian "ought" to be knocking at the front door. And both women felt their ignorant, puzzled inferiority in these recondite matters of travel, and the comfort of having an omniscient male in the house.

Then slightly drawing up his dark blue trousers with an accustomed movement, he carefully sat down on the Chesterfield, and stroked his soft black moustache (which was estimably long for a fellow of twenty-three) and patted his black hair.

"Rachel, you didn't fasten that landing window, after all!" said Mrs. Maldon, looking over Louis' head at the lady companion, who hesitated modestly near the door. "I've tried, but I couldn't."

"Neither could I, Mrs. Maldon," said Rachel. "I was thinking perhaps Mr. Fores wouldn't mind—"

She did not explain that her failure to fasten the window had been more or less deliberate, since, while actually tugging at the window, she had been visited by the sudden delicious thought: "How nice it would be to ask Louis Fores to do this hard thing for me!"

And now she had asked him.

"Certainly!" Louis jumped to his feet, and off he went upstairs. Most probably, if the sudden delicious thought had not skipped into Rachel's brain, he would never have made that critical ascent to the first floor.

A gas-jet burned low on the landing.

"Let's have a little light on the subject," he cheerfully muttered to himself, as he turned on the gas to the full.

Then in the noisy blaze of yellow and blue light he went to the window and with a single fierce wrench he succeeded in pulling the catch into position. He was proud of his strength. It pleased him to think of the weakness of women; it pleased him to anticipate the impressed thanks of the weak women for this exertion of his power on their behalf. "Have you managed it so soon?" his aunt would exclaim, and he would answer in a carefully offhand way, "Of course. Why not?"

He was about to descend, but he remembered that he must not leave the gas at full. With his hand on the tap, he glanced perfunctorily around the little landing. The door of Mrs. Maldon's bedroom was in front of him, at right angles to the window. By the door, which was ajar, stood a cane-seated chair. Underneath the chair he perceived a whitish package or roll that seemed to be out of place there on the floor. He stooped and picked it up. And as the paper rustled peculiarly in his hand, he could feel his heart give a swift bound. He opened the roll. It consisted of nothing whatever but bank-notes. He listened intently, with ear cocked and rigid limbs, and he could just catch the soothing murmur of women's voices in the parlour beneath the reverberating, solemn pulse of the lobby clock.

IV

Louis Fores had been intoxicated into a condition of poesy. He was deliciously incapable of any precise thinking; he could not formulate any theory to account for the startling phenomenon of a roll of bank-notes loose under a chair on a first-floor landing of his great-aunt's house; he could not even estimate the value of the roll—he felt only that it was indefinitely prodigious. But he had the most sensitive appreciation of the exquisite beauty of those pieces of paper. They were not merely beautiful because they stood for delight and indulgence, raising lovely visions of hosiers' and jewellers' shops and the night interiors of clubs and restaurants—raising one clear vision of himself clasping a watch-bracelet on the soft arm of Rachel who had so excitingly smiled upon him a moment ago. They were beautiful in themselves; the aspect and very texture of them were beautiful—surpassing pictures and fine scenery. They were the most poetic things in the world. They transfigured the narrow, gaslit first-floor landing of his great-aunt's house into a secret and unearthly grove of bliss. He was drunk with quivering emotion.

And then, as he gazed at the divine characters printed in sable on the rustling whiteness, he was aware of a stab of ugly, coarse pain. Up to the instant of beholding those bank-notes he had been convinced that his operations upon the petty-cash book would be entirely successful and that the immediate future of Horrocleave's was assured of tranquillity; he had been blandly certain that Horrocleave held no horrid suspicion against him, and that even if Horrocleave's pate did conceal a dark thought, it would be conjured at once away by the superficial reasonableness of the falsified accounts. But now his mind was terribly and inexplicably changed, and it seemed to him impossible to gull the acute and mighty Horrocleave. Failure, exposure, disgrace, ruin, seemed inevitable—and also intolerable. It was astonishing that he should have deceived himself into an absurd security. The bank-notes, by some magic virtue which they possessed, had opened his eyes to the truth. And they presented themselves as absolutely indispensable to him. They had sprung from naught, they belonged to nobody, they existed without a creative cause in the material world—and they were indispensable to him! Could it be conceived that he should lose his high and brilliant position in the town, that two policemen should hustle him into the black van, that the gates of a prison should clang behind him? It could not be conceived. It was monstrously inconceivable.... The bank-notes ... he saw them wavy, as through a layer of hot air.

A heavy knock on the front door below shook him and the floor and the walls. He heard the hurried feet of Rachel, the opening of the door, and Julian's harsh, hoarse voice. Julian, then, was not quite an hour late, after all. The stir in the lobby seemed to be enormous, and very close to him; Mrs. Maldon had come forth from the parlour to greet Julian on his birthday.... Louis stuck the bank-notes into the side pocket of his coat. And as it were automatically his mood underwent a change, violent and complete. "I'll teach the old lady to drop notes all over the place," he said to himself. "I'll just teach her!" And he pictured his triumph as a wise male when, during the course of the feast, his great-aunt should stumble on her loss and yield to senile feminine agitation, and he should remark superiorly, with elaborate calm: "Here is your precious money, auntie. A good thing it was I and not burglars who discovered it. Let this be a lesson to you!... Where was it? It was on the landing carpet, if you please! That's where it was!" And the nice old creature's pathetic relief!

As he went jauntily downstairs there remained nothing of his mood of intoxication except a still thumping heart.

CHAPTER III
THE FEAST

I

· The dramatic moment of the birthday feast came nearly at the end of the meal when Mrs. Maldon, having in mysterious silence disappeared for a space to the room behind, returned with due pomp bearing a parcel in her dignified hands. During her brief absence Louis, Rachel, and Julian—hero of the night—had sat mute and somewhat constrained round the debris of the birthday pudding. The constraint was no doubt due partly to Julian's characteristic and notorious grim temper, and partly to mere anticipation of a solemn event.

Julian Maldon in particular was self-conscious. He hated intensely to be self-conscious, and his feeling towards every witness of his self-consciousness partook always of the homicidal. Were it not that civilization has the means to protect itself, Julian might have murdered defenceless aged ladies and innocent young girls for the simple offence of having seen him blush.

He was a perfect specimen of a throw-back to original ancestry. He had been born in London, of an American mother, and had spent the greater part of his life in London. Yet London and his mother seemed to count for absolutely nothing at all in his composition. At the age of seventeen his soul, quitting the exile of London, had come to the Five Towns with a sigh of relief as if at the assuagement of a long nostalgia, and had dropped into the district as into a socket. In three months he was more indigenous than a native. Any experienced observer who now chanced at a week-end to see him board the Manchester express at Euston would have been able to predict from his appearance that he would leave the train at Knype. He was an undersized man, with a combative and suspicious face. He regarded the world with crafty pugnacity from beneath frowning eyebrows. His expression said: "Woe betide the being who tries to get the better of me!" His expression said: "Keep off!" His expression said: "I am that I am. Take me or leave me, but preferably leave me. I loathe fuss, pretence, flourishes—any and every form of damned nonsense."

He had an excellent heart, but his attitude towards it was the attitude of his great-grandmother towards her front parlour—he used it as little as possible, and kept it locked up like a shame. In brief, he was more than a bit of a boor. And boorishness being his chief fault, he was quite naturally proud of it, counted it for the finest of all qualities, and scorned every manifestation of its opposite. To prove his inward sincerity he deemed it right to flout any form of external grace—such as politeness, neatness, elegance, compliments, small-talk, smooth words, and all ceremonial whatever. He would have died in torment sooner than kiss. He was averse even from shaking hands, and when he did shake hands he produced a carpenter's vice, crushed flesh and bone together, and flung the intruding pulp away. His hat was so heavy on his head that only by an exhausting and supreme effort could he raise it to a woman, and after the odious accident he would feel as humiliated as a fox-terrier after a bath. By the kind hazard of fate he had never once encountered his great-aunt in the street. He was superb in enmity—a true hero. He would quarrel with a fellow and say, curtly, "I'll never speak to you again"; and he never would speak to that fellow again. Were the last trump to blow and all the British Isles to be submerged save the summit of Snowdon, and he and that fellow to find themselves alone and safe together on the peak, he could still be relied upon never to speak to that fellow again. Thus would he prove that he was a man of his word and that there was no nonsense about him.

Strange though it may appear to the thoughtless, he was not disliked—much less ostracised. Codes differ. He conformed to one which suited the instincts of some thirty thousand other adult males in the Five Towns. Two strapping girls in the warehouse of his manufactory at Knype quarrelled over him in secret as the Prince Charming of those parts. Yet he had never addressed them except to inform them that if they didn't mind their p's and q's he would have them flung off the "bank" [manufactory]. Rachel herself had not yet begun to be prejudiced against him.

This monster of irascible cruelty regarded himself as a middle-aged person. But he was only twenty-five that day, and he did not look more, either, despite a stiff, strong moustache. He too, like Louis and Rachel, had the gestures of youth—the unconsidered, lithe movements of limb, the wistful, unteachable pride of his age, the touching self-confidence. Old Mrs. Maldon was indeed old among them.

II

She sat down in all her benevolent stateliness and with a slightly irritating deliberation undid the parcel, displaying a flattish leather case about seven inches by four, which she handed formally to Julian Maldon, saying as she did so—

"From your old auntie, my dear boy, with her loving wishes. You have now lived just a quarter of a century."

And as Julian, awkwardly grinning, fumbled with the spring-catch of the case, she was aware of having accomplished a great and noble act of surrender. She hoped the best from it. In particular, she hoped that she had saved the honour of her party and put it at last on a secure footing of urbane convivial success. For that a party of hers should fail in giving pleasure to every member of it was a menace to her legitimate pride. And so far fate had not been propitious. The money in the house had been, and was, on her mind. Then the lateness of the guests had disturbed her. And then Julian had aggrieved her by a piece of obstinacy very like himself. Arriving straight from a train journey, he had wanted to wash. But he would not go to the specially prepared bedroom, where a perfect apparatus awaited him. No, he must needs take off his jacket in the back room and roll up his sleeves and stamp into the scullery and there splash and rub like a stableman, and wipe himself on the common rough roller-towel. He said he preferred the "sink." (Offensive word! He would not even say "slop-stone," which was the proper word. He said "sink," and again "sink.")

And then, when the meal finally did begin Mrs. Maldon's serviette and silver serviette-ring had vanished. Impossible to find them! Mr. Batchgrew had of course horribly disarranged the table, and in the upset the serviette and ring might have fallen unnoticed into the darkness beneath the table. But no search could discover them. Had the serviette and ring ever been on the table at all? Had Rachael perchance forgotten them? Rachael was certain that she had put them on the table. She remembered casting away a soiled serviette and replacing it with a clean one in accordance with Mrs. Maldon's command for the high occasion. She produced the soiled serviette in proof. Moreover, the ring was not in the serviette drawer of the sideboard. Renewed search was equally sterile.... At one moment Mrs. Maldon thought that she herself had seen the serviette and ring on the table early in the evening; but at the next she thought she had not. Conceivably Mr. Batchgrew had taken them in mistake. Yes, assuredly, he had taken them in mistake—somehow! And yet it was inconceivable that he had taken a serviette and ring in mistake. In mistake for what? No!...

Mystery! Excessively disconcerting for an old lady! In the end Rachel provided another clean serviette, and the meal commenced. But Mrs. Maldon had not been able to "settle down" in an instant. The wise, pitying creatures in their twenties considered that it was absurd for her to worry herself about such a trifle. But was it a trifle? It was rather a denial of natural laws, a sinister miracle. Serviette-rings cannot walk, nor fly, nor be annihilated. And further, she had used that serviette-ring for more than twenty years. However, the hostess in her soon triumphed over the foolish old lady, and taken the head of the board with aplomb.

And indeed aplomb had been required. For the guests behaved strangely—unless it was that the hostess was in a nervous mood for fancying trouble! Julian Maldon was fidgety and preoccupied. And Louis himself— usually a model guest—was also fidgety and preoccupied. As for Rachel, the poor girl had only too obviously lost her head about Louis. Mrs. Maldon had never seen anything like it, never!

III

Julian, having opened the case, disclosed twin brier pipes, silver-mounted, with alternative stems of various lengths and diverse mouthpieces—all reposing on soft couches of fawn-tinted stuff, with a crimson, silk-lined lid to serve them for canopy. A rich and costly array! Everybody was impressed, even startled. For not merely was the gift extremely handsome—it was more than a gift; it symbolized the end of an epoch in those lives. Mrs. Maldon had been no friend of tobacco. She had lukewarmly permitted cigarettes, which Louis smoked, smoking naught else. But cigars she had discouraged, and pipes she simply would not have! Now, Julian smoked nothing but a pipe. Hence in his great-aunt's parlour he had not smoked; in effect he had been forbidden to smoke there. The theory that a pipe was vulgar had been stiffly maintained in that sacred parlour. In the light of these facts did not Mrs. Maldon's gift indeed shine as a great and noble act of surrender? Was it not more than a gift, and entitled to stagger beholders? Was it not a sublime proof that the earth revolves and the world moves?

Mrs. Maldon was as susceptible as any one to the drama of the moment, perhaps more than any one. She thrilled and became happy as Julian in silence minutely examined the pipes. She had taken expert advice before purchasing, and she was tranquil as to the ability of the pipes to withstand criticism. They bore the magic triple initials of the first firm of brier-pipe makers in the world—initials as famous and as welcome on the plains of Hindustan as in the Home Counties or the frozen zone. She gazed round the table with increasing satisfaction. Louis, who was awkwardly fixed with regard to the light, the shadow of his bust falling always across his plate, had borne that real annoyance with the most charming good-humour. He was a delight to the eye; he had excellent qualities, especially social qualities. Rachel sat opposite to the hostess—an admirable girl in most ways, a splendid companion, and a sound cook. The meal had been irreproachable, and in the phrase of the *Signal* "ample justice had been done" to it. Julian was on the hostess's left, with his back to the window and to the draught. A good boy, a sterling boy, if peculiar! And there they were all close together, intimate, familiar, mutually respecting; and the perfect parlour was round about them: a domestic organism, honest, dignified, worthy, more than comfortable. And she, Elizabeth Maldon, in her old age, was the head of it, and the fount of good things.

"Thank ye!" ejaculated Julian, with a queer look askance at his benefactor. "Thank ye, aunt!"

It was all he could get out of his throat, and it was all that was expected of him. He hated to give thanks—and he hated to be thanked. The grandeur of the present flattered him. Nevertheless he regarded it as essentially absurd in its pretentiousness. The pipes were A1, but could a man carry about a huge contraption like that? All a man needed was an A1 pipe, which, if he had any sense, he would carry loose in his pocket with his pouch—and be hanged to morocco cases and silk linings!

"Stoke up, my hearties!" said Louis, drawing forth a gun-metal cigarette-case, which was chained to his person by a kind of cable.

Undoubtedly the case of pipes represented for Julian a triumph over Louis, or, at least, justice against Louis. For obvious reasons Julian had not quarrelled with a rich and affectionate great-aunt because she had accorded to Louis the privilege of smoking in her parlour what he preferred to smoke, while refusing a similar privilege to himself. But he had resented the distinction. And his joy in the spectacular turn of the wheel was vast. For that very reason he hid it with much care. Why should he bubble over with gratitude for having been at last treated fairly? It would be pitiful to do so. Leaving the case open upon the table, he pulled a pouch and an old pipe from his pocket, and began to fill the pipe. It was inexcusable, but it was like him—he had to do it.

"But aren't you going to try one of the new ones?" asked Mrs. Maldon, amiably but uncertainly.

"No," said he, with cold nonchalance. Upon nobody in the world had the sweet magic of Mrs. Maldon's demeanour less influence than upon himself. "Not now. I want to enjoy my smoke, and the first smoke out of a new pipe is never any good."

It was very true, but far more wanton than true. Mrs. Maldon in her ignorance could not appreciate the truth, but she could appreciate its wantonness. She was wounded—silly, touchy old thing! She was wounded, and she hid the wound.

Rachel flushed with ire against the boor.

"By the way," Mrs. Maldon remarked in a light, indifferent tone, just as though the glory of the moment had not been suddenly rent and shrivelled. "I didn't see your portmanteau in the back room just now, Julian. Has any one carried it upstairs? I didn't hear any one go upstairs."

"I didn't bring one, aunt," said Julian.

"Not bring—"

"I was forgetting to tell ye. I can't sleep here to-night. I'm off to South Africa to-morrow, and I've got a lot of things to fix up at my digs to-night." He lit the old pipe from a match which Louis passed to him.

"To South Africa?" murmured Mrs. Maldon, aghast. And she repeated, "South Africa?" To her it was an incredible distance. It was not a place—it was something on the map. Perhaps she had never imaginatively realized that actual people did in fact go to South Africa. "But this is the first I have heard of this!" she said. Julian's extraordinary secretiveness always disturbed her.

"I only got the telegram about my berth this morning," said Julian, rather sullenly on the defensive.

"Is it business?" Mrs. Maldon asked.

"You may depend it isn't pleasure, aunt," he answered, and shut his lips tight on the pipe.

After a pause Mrs. Maldon tried again.

"Where do you sail from?"

Julian answered—

"Southampton."

There was another pause. Louis and Rachel exchanged a glance of sympathetic dismay at the situation.

Mrs. Maldon then smiled with plaintive courage.

"Of course if you can't sleep here, you can't," said she benignly. "I can see that. But we were quite counting on having a man in the house to-night—with all these burglars about—weren't we, Rachel?" Her grimace became, by an effort, semi-humorous.

Rachel diplomatically echoed the tone of Mrs. Maldon, but more brightly, with a more frankly humorous smile—

"We were, indeed!"

But her smile was a masterpiece of duplicity, somewhat strange in a girl so downright; for beneath it burned hotly her anger against the brute Julian.

"Well, there it is!" Julian gruffly and callously summed up the situation, staring at the inside of his teacup.

"Propitious moment for getting a monopoly of door-knobs at the Cape, I suppose?" said Louis quizzically. His cousin manufactured, among other articles, white and jet door-knobs.

"No need for you to be so desperately funny!" snapped Julian, who detested Louis' brand of facetiousness. It was the word "propitious" that somehow annoyed him—it had a sarcastic flavour, and it was "Louis all over."

"No offence, old man!" Louis magnanimously soothed him. "On the contrary, many happy returns of the day." In social intercourse the younger cousin's good-humour and suavity were practically indestructible.

But Julian still scowled.

Rachel, to make a tactful diversion, rose and began to collect plates. The meal was at an end, and for Mrs. Maldon it had closed in ignominy. From her quarter of the table she pushed crockery towards Rachel with a gesture of disillusion; the courage to smile had been but momentary. She felt old—older than she had ever felt before. The young generation presented themselves to her as almost completely enigmatic. She admitted that they were foreign to her, that she could not comprehend them at all. Each of the three at her table was entirely free and independent—each could and did act according to his or her whim, and none could say them nay. Such freedom seemed unreal. They were children playing at life, and playing dangerously. Hundreds of times, in conversation with her coevals, she had cheerfully protested against the banal complaint that the world had changed of late years. But now she felt grievously that the world was different—that it had indeed deteriorated since her young days. She was fatigued by the modes of thought of these youngsters, as a nurse or mother is fatigued by too long a spell of the shrillness and the *naïveté* of a family of infants. She wanted repose.... Was it conceivable that when, with incontestable large-mindedness, she had given a case of pipes to Julian, he should first put a slight on her gift and then, brusquely leaving her in the lurch, announce his departure for South Africa, with as much calm as though South Africa were in the next street?... And the other two were guilty in other ways, perhaps more subtly, of treason against forlorn old age.

And then Louis, in taking the slop-basin from her trembling fingers, to pass it to Rachel, gave her one of his adorable, candid, persuasive, sympathetic smiles. And lo! she was enheartened once more. And she remembered that dignity and kindliness had been the watchwords of her whole life, and that it would be shameful to relinquish the struggle for an ideal at the very threshold of the grave. She began to find excuses for Julian. The dear lad must have many business worries. He was very young to be at the head of a manufacturing concern. He had a remarkable brain—worthy of the family. Allowances must be made for him. She must not be selfish.... And assuredly that serviette and ring would reappear on the morrow.

"I'll take that out," said Louis, indicating the tray which Rachel had drawn from concealment under the Chesterfield, and which was now loaded. Mrs. Maldon employed an old and valued charwoman in the mornings. Rachel accomplished all the rest of the housework herself, including cookery, and she accomplished it with the stylistic smartness of a self-respecting lady-help.

"Oh no!" said she. "I can carry it quite easily, thanks."

Louis insisted masculinely—

"I'll take that tray out."

And he took it out, holding his head back as he marched, so that the smoke of the cigarette between his lips should not obscure his eyes. Rachel followed with some oddments. Behold those two away together in the seclusion of the kitchen; and Mrs. Maldon and Julian alone in the parlour!

"Very fine!" muttered Julian, fingering the magnificent case of pipes. Now that there were fewer spectators, his tongue was looser, and he could relent.

"I'm so glad you like it," Mrs. Maldon responded eagerly.

The world was brighter to her, and she accepted Julian's amiability as Heaven's reward for her renewal of courage.

IV

"Auntie-" began Louis, with a certain formality.

"Yes?"

Mrs. Maldon had turned her chair a little towards the fire. The two visitants to the kitchen had reappeared. Rachel with a sickle-shaped tool was sedulously brushing the crumbs from the damask into a silver tray. Louis had taken the poker to mend the fire.

He said, nonchalantly—

"If you'd care for me to stay the night here instead of Julian, I will."

"Well—" Mrs. Maldon was unprepared for this apparently quite natural and kindly suggestion. It perturbed, even frightened her by its implications. Had it been planned in the kitchen between those two? She wanted to accept it; and yet another instinct in her prompted her to decline it absolutely and at once. She saw Rachel flushing as the girl industriously continued her task without looking up. To Mrs. Maldon it seemed that those two, under the impulsion of Fate, were rushing towards each other at a speed far greater than she had suspected.

Julian stirred on his chair, under the sharp irritation caused by Louis' proposal. He despised Louis as a boy of no ambition—a butterfly being who had got no farther than the adolescent will-to-live, the desire for self-indulgence, whereas he, Julian, was profoundly conscious of the will-to-dominate, the hunger for influence and power. And also he was jealous of Louis on various counts. Louis had come to the Five Towns years after Julian, and had almost immediately cut a figure therein; Julian had never cut a figure. Julian had been the sole resident great-nephew of a benevolent aunt, and Louis had arrived and usurped at least half the advantages of the relationship, if not more; Louis lived several miles nearer to his aunt. Julian it was who, through his acquaintance with Rachel's father and her masterful sinister brother, had brought her into touch with Mrs. Maldon.

Rachel was Julian's creation, so far as his aunt was concerned. Julian had no dislike for Rachel; he had even been thinking of her favourably. But Louis had, as it were, appropriated her ... From the steely conning-tower of his brows Julian had caught their private glances at the table. And Louis was now carrying trays for her, and hobnobbing with her in the kitchen! Lastly, because Julian could not pass the night in the house, Louis, the interloper, had the effrontery to offer to fill his place—on some preposterous excuse about burglars! And the fellow was so polite and so persuasive, with his finicking eloquence. By virtue of a strange faculty not uncommon in human nature Julian loathed Louis' good manners and appearance—and acutely envied them.

He burst out with scarcely controlled savagery—

"A lot of good you'd be with burglars!"

The women were outraged by his really shocking rudeness. Rachel bit her lip and began to fold up the cloth. Mrs. Maldon's head slightly trembled. Louis alone maintained a perfect equanimity. It was as if he were invulnerable.

"You never know!" he smiled amiably, and shrugged his shoulders. Then he finished his operation on the fire.

"I'm sure it's very kind and thoughtful of you, Louis," said Mrs. Maldon, driven to acceptance by Julian's monstrous behaviour.

"Moreover," Louis urbanely continued, smoothing down his trousers with a long perpendicular caress as he usually did after any bending— "moreover, there's always my revolver."

He gave a short laugh.

"Revolver!" exclaimed Mrs. Maldon, intimidated by the mere name. Then she smiled, in an effort to reassure herself. "Louis, you are a tease. You really shouldn't tease me."

"I'm not," said Louis, with that careful air of false blank casualness which he would invariably employ for his more breath-taking announcements. "I always carry a loaded revolver."

The fearful word "loaded" sank into the heart of the old woman, and thrilled her. It was a fact that for some weeks past Louis had been carrying a revolver. At intervals the craze for firearms seizes the fashionable youth of a provincial town, like the craze for marbles at school, and then dies away. In the present instance it had been originated by the misadventure of a dandy with an out-of-work artisan on the fringe of Hanbridge. Nothing could be more correct than for a man of spirit and fashion thus to arm himself in order to cow the lower orders and so cope with the threatened social revolution.

"You *don't*, Louis!" Mrs. Maldon deprecated.

"I'll show you," said Louis, feeling in his hip pocket.

"*Please!*" protested Mrs. Maldon, and Rachel covered her face with her hands and drew back from Louis' sinister gesture. "Please don't *show* it to us!" Mrs. Maiden's tone was one of imploring entreaty. For an instant she was just like a sentimentalist who resents and is afraid of hearing the truth. She obscurely thought that if she resolutely refused to see the revolver it would somehow cease to exist. With a loaded revolver in the house the situation seemed more dangerous and more complicated than ever. There was something absolutely terrifying in the conjuncture of a loaded revolver and a secret hoard of bank-notes.

"All right! All right!" Louis relented.

Julian cut across the scene with a gruff and final—

"I must clear out of this!"

He rose.

"Must you?" said his aunt.

She did not unduly urge him to delay, for the strain of family life was exhausting her.

"I must catch the 9.48," said Julian, looking at the clock and at his watch.

Herein was yet another example of the morbid reticence which so pained Mrs. Maldon. He must have long before determined to catch the 9.48; yet he had said nothing about it till the last moment! He had said nothing even about South Africa until the news was forced from him. It had been arranged that he should come direct to Bursley station from his commercial journey in Yorkshire and Derbyshire, pass the night at his aunt's house, which was conveniently near the station, and proceed refreshed to business on the morrow. A neat arrangement, well suiting the fact of his birthday! And now he had broken it in silence, without a warning, with the baldest possible explanation! His aunt, despite her real interest in him, could never extract from him a clear account of his doings and his movements. And this South African excursion was the last and worst illustration of his wilful cruel harshness to her.

Nevertheless, the extreme and unimaginable remoteness of South Africa seemed to demand a special high formality in bidding him adieu, and she rendered it. If he would not permit her to superintend his packing (he had never even let her come to his rooms!), she could at least superintend the putting on of his overcoat. And she did. And instead of quitting him as usual at the door of the parlour, she insisted on going to the front door and opening it herself. She was on her mettle. She was majestic and magnificent. By refusing to see his ill-breeding she actually did terminate its existence. She stood at the open front door with the three young ones about her, and by the force of her ideal the front door became the portal of an embassy and Julian's departure a ceremony of state. He had to shake hands all round. She raised her cheek, and he had to kiss. She said, "God bless you!" and he had to say, "Thank you."

As he was descending the outer steps, the pipe-case clipped under his arm, Louis threw at him—

"I say, old man!"

"What?" He turned round with sharp defiance beneath the light of the street-lamp.

"How are you going to get to London to-morrow morning in time for the boat-train at Waterloo, if you're staying at Knype to-night."

Louis travelled little, but it was his foible to be learned in boat-trains and "connections."

"A friend o' mine's motoring me to Stafford at five to-morrow morning, if you want to know. I shall catch the Scotch express. Anything else?"

"Oh!" muttered Louis, checked.

Julian clanked the gate and vanished up the street, Mrs. Maldon waving.

"What friend? What motor?" reflected Mrs. Maldon sadly. "He is incorrigible with his secretiveness."

"Mrs. Maldon," said Rachel anxiously, "you look pale. Is it being in this draught?" She shut the door.

Mrs. Maldon sighed and moved away. She hesitated at the parlour door and then said—

"I must go upstairs a moment."

CHAPTER IV
IN THE NIGHT

I

Louis stood hesitant and slightly impatient in the parlour, alone. A dark blue cloth now covered the table, and in the centre of it was a large copper jar containing an evergreen plant. Of the feast no material trace remained except a few crumbs on the floor. But the room was still pervaded by the emotional effluence of the perturbed souls who had just gone; and Louis felt it, though without understanding.

Throughout the evening he had of course been preoccupied by the consciousness of having in his pocket bank-notes to a value unknown. Several times he had sought for a suitable opportunity to disclose his exciting secret. But he had found none. In practice he could not say to his aunt, before Julian and Rachel: "Auntie, I picked up a lot of bank-notes on the landing. You really ought to be more careful!" He could not even in any way refer to them. The dignity of Mrs. Maldon had intimidated him. He had decided, after Julian's announcement of departure, that he would hand them over to her, simply and undramatically and with no triumphant air, as soon as he and she should for a moment be alone together. Then Mrs. Maldon vanished upstairs. And she had not returned. Rachel also had vanished. And he was waiting.

He desired to examine the notes, to let his eyes luxuriously rest upon them, but he dared not take them from his pocket lest one or other of the silent-footed women might surprise him by a sudden entrance. He fingered them as they lay in their covert, and the mere feel of them, raised exquisite images in his mind; and at the same time the whole room and every object in the room was transformed into a secret witness which spied upon him, disquieted him, and warned him. But the fact that the notes were intact, that nothing irremediable had occurred, reassured him and gave him strength, so that he could defy the suspicions of those senseless surrounding objects.

Within the room there was no sound but the faint regular hiss of the gas and an occasional falling together of coal in the weakening fire. Overhead, from his aunt's bedroom, vague movements were perceptible. Then these ceased, absolutely. The tension, increasing, grew too much for him, and with a curt gesture, and a self-conscious expression between a smile and a frown, he left the parlour and stood to listen in the lobby. Not for several seconds did he notice the heavy ticking of the clock, close to his ear, nor the chill draught that came under the front door. He gazed up into the obscurity at the top of the stairs. The red glow of the kitchen fire, in the distance to the right of the stairs, caught his attention at intervals. He was obsessed, almost overpowered, by the mysteriousness of the first floor. What had happened? What was happening? And suddenly an explanation swept into his brain—the obvious explanation. His aunt had missed the bank-notes and was probably at that very instant working herself into an anguish. What ought he to do? Should he run up and knock at her door? He was spared a decision by the semi-miraculous appearance of Rachel at the top of the stairs. She started.

"Oh! How you frightened me!" she exclaimed in a low voice.

He answered weakly, charmingly—

"Did I?"

"Will you please come and speak to Mrs. Maldon? She wants you."

"In her room?"

Rachel nodded and disappeared before he could ask another question. With heart beating he ascended the stairs by twos. Through the half-open door of the faintly lit room which he himself would occupy he could hear Rachel active. And then he was at the closed door of his aunt's room. "I must be jolly careful how I do it!" he thought as he knocked.

II

He was surprised, and impressed, to see Mrs. Maldon in bed. She lay on her back, with her striking head raised high on several pillows. Nothing else of her was visible; the purple eider-down covered the whole bed without a crease.

"Hello, auntie!" he greeted her, instinctively modifying his voice to the soft gentleness proper to the ordered and solemn chamber.

Mrs. Maldon, moving her head, looked at him in silence. He tiptoed to the foot of the bed and leaned on it gracefully. And as in the parlour his shadow had fallen on the table, so now, with the gas just behind him, it fell on the bed. The room was chilly and had a slight pharmaceutical odour.

Mrs. Maldon said, with a weak effort—

"I was feeling faint, and Rachel thought I'd better get straight to bed. I'm an old woman, Louis."

"She hasn't missed them!" he thought in a flash, and said, aloud—

"Nothing of the sort, auntie."

He was aware of the dim reflection of himself in the mirror of the immense Victorian mahogany wardrobe to his left.

Mrs. Maldon again hesitated before speaking.

"You aren't ill, are you, auntie?" he said in a cheerful, friendly whisper. He was touched by the poignant pathos of her great age and her debility. It rent his heart to think that she had no prospect but the grave.

She murmured, ignoring his question—

"I just wanted to tell you that you needn't go down home for your night things—unless you specially want to, that is. I have all that's necessary here, and I've given orders to Rachel."

"Certainly, auntie. I won't leave the house. That's all right."

No, she assuredly had not missed the notes! He was strangely uplifted. He felt almost joyous in his relief. Could he tell her now as she lay in her bed? Impossible! He would tell her in the morning. It would be cruel to disturb her now with such a revelation of her own negligence. He vibrated with sympathy for her, and he was proud to think that she appreciated the affectionate, comprehending, subdued intimacy of his attitude towards her as he leaned gracefully on the foot of the bed, and that she admired him. He did not know, or rather he absolutely did not realize, that she was acquainted with aught against his good fame. He forgot his sins with the insouciance of an animal.

"Don't stay up too late," said Mrs. Maldon, as it were dismissing him. "A long night will do you no harm for once in a way." She smiled. "I know you'll see that everything's locked up."

He nodded soothingly, and stood upright.

"You might turn the gas down, rather low."

He tripped to the gas-bracket and put the room in obscurity. The light of the street lamp irradiated the pale green blinds of the two windows.

"That do?"

"Nicely, thank you! Good-night, my dear. No, I'm not ill. But you know I have these little attacks. And then bed's the best place for me." Her voice seemed to expire.

He crept across the wide carpet and departed with the skill of a trained nurse, and inaudibly closed the door.

From the landing the whole of the rest of the house seemed to offer itself to him in the night as an enigmatic and alluring field of adventure ... Should he drop the notes under the chair on the landing, where he had found them?... He could not! He could not!... He moved to the head of the stairs, past the open door of the spare bedroom, which was now dark. He stopped at the head of the stairs, and then descended. The kitchen was lighted.

"Are you there?" he asked.

"Yes," replied Rachel.

"May I come?"

"Why, of course!" Her voice trembled.

He went towards the other young creature in the house. The old one lay above, in a different world remote and foreign. He and Rachel had the ground floor and all its nocturnal enchantment to themselves.

III

Mechanically, as he went into the kitchen, he drew his cigarette-case from his pocket. It was the proper gesture of a man in any minor crisis. He was not a frequenter of kitchens, and this visit, even more than the brief first one, seemed to him to be adventurous.

Mrs. Maldon's kitchen—or rather Rachel's—was small, warm (though the fire was nearly out), and agreeable to the eye. On the left wall was a deal dresser full of crockery, and on the right, under the low window, a narrow deal table. In front, opposite the door, gleamed the range, and on either side of the range were cupboards with oak-grained doors. There was a bright steel fender before the range, and then a hearth-rug on which stood an oak rocking-chair. The floor was a friendly chequer of red and black tiles. On the high mantelpiece were canisters and an alarm-clock and utensils; sundry other utensils hung on the walls, among the coloured images of sweet girls and Norse-like men offered by grocers and butchers under the guise of almanacs; and cupboard doors ajar dimly disclosed other utensils still, so that the kitchen had the effect of a novel, comfortable kind of workshop; which effect was helped by the clothes-drier that hung on pulley-ropes from the ceiling, next to the gas-pendant and to a stalactite of onions.

The uncurtained window, instead of showing black, gave on another interior, whitewashed, and well illuminated by the kitchen gas. This other interior had, under a previous tenant of the property, been a lean-to greenhouse, but Mrs. Maldon esteeming a scullery before a greenhouse, it had been modified into a scullery. There it was that Julian Maldon had preferred to make his toilet. One had to pass through the scullery in order to get from the kitchen into the yard. And the light of day had to pass through the imperfectly transparent glass roof of the scullery in order to reach the window of the unused room behind the parlour; and herein lay the reason why that room was unused, it being seldom much brighter than a crypt.

At the table stood Rachel, in her immense pinafore-apron, busy with knives and forks and spoons, and an enamel basin from which steam rose gently. Louis looked upon Rachel, and for the first time in his life liked an apron! It struck him as an exceedingly piquant addition to the young woman's garments. It suited her; it set off the tints of her notable hair; and it suited the kitchen. Without delaying her work, Rachel made the protector of the house very welcome. Obviously she was in a high state of agitation. For an instant Louis feared that the agitation was due to anxiety on account of Mrs. Maldon.

"Nothing serious up with the old lady, is there?" he asked, pinching the cigarette to regularize the tobacco in it.

"Oh, *no!*"

The exclamation in its absolute sincerity dissipated every trace of his apprehension. He felt gay, calmly happy, and yet excited too. He was sure, then, that Rachel's agitation was a pleasurable agitation. It was caused solely by his entrance into the kitchen, by the compliment he was paying to her kitchen! Her eyes glittered; her face shone; her little movements were electric; she was intensely conscious of herself—all because he had come into her kitchen! She could not conceal—perhaps she did not wish to conceal—the joy that his near presence inspired. Louis had had few adventures, very few, and this experience was exquisite and wondrous to him. It roused, not the fatuous coxcomb, nor the Lothario, but that in him which was honest and high-spirited. A touch of the male's vanity, not surprising, was to be excused.

"Mrs. Maldon," said Rachel, "had an idea that it was *me* who suggested your staying all night instead of your cousin." She raised her chin, and peered at nothing through the window as she rubbed away at a spoon.

"But when?" Louis demanded, moving towards the fire. It appeared to him that the conversation had taken a most interesting turn.

"When?... When you brought the tray in here for me, I suppose."

"And I suppose you explained to her that I had the idea all out of my own little head?"

"I told her that I should never have dreamed of asking such a thing!" The susceptible and proud young creature indicated that the suggestion was one of Mrs. Maldon's rare social errors, and that Mrs. Maldon had had a narrow escape of being snubbed for it by the woman of the world now washing silver. "I'm no more afraid of burglars than you are," Rachel added. "I should just like to catch a burglar here—that I should!"

Louis indulgently doubted the reality of this courage. He had been too hastily concluding that what Rachel resented was an insinuation of undue interest in himself, whereas she now made it seem that she was objecting merely to any reflection upon her valour: which was much less exciting to him. Still, he thought that both causes might have contributed to her delightful indignation.

"Why was she so keen about having one of us to sleep here to-night?" Louis inquired.

"Well, I don't know that she was," answered Rachel. "If you hadn't said anything—"

"Oh, but do you know what she said to me upstairs?"

"No."

"She didn't want me even to go back to my digs for my things. Evidently she doesn't care for the house to be left even for half an hour."

"Well, of course old people are apt to get nervous, you know—especially when they're not well."

"Funny, isn't it?"

There was perfect unanimity between them as to the irrational singularity and sad weakness of aged persons.

Louis remarked—

"She said you would make everything right for me upstairs."

"I have done—I hope," said Rachel.

"Thanks awfully!"

One part of the table was covered with newspaper. Suddenly Rachel tore a strip off the newspaper, folded the strip into a spill, and, lighting it at the gas, tendered it to Louis' unlit cigarette.

The climax of the movement was so quick and unexpected as almost to astound Louis. For he had been standing behind her, and she had not turned her head before making the spill. Perhaps there was a faint reflection of himself in the window. Or perhaps she had eyes in her hair. Beyond doubt she was a strange, rare, angelic girl. The gesture with which she modestly offered the spill was angelic; it was divine; it was one of those phenomena which persist in a man's memory for decades. At the very instant of its happening he knew that he should never forget it.

The man of fashion blushed as he inhaled the first smoke created by her fire.

Rachel dropped the heavenly emblem, all burning, into the ash-bin of the range, and resumed her work.

Louis coughed. "Any law against sitting down?" he asked.

"You're very welcome," she replied primly.

"I didn't know I might smoke," he said.

She made no answer at first, but just as Louis had ceased to expect an answer, she said—

"I should think if you can smoke in the sitting-room you can smoke in the kitchen—shouldn't you?"

"I should," said he.

There was silence, but silence not disagreeable. Louis, lolling in the chair, and slightly rocking it, watched Rachel at her task. She completely immersed spoons and forks in the warm water, and then rubbed them with a brush like a large nail-brush, giving particular attention to the inside edges of the prongs of the forks; and then she laid them all wet on a thick cloth to the right of the basin. But of the knives she immersed only the blades, and took the most meticulous care that no drop of water should reach the handles.

"I never knew knives and forks and things were washed like that," observed Louis.

"They generally aren't," said Rachel. "But they ought to be. I leave all the other washing-up for the charwoman in the morning, but I wouldn't trust these to her." (The charwoman had been washing up cutlery since before Rachel was born.) "They're all alike," said Rachel.

Louis acquiesced sagely in this broad generalization as to charwomen.

"Why don't you wash the handles of the knives?" he queried.

"It makes them come loose."

"Really?"

"Do you mean to say you didn't know that water, especially warm water with soda in it, loosens the handles?" She showed astonishment, but her gaze never left the table in front of her.

"Not me!"

"Well, I should have thought that everybody knew that. Some people use a jug, and fill it up with water just high enough to cover the blades, and stick the knives in to soak. But I don't hold with that because of the steam, you see. Steam's nearly as bad as water for the handles. And then some people drop the knives wholesale into a basin just for a second, to wash the handles. But I don't hold with that, either. What I say is that you can get the handles clean with the cloth you wipe them dry with. That's what I say."

"And so there's soda in the water?"

"A little."

"Well, I never knew that either! It's quite a business, it seems to me."

Without doubt Louis' notions upon domestic work were being modified with extreme rapidity. In the suburb from which he sprang domestic work— and in particular washing up—had been regarded as base, foul, humiliating, unmentionable—as toil that any slut might perform anyhow. It would have been inconceivable to him that he should admire a girl in the very act of washing up. Young ladies, even in exclusive suburban families, were sometimes forced by circumstances to wash up—of that he was aware—but they washed up in secret and in shame, and it was proper for all parties to pretend that they never had washed up. And here was Rachel converting the horrid process into a dignified and impressive ritual. She made it as fine as fine needlework—so exact, so dainty, so proud were the motions of her fingers and her forearms. Obviously washing up was an art, and the delicate operation could not be scamped nor hurried ...

The triple pile of articles on the cloth grew slowly, but it grew; and then Rachel, having taken a fresh white cloth from a hook, began to wipe, and her wiping was an art. She seemed to recognize each fork as a separate individuality, and to attend to it as to a little animal. Whatever her view of charwomen, never would she have said of forks that they were all alike.

Louis felt in his hip pocket for his reserve cigarette-case.

And Rachel immediately said, with her back to him—

"Have you really got a revolver, or were you teasing—just now in the parlour?"

It was then that he perceived a small unframed mirror, hung at the height of her face on the broad, central, perpendicular bar of the old-fashioned window-frame. Through this mirror the chit—so he named her in his mind at the instant—had been surveying him!

"Yes," he said, producing the second cigarette-case, "I was only teasing." He lit a fresh cigarette from the end of the previous one.

"Well," she said, "you did frighten Mrs. Maldon. I was so sorry for her."

"And what about you? Weren't you frightened?"

"Oh no! I wasn't frightened. I guessed, somehow, you were only teasing."

"Well, I just wasn't teasing, then!" said Louis, triumphantly yet with benevolence. And he drew a revolver from his pocket.

She turned her head now, and glanced neutrally at the incontestable revolver for a second. But she made no remark whatever, unless the pouting of her tightly shut lips and a mysterious smile amounted to a remark.

Louis adopted an indifferent tone—

"Strange that the old lady should be so nervous just to-night—isn't it?— seeing these burglars have been knocking about for over a fortnight. Is this the first time she's got excited about it?"

"Yes, I think it is," said Rachel faintly, as it were submissively, with no sign of irritation against him.

With their air of worldliness and mature wisdom they twittered on like a couple of sparrows—inconsequently, capriciously; and nothing that they said had the slightest originality, weight, or importance. But they both thought that their conversation was full of significance; which it was, though they could not explain it to themselves. What they happened to say did not matter in the least. If they had recited the Koran to each other the inexplicable significance of their words would have been the same.

Rachel faced him again, leaning her hands behind her on the table, and said with the most enchanting, persuasive friendliness—

"I wasn't frightened—truly! I don't know why I looked as though I was."

"You mean about the revolver—in the sitting-room?" He jumped nimbly back after her to the revolver question.

"Yes. Because I'm quite used to revolvers, you know. My brother had one. Only his was a Colt—one of those long things."

"Your brother, eh?"

"Yes. Did you know him?"

"I can't say I did," Louis replied, with some constraint.

Rachel said with generous enthusiasm—

"He's a wonderful shot, my brother is!"

Louis was curiously touched by the warmth of her reference to her brother. In the daily long monotonous column of advertisements headed succinctly "Money" in the *Staffordshire Signal*, there once used to appear the following invitation: "**WE NEVER REFUSE** a loan to a responsible applicant. No fussy inquiries. Distance no objection. Reasonable terms. Strictest privacy. £3 to £10,000. Apply personally or by letter. Lovelace Curzon, 7 Colclough Street, Knype." Upon a day Louis had chosen that advertisement from among its rivals, and had written to Lovelace Curzon. But on the very next day he had come into his thousand pounds, and so had lost the advantage of business relations with Lovelace Curzon. Lovelace Curzon, as he had learnt later, was Reuben Fleckring, Rachel's father. Or, more accurately, Lovelace Curzon was Reuben Fleckring, junior, Rachel's brother, a young man in a million. Reuben, senior, had been for many years an entirely mediocre and ambitionless clerk in a large works where Julian Maldon had learnt potting, when Reuben, junior (whom he blindly adored), had dragged him out of clerkship, and set him up as the nominal registered head of a money-lending firm. An amazing occurrence! At that time Reuben, junior, was a minor, scarcely eighteen. Yet his turn for finance had been such that he had already amassed reserves, and—without a drop of Jewish blood in his veins—possessed confidence enough to compete in their own field with the acutest Hebrews of the district. Reuben, senior, was the youth's tool.

In a few years Lovelace Curzon had made a mighty and terrible reputation in the world where expenditures exceed incomes. And then the subterranean news of the day—not reported in the *Signal*—was that something serious had happened to Lovelace Curzon. And the two Fleckrings went to America, the father, as usual, hypnotized by the son. And they left no wrack behind save Rachel.

It was at this period—only a few months previous to the opening of the present narrative—that the district had first heard aught of the womenfolk of the Fleckrings. An aunt—Reuben, senior's, sister, it appeared—had died several years earlier, since when Rachel had alone kept house for her brother and her father. According to rumour the three had lived in the simplicity of relative poverty, utterly unvisited except by clients. No good smell of money had ever escaped from the small front room which was employed as an office into the domestic portion of the house. It was alleged that Rachel had existed in perfect ignorance of all details of the business. It was also alleged that when the sudden crisis arrived, her brother had told her that she would not be taken to America, and that, briefly, she must shift for herself in the world. It was alleged further that he had given her forty-five pounds. (Why forty-five pounds and not fifty, none knew.) The whole affair had begun and finished—and the house was sold up—in four days. Public opinion in the street and in Knype blew violently against the two Reubens, but as they were on the Atlantic it did not affect them. Rachel, with scarcely an acquaintance in the world in which she was to shift for herself, found that she had a streetful of friends! It transpired that everybody had always divined that she was a girl of admirable efficient qualities. She behaved as though her brother and father had behaved in quite a usual and proper manner. Assistance in the enterprise of shifting for herself she welcomed, but not sympathy. The devotion of the Fleckring women began to form a legend. People said that Rachel's aunt had been another such creature as Rachel.

Hence the effect on Louis, who, through his aunt and his cousin, was acquainted with the main facts and surmises, of Rachel's glowing reference to the vanished Reuben.

"Where did your brother practise?" he asked.

"In the cellar."

"Of course it's easier with a long barrel."

"Is it?" she said incredulously. "You should see my brother's score-card the first time he shot at that new miniature rifle-range in Hanbridge!"

"Why? Is it anything special?"

"Well, you should see it. Five bulls, all cutting into each other."

"I should have liked to see that."

"I've got it upstairs in my trunk," said she proudly. "I dare say I'll show you it some time."

"I wish you would," he urged.

Such loyalty moved him deeply. Louis had had no sisters, and his youthful suburban experience of other people's sisters had not fostered any belief that loyalty was an outstanding quality of sisters. Like very numerous young men of the day, he had passed an unfavourable judgment upon young women. He had found them greedy for diversion, amazingly ruthless in their determination to exact the utmost possible expensiveness of pleasure in return for their casual society, hard, cruelly clever in conversation, efficient in certain directions, but hating any sustained effort, and either socially or artistically or politically snobbish. Snobs all! Money-worshippers all!... Well, nearly all! It mattered not whether you were one of the dandies or one of the hatless or Fletcherite corps that lolled on foot or on bicycles, or shot on motor-cycles, through the prim streets of the suburb—the young women would not remain in dalliance with you for the mere sake of your beautiful eyes. Because they were girls they would take all that you had and more, and give you nothing but insolence or condescension in exchange. Such was Louis' judgment, and scores of times he had confirmed it in private saloon-lounge talk with his compeers. It had not, however, rendered the society of these unconscionable and cold female creatures distasteful to him. Not a bit! He had even sought it and been ready to pay for that society in the correct manner—even to imperturbably beggaring himself of his final sixpence in order to do the honours of the latest cinema. Only, he had a sense of human superiority. It certainly did not occur to him that in the victimized young men there might exist faults which complemented those of the parasitic young women.

And now he contrasted these young women with Rachel! And he fell into a dreamy mood of delight in her.... Her gesture in lighting his cigarette!

Marvellous! Tear-compelling!... Flippancy dropped away from him.... She liked him. With the most alluring innocence, she did not conceal that she liked him. He remembered that the last time he called at his aunt's he had remarked something strange, something disturbing, in Rachel's candid demeanour towards himself. He had made an impression on her! He had given her the lightning-stroke! No shadow of a doubt as to his own worthiness crossed his mind.

What did cross his mind was that she was not quite of his own class. In the suburb, where "sets" are divided one from another by unscalable barriers, she could not have aspired to him. But in the kitchen, now become the most beautiful and agreeable and romantic interior that he had ever seen—in the kitchen he could somehow perceive with absolute clearness that the snobbery of caste was silly, negligible, laughable, contemptible. Yes, he could perceive all that! Life in the kitchen seemed ideal—life with that loyalty and that candour and that charm and that lovely seriousness! Moreover, he could teach her. She had already blossomed—in a fortnight. She was blossoming. She would blossom further.

Odd that, when he had threatened to pull out a revolver, she, so accustomed to revolvers, should have taken a girlish alarm! That queer detail of her behaviour was extraordinarily seductive. But far beyond everything else it was the grand loyalty of her nature that drew him. He wanted to sink into it as into a bed of down. He really needed it. Enveloped in that loving loyalty of a creature who gave all and demanded nothing, he felt that he could truly be his best self, that he could work marvels. His eyes were moist with righteous ardour.

The cutlery reposed in a green-lined basket. She had doffed the apron and hung it behind the scullery door. With all the delicious curves of her figure newly revealed, she was reaching the alarm-clock down from the mantelpiece, and then she was winding it up. The ratchet of the wheel clacked, and the hurried ticking was loud. In the grate of the range burned one spot of gloomy red.

"Your bedtime, I suppose?" he murmured, rising elegantly.

She smiled. She said—

"Shall you lock up, or shall I?"

"Oh! I think I know all the tricks," he replied, and thought, "She's a pretty direct sort of girl, anyway!"

IV

About an hour later he went up to his room. It was a fact that everything had been made right for him. The gas burned low. He raised it, and it shone directly upon the washstand, which glittered with the ivory glaze of large earthenware, and the whiteness of towels that displayed all the creases of their folding. There was a new cake of soap in the ample soap-dish, and a new tooth-brush in a sheath of transparent paper lay on the marble. "Rather complete this!" he reflected. The nail-brush—an article in which he specialized—was worn, but it was worn evenly and had cost good money. The water-bottle dazzled him; its polished clarity was truly crystalline. He could not remember ever having seen a toilet array so shining with strict cleanness. Indeed, it was probable that he had never set eyes on an absolutely clean water-bottle before; the qualities associated with water-bottles in his memory were semi-opacity and spottiness.

The dressing-table matched the washstand. A carriage clock in leather had been placed on the mantelpiece. In front of the mantelpiece was an old embroidered fire-screen. Peeping between the screen and the grate, he saw that a fire had been scientifically laid, ready for lighting; but some bits of paper and oddments on the top of the coal showed that it was not freshly laid. The grate had a hob at one side, and on this was a small, bright tin kettle. The bed was clearly a good bed, resilient, softly garnished. On it was stretched a long, striped garment of flannel, with old-fashioned pearl buttons at neck and sleeves. An honest garment, quite surely unshrinkable! No doubt in the sixties, long before the mind of man had leaped to the fine perverse conception of the decorated pyjama, this garment had enjoyed the fullest correctness. Now, after perhaps forty years in the cupboards of Mrs. Maldon, it seemed to recall the more excellent attributes of an already forgotten past, and to rebuke what was degenerate in the present.

Louis, ranging over his experiences in the disorderly and mean pretentiousness of the suburban home, and in the discomfort of various lodgings, appreciated the grave, comfortable benignity of that bedroom. Its appeal to his senses was so strong that it became for him almost luxurious. The bedroom at his latest lodgings was full of boot-trees and trouser-stretchers and coat-holders, but it was a paltry thing and a grimy. He saw the daily and hourly advantages of marriage with a loving, simple woman whose house was her pride. He had a longing for solidities, certitudes, and righteousness.

Musing delectably, he drew aside the crimson curtain from the window and beheld the same prospect that Rachel had beheld on her walk towards Friendly Street—the obscurity of the park, the chain of lamps down the slope of Moorthorne Road, and the distant fires of industry still farther beyond, towards Toft End. He had hated the foul, sordid, ragged prospects and vistas of the Five Towns when he came new to them from London, and he had continued to hate them. They desolated him. But to-night he thought of them sympathetically. It was as if he was divining in them for the first time a recondite charm. He remembered what an old citizen named Dain had said one evening at the Conservative Club: "People may say what they choose about Bursley. I've just returned from London and I tell thee I was glad to get back. I *like* Bursley." A grotesque saying, he had thought, then. Yet now he positively felt himself capable of sharing the sentiment. Rachel in the kitchen, and the kitchen in town, and the town amid those scarred and smoking hillocks!... Invisible phenomena! Mysterious harmonies! The influence of the night solaced and uplifted him and bestowed on him new faculties of perception.

At length, deciding, after characteristic procrastination, that he must really go to bed, he wound up his watch and put it on the dressing-table. His pockets had to be emptied and his clothes hung or folded. His fingers touched the notes in the left-hand outside pocket of his coat. Not for one instant had the problem of the bank-notes been absent from his mind. Throughout the conversation with Rachel, throughout the interval between her retirement and his own, throughout his meditations in the bedroom, he had not once escaped from the obsession of the bank-notes and their problem. He knew now how the problem must be solved. There was, after all, only one solution, and it was extremely simple. He must put the notes back where he had found them, underneath the chair on the landing. If advisable, he might rediscover them in the morning and surrender them immediately. But they must not remain in his room during the night. He must not examine them—he must not look at them.

He approached the door quickly, lest he might never reach the door. But he was somehow forced to halt at the wardrobe, to see if it had coat-holders. It had one coat-holder.... His hand was on the door-knob. He turned it with every species of precaution—and it complained loudly in the still night. The door opened with a terrible explosive noise of protest. He gazed into the darkness of the landing, and presently, by the light from the bedroom, could distinguish the vague boundaries of it. The chair, invisible, was on the left. He opened the door wider to the nocturnal riddle of the house. His hand clasped the notes in his pocket. No sound! He listened for the ticking of the lobby clock and could not catch it. He listened more intently. It was impossible that he should not hear the ticking of the lobby clock. Was he dreaming? Was he under some delusion? Then it occurred to him that the lobby clock must have run down or otherwise stopped. Clocks did stop.... And then his heart bounded and his flesh crept. He had heard footsteps somewhere below. Or were the footsteps merely in his imagination?

Alone in the parlour, after Rachel had gone to bed, he had spent some time in gazing at the *Signal*; for there had been absolutely nothing else to do, and he could not have thought of sleep at such an early hour. It is true that, with his intense preoccupations, he had for the most part gazed uncomprehendingly at the *Signal*. The tale of the latest burglaries, however, had by virtue of its intrinsic interest reached his brain through his eyes, and had impressed him, despite preoccupations. And now, as he stood in the gloom at the door of his bedroom and waited feverishly for the sound of more footsteps, it was inevitable that visions of burglars should disturb him.

The probability of burglars visiting any particular house in the town was infinitely slight—his common sense told him that. But supposing—just supposing that they actually had chosen his aunt's abode for their prey!... Conceivably they had learnt that Mrs. Maldon was to have a large sum of money under her roof. Conceivably a complex plan had been carefully laid. Conceivably one of the great burglaries of criminal history might be in progress. It was not impossible. No wonder that, with bank-notes loose all over the place, his shockingly negligent auntie should have special qualms concerning burglars on that night of all nights! Fortunate indeed that he carried a revolver, that the revolver was loaded, and that he had some skill to use it! A dramatic surprise—his gun and the man behind it—for burglars who had no doubt counted on having to deal with a mere couple of women! He had but to remove his shoes and creep down the stairs. He felt at the revolver in his pocket. Often had he pictured himself in the act of calmly triumphing over burglars or other villains.

Then, with no further hesitation, he silently closed the door—on the inside!... How could there be burglars in the house? The suspicion was folly. What he had heard could be naught but the nocturnal cracking and yielding of an old building at night. Was it not notorious that the night was full of noises? And even if burglars had entered!... Better, safer, to ignore them! They could not make off with a great deal, for the main item of prey happened to be in his own pocket. Let them search for the treasure! If they had the effrontery to come searching in his bedroom, he would give them a reception! Let them try! He looked at the revolver, holding it beneath the gas. Could he aim it at a human being?...

Or—another explanation—possibly Rachel, having forgotten something or having need of something, had gone downstairs for it. He had not thought of that. But what more natural? Sudden toothache—a desire for laudanum—a visit to a store cupboard: such was the classic order of events.

He listened, secure within the four walls of his bedroom. He smiled. He could have fancied that he heard an electric bell ring ever so faintly at a distance—in the next house, in the next world.

He laughed to himself.

Then at length he moved again towards the door; and he paused in front of it. There were no burglars! The notion of burglars was idiotic! He must put the notes back under the chair. His whole salvation depended upon his putting the notes back under the chair on the landing!... An affair of two seconds!... With due caution he opened the door. And simultaneously, at the very selfsame instant, he most distinctly heard the click of the latch of his aunt's bedroom door, next his own! Now, in a horrible quandary, trembling and perspiring, he felt completely nonplussed. He pushed his own door to, but without quite closing it, for fear of a noise; and edged away from it towards the fireplace.

Had his aunt wakened up, and felt a misgiving about the notes, and found that they were not where they ought to be?

No further sound came though the crack of his door. In the dwelling absolute silence seemed to be established. He stood thus for an indefinite period in front of the fireplace, the brain's action apparently suspended, until his agitation was somewhat composed. And then, because he had no clear plan in his head, he put his hand into the pocket containing the notes and drew them out. And immediately he was aware of a pleasant feeling of relief, as one who, after battling against a delicious and shameful habit, yields and is glad. The beauty of the notes was eternal; no use could stale it. Their intoxicating effect on him was just as powerful now as before supper. And now, as then, the mere sight of them filled him with a passionate conviction that without them he would be ruined. His tricks to destroy the suspicions of Horrocleave could not possibly be successful. Within twenty-four hours he might be in prison if he could not forthwith command a certain sum of money. And even possessing the money, he would still have an extremely difficult part to play. It would be necessary for him to arrive early at the works, to change notes for gold in the safe, to erase many of his pencilled false additions, to devise a postponement of his crucial scene with Horrocleave, and lastly to invent a plausible explanation of the piling up of a cash reserve.

If he had not been optimistic and an incurable procrastinator and a believer in luck at the last moment, he would have seen that nothing but a miracle could save him if Horrocleave were indeed suspicious. Happily for his peace of mind, he was incapable of looking a fact in the face. Against all reason he insisted to himself that with the notes he might reach salvation. He did not trouble even to estimate the chances of the notes being traced by their numbers. Such is the magic force of a weak character.

But he powerfully desired not to steal the notes, or any of them. The image of Rachel rose between him and his temptation. Her honesty, candour, loyalty, had revealed to him the beauty of the ways of righteousness. He had been born again in her glance. He swore he would do nothing unworthy of the ideal she had unconsciously set up in him. He admitted that it was supremely essential for him to restore the notes to the spot whence he had removed them.... And yet—if he did so, and was lost? What then? For one second he saw himself in the dock at the police-court in the town hall. Awful hallucination! If it became reality, what use, then, his obedience to the new ideal? Better to accomplish this one act of treason to the ideal in order to be able for ever afterwards to obey it and to look Rachel in the eyes! Was it not so? He wanted advice, he wanted to be confirmed in his own opportunism, as a starving beggar may want food.

And in the midst of all this torture of his vacillations, he was staggered and overwhelmed by the sudden noise of Mrs. Maldon's door brusquely opening, and of an instant loud, firm knock on his own door. The silence of the night was shattered as by an earthquake.

Almost mechanically he crushed the notes in his left hand—crushed them into a ball; and the knuckles of that hand turned white with the muscular tension.

"Are you up?" a voice demanded. It was Rachel's voice.

"Ye-es," he answered, and held his left hand over the screen in front of the fireplace.

"May I come in?"

And with the word she came in. She was summarily dressed, and very pale, and her hair, more notable than ever, was down. As she entered he opened his hand and let the ball of notes drop into the littered grate.

V

"Anything the matter?" he asked, moving away from the region of the hearth-rug.

She glanced at him with a kind of mild indulgence, as if to say: "Surely you don't suppose I should be wandering about in the night like this if nothing was the matter!"

She replied, speaking quickly and eagerly—"I'm so glad you aren't in bed. I want you to go and fetch the doctor—at once."

"Auntie ill?"

She gave him another glance like the first, as if to say: "*I'm* not ill, and *you* aren't. And Mrs. Maldon is the only other person in the house—"

"I'll go instantly," he added in haste. "Which doctor?"

"Yardley in Park Road. It's near the corner of Axe Street. You'll know it by the yellow gate—even if his lamp isn't lighted."

"I thought old Hawley up at Hillport was auntie's doctor."

"I believe he is, but you couldn't get up to Hillport in less than half an hour, could you?"

"Not so serious as all that, is it?"

"Well, you never know. Best to be on the safe side. It's not quite like one of her usual attacks. She's been upset. She actually went downstairs."

"I thought I heard somebody. Did you hear her, then?"

"No, she rang for me afterwards. There's a little electric bell over my bed, from her room."

"And I heard that too," said Louis.

"Will you ask Dr. Yardley to come at once?"

"I'm off," said he. "What a good thing I wasn't in bed!"

"What a good thing you're here at all!" Rachel murmured, suddenly smiling.

He was waiting anxiously for her to leave the room again. But instead of leaving it she came to the fireplace and looked behind the screen. He trembled.

"Oh! That kettle *is* there! I thought it must be!" And picked it up.

Then, with the kettle in one hand, she went to a large cupboard let into the wall opposite the door, and opened it.

"You know Park Road, I suppose?" she turned to him.

"Yes, yes, I'm off!"

He was obliged to go, surrendering the room to her. As he descended the stairs he heard her come out of the room. She was following him downstairs. "Don't bang the door," she whispered. "I'll come and shut it after you."

The next moment he had undone the door and was down the front steps and in the solitude of Bycars Lane. He ran up the street, full of the one desire to accomplish his errand and be back again in the spare bedroom alone. The notes were utterly safe where they lay, and yet—astounding events might happen. Was it not a unique coincidence that on this very night and no other his aunt should fall ill, and that as a result Rachel should take him unawares at the worst moment of his dilemma? And further, could it be the actual fact, as he had been wildly guessing only a few minutes earlier, that his aunt had at last missed the notes? Could it be that it was this discovery which had upset her and brought on an attack?... An attack of what?

He swerved at the double into Park Road, which was a silent desert watched over by forlorn gaslamps. He saw the yellow gate. The yellow gate clanked after him. He searched in the deep shadow of the porch for the button of the night bell, and had to strike a match in order to find it. He rang; waited and waited, rang again; waited; rang a third time, keeping his finger hard on the button. Then arose and expired a flickering light in the hall of the house.

"That'll do! That'll do! You needn't wear the bell out." He could hear the irritated accents through the glazed front door.

A dim figure in a dressing-gown opened.

"Are you Dr. Yardley?" Louis gasped between rapid breaths.

"What is it?" The question was savage.

With his extraordinary instinctive amiability Louis smiled naturally and persuasively.

"You're wanted at Mrs. Maldon's, Bycars. Awfully sorry to disturb you."

"Oh!" said the dressing-gown in a changed, interested tone. "Mrs. Maldon's! Right. I'll follow you."

"You'll come at once?" Louis urged.

"I shall come at once."

The door was curtly closed.

"So that's how you call a doctor in the middle of the night!" thought Louis, and ran off. He had scarcely deciphered the man's face.

The return, being chiefly downhill, was less exhausting. As he approached his aunt's house he saw that there was a light on the ground floor as well as in the front bedroom. The door opened as he swung the gate. The lobby gas had been lighted. Rachel was waiting for him. Her hair was tied up now. The girl looked wise, absurdly so. It was as though she was engaged in the act of being equal to the terrible occasion.

"He's coming," said Louis.

"You've been frightfully quick!" said she, as if triumphantly. She appeared to glory in the crisis.

He passed within as she held the door. He was frantic to rush upstairs to the fireplace in his room; but he had to seem deliberate.

"And what next?" he inquired.

"Well, nothing. It'll be best for you to sit in your bedroom for a bit. That's the only place where there's a fire—and it's rather chilly at this time of night."

"A fire?" he repeated, incredulous and yet awe-struck.

"I knew you wouldn't mind," said she. "It just happened there wasn't two drops of methylated spirits left in the house, and as there was a fire laid in your room, I put a match to it. I must have hot water ready, you see. And Mrs. Maldon only has one of those old-fashioned gas-stoves in her bedroom—"

"I see," he agreed.

They mounted the steps together. The grate in his room was a mass of pleasant flames, in the midst of which gleamed the bright kettle.

"How is she now?" He asked in a trance. And he felt as though it was another man in his own body who was asking.

"Oh! It's not very serious, I hope," said Rachel, kneeling to coax the fire with a short, wiry poker. "Only you never know. I'm just going in again.... She seems to lose all her vitality—that's what's apt to frighten you."

The girl looked wise—absurdly, deliciously wise. The spectacle of her engaged in the high act of being equal to the occasion was exquisite. But Louis had no eye for it.

CHAPTER V
NEWS OF THE NIGHT

I

The next morning, Mrs. Tarns, the charwoman whom Rachel had expressly included in the dogma that all charwomen are alike, was cleaning the entranceway to Mrs. Maldon's house. She had washed and stoned the steep, uneven flight of steps leading up to the front door, and the flat space between them and the gate; and now, before finishing the step down to the footpath, she was wiping the grimy ledges of the green iron gate itself.

Mrs. Tarns was a woman of nearly sixty, stout and—in appearance—untidy and dirty. The wet wind played with grey wisps of her hair, and with her coarse brown apron, beneath which her skirt was pinned up. Human eye so seldom saw her without a coarse brown apron that, apronless, she would have almost seemed (like Eve) to be unattired. It and a pail were the insignia of her vocation.

She was accomplished and conscientious; she could be trusted; despite appearances, her habits were cleanly. She was also a woman of immense experience. In addition to being one of the finest exponents of the art of step-stoning and general housework that the Five Towns could show, she had numerous other talents. She was thoroughly accustomed to the supreme spectacles of birth and death, and could assist thereat with dignity and skill. She could turn away the wrath of rent-collectors, rate-collectors, school-inspectors, and magistrates. She was an adept in enticing an inebriated husband to leave a public-house. She could feed four children for a day on sevenpence, and rise calmly to her feet after having been knocked down by one stroke of a fist. She could go without food, sleep, and love, and yet thrive. She could give when she had nothing, and keep her heart sweet amid every contagion. Lastly, she could coax extra sixpences out of a pawnbroker. She had never had a holiday, and almost never failed in her duty. Her one social fault was a tendency to talk at great length about babies, corpses, and the qualities of rival soaps. All her children were married. Her husband had gone in a box to a justice whose anger Mrs. Tam's simple tongue might not soothe. She lived alone. Six half-days a week she worked about the house of Mrs. Maldon from eight to one o'clock, for a shilling per half-day and her breakfast. But if she chose to stay for it she could have dinner—and a good one—on condition that she washed up afterwards. She often stayed. After over forty years of incessant and manifold expert labour she was happy and content in this rich reward.

A long automobile came slipping with noiseless stealth down the hill, and halted opposite the gate, in silence, for the engine had been stopped higher up. Mrs. Tams, intimidated by the august phenomenon, ceased to rub, and in alarm watched the great Thomas Batchgrew struggle unsuccessfully with the handle of the door that imprisoned him. Mrs. Tams was a born serf, and her nature was such that she wanted to apologize to Thomas Batchgrew for the naughtiness of the door. For her there was something monstrous in a personage like Thomas Batchgrew being balked in a desire, even for a moment, by a perverse door-catch. Not that she really respected Thomas Batchgrew! She did not, but he was a member of the sacred governing class. The chauffeur—not John's Ernest, but a professional—flashed round the front of the car and opened the door with obsequious haste. For Thomas Batchgrew had to be appeased. Already a delay of twenty minutes—due to a defective tire and to the inexcusable absence of the spanner with which the spare wheel was manipulated—had aroused his just anger.

Mrs. Tarns pulled the gate towards herself and, crushed behind it, curtsied to Thomas Batchgrew. This curtsy, the most servile of all Western salutations, and now nearly unknown in Five Towns, consisted in a momentary shortening of the stature by six inches, and in nothing else. Mrs. Tams had acquired it in her native village of Sneyd, where an earl held fast to that which was good, and she had never been able to quite lose it. It did far more than the celerity of the chauffeur to appease Thomas Batchgrew.

Snorting and self-conscious, and with his white whiskers flying behind him, he stepped in his two overcoats across the narrow, muddy pavement and on to Mrs. Tarn's virgin stonework, and with two haughty black footmarks he instantly ruined it. The tragedy produced no effect on Mrs. Tams. And indeed nobody in the Five Towns would have been moved by it. For the social convention as to porticoes enjoined, not that they should remain clean, but simply that they should show evidence of having been clean at some moment early in each day. It mattered not how dirty they were in general, provided that the religious and futile rite of stoning had been demonstrably performed during the morning.

Mrs. Tams adroitly moved her bucket, aside, though there was plenty of room for feet even larger than those of Thomas Batchgrew, and then waited to be spoken to. She was not spoken to. Mr. Batchgrew, after hesitating and clearing his throat, proceeded up the steps, defiling them. As he did so Mrs. Tams screwed together all her features and clenched her hands as if in agony, and stared horribly at the open front door, which was blowing to. It seemed that she was trying to arrest the front door by sheer force of muscular contraction. She did not succeed. Gently the door closed, with a firm click of its latch, in face of Mr. Batchgrew.

"Nay, nay!" muttered Mrs. Tarns, desolated.

And Mr. Batchgrew, once more justly angered, raised his hand to the heavy knocker.

"Dunna' knock, mester! Dunna' knock!" Mrs. Tarns implored in a whisper. "Missis is asleep. Miss Rachel's been up aw night wi' her, seemingly, and now her's gone off in a doze like, and Miss Rachel's resting, too, on th' squab i' th' parlor. Doctor was fetched."

Apparently charging Mrs. Tarns with responsibility for the illness, Mr. Batchgrew demanded severely—

"What was it?"

"One o' them attacks as her has," said Mrs. Tarns with a meekness that admitted she could offer no defence, "only wuss!"

"Hurry round to th' back door and let me in."

"I doubt back door's bolted on th' inside," said Mrs. Tarns with deep humility.

"This is ridiculous," said Mr. Batchgrew, truly. "Am I to stand here all day?" And raised his hand to the knocker.

Mrs. Tarns with swiftness darted up the steps and inserted a large, fat, wet hand between the raised knocker and its bed. It was the sublime gesture of a martyr, and her large brown eyes gazed submissively, yet firmly, at Mr. Batchgrew with the look of a martyr. She had nothing to gain by the defiance of a great man, but she could not permit her honoured employer to be wakened. She was accustomed to emergencies, and to desperate deeds therein, and she did not fail now in promptly taking the right course, regardless of consequences. Somewhat younger than Mr. Batchgrew in years, she was older in experience and in wisdom. She could do a thousand things well; Mr. Batchgrew could do nothing well. At that very moment she conquered, and he was beaten. Yet her brown eyes and even the sturdy uplifted arm cringed to him, and asked in abasement to be forgiven for the impiety committed. From her other hand a cloth dripped foul water on to the topmost step.

And then the door yielded. Thomas Batchgrew and Mrs. Tarns both abandoned the knocker. Rachel, pale as a lily, stern, with dilated eyes, stood before them. And Mr. Batchgrew realized, as he looked at her against the dark, hushed background of the stairs, that Mrs. Maldon was indeed ill. Mrs. Tams respectfully retired down the steps. A mightier than she, the young, naïve, ignorant girl, to whom she could have taught everything save possibly the art of washing cutlery, had relieved her of responsibility.

"You can't see her," said Rachel in a low tone, trembling.

"But—but—" Thomas Batchgrew spluttered, ineffectively. "D'you know I'm her trustee, miss? Let me come in."

Rachel would not take her hand off the inner knob.

There was the thin, far-off sound of an electric bell, breaking the silence of the house. It was the bell in Rachel's bedroom, rung from Mrs. Maldon's bedroom. And at this mysterious signal from the invalid, this faint proof that the hidden sufferer had consciousness and volition, Rachel started and Thomas Batchgrew started.

"Her bell!" Rachel exclaimed, and fled upstairs.

In the large bedroom Mrs. Maldon lay apparently at ease.

"Did they waken you?" cried Rachel, distressed.

"Who is there, dear?" Mrs. Maldon asked, in a voice that had almost recovered from the weakness of the night, Rachel was astounded.

"Mr. Batchgrew."

"I must see him," said the old lady.

"But—"

"I must see him at once," Mrs. Maldon repeated. "At once. Kindly bring him up." And she added, in a curiously even and resigned tone, "I've lost all that money!"

II

"Nay," said Mrs. Maldon to Thomas Batchgrew, "I'm not going to die just yet."

Her voice was cheerful, even a little brisk, and she spoke with a benign smile in the tranquil accents of absolute conviction. But she did not move her head; she waited to look at Thomas Batchgrew until he came within her field of vision at the foot of the bed. This quiescence had a disconcerting effect, contradicting her voice.

She was lying on her back, in the posture customary to her, the arms being stretched down by the sides under the bed-quilt. Her features were drawn slightly askew; the skin was shiny; the eyes stared as though Mrs. Maldon had been a hysterical subject. It was evident that she had passed through a tremendous physical crisis. Nevertheless, Rachel was still astounded at the change for the better in her, wrought by sleep and the force of her obstinate vitality.

The contrast between the scene which Thomas Batchgrew now saw and the scene which had met Rachel in the night was so violent as to seem nearly incredible. Not a sign of the catastrophe remained, except in Mrs. Maldon's face, and in some invalid gear on the dressing-table, for Rachel had gradually got the room into order. She had even closed and locked the wardrobe.

On answering Mrs. Maldon's summons in the night, Rachel had found the central door of the wardrobe swinging and the sacred big drawer at the bottom of that division only half shut, and Mrs. Maldon in a peignoir lying near it on the floor, making queer inhuman noises, not moans, but a kind of anxious, inarticulate entreaty, and shaking her head constantly to the left—never to the right. Mrs. Maldon had recognized Rachel, and had seemed to implore with agonized intensity her powerful assistance in some nameless and hopeless tragic dilemma. The sight—especially of the destruction of the old woman's dignity—was dreadful to such an extent that Rachel did not realize its effect on herself until several hours afterwards. At the moment she called on the immense reserves of her self-confidence to meet the situation—and she met it, assisting her pride with the curious pretence, characteristic of the Five Towns race, that the emergency was insufficient to alarm in the slightest degree a person of sagacity and sang-froid.

She had restored Mrs. Maldon to her bed and to some of her dignity. But the horrid symptoms were not thereby abated. The inhuman noises and the distressing, incomprehensible appeal had continued. Immediately Rachel's back was turned Mrs. Maldon had fallen out of bed. This happened three times, so that clearly the sufferer was falling out of bed under the urgency of some half-conscious purpose. Rachel had soothed her. And once she had managed to say with some clearness the words, "I've been downstairs." But when Rachel went back to the room from dispatching Louis for the doctor, she was again on the floor. Louis' absence from the house had lasted an intolerable age, but the doctor had followed closely on the messenger, and already the symptoms had become a little less acute. The doctor had diagnosed with rapidity. Supervening upon her ordinary cardiac attack after supper, Mrs. Maldon had had, in the night, an embolus in one artery of the brain. The way in which the doctor announced the fact showed to Rachel that nothing could easily have been more serious. And yet the mere naming of the affliction eased her, although she had no conception of what an embolus might be. Dr. Yardley had remained until four o'clock, when Mrs. Maldon, surprisingly convalescent, dropped off to sleep. He remarked that she might recover.

At eight o'clock he had come back. Mrs. Maldon was awake, but had apparently no proper recollection of the events of the night, which even to Rachel had begun to seem unreal, like a waning hallucination. The doctor gave orders, with optimism, and left, sufficiently reassured to allow himself to yawn. At a quarter past eight Louis had departed to his own affairs, on Rachel's direct suggestion. And when Mrs. Tams had been informed of the case so full of disturbing enigmas, while Rachel and she drank tea together in the kitchen, the daily domestic movement of the house was partly resumed, from vanity, because Rachel could not bear to sit idle nor to admit to herself that she had been scared to a standstill.

And now Mrs. Maldon, in full possession of her faculties, faced Thomas Batchgrew for the interview which she had insisted on having. And Rachel waited with an uncanny apprehension, her ears full of the mysterious and frightful phrase, "I've lost all that money."

III

Mrs. Maldon, after a few words had passed as to her illness, used exactly the same phrase again—"I've lost all that money!"

Mr. Batchgrew snorted, and glanced at Rachel for an explanation.

"Yes. It's all gone," proceeded Mrs. Maldon with calm resignation. "But I'm too old to worry. Please listen to me. We lost my serviette and ring last evening at supper. Couldn't find it anywhere. And in the night it suddenly occurred to me where it was. I've remembered everything now, almost, and I'm quite sure. You know you first told me to put the money in my wardrobe. Now before you said that, I had thought of putting it on the top of the cupboard to the right of the fireplace in the back room downstairs. I thought that would be a good place for it in case burglars *did* come. No burglar would ever think of looking there."

"God bless me!" Mr. Batchgrew muttered, scornfully protesting.

"It couldn't possibly be seen, you see. However, I thought I ought to respect your wish, and so I decided I'd put part of it on the top of the cupboard, and part of it underneath a lot of linen at the bottom of the drawer in my wardrobe. That would satisfy both of us."

"Would it!" exclaimed Mr. Batchgrew, without any restraint upon his heavy, rolling voice.

"Well, I must have picked up the serviette and ring with the bank-notes, you see. I fear I'm absent-minded like that sometimes. I know I went out of the sitting-room with both hands full. I know both hands were occupied, because I remember when I went into the back room I didn't turn the gas up, and I pushed a chair up to the cupboard with my knee, for me to stand on. I'm certain I put some of the notes on the top of the cupboard. Then I came upstairs. The window on the landing was rattling, and I put the other part of the money on the chair while I tried to fasten the window. However, I couldn't fasten it. So I left it. And then I thought I picked up the money again off the chair and came in here and hid it at the bottom of the drawer and locked the wardrobe."

"You thought!" said Thomas Batchgrew, gazing at the aged weakling as at an insane criminal. "Was this just after I left?"

Mrs. Maldon nodded apologetically.

"When I woke up the first time in the night, it struck me like a flash: Had I taken the serviette and ring up with the notes? I *am* liable to do that sort of thing. I'm an old woman—it's no use denying it." She looked plaintively at Rachel, and her voice trembled. "I got up. I was bound to get up, and I turned the gas on, and there the serviette and ring were at the bottom of the drawer, but no money! I took everything out of the drawer, piece by piece, and put it back again. I simply cannot tell you how I felt! I went out to the landing with a match. There was no money there. And then I went downstairs in the dark. I never knew it to be so dark, in spite of the street-lamp. I knocked against the clock. I nearly knocked it over. I managed to light the gas in the back room. I made sure that I must have left *all* the notes on the top of the cupboard instead of only part of them. But there was nothing there at all. Nothing! Then I looked all over the sitting-room floor with a candle. When I got upstairs again I didn't know what I was doing. I knew I was going to be ill, and I just managed to ring the bell for dear Rachel, and the next thing I remember was I was in bed here, and Rachel putting something hot to my feet—the dear child!"

Her eyes glistened with tears. And Rachel too, as she pictured the enfeebled and despairing incarnation of dignity colliding with grandfather's clocks in the night and climbing on chairs and groping over carpets, had difficulty not to cry, and a lump rose in her throat. She was so moved by compassion that she did not at first feel the full shock of the awful disappearance of the money.

Mr. Batchgrew, for the second time that morning unequal to a situation, turned foolishly to the wardrobe, clearing his throat and snorting.

"It's on one of the sliding trays," said Mrs. Maldon.

"What's on one of the sliding trays?"

"The serviette."

Rachel, who was nearest, opened the wardrobe and immediately discovered the missing serviette and ring, which had the appearance of a direct dramatic proof of Mrs. Maldon's story.

Mr. Batchgrew exclaimed, indignant—

"I never heard such a rigmarole in all my born days." And then, angrily to Rachel, "Go down and look on th' top o' th' cupboard, thee!"

Rachel hesitated.

"I'm quite resigned," said Mrs. Maldon placidly. "It's a punishment on me for hardening my heart to Julian last night. It's a punishment for my pride."

"Now, then!" Mr. Batchgrew glared bullyingly at Rachel, who vanished.

In a few moments she returned.

"There's nothing at all on the top of the cupboard."

"But th' money must be somewhere," said Mr. Batchgrew savagely. "Nine hundred and sixty-five pun. And I've arranged to lend out that money again, at once! What am I to say to th' mortgagor? Am I to tell him as I've lost it?... No! I never!"

Mrs. Maldon murmured—

"Nay, nay! It's no use looking at me. I thought I should never get over it in the night. But I'm quite resigned now."

Rachel, standing near the door, could observe both Mrs. Maldon and Thomas Batchgrew, and was regarded by neither of them. And while, in the convulsive commotion of her feelings, her sympathy for and admiration of Mrs. Maldon became poignant, she was thrilled by the most intense scorn and disgust for Thomas Batchgrew. The chief reason for her abhorrence was the old man's insensibility to the angelic submission, the touching fragility, the heavenly meekness and tranquillity, of Mrs. Maldon as she lay there helpless, victimized by a paralytic affliction. (Rachel wanted to forget utterly the souvenir of Mrs. Maldon's paroxysm in the night, because it slurred the unmatched dignity of the aged creature.) Another reason was the mere fact that Mr. Batchgrew had insisted on leaving the money in the house. Who but Mr. Batchgrew would have had the notion of saddling poor old Mrs. Maldon with the custody of a vast sum of money? It was a shame; it was positively cruel! Rachel was indignantly convinced that he alone ought to be made responsible for the money. And lastly, she loathed and condemned him for the reason that he was so obviously unequal to the situation. He could not handle it. He was found out. He was disproved, He did not know what to do. He could only mouth, strut, bully, and make rude noises. He could not even keep decently around him the cloak of self-importance. He stood revealed to Mrs. Maldon and Rachel as he had sometimes stood revealed to his dead wife and to his elder children and to some of his confidential, faithful employees. He was an offence in the delicacy of the bedroom. If the rancour of Rachel's judgment had been fierce enough to strike him to the floor, assuredly his years would not have saved him! And yet Mrs. Maldon gazed at him with submissive and apologetic gentleness! Foolish saint! Fancy *her* (thought Rachel) hardening her heart to Julian! Rachel longed to stiffen her with some backing of her own harsh common sense. And her affection for Mrs. Maldon grew passionate and half maternal.

IV

Thomas Batchgrew was saying —

"It beats me how anybody in their senses could pick up a serviette and put it way for a pile o' bank-notes." He scowled. "However, I'll go and see Snow. I'll see what Snow says. I'll get him to come up with one of his best men — Dickson, perhaps."

"Thomas Batchgrew!" cried Mrs. Maldon with sudden disturbing febrile excitement. "You'll do no such thing. I'll have no police prying into this affair. If you do that I shall just die right off."

And her manner grew so imperious that Mr. Batchgrew was intimidated.

"But—but—"

"I'd sooner lose all the money!" said Mrs. Maldon, almost wildly.

She blushed. And Rachel also felt herself to be blushing, and was not sure whether she knew why she was blushing. An atmosphere of constraint and shame seemed to permeate the room.

Mr. Batchgrew growled—

"The money must be in the house. The truth is, Elizabeth, ye don't know no more than that bedpost where ye put it."

And Rachel agreed eagerly—

"Of course it *must* be in the house! I shall set to and turn everything out. Everything!"

"Ye'd better!" said Thomas Batchgrew.

"That will be the best thing, dear—perhaps," said Mrs. Maldon, indifferent, and now plainly fatigued.

Every one seemed determined to be convinced that the money was in the house, and to employ this conviction as a defence against horrible dim suspicions that had inexplicably emerged from the corners of the room and were creeping about like menaces.

"Where else should it be?" muttered Batchgrew, sarcastically, after a pause, as if to say, "Anybody who fancies the money isn't in the house is an utter fool."

Mrs. Maldon had closed her eyes.

There was a faint knock at the door. Rachel turned instinctively to prevent a possible intruder from entering and catching sight of those dim suspicions before they could be driven back into their dark corners. Then she remembered that she had asked Mrs. Tams to bring up some Revalenta Arabica food for Mrs. Maldon as soon as it should be ready. And she sedately opened the door. Mrs. Tams, with her usual serf-like diffidence, remained invisible, except for the hand holding forth the cup. But her soft voice, charged with sensational news, was heard—

"Mrs. Grocott's boy next door but one has just been round to th' back to tell me as there was a burglary down the Lane last night."

As Rachel carried the food across to the bed, she could not help saying, though with feigned deference, to Mr. Batchgrew—

"You told us last night that there wouldn't *be* any more burglaries, Mr. Batchgrew."

The burning tightness round the top of her head, due to fatigue and lack of sleep, seemed somehow to brace her audacity, and to make her careless of consequences.

The trustee and celebrity, though momentarily confounded, was recovering himself now. He determined to crush the pert creature whose glance had several times incommoded him. He said severely—

"What's a burglary down the Lane got to with us and this here money?"

"Us and the money!" Rachel repeated evenly. "Nothing, only when I came downstairs in the night the greenhouse door was open." (The scullery was still often called the greenhouse.) "And I'd locked it myself!"

A troubling silence followed, broken by Mr. Batchgrew's uneasy grunts as he turned away to the window, and by the clink of the spoon as Rachel helped Mrs. Maldon to take the food.

At length Mr. Batchgrew asked, staring through the window—

"Did ye notice the dust on top o' that cupboard? Was it disturbed?"

Hesitating an instant, Rachel answered firmly, without turning her head—

"I did ... It was ... Of course."

Mrs. Maldon made no sign of interest.

Mr. Batchgrew's boots creaked to and fro in the room.

"And what's Julian got to say for himself?" he asked, not addressing either woman in particular.

"Julian wasn't here. He didn't stay the night. Louis stayed instead," answered Mrs. Maldon, faintly, without opening her eyes.

"What? What? What's this?"

"Tell him, dear, how it was," said Mrs. Maldon, still more faintly.

Rachel obeyed, in agitated, uneven tones.

CHAPTER VI
THEORIES OF THE THEFT

I

The inspiring and agreeable image of Rachel floated above vast contending forces of ideas in the mind of Louis Fores as he bent over his petty-cash book amid the dust of the vile inner office at Horrocleave's; and their altercation was sharpened by the fact that Louis had not had enough sleep. He had had a great deal more sleep than Rachel, but he had not had what he was in the habit of calling his "whack" of it. Although never in a hurry to go to bed, he appreciated as well as any doctor the importance of sleep in the economy of the human frame, and his weekly average of repose was high; he was an expert sleeper.

He thirsted after righteousness, and the petty-cash book was permeated through and through with unrighteousness; and it was his handiwork. Of course, under the unconscious influence of Rachel, seen in her kitchen and seen also in various other striking aspects during the exciting night, he might have bravely exposed the iniquity of the petty-cash book to Jim Horrocleave, and cleared his conscience, and then gone and confessed to Rachel, and thus prepared the way for the inner peace and a new life. He would have suffered—there was indeed a possibility of very severe suffering—but he would have been a free man—yes, free even if in prison, and he would have followed the fine tradition of rectitude, exhorting the respect and admiration of all true souls, etc. He had read authentic records of similar deeds. What stopped him from carrying out the programme of honesty was his powerful worldly common sense. Despite what he had read, and despite the inspiring image of Rachel, his common sense soon convinced him that confession would be an error of judgment and quite unremunerative for, at any rate, very many years. Hence he abandoned regretfully the notion of confession, as a beautifully impossible dream. But righteousness was not thereby entirely denied to him; his thirst for it could still be assuaged by the device of an oath to repay secretly to Horrocleave every penny that he had stolen from Horrocleave, which oath he took—and felt better and worthier of Rachel.

He might, perhaps, have inclined more effectually towards confession had not the petty-cash book appeared to him in the morning light as an admirably convincing piece of work. It had the most innocent air, and was markedly superior to his recollection of it. On many pages he himself could scarcely detect his own traces. He began to feel that he could rely pretty strongly on the cleverness of the petty-cash book. Only four blank pages remained in it. A few days more and it would be filled up, finished, labelled with a gummed white label showing its number and the dates of its first and last entries, shelved and forgotten. A pity that Horrocleave's suspicions had not been delayed for another month or so, for then the book might have been mislaid, lost, or even consumed in a conflagration! But never mind! A certain amount of ill luck fell to every man, and he would trust to his excellent handicraft in the petty-cash book. It was his only hope in the world, now that the mysterious and heavenly bank-notes were gone.

His attitude towards the bank-notes was, quite naturally, illogical and self-contradictory. While the bank-notes were in his pocket he had in the end seen three things with clearness. First, the wickedness of appropriating them. Second, the danger of appropriating them—having regard to the prevalent habit of keeping the numbers of bank-notes. Third, the wild madness of attempting to utilize them in order to replace the stolen petty cash, for by no ingenuity could the presence of a hoard of over seventy pounds in the petty-cash box have been explained. He had perfectly grasped all that; and yet, the notes having vanished, he felt forlorn, alone, as one who has lost his best friend—a prop and firm succour in a universe of quicksands.

In the matter of the burning of the notes his conscience did not accuse him. On the contrary, he emerged blameless from the episode. It was not he who first had so carelessly left the notes lying about. He had not searched for them, he had not purloined them. They had been positively thrust upon him. His intention in assuming charge of them for a brief space was to teach some negligent person a lesson. During the evening Fate had given him no opportunity to produce them. And when in the night, with honesty unimpeachable, he had decided to restore them to the landing, Fate had intervened once more. At each step of the affair he had acted for the best in difficult circumstances. Persons so ill-advised as to drop bank-notes under chairs must accept all the consequences of their act. Who could have foreseen that while he was engaged on the philanthropic errand of fetching a doctor for an aged lady Rachel would light a fire under the notes?... No, not merely was he without sin in the matter of the bank-notes, he was rather an ill-used person, a martyr deserving of sympathy. And, further, he did not regret the notes; he was glad they were gone. They could no longer tempt him now, and their disappearance would remain a mystery for ever. So far as they were concerned, he could look his aunt or anybody else in the face without a tremor. The mere destruction of the immense, undetermined sum of money did not seriously ruffle him. As an ex-bank clerk he was aware that though an individual would lose, the State, through the Bank of England, would correspondingly gain, and thus for the nonce he had the large sensation of a patriot.

II

Axon, the factotum of the counting-house, came in from the outer office, with a mien composed of mirth and apprehension in about equal parts. If Axon happened to be a subject of a conversation and there was any uncertainty as to which Axon out of a thousand Axons he might be, the introducer of the subject would always say, "You know—sandy-haired fellow." This described him—hair, beard, moustache. Sandy-haired men have no age until they are fifty-five, and Axon was not fifty-five. He was a pigeon-flyer by choice, and a clerk in order that he might be a pigeon-flyer. His fault was that, with no moral right whatever to do so, he would treat Louis Fores as a business equal in the office and as a social equal in the street.

He sprang upon Louis now as one grinning valet might spring upon another, enormous with news, and whispered—

"I say, guv'nor's put his foot through them steps from painting-shop and sprained his ankle. Look out for ructions, eh? Thank the Lord it's a half-day!" and then whipped back to his own room.

On any ordinary Saturday morning Louis by a fine frigidity would have tried to show to the obtuse Axon that he resented such demeanour towards himself on the part of an Axon, assuming as it did that the art-director of the works was one of the servile crew that scuttled about in terror if the ferocious Horrocleave happened to sneeze. But to-day the mere sudden information that Horrocleave was on the works gave him an unpleasant start and seriously impaired his presence of mind. He had not been aware of Horrocleave's arrival. He had been expecting to hear Horrocleave's step and voice, and the rustle of him hanging up his mackintosh outside

(Horrocleave always wore a mackintosh instead of an overcoat), and all the general introductory sounds of his advent, before he finally came into the inner room. But, now, for aught Louis knew, Horrocleave might already have been in the inner room, before Louis. He was upset. The enemy was not attacking him in the proper and usual way.

And the next instant, ere he could collect and reorganize his forces, he was paralysed by the footfall of Horrocleave, limping, and the bang of a door.

And Louis thought—

"He's in the outer office. He's only got to take his mackintosh off, and then I shall see his head coming through this door, and perhaps he'll ask me for the petty-cash book right off."

But Horrocleave did not even pause to remove his mackintosh. In defiance of immemorial habit, being himself considerably excited and confused, he stalked straight in, half hopping, and sat down in his frowsy chair at his frowsy desk, with his cap at the back of his head. He was a spare man, of medium height, with a thin, shrewd face and a constant look of hard, fierce determination.

And there was Louis staring like a fool at the open page of the petty-cash book, incriminating himself every instant.

"Hello!" said Louis, without looking round. "What's up?"

"What's up?" Horrocleave scowled. "What d'ye mean?"

"I thought you were limping just the least bit in the world," said Louis, whose tact was instinctive and indestructible.

"Oh, *that!*" said Horrocleave, as though nothing was farther from his mind than the peculiarity of his gait that morning. He bit his lip.

"Slipped over something?" Louis suggested.

"Aye!" said Horrocleave, somewhat less ominously, and began to open his letters.

Louis saw that he had done well to feign ignorance of the sprain and to assume that Horrocleave had slipped, whereas in fact Horrocleave had put his foot through a piece of rotten wood. Everybody in the works, upon pain of death, would have to pretend that the employer had merely slipped, and that the consequences were negligible. Horrocleave had already nearly eaten an old man alive for the sin of asking whether he had hurt himself!

And he had not hurt himself because two days previously he had ferociously stopped the odd-man of the works from wasting his time in mending just that identical stair, and had asserted that the stair was in excellent condition. Horrocleave, though Napoleonic by disposition, had a provincial mind, even a Five Towns mind. He regarded as sheer loss any expenditure on repairs or renewals or the processes of cleansing. His theory was that everything would "do" indefinitely. He passed much of his time in making things "do." His confidence in the theory that things could indeed be made to "do" was usually justified, but the steps from the painting-shop—a gimcrack ladder with hand-rail, attached somehow externally to a wall—had at length betrayed it. That the accident had happened to himself, and not to a lad balancing a plankful of art-lustre ware on one shoulder, was sheer luck. And now the odd-man, with the surreptitious air of one engaged in a nefarious act, was putting a new tread on the stairs. Thus devoutly are the Napoleonic served!

Horrocleave seemed to weary of his correspondence.

"By the by," he said in a strange tone, "let's have a look at that petty-cash book."

Louis rose, and with all his charm, with all the elegance of a man intended by Nature for wealth and fashion instead of a slave on a foul pot-bank, gave up the book. It was like giving up hope to the last vestige, like giving up the ghost. He saw with horrible clearness that he had been deceiving himself, that Horrocleave's ruthless eye could not fail to discern at the first glance all his neat dodges, such as additions of ten to the shillings, and even to the pounds here and there, and ingenious errors in carrying forward totals from the bottom of one page to the top of the next. He began to speculate whether Horrocleave would be content merely to fling him out of the office, or whether he would prosecute. Prosecution seemed much more in accordance with the Napoleonic temperament, and yet Louis could not, then, conceive himself the victim of a prosecution.... Anybody else, but not Louis Fores!

Horrocleave, his elbow on the table, leaned his head on his hand and began to examine the book. Suddenly he looked up at Louis, who could not move and could not cease from agreeably smiling.

Said Horrocleave in a still more peculiar tone—

"Just ask Axon whether he means to go fetch wages to-day or to-morrow. Has he forgotten it's Saturday morning?"

Louis shot away into the outer office, where Axon was just putting on his hat to go to the bank.

Alone in the outer office Louis wondered. The whole of his vitality was absorbed in the single function of wondering. Then through the thin slit of the half-open door between the top and the middle hinges, he beheld Horrocleave bending in judgment over the book. And he gazed at the vision in the fascination of horror. In a few moments Horrocleave leaned back, and Louis saw that his face had turned paler. It went almost white. Horrocleave was breathing strangely, his arms dropped downward, his body slipped to one side, his cap fell off, his eyes shut, his mouth opened, his head sank loosely over the back of the chair like the head of a corpse. He had fainted. The thought passed through Louis' mind that stupefaction at the complex unrighteousness of the petty-cash records had caused Horrocleave to lose consciousness. Then the true explanation occurred to him. It was the pain in his ankle that had overcome the heroic sufferer. Louis had desired to go to his aid, but he could not budge from his post. Presently the colour began slowly to return to Horrocleave's cheek; his eyes opened; he looked round sleepily and then wildly; and then he rubbed his eyes and yawned. He remained quiescent for several minutes, while a railway lorry thundered through the archway and the hoofs of the great horse crunched on shawds in the yard. Then he called, in a subdued voice—

"Louis! Where the devil are ye?"

Louis re-entered the room, and as he did so Horrocleave shut the petty-cash book with an abrupt gesture.

"Here, take it!" said he, pushing the book away.

"Is it all right?" Louis asked.

Horrocleave nodded. "Well, I've checked about forty additions." And he smiled sardonically.

"I think you might do it a bit oftener," said Louis, and then went on: "I say, don't you think it might be a good thing if you took your boot off. You never know, when you've slipped, whether it won't swell—I mean the ankle."

"Bosh!" exclaimed Horrocleave, with precipitation, but after an instant added thoughtfully: "Well, I dun'no'. Wouldn't do any harm, would it? I say—get me some water, will you? I don't know how it is, but I'm as thirsty as a dog."

The heroic martyr to the affirmation that he had not hurt himself had handsomely saved his honour. He could afford to relax a little now the rigour of consistency in conduct. With twinges and yawns he permitted Louis to help him with the boot and to put an art-lustre cup to his lips.

Louis was in the highest spirits. He had seen the gates of the Inferno, and was now snatched up to Paradise. He knew that Horrocleave had never more than half suspected him, and that the terrible Horrocleave pride would prevent Horrocleave from asking for the book again. Henceforth, saved by a miracle, he could live in utter rectitude; he could respond freely to the inspiring influence of Rachel, and he would do so. He smiled at his previous fears, and was convinced, by no means for the first time, that a Providence watched over him because of his good intentions and his nice disposition—that nothing really serious could ever occur to Louis Fores. He reflected happily that in a few days he would begin a new petty-cash book—and he envisaged it as a symbol of his new life. The future smiled. He made sure that his aunt Maldon was dying, and though he liked her very much and would regret her demise, he could not be expected to be blind to the fact that a proportion of her riches would devolve on himself. Indeed, in unluckily causing a loss of money to his aunt Maldon he had in reality only been robbing himself. So that there was no need for any kind of remorse. When the works closed for the week-end, he walked almost serenely up to Bycars for news—news less of his aunt's condition than of the discovery that a certain roll of bank-notes had been mislaid.

III

The front door was open when Louis arrived at Mrs. Maldon's house, and he walked in. Anybody might have walked in. There was nothing unusual in this; it was not a sign that the mistress of the house was ill in bed and its guardianship therefore disorganized. The front doors of Bursley— even the most select—were constantly ajar and the fresh wind from off the pot-bank was constantly blowing through those exposed halls and up those staircases. For the demon of public inquisitiveness is understood in the Five Towns to be a nocturnal demon. The fear of it begins only at dusk. A woman who in the evening protects her parlour like her honour, will, while the sun is above the horizon, show the sacred secrets of the kitchen itself to any one who chooses to stand on the front step.

Louis put his hat and stick on the oak chest, and with a careless, elegant gesture brushed back his dark hair. The door of the parlour was slightly ajar. He pushed it gently open, and peeped round it with a pleasant arch expression, on the chance of there being some one within.

Rachel was lying on the Chesterfield. Her left cheek, resting on her left hand, was embedded in the large cushion. A large coil of her tawny hair, displaced, had spread loosely over the dark green of the sofa. The left foot hung limp over the edge of the sofa; the jutting angle of the right knee divided sharply the drapery of her petticoat into two systems, and her right shoe with its steel buckle pressed against the yielding back of the Chesterfield. The right arm lay lissom like a snake across her breast. All her muscles were lax, and every full curve of her body tended downward in response to the negligent pose. Her eyes were shut, her face flushed; and her chest heaved with the slow regularity of her deep, unconscious breathing.

Louis as he gazed was enchanted. This was not Miss Fleckring, the companion and household help of Mrs. Maldon, but a nymph, a fay, the universal symbol of his highest desire.... He would have been happy to kiss the glinting steel buckle, so feminine, so provocative, so coy. The tight rounded line of the waist, every bend of the fingers, the fall of the eye-lashes—all were exquisite and precious to him after the harsh, unsatisfying, desolating masculinity of Horrocleave's. This was the divine reward of Horrocleave's, the sole reason of Horrocleave's. Horrocleave's only existed in order that this might exist and be maintained amid cushions and the softness of calm and sequestered interiors, waiting for ever in acquiescence for the arrival of manful doers from Horrocleave's. The magnificent pride of male youth animated Louis. He had not a care in the world. Even his long-unpaid tailor's bill was magically abolished. He was an embodiment of exulting hope and fine aspirations.

Rachel stirred, dimly aware of the invasion. And Louis, actuated by the most delicate regard for her sensitive modesty, vanished back for a moment into the hall, until she should have fitted herself for his beholding.

Mrs. Tams had come from somewhere into the hall. She was munching a square of bread and cold bacon, and she curtsied, exclaiming—

"It's never Mester Fores! That's twice her's been woke up this day!"

"Who's there?" Rachel called out, and her voice had the breaking, bewildered softness of a woman's in the dark, emerging from a dream.

"Sorry! Sorry!" said Louis, behind the door.

"It's all right," she reassured him.

He returned to the room. She was sitting upright on the sofa, her arms a little extended and the tips of her fingers touching the sofa. The coil of her hair had been arranged. The romance of the exciting night still clung to her, for Louis; but what chiefly seduced him was the mingling in her mien of soft confusion and candid, sturdy honesty and dependableness. He felt that here was not only a ravishing charm, but a source of moral strength from which he could draw inexhaustibly that which he had had a slight suspicion he lacked. He felt that here was joy and salvation united, and it seemed too good to be true. Strange that when she greeted him at the door-step on the previous evening, he had imagined that she was revealing herself to him for the first time; and again later, in the kitchen, he had imagined that she was revealing herself to him for the first time; and again, still later, in the sudden crisis at his bedroom door, he had imagined that she was revealing herself to him for the first time. For now he perceived that he had never really seen her before; and he was astounded and awed.

"Auntie still on the up-grade?" he inquired, using all his own charm. He guessed, of course, that Mrs. Maldon must be still better, and he was very glad, although, if she recovered, it would be she and not himself that he had deprived of bank-notes.

"Oh yes, she's better," said Rachel, not moving from the sofa; "but have you heard what's happened?"

In spite of himself he trembled, awaiting the disclosure. "Now for the bank-notes!" he reflected, bracing his nerves. He shook his head.

She told him what had happened; she told him at length, quickening her speech as she proceeded. And for a few moments it was as if he was being engulfed by an enormous wave, and would drown. But the next instant he recollected that he was on dry land, safe, high beyond the reach of any catastrophe. His position was utterly secure. The past was past; the leaf was turned. He had but to forget, and he was confident of his ability to forget. The compartments of his mind were innumerable, and as separate as the dungeons of a mediaeval prison.

"Isn't it awful?" she murmured.

"Well, it is rather awful!"

"Nine hundred and sixty-five pounds! Fancy it!"

The wave approached him again as she named the sum. Nevertheless, he never once outwardly blenched. As he had definitely put away unrighteousness, so his face showed no sign of guilt. Like many ingenuous-minded persons, he had in a high degree the faculty of appearing innocent—except when he really was innocent.

"If you ask me," said Rachel, "she never took any of the notes upstairs at all; she left them all somewhere downstairs and only took the serviette upstairs."

"Yes," he agreed thoughtfully, wondering whether on the other hand, Mrs. Maldon had not taken all the notes upstairs, and left none of them downstairs. Was it possible that in that small roll, in that crushed ball that he had dropped into the grate, there was nearly a thousand pounds—the equivalent of an income of a pound a week for ever and ever?... Never mind! The incident, so far as he was concerned, was closed. The dogma of his future life would be that the bank-notes had never existed.

"And I've looked *ev'*rywhere!" Rachel insisted with strong emphasis.

Louis remarked, thoughtfully, as though a new aspect of the affair was presenting itself to him—

"It's really rather serious, you know!"

"I should just say it was—as much money as that!"

"I mean," said Louis, "for everybody. That is to say, Julian and me. We're involved."

"How can you be involved? You didn't even know it was in the house."

"No. But the old lady might have dropped it. I might have picked it up. Julian might have picked it up. Who's to prove—"

She cut in coldly—

"Please don't talk like that!"

He smiled with momentary constraint. He said to himself—

"It won't do to talk to this kind of girl like that. She won't stand it.... Why, she wouldn't even *dream* of suspicion falling on herself—wouldn't dream of it."

After a silence he began—

"Well—" and made a gesture to imply that the enigma baffled him.

"I give it up!" breathed Rachel intimately. "I fairly give it up!"

"And of course that was the cause of her attack?" he said suddenly, as if the idea had just occurred to him.

Rachel nodded—"Evidently."

"Well," said he, "I'll look in again during the afternoon. I must be getting along for my grub." He was hoping that he had not unintentionally brought about his aunt's death.

"Not had your dinner!" she cried. "Why! It's after half-past two!"

"Oh, well, you know ... Saturday...."

"I shall get you a bit of dinner here," she said. "And then perhaps Mrs. Maldon will be waking up. Yes," she repeated, positively, "I shall get you a bit of dinner here, myself. Mrs. Maldon would not be at all pleased if I didn't."

"I'm frightfully hungry," he admitted.

And he was.

When she had left the parlour he perceived evidences here and there that she had been hunting up hill and down dale for the notes; and he went into the back room with an earnest, examining air, as though he might find part of the missing hoard, after all, in some niche overlooked by Rachel. He would have preferred to think that Mrs. Maldon had not taken the whole of the money upstairs, but reflection did much to convince him that she had. It was infinitely regrettable that he had not counted his treasure-trove under the chair.

IV

The service of his meal, which had the charm of a picnic, was interrupted by the arrival of the doctor, whose report on the invalid, however, was so favourable that Louis could quite dismiss the possibly homicidal aspect of his dealings with the bank-notes. The shock of the complete disappearance of the vast sum had perhaps brought Mrs. Maldon to the brink of death, but she had edged safely away again, in accordance with her own calm prophecy that very morning. When the doctor had gone, and the patient was indulged in her desire to be left alone for sleep, Louis very slowly and luxuriously finished his repast, with Rachel sitting opposite to him, in Mrs. Maldon's place, at the dining-table. He lit a cigarette and, gracefully leaning his elbows on the table, gazed at her through the beautiful grey smoke-veil, which was like the clouds of Paradise.

What thrilled Louis was the obvious fact that he fascinated her. She was transformed under his glance. How her eyes shone! How her cheek flushed and paled! What passionate vitality found vent in her little gestures! But in the midst of this transformation her honesty, her loyalty, her exquisite ingenuousness, her superb dependability remained. She was no light creature, no flirt nor seeker after dubious sensations. He felt that at last he was appreciated by one whose appreciation was tremendously worth having. He was confirmed in that private opinion of himself that no mistakes hitherto made in his career had been able to destroy. He felt happy and confident as never before.

Luck, of course; but luck deserved! He could marry this unique creature and be idolized and cherished for the rest of his life. In an instant, from being a scorner of conjugal domesticity, he became a scorner of the bachelor's existence, with its immeasurable secret ennui hidden beneath the jaunty cloak of a specious freedom—freedom to be bored, freedom to fret, and long and envy, freedom to eat ashes and masticate dust! He would marry her. Yes, he was saved, because he was loved. And he meant to be worthy of his regenerate destiny. All the best part of his character came to the surface and showed in his face. But he did not ask his heart whether he was or was not in love with Rachel. The point did not present itself. He certainly never doubted that he was seeing her with a quite normal vision.

Their talk went through and through the enormous topic of the night and day, arriving at no conclusion whatever, except that there was no conclusion—not even a theory of a conclusion. (And the Louis who now discussed the case was an innocent, reborn Louis, quite unconnected with the Louis of the previous evening; he knew no more of the inwardness of the affair than Rachel did. Of such singular feats of doubling the personality is the self-deceiving mind capable.) After a time it became implicit in the tone of their conversation that the mysterious disappearance in a small, ordinary house of even so colossal a sum as nine hundred and sixty-five pounds did not mean the end of the world. That is to say, they grew accustomed to the situation. Louis, indeed, permitted himself to suggest, as a man of the large, still-existing world, that Rachel should guard against over-estimating the importance of the sum. True, as he had several times reflected, it did represent an income of about a pound a week! But, after all, what was a pound a week, viewed in a proper perspective?...

Louis somehow glided from the enormous topic to the topic of the newest cinema—Rachel had never seen a cinema, except a very primitive one, years earlier—and old Batchgrew was mentioned, he being notoriously a cinema magnate. "I cannot stand that man," said Rachel with a candour that showed to what intimacy their talk had developed. Louis was delighted by the explosion, and they both fell violently upon Thomas Batchgrew and found intense pleasure in destroying him. And Louis was saying to himself, enthusiastically, "How well she understands human nature!"

So that when old Batchgrew, without any warning or preliminary sound, stalked pompously into the room their young confusion was excessive. They felt themselves suddenly in the presence of not merely a personal adversary, but of an enemy of youth and of love and of joy—of a being mysterious and malevolent who neither would nor could comprehend them. And they were at once resentful and intimidated.

During the morning Councillor Batchgrew had provided himself—doubtless by purchase, since he had not been home—with a dandiacal spotted white waistcoat in honour of the warm and sunny weather. This waistcoat by its sprightly unsuitability to his aged uncouthness, somehow intensified the sinister quality of his appearance.

"Found it?" he demanded tersely.

Rachel, strangely at a loss, hesitated and glanced at Louis as if for succour.

"No, I haven't, Mr. Batchgrew," she said. "I haven't, I'm sure. And I've turned over every possible thing likely or unlikely."

Mr. Batchgrew growled—

"From th' look of ye I made sure that th' money had turned up all right—ye were that comfortable and cosy! Who'd guess as nigh on a thousand pound's missing out of this house since last night!"

The heavy voice rolled over them brutally. Louis attempted to withstand Mr. Batchgrew's glare, but failed. He was sure of the absolute impregnability of his own position; but the clear memory of at least one humiliating and disastrous interview with Thomas Batchgrew in the past robbed Louis' eye of its composure. The circumstances under which he had left the councillor's employ some years ago were historic and unforgettable.

"I came in back way instead of front way," said Thomas Batchgrew, "because I thought I'd have a look at that scullery door. Kitchen's empty."

"What about the scullery door?" Louis lightly demanded.

Rachel murmured—

"I forgot to tell you; it was open when I came down in the middle of the night." And then she added: "Wide open."

"Upon my soul!" said Louis slowly, with marked constraint. "I really forget whether I looked at that door before I went to bed. I know I looked at all the others."

"I'd looked at it, anyway," said Rachel defiantly, gazing at the table.

"And when you found it open, miss," pursued Thomas Batchgrew, "what did ye do?"

"I shut it and locked it."

"Where was the key?"

"In the door."

"Lock in order?"

"Yes."

"Well, then, how could it have been opened from the outside? There isn't a mark on the door, outside *or* in."

"As far as that goes, Mr. Batchgrew," said Rachel, "only last week the key fell out of the lock on the inside and slid down the brick floor to the outside—you know there's a slope. And I had to go out of the house by the front and the lamplighter climbed over the back gate for me and let me into the yard so that I could get the key again. That might have happened last night. Some one might have shaken the key out, and pulled it under the door with a bit of wire or something."

"That won't do," Thomas Batchgrew stopped her. "You said the key was in the door on the inside."

"Well, when they'd once opened the door from the outside, couldn't they have put the key on the inside again?"

"They? Who?"

"Burglars."

Thomas Batchgrew repeated sarcastically—

"Burglars! Burglars!" and snorted.

"Well, Mr. Batchgrew, either burglars must have been at work," said Louis, who was fascinated by Rachel's surprising news and equally surprising theory—"either burglars must have been at work," he repeated impressively, "*or*—the money is still in the house. That's evident."

"Is it?" snarled Batchgrew. "Look here, miss, and you, young Fores, I didn't make much o' this this morning, because I thought th' money 'ud happen be found. But seeing as it isn't, and *as* we're talking about it, what time was the rumpus last night?"

"What time?" Rachel muttered. "What time was it, Mr. Fores?"

"I dun'no'," said Louis. "Perhaps the doctor would know."

"Oh!" said Rachel, "Mrs. Tams said the hall clock had stopped; that must have been when Mrs. Maldon knocked up against it."

She went to the parlour door and opened it, displaying the hall clock, which showed twenty-five minutes past twelve. Louis had crept up behind Mr. Batchgrew, who in his inapposite white waistcoat stood between the two lovers, stertorous with vague anathema.

"So that was the time," said he. "And th' burglars must ha' been and gone afore that. A likely thing burglars coming at twelve o'clock at night, isn't it? And I'll tell ye summat else. Them burglars was copped last night at Knype at eleven o'clock when th' pubs closed, if ye want to know—the whole gang of three on 'em."

"Then what about that burglary last night down the Lane?" Rachel asked sharply.

"Oh!" exclaimed Louis. "Was there a burglary down the Lane last night? I didn't know that."

"No, there wasn't," said Batchgrew ruthlessly. "That burglary was a practical joke, and it's all over the town. Denry Machin had a hand in that affair, and by now I dare say he wishes he hadn't."

"Still, Mr. Batchgrew," Louis argued superiorly, with the philosophic impartiality of a man well accustomed to the calm unravelling of crime, "there may be other burglars in the land beside just those three." He would not willingly allow the theory of burglars to crumble. Its attractiveness increased every moment.

"There may and there mayn't, young Fores," said Thomas Batchgrew. "Did *you* hear anything of 'em?"

"No, I didn't," Louis replied restively.

"And yet you ought to have been listening out for 'em."

"Why ought I to have been listening out for them?"

"Knowing there was all that money in th' house."

"Mr. Fores didn't know," said Rachel.

Louis felt himself unjustly smirched.

"It's scarcely an hour ago," said he, "that I heard about this money for the first time." And he felt as innocent and aggrieved as he looked.

Mr. Batchgrew smacked his lips loudly.

"Then," he announced, "I'm going down to th' police-station, to put it i' Snow's hands."

Rachel straightened herself.

"But surely not without telling Mrs. Maldon?"

Mr. Batchgrew fingered his immense whiskers.

"Is she better?" he inquired threateningly. This was his first sign of interest in Mrs. Maldon's condition.

"Oh, yes; much. She's going on very well. The doctor's just been."

"Is she asleep?"

"She's resting. She may be asleep."

"Did ye tell her ye hadn't found her money?"

"Yes."

"What did she say?"

"She didn't say anything."

"It might be municipal money, for all she seems to care!" remarked Thomas Batchgrew, with a short, bitter grin. "Well, I'll be moving to th' police-station. I've never come across aught like this before, and I'm going to get to the bottom of it."

Rachel slipped out of the door into the hall.

"Please wait a moment, Mr. Batchgrew," she whispered timidly.

"What for?"

"Till I've told Mrs. Maldon."

"But if her's asleep?"

"I must waken her. I couldn't think of letting you go to the police-station without letting her know—after what she said this morning."

Rachel waited. Mr. Batchgrew glanced aside.

"Here! Come here!" said Mr. Batchgrew in a different tone. The fact was that, put to the proof, he dared not, for all his autocratic habit, openly disobey the injunction of the benignant, indifferent, helpless Mrs. Maldon. "Come here!" he repeated coarsely. Rachel obeyed, shamefaced despite herself. Batchgrew shut the door. "Now," he said grimly, "what's your secret? Out with it. I know you and her's got a secret. What is it?"

Rachel sat down on the sofa, hid her face in her hands, and startled both men by a sob. She wept with violence. And then through her tears, and half looking up, she cried out passionately: "It's all your fault. Why did you leave the money in the house at all? You know you'd no right to do it, Mr. Batchgrew!"

The councillor was shaken out of his dignity by the incredible impudence of this indictment from a chit like Rachel. Similar experiences, however, had happened to him before; for, though as a rule people most curiously conspired with him to keep up the fiction that he was sacred, at rare intervals somebody's self-control would break down, and bitter, inconvenient home truths would resound in the ear of Thomas Batchgrew. But he would recover himself in a few moments, and usually some diversion would occur to save him—he was nearly always lucky. A diversion occurred now, of the least expected kind. The cajoling tones of Mrs. Tams were heard on the staircase.

"Nay, ma'am! Nay, ma'am! This'll never do. Must I go on my bended knees to ye?"

And then the firm but soft voice of Mrs. Maldon—

"I must speak to Mr. Batchgrew. I must have Mr. Batchgrew here at once. Didn't you hear me call and call to you?"

"That I didn't, ma'am! I was beating the feather bed in the back bedroom. Nay, not a step lower do you go, ma'am, not if I lose me job for it."

Thomas Batchgrew and Louis were already out in the hall. Half-way down the stairs stood Mrs. Maldon, supporting herself by the banisters and being supported by Mrs. Tams. She was wearing her pink peignoir with white frills at the neck and wrists. Her black hair was loose on her shoulders like the hair of a young girl. Her pallid and heavily seamed features with the deep shining eyes trembled gently, as if in response to a distant vibration. She gazed upon the two silent men with an expression that united benignancy with profound inquietude and sadness. All her past life was in her face, inspiring it with strength and sorrow.

"Mr. Batchgrew," she said. "I've heard your voice for a long time. I want to speak to you."

And then she turned, yielded to the solicitous alarm of Mrs. Tams, climbed feebly up the stairs, and vanished round the corner at the top. And Mrs. Tams, putting her frowsy head for an instant over the hand-rail, stopped to adjure Mr. Batchgrew—

"Eh, mester; ye'd better stop where ye are awhile."

From the parlour came the faint sobbing of Rachel.

The two men had not a word to say. Mr. Batchgrew grunted, vacillating. It seemed as if the majestic apparition of Mrs. Maldon had rebuked everything that was derogatory and undignified in her trustee, and that both he and Louis were apologizing to the empty hall for being common, base creatures. Each of them—and especially Louis—had the sense of being awakened to events of formidable grandeur whose imminence neither had suspected. Still assuring himself that his position was absolutely safe, Louis nevertheless was aware of a sinking in the stomach. He could rebut any accusation. "And yet ...!" murmured his craven conscience. What could be the enigma between Mrs. Maldon and Rachel? He was now trying to convince himself that Mrs. Maldon had in fact divided the money into two parts, of which he had handled only one, and that the impressive mystery had to do with the other part of the treasure, which he had neither seen nor touched. How, then, could he personally be threatened? "And yet!..." said his conscience again.

In about a minute Mrs. Tarns reappeared at the head of the stairs.

"Her *will* have ye, mester!" said she to the councillor.

Thomas Batchgrew mounted after her.

Louis made a noise with his tongue as if starting a horse, and returned to the parlour.

Rachel, still on the sofa, showed her wet face.

"I've got no secret," she said passionately. "And I'm sure Mrs. Maldon hasn't. What's he driving at?"

The natural freedom of her gestures and vehement accent was enchanting to Louis.

She jumped from the Chesterfield and ran away upstairs, flying. He followed to the lobby, and saw her dash into her own room and feverishly shut the door, which was in full view at the top of the stairs. And Louis thought he had never lived in any moment so exquisite and so alarming as that moment.

He was now alone on the ground floor. He caught no sound from above.

"Well, I'd better get out of this," he said to himself. "Anyhow, I'm all right!... What a girl! Terrific!" And, lighting a fresh cigarette, he left the house.

V

"And now what's amiss?" Thomas Batchgrew demanded, alone with Mrs. Maldon in the tranquillity of the bedroom.

Mrs. Maldon lay once more in bed; the bedclothes covered her without a crease, and from the neat fold-back of the white sheet her wrinkled ivory face and curving black hair emerged so still and calm that her recent flight to the stairs seemed unreal, impossible. The impression her mien gave was that she never had moved and never would move from the bed. Thomas Batchgrew's blusterous voice frankly showed acute irritation. He was angry because nine hundred and sixty-five pounds had monstrously vanished, because the chance of a good investment was lost, because Mrs. Maldon tied his hands, because Rachel had forgotten her respect and his dignity in addressing him; but more because he felt too old to impose himself by sheer rough-riding, individual force on the other actors in the drama, and still more because he, and nobody else, had left the nine hundred and sixty-five pounds in the house. What an orgy of denunciation he would have plunged into had some other person insisted on leaving the money in the house with a similar result!

Mrs. Maldon looked up at him with a glance of compassion. She was filled with pity for him because he had arrived at old age without dignity and without any sense of what was fine in life; he was not even susceptible to the chastening influences of a sick-room. She knew, indeed, that he hated and despised sickness in others, and that when ill himself he became a moaning mass of cowardice and vituperation. And in her heart she invented the most wonderful excuses for him, and transformed him into a martyr of destiny who had suffered both through ancestry and through environment. Was it his fault that he was thus tragically defective? So that by the magic power of her benevolence he became dignified in spite of himself.

She said—

"Mr. Batchgrew, I want you to oblige me by not discussing my affairs with any one but me."

At that moment the front door closed firmly below, and the bedroom vibrated.

"Is that Louis going?" she asked.

Batchgrew went to the window and looked downward, lowering the pupils as far as possible so as to see the pavement.

"It's Louis going," he replied.

Mrs. Maldon sighed relief.

Mr. Batchgrew said no more.

"What were you talking about downstairs to those two?" Mrs. Maldon went on carefully.

"What d'ye suppose we were talking about?" retorted Batchgrew, still at the window. Then he turned towards her and proceeded in an outburst: "If you want to know, missis, I was asking that young wench what the secret was between you and her."

"The secret? Between Rachel and me?"

"Aye! Ye both know what's happened to them notes, and ye've made it up between ye to say nowt!"

Mrs. Maldon answered gravely—

"You are quite mistaken. I know nothing, and I'm sure Rachel doesn't. And we have made nothing up between us. How can you imagine such things?"

"Why don't ye have the police told?"

"I cannot do with the police in my house."

Mr. Batchgrew approached the bed almost threateningly.

"I'll tell you why ye won't have the police told. Because ye know Louis Fores has taken your money. It's as plain as a pikestaff. Ye put it on the chair on the landing here, and ye left it there, and he came along and pocketed it." Mrs. Maldon essayed to protest, but he cut her short. "Did he or did he not come upstairs after ye'd been upstairs yourself?"

As Mrs. Maldon hesitated, Thomas Batchgrew began to feel younger and more impressive.

"Yes, he did," said Mrs. Maldon at length. "But only because I asked him to come up—to fasten the window."

"What window?"

"The landing window."

Mr. Batchgrew, startled and delighted by this unexpected confirmation of his theory, exploded—

"Ha!... And how soon was that after ye'd been upstairs with the notes?"

"It was just afterwards."

"Ha!... I don't mind telling ye I've been suspecting that young man ever since this morning. I only learnt just now as he was in th' house all night. That made me think for a moment as he'd done it after ye'd all gone to bed. And for aught I know he may have. But done it some time he has, and you know it as well as I do, Elizabeth."

Mrs. Maldon maintained her serenity.

"We may be unjust to him. I should never forgive myself if I was. He has a very good side to him, has Louis!"

"I've never seen it," said Mr. Batchgrew, still growing in authority. "He began as a thief and he'll end as a thief, if it's no worse."

"Began as a thief?" Mrs. Maldon protested.

"Well, what d'ye suppose he left the bank for?"

"I never knew quite why he left the bank. I always understood there was some unpleasantness."

"If ye didn't know, it was because ye didn't want to know. Ye never do want to know these things. 'Unpleasantness!' There's only one sort of unpleasantness with the clerks in a bank!... I know, anyhow, because I took the trouble to find out for myself, when I had that bother with him in my own office. And a nice affair that was, too!"

"But you told me at the time that his books were all right with you. Only you preferred not to keep him." Mrs. Maiden's voice was now plaintive.

Thomas Batchgrew came close to the bed and leaned on the foot of it.

"There's some things as you won't hear, Elizabeth. His books were all right, but he'd made 'em all right. I got hold of him afore he'd done more than he could undo—that's all. There's one trifle as I might ha' told ye if ye hadn't such a way of shutting folks up sometimes, missis. I'll tell ye now.

Louis Fores went down on his knees to me in my office. On his knees, and all blubbing. What about that?"

Mrs. Maldon replied—

"You must have been glad ever since that you did give the poor boy another chance."

"There's nothing I've regretted more," said Thomas Batchgrew, with a grimness that became him. "I heard last week he's keeping books and handling cash for Horrocleave nowadays. I know how that'll end! I'd warn Horrocleave, but it's no business o' mine, especially as ye made me help ye to put him into Horrocleave's.... There's half a dozen people in this town and in Hanbridge that can add up Louis Fores, and have added him up! And now he's robbed ye in yer own house. But it makes no matter. He's safe enough!" He sardonically snorted. "He's safe enough. We canna' even stop the notes without telling the police, and ye won't have the police told. Oh, no! He's managed to get on th' right side o' you. However, he'll only finish in one way, that chap will, whether you and me's here to see it or not."

Mr. Batchgrew had grown really impressive, and he knew it.

"Don't let us be hard," pleaded Mrs. Maldon. And then, in a firmer, prouder voice: "There will be no scandal in my family, Mr. Batchgrew, as long as I live."

Mr. Batchgrew's answer was superb in its unconscious ferocity—

"That depends how long ye live."

His meaningless eyes rested on her with frosty impartiality, as he reflected—

"I wonder how long she'll last."

He felt strong; he felt immortal. Exactly like Mrs. Maldon, he was convinced that he was old only by the misleading arithmetic of years, that he was not really old, and that there was a subtle and vital difference between all other people of his age and himself. As for Mrs. Maldon, he regarded her as a mere poor relic of an organism.

"At our age," Mrs. Maldon began, and paused as if collecting her thoughts.

"At our age! At our age!" he repeated, sharply deprecating the phrase.

"At our age," said Mrs. Maldon, with slow insistence, "we ought not to be hard on others. We ought to be thinking of our own sins."

But, although Mrs. Maldon was perhaps the one person on earth whom he both respected and feared, Thomas Batchgrew listened to her injunction only with rough disdain. He was incapable of thinking of his own sins. While in health, he was nearly as unaware of sin as an animal.

Nevertheless, he turned uneasily in the silence of the pale room, so full of the shy and prim refinement of Mrs. Maldon's individuality. He could talk morals to others in the grand manner, and with positive enjoyment, but to be sermonized himself secretly exasperated him because it constrained him and made him self-conscious. Invariably, when thus attacked, he would execute a flank movement.

He said bluntly—

"And I suppose ye'll let him marry this Rachel girl if he's a mind to!"

Slowly a deep flush covered Mrs. Maldon's face.

"What makes you say that?" she questioned, with rising agitation.

"I have but just seen 'em together."

Mrs. Maldon moved nervously in the bed.

"I should never forgive myself if I stood by and let Louis marry Rachel," she said, and there was a sudden desperate urgency in her voice.

"Isn't she good enough for a nephew o' yours?"

"She's good enough for any man," said Mrs. Maldon quietly.

"Then it's him as isna' good enough! And yet, if he's got such a good side to him as ye say—" Mr. Batchgrew snorted.

"He's not suited to her—not at all."

"Now, missis," said Mr. Batchgrew in triumph, "at last we're getting down to your real opinion of young Fores."

"I feel I'm responsible for Rachel, and—What ought I to do about it?"

"Do? What can a body do when a respectable young woman wi' red hair takes a fancy to a youth? Nowt, Elizabeth. That young woman'll marry Louis Fores, and ye can take it from me."

"But why do you say a thing like that? I only began to notice anything myself last night."

"She's lost her head over him, that's all. I caught 'em just now.... As thick as thieves in your parlour!"

"But I'm by no means sure that he's smitten with her."

"What does it matter whether he is or not? She's lost her head over him, and she'll have him. It doesn't want a telescope to see as far as that."

"Well, then, I shall speak to her—I shall speak to her to-morrow morning, after she's had a good night's rest, when I feel stronger."

"Ay! Ye may! And what shalt say?"

"I shall warn her. I think I shall know how to do it," said Mrs. Maldon, with a certain air of confidence amid her trouble. "I wouldn't run the risk of a tragedy for worlds."

"It's no *risk* of a tragedy, as ye call it," said Thomas Batchgrew, very pleased with his own situation in the argument. "It's a certainty. She'll believe him afore she believes you, whatever ye say. You mark me. It's a certainty."

After elaborate preparations of his handkerchief, he blew his nose loudly, because blowing his nose loudly affected him in an agreeable manner.

A few minutes later he left, saying the car would be waiting for him at the back of the Town Hall. And Mrs. Maldon lay alone until Mrs. Tams came in with a tray.

"An' I hope that's enough company for one day!" said Mrs. Tarns. "Now, sup it up, do!"

CHAPTER VII
THE CINEMA

I

That evening Rachel sat alone in the parlour, reclining on the Chesterfield over the *Signal*. She had picked up the *Signal* in order to read about captured burglars, but the paper contained not one word on the subject, or on any other subject except football. The football season had commenced in splendour, and it happened to be the football edition of the *Signal* that the paper-boy had foisted upon Mrs. Maldon's house. Despite repeated and positive assurances from Mrs. Maldon that she wanted the late edition and not the football edition on Saturday nights, the football edition was usually delivered, because the paper-boy could not conceive that any customer could sincerely not want the football edition. Rachel was glancing in a torpid condition at the advertisements of the millinery and trimming shops.

She would have been more wakeful could she have divined the blow which she had escaped a couple of hours before. Between five and six o'clock, when she was upstairs in the large bedroom, Mrs. Maldon had said to her, "Rachel—" and stopped. "Yes, Mrs. Maldon," she had replied. And Mrs. Maldon had said, "Nothing." Mrs. Maldon had desired to say, but in words carefully chosen: "Rachel, I've never told you that Louis Fores began life as a bank clerk, and was dismissed for stealing money. And even since then his conduct has not been blameless." Mrs. Maldon had stopped because she could not find the form of words which would permit her to impart to her paid companion this information about her grand-nephew. Mrs. Maldon, when the moment for utterance came, had discovered that she simply could not do it, and all her conscientious regard for Rachel and all her sense of duty were not enough to make her do it. So that Rachel, unsuspectingly, had been spared a tremendous emotional crisis. By this time she had grown nearly accustomed to the fact of the disappearance of the money. She had completely recovered from the hysteria caused by old Batchgrew's attack, and was, indeed, in the supervening calm, very much ashamed of it.

She meant to doze, having firmly declined the suggestion of Mrs. Tams that she should go to bed at seven o'clock, and she was just dropping the paper when a tap on the window startled her. She looked in alarm at the window, where the position of one of the blinds proved the correctness of Mrs. Maldon's secret theory that if Mrs. Maldon did not keep a personal watch on the blinds they would never be drawn properly. Eight inches of black pane showed, and behind that dark transparency something vague and pale. She knew it must be the hand of Louis Fores that had tapped, and she could feel her heart beating. She flew on tiptoe to the front door, and cautiously opened it. At the same moment Louis sprang from the narrow space between the street railings and the bow window on to the steps. He raised his hat with the utmost grace.

"I saw your head over the arm of the Chesterfield," he said in a cheerful, natural low voice. "So I tapped on the glass. I thought if I knocked at the door I might waken the old lady. How are things to-night?"

In those few words he perfectly explained his manner of announcing himself, endowing it with the highest propriety. Rachel's misgivings were soothed in an instant. Her chief emotion was an ecstatic pride—because he had come, because he could not keep away, because she had known that he would come, that he must come. And in fact was it not his duty to come? Quietly he came into the hall, quietly she closed the door, and when they were shut up together in the parlour they both spoke in hushed voices, lest the invalid should be disturbed. And was not this, too, highly proper?

She gave him the news of the house and said that Mrs. Tams was taking duty in the sick-room till four o'clock in the morning, and herself thenceforward, but that the invalid gave no apparent cause for apprehension.

"Old Batch been again?" asked Louis, with a complete absence of any constraint.

She shook her head.

"You'll find that money yet—somewhere, when you're least expecting it," said he, almost gaily.

"I'm sure we shall," she agreed with conviction.

"And how are *you*?" His tone became anxious and particular. She blushed deeply, for the outbreak of which she had been guilty and which he had witnessed, then smiled diffidently.

"Oh, I'm all right."

"You look as if you wanted some fresh air—if you'll excuse me saying so."

"I haven't been out to-day, of course," she said.

"Don't you think a walk—just a breath—would do you good!"

Without allowing herself to reflect, she answered—

"Well, I ought to have gone out long ago to get some food for to-morrow, as it's Sunday. Everything's been so neglected to-day. If the doctor happened to order a cutlet or anything for Mrs. Maldon, I don't know what I should do. Truly I ought to have thought of it earlier."

She seemed to be blaming herself for neglectfulness, and thus the enterprise of going out had the look of an act of duty. Her sensations bewildered her.

"Perhaps I could walk down with you and carry parcels. It's a good thing it's Saturday night, or the shops might have been closed."

She made no answer to this, but stood up, breathing quickly.

"I'll just speak to Mrs. Tams."

Creeping upstairs, she silently pushed open the door of Mrs. Maldon's bedroom. The invalid was asleep. Mrs. Tams, her hands crossed in her comfortable lap, and her mouth widely open, was also asleep. But Mrs. Tams was used to waking with the ease of a dog. Rachel beckoned her to the door. Without a sound the fat woman crossed the room.

"I'm just going out to buy a few things we want," said Rachel in her ear, adding no word as to Louis Fores.

Mrs. Tams nodded.

Rachel went to her bedroom, turned up the gas, straightened her hair, and put on her black hat, and her blue jacket trimmed with a nameless fur, and picked up some gloves and her purse. Before descending she gazed at herself for many seconds in the small, slanting glass. Coming downstairs, she took the marketing reticule from its hook in the kitchen passage. Then she went back to the parlour and stood in the doorway, speechless, putting on her gloves rapidly.

"Ready?"

She nodded.

"Shall I?" Louis questioned, indicating the gas.

She nodded again, and, stretching to his full height, he managed to turn the gas down without employing a footstool as Rachel was compelled to do.

"Wait a moment," she whispered in the hall, when he had opened the front door. These were the first words she had been able to utter. She went to the kitchen for a latch-key. Inserting this latch-key in the keyhole on the outside, and letting Louis pass in front of her, she closed the front door with very careful precautions against noise, and withdrew the key.

"I'll take charge of that if you like," said Louis, noticing that she was hesitating where to bestow it.

She gave it up to him with a violent thrill. She was intensely happy and intensely fearful. She was only going out to do some shopping; but the door was shut behind her, and at her side was this magic, mysterious being, and the nocturnal universe lay around. Only twenty-four hours earlier she had shut the door behind her and gone forth to find Louis. And now, having found him, he and she were going forth together like close friends. So much had happened in twenty-four hours that the previous night seemed to be months away.

II

Instead of turning down Friendly Street, they kept straight along the lane till, becoming suddenly urban, it led them across tram-lines and Turnhill Road, and so through a gulf or inlet of the market-place behind the Shambles, the Police Office, and the Town Hall, into the market-place itself, which in these latter years was recovering a little of the commercial prestige snatched from it half a century earlier by St. Luke's Square. Rats now marauded in the empty shops of St. Luke's Square, while the market-place glittered with custom, and the electric decoy of its façades lit up strangely the lower walls of the black and monstrous Town Hall.

Innumerable organized activities were going forward at that moment in the serried buildings of the endless confused streets that stretched up hill and down dale from one end of the Five Towns to the other—theatres, Empire music-halls, Hippodrome music-halls, picture-palaces in dozens, concerts, singsongs, spiritualistic propaganda, democratic propaganda, skating-rinks, Wild West exhibitions, Dutch auctions, and the private séances in dubious quarters of "psychologists," "clair-voyants," "scientific palmists," and other rascals who sold a foreknowledge of the future for eighteenpence or even a shilling. Viewed under certain aspects, it seemed indeed that the Five Towns, in the week-end desertion of its sordid factories, was reaching out after the higher life, the subtler life, the more elegant life of greater communities; but the little crowds and the little shops of Bursley market-place were nevertheless a proof that a tolerable number of people were still mainly interested in the primitive elemental enterprise of keeping stomachs filled and skins warm, and had no thought beyond it. In Bursley market-place the week's labour was being translated into food and drink and clothing by experts who could distinguish infallibly between elevenpence-halfpenny and a shilling. Rachel was such an expert. She forced her thoughts down to the familiar, sane, safe subject of shopping, though to-night her errands were of the simplest description, requiring no brains. But she could not hold her thoughts. A voice was continually whispering to her—not Louis Fores' voice, but a voice within herself, that she had never clearly heard before. Alternatively she scorned it and trembled at it.

She stopped in front of the huge window of Wason's Provision Emporium.

"Is this the first house of call?" asked Louis airily, swinging the reticule and his stick together.

"Well—" she hesitated. "Mrs. Tams told me they were selling Singapore pineapple at sevenpence-halfpenny. Mas. Maldon fancies pineapple. I've known her fancy a bit of pineapple when she wouldn't touch anything else.... Yes, there it is!"

In fact, the whole of the upper half of Wason's window was yellow with tins of preserved pineapple. And great tickets said: "Delicious chunks, 7 1/2d. per large tin. Chunks, 6 1/2d. per large tin."

Customers in ones and twos kept entering and leaving the shop. Rachel moved on towards the door, which was at the corner of the Cock yard, and looked within. The long double counters were being assailed by a surging multitude who fought for the attention of prestidigitatory salesmen.

"Hm!" murmured Rachel. "That may be all very well for Mrs. Tams...."

A moment later she said—

"It's always like that with Wason's shops for the first week or two!"

And her faintly sarcastic tone of a shrewd housewife immediately set Wason in his place—Wason with his two hundred and sixty-five shops, and his racing-cars, and his visits to kings and princes. Wason had emporia all over the kingdom, and in particular at Knype, Hanbridge, and Longshaw.

And now he had penetrated to Bursley, sleepiest of the Five. His method was to storm a place by means of electricity, full-page advertisements in newspapers, the power of his mere name, and a leading line or so. At Bursley his leading line was apparently "Singapore delicious chunks at 7-1/2d. per large tin." Rachel knew Wason; she had known him at Knype. And she was well aware that his speciality was second-rate. She despised him. She despised that multitude of simpletons who, full of the ancient illusion that somewhere something can regularly be had for nothing, imagined that Wason's bacon and cheese were cheap because he sold preserved pineapple at a penny less than anybody else in the town. And she despised the roaring, vulgar success of advertising and electricity. She had in her some tincture of the old nineteenth century, which loved the decency of small, quiet things. And in the prim sanity of her judgment upon Wason she forgot for a few instants that she was in a dream, and that the streets and the whole town appeared strange and troubling to her, and that she scarcely knew what she was doing, and that the most seductive and enchanting of created men was at her side and very content to be at her side. And also the voice within her was hushed.

She said—

"I don't see the fun of having the clothes torn off my back to save a penny. I think I shall go to Malkin's. I'll get some cocoa there, too. Mrs. Tams simply lives for cocoa."

And Louis archly answered—

"I've always wondered what Mrs. Tams reminds me of. Now I know. She's exactly like a cocoa-tin dented in the middle."

She laughed with pleasure, not because she considered the remark in the least witty, but because it was so characteristic of Louis Fores. She wished humbly that she could say things just like that, and with caution she glanced up at him.

They went into Ted Malkin's sober shop, where there was a nice handful of customers, in despite of Wason only five doors away. And no sooner had Rachel got inside than she was in the dream again, and the voice resumed its monotonous phrase, and she blushed. The swift change took her by surprise and frightened her. She was not in Bursley, but in some forbidden city without a name, pursuing some adventure at once shameful and delicious. A distinct fear seized her. Her self-consciousness was intense.

And there was young Ted Malkin in his starched white shirt-sleeves and white apron and black waistcoat and tie, among his cheeses and flitches, every one of which he had personally selected and judged, weighing a piece of cheddar in his honourable copper-and-brass scales. He was attending to two little girls. He nodded with calm benevolence to Rachel and then to Louis Fores. It is true that he lifted his eyebrows—a habit of his—at sight of Fores, but he did so in a quite simple, friendly, and justifiable manner, with no insinuations.

"In one moment, Miss Fleckring," said he.

And as he rapidly tied up the parcel of cheese and snapped off the stout string with a skilled jerk of the hand, he demanded calmly—

"How's Mrs. Maldon to-night?"

"Much better," said Rachel, "thank you."

And Louis Fores joined easily in—

"You may say, very much better."

"That's rare good news! Rare good news!" said Malkin. "I heard you had an anxious night of it.... Go across and pay at the other counter, my dears." Then he called out loudly—"One and seven, please."

The little girls tripped importantly away.

"Yes, indeed," Rachel agreed. The tale of the illness, then, was spread over the town! She was glad, and her self-consciousness somehow decreased. She now fully understood the wisdom of Mrs. Maldon in refusing to let the police be informed of the disappearance of the money. What a fever in the shops of Bursley—even in the quiet shop of Ted Malkin—if the full story got abroad!

"And what is it to be to-night, Miss Fleckring? These aren't quite your hours, are they? But I suppose you've been very upset."

"Oh," said Rachel, "I only want a large tin of Singapore Delicious Chunks, please."

But if she had announced her intention of spending a thousand pounds in Ted Malkin's shop she would not have better pleased him. He beamed. He desired the whole shop to hear that order, for it was the vindication of honest, modest trading—of his father's methods and his own. His father, himself, and about a couple of other tradesmen had steadily fought the fight of the market-place against St. Luke's Square in the day of its glory, and more recently against the powerfully magnetic large shops at Hanbridge, and they had not been defeated. As for Ted Malkin, he was now beyond doubt the "best" provision-dealer and grocer in the town, and had drawn ahead even of "Holl's" (as it was still called), the one good historic shop left in Luke's Square. The onslaught of Wason had alarmed him, though he had pretended to ignore it. But he was delectably reassured by this heavenly incident of the representative of one of his most distinguished customers coming into the shop and deliberately choosing to buy preserved pineapple from him at 8-1/2d. when it could be got thirty yards away for 7 1/2d. Rachel read his thoughts plainly. She knew well enough that she had done rather a fine thing, and her demeanour showed it. Ted Malkin enveloped the tin in suitable paper.

"Sure there's nothing else?"

"Not at this counter."

He gave her the tin, smiled, and as he turned to the next waiting customer, called out—

"Singapore Delicious, eight and a half pence."

It was rather a poor affair, that tin—a declension from the great days of Mrs. Maldon's married life, when she spent freely, knowing naught of her husband's income except that it was large and elastic. In those days she would buy a real pineapple, entire, once every three weeks or so, costing five, six, seven, or eight shillings—gorgeous and spectacular fruit. Now she might have pineapple every day if she chose, but it was not quite the same pineapple. She affected to like it, she did like it, but the difference between the old pineapple and the new was the saddening difference, for Mrs. Maldon's secret heart, between the great days and the paltry, facile convenience of the twentieth century.

It was to his aunt, who presided over the opposite side of the shop, including the cash-desk, that Ted Malkin proclaimed in a loud voice the amounts of purchases on his own side. Miss Malkin was a virgin of fifty-eight years' standing, with definite and unchangeable ideas on every subject on earth or in heaven except her own age. As Rachel, followed by Louis Fores, crossed the shop, Miss Malkin looked at them and closed her lips, and lowered her eyelids, and the upper part of her body seemed to curve slightly, with the sinuosity of a serpent—a strange, significant movement, sometimes ill described as "bridling."

The total effect was as though Miss Malkin had suddenly clicked the shutters down on all the windows of her soul and was spying at Rachel and Louis Fores through a tiny concealed orifice in the region of her eye. It was nothing to Miss Malkin that Rachel on that night of all nights had come in to buy Singapore Delicious Chunks at 8-1/2d. It was nothing to her that Mrs. Maldon had had "an attack." Miss Malkin merely saw Rachel and Fores gadding about the town together of a Saturday night while Mrs. Maldon was ill in bed. And she regarded Ted's benevolence as the benevolence of a simpleton. Between Miss Malkin's taciturnity and the voice within her Rachel had a terrible three minutes. She was "sneaped"; which fortunately made her red hair angry, so that she could keep some of her dignity. Louis Fores seemed to be quite unconscious that a fearful scene was enacting between Miss Malkin and Rachel, and he blandly insisted on taking the pineapple-tin and the cocoa-tin and slipping them into the reticule, as though he had been shopping with Rachel all his life and there was a perfect understanding between them. The moral effect was very bad. Rachel blushed again.

When she emerged from the shop she had the illusion of being breathless, and in the midst of a terrific adventure the end of which none could foresee. She was furious against Miss Malkin and against herself. Yet she indignantly justified herself. Was not Louis Fores Mrs. Maiden's nephew, and were not he and she doing the best thing they could together under the difficult circumstances of the old lady's illness? If she was not to co-operate with the old lady's sole relative in Bursley, with whom was she to co-operate? In vain such justifications!... She murderously hated Miss Malkin. She said to herself, without meaning it, that no power should induce her ever to enter the shop again.

And she thought: "I can't possibly go into another shop to-night—I can't possibly do it! And yet I must. Why am I such a silly baby?"

As they walked slowly along the pavement she was in the wild dream anew, and Louis Fores was her only hope and reliance. She clung to him, though not with her arm. She seemed to know him very intimately, and still he was more enigmatic to her than ever he had been.

As for Louis, beneath his tranquil mien of a man of experience and infinite tact, he was undergoing the most extraordinary and delightful sensations, keener even than those which had thrilled him in Rachel's kitchen on the previous evening. The social snob in him had somehow suddenly expired, and he felt intensely the strange charm of going shopping of a Saturday night with a young woman, and making a little purchase here and a little purchase there, and thinking about halfpennies. And in his fancy he built a small house to which he and Rachel would shortly return, and all the brilliant diversions of bachelordom seemed tame and tedious compared to the wondrous existence of this small house.

"Now I have to go to Heath's the butcher's," said Rachel, determined at all costs to be a woman and not a silly baby. After that plain announcement her cowardice would have no chance to invent an excuse for not going into another shop.

But she added—

"And that'll be all."

"I know Master Bob Heath. Known him a long time," said Louis Fores, with amusement in his voice, as though to imply that he could relate strange and titillating matters about Heath if he chose, and indeed that he was a mine of secret lore concerning the citizens.

The fact was that he had travelled once to Woore races with the talkative Heath, and that Heath had introduced him to his brother Stanny Heath, a local book-maker of some reputation, from whom Louis had won five pounds ten during the felicitous day. Ever afterwards Bob Heath had effusively saluted Louis on every possible occasion, and had indeed once stopped him in the street and said: "My brother treated you all right, didn't he? Stanny's a true sport." And Louis had to be effusive also. It would never do to be cold to a man from whose brother you had won—and received— five pounds ten on a racecourse.

So that when Louis followed Rachel into Heath's shop at the top of Duck Bank the fat and happy Heath gave him a greeting in which astonishment and warm regard were mingled. The shop was empty of customers, and also it contained little meat, for Heath's was not exactly a Saturday-night trade. Bob Heath, clothed from head to foot in slightly blood-stained white, stood behind one hacked counter, and Mrs. Heath, similarly attired, and rather stouter, stood behind the other; and each possessed a long steel which hung from an ample loose girdle.

Heath, a man of forty, had a salute somewhat military in gesture, though conceived in a softer, more accommodating spirit. He raised his chubby hand to his forehead, but all the muscles of it were lax and the fingers loosely curved; at the same time he drew back his left foot and kicked up the heel a few inches. Louis amiably responded. Rachel went direct to Mrs. Heath, a woman of forty-five. She had never before seen Heath in the shop.

"Doing much with the gees lately, Mr. Fores?" Heath inquired in a cheerful, discreet tone.

"Not me!"

"Well, I can't say I've had much luck myself, sir."

The conversation was begun in proper form. Through it Louis could hear Rachel buying a cutlet, and then another cutlet, from Mrs. Heath, and protesting that five-pence was a good price and all she desired to pay even for the finest cutlet in the shop. And then Rachel asked about sweetbreads. Heath's voice grew more and more confidential and at length, after a brief pause, he whispered —

"Ye're not married, are ye, sir? Excuse the liberty."

It was a whisper, but one of those terrible, miscalculated whispers that can be heard for miles around, like the call of the cuckoo. Plainly Heath was not aware of the identity of Rachel Fleckring. And in his world, which was by no means the world of his shop and his wife, it was incredible that a man should run round shopping with a woman on a Saturday night unless he was a husband on unescapable duty.

Louis shook his head.

Mrs. Heath called out in severe accents which were a reproof and a warning: "Got a sweetbread, Robert? It's for Mrs. Maldon."

The clumsy fool understood that he had blundered.

He had no sweetbread—not even for Mrs. Maldon. The cutlets were wrapped in newspaper, and Louis rather self-consciously opened the maw of the reticule for them.

"No offence, I hope, sir," said Heath as the pair left the shop, thus aggravating his blunder. Louis and Rachel crossed Duck Bank in constrained silence. Rachel was scarlet. The new cinema next to the new Congregational chapel blazed in front of them.

"Wouldn't care to look in here, I suppose, would you?" Louis imperturbably suggested.

Rachel did not reply.

"Only for a quarter of an hour or so," said Louis.

Rachel did not venture to glance up at him. She was so agitated that she could scarcely speak.

"I don't think so," she muttered.

"Why not?" he exquisitely pleaded. "It will do you good."

She raised her head and saw the expression of his face, so charming, so provocative, so persuasive. The voice within her was insistent, but she would not listen to it. Nobody had ever looked at her as Louis was looking at her then. The streets, the town faded. She thought: "Whatever happens, I cannot withstand that face." She was feverishly happy, and at the same time ravaged by both pain and fear. She became a fatalist. And she abandoned the pretence that she was not the slave of that face. Her eyes grew candidly acquiescent, as if she were murmuring to him, "I am defenceless against you."

III

It was not surprising that Rachel, who never in her life had beheld at close quarters any of the phenomena of luxury, should blink her ingenuous eyes at the blinding splendour of the antechambers of the Imperial Cinema de Luxe. Eyes less ingenuous than hers had blinked before that prodigious dazzlement. Even Louis, a man of vast experience and sublime imperturbability, visiting the Imperial on its opening night, had allowed the significant words to escape him, "Well, I'm blest!" — proof enough of the triumph of the Imperial!

The Imperial had set out to be the most gorgeous cinema in the Five Towns; and it simply was. Its advertisements read: "There is always room at the top." There was. Over the ceiling of its foyer enormous crimson peonies expanded like tropic blooms, and the heart of each peony was a sixteen-candle-power electric lamp. No other two cinemas in the Five Towns, it was reported, consumed together as much current as the Imperial de Luxe; and nobody could deny that the degree of excellence of a cinema is finally settled by its consumption of electricity.

Rachel now understood better the symbolic meaning of the glare in the sky caused at night by the determination of the Imperial to make itself known. She had been brought up to believe that, gas being dear, no opportunity should be lost of turning a jet down, and that electricity was so dear as to be inconceivable in any house not inhabited by crass spendthrift folly. She now saw electricity scattered about as though it were as cheap as salt. She saw written in electric fire across the inner entrance the beautiful sentiment, "Our aim is to please YOU." The "you" had two lines of fire under it. She saw, also, the polite nod of the official, dressed not less glitteringly than an Admiral of the Fleet in full uniform, whose sole duty in life was to welcome and reassure the visitor. All this in Bursley, which even by Knype was deemed an out-of-the-world spot and home of sordid decay! In Hanbridge she would have been less surprised to discover such marvels, because the flaunting modernity of Hanbridge was notorious. And her astonishment would have been milder had she had been in the habit of going out at night. Like all those who never went out at night, she had quite failed to keep pace with the advancing stride of the Five Towns on the great road of civilization.

More impressive still than the extreme radiance about her was the easy and superb gesture of Louis as, swinging the reticule containing pineapple, cocoa, and cutlets, he slid his hand into his pocket and drew therefrom a coin and smacked it on the wooden ledge of the ticket-window—gesture of a man to whom money was naught provided he got the best of everything. "Two!" he repeated, with slight impatience, bending down so as to see the young woman in white who sat in another world behind gilt bars. He was paying for Rachel! Exquisite experience for the daughter and sister of Fleckrings! Experience unique in her career! And it seemed so right and yet so wondrous, that he should pay for her!... He picked up the change, and without a glance at them dropped the coins into his pocket. It was a glorious thing to be a man! But was it not even more glorious to be a girl and the object of his princely care?... They passed a heavy draped curtain, on which was a large card, "Tea-Room," and there seemed to be celestial social possibilities behind that curtain, though indeed it bore another and smaller card: "Closed after six o'clock"—the result of excessive caution on the part of a kill-joy Town Council. A boy in the likeness of a midshipman took halves of the curving tickets and dropped them into a tin box, and then next Rachel was in a sudden black darkness, studded here and there with minute glowing rubies that revealed the legend: "Exit. Exit. Exit."

Row after row of dim, pale, intent faces became gradually visible, stretching far back-into complete obscurity; thousands, tens of thousands of faces, it seemed—for the Imperial de Luxe was demonstrating that Saturday night its claim to be "the fashionable rage of Bursley." Then mysterious laughter rippled in the gloom, and loud guffaws shot up out of the rippling. Rachel saw nothing whatever to originate this mirth until an attendant in black with a tiny white apron loomed upon them out of the darkness, and, beckoning them forward, bent down, and indicated two empty places at the end of a row, and the great white scintillating screen of the cinema came into view. Instead of being at the extremity it was at the beginning of the auditorium. And as Rachel took her seat she saw on the screen—which was scarcely a dozen feet away—a man kneeling at the end of a canal-lock, and sucking up the water of the canal through a hose-pipe; and this astoundingly thirsty man drank with such rapidity that the water, with huge boats floating on it, subsided at the rate of about a foot a second, and the drinker waxed enormously in girth. The laughter grew uproarious. Rachel herself gave a quick, uncontrolled, joyous laugh, and it was as if the laugh had been drawn out of her violently unawares. Louis Fores also laughed very heartily.

"Cute idea, that!" he whispered.

When the film was cut off Rachel wanted to take back her laugh. She felt a little ashamed of having laughed at anything so silly.

"How absurd!" she murmured, trying to be serious.

Nevertheless she was in bliss. She surrendered herself to the joy of life, as to a new sensation. She was intoxicated, ravished, bewildered, and quite careless. Perhaps for the first time in her adult existence she lived without reserve or preoccupation completely in and for the moment. Moreover the hearty laughter of Louis Fores helped to restore her dignity. If the spectacle was good enough for him, with all his knowledge of the world, to laugh at, she need not blush for its effect on herself. And in another ten seconds, when the swollen man, staggering along a wide thoroughfare, was run down by an automobile and squashed flat, while streams of water inundated the roadway, she burst again into free laughter, and then looked round at Louis, who at the same instant looked round at her, and they exchanged an intimate smiling glance. It seemed to Rachel that they were alone and solitary in the crowded interior, and that they shared exactly the same tastes and emotions and comprehended one another profoundly and utterly; her confidence in him, at that instant, was absolute, and enchanting to her. Half a minute later the emaciated man was in a room and being ecstatically kissed by a most beautiful and sweetly shameless girl in a striped shirtwaist; it was a very small room, and the furniture was close upon the couple, giving the scene an air of delightful privacy. And then the scene was blotted out and gay music rose lilting from some unseen cave in front of the screen.

Rachel was rapturously happy. Gazing along the dim rows, she descried many young couples, without recognizing anybody at all, and most of these couples were absorbed in each other, and some of the girls seemed so elegant and alluring in the dusk of the theatre, and some of the men so fine in their manliness! And the ruby-studded gloom protected them all, including Rachel and Louis, from the audience at large.

The screen glowed again. And as it did so Louis gave a start.

"By Jove!" he said, "I've left my stick somewhere. It must have been at Heath's. Yes, it was. I put it on the counter while I opened this net thing. Don't you remember? You were taking some money out of your purse." Louis had a very distinct vision of his Rachel's agreeably gloved fingers primly unfastening the purse and choosing a shilling from it.

"How annoying!" murmured Rachel feelingly.

"I wouldn't lose that stick for a five-pound note." (He had a marvellous way of saying "five-pound note.") "Would you mind very much if I just slip over and get it, before he shuts? It's only across the road, you know."

There was something in the politeness of the phrase "mind *very much*" that was irresistible to Rachel. It caused her to imagine splendid drawing-rooms far beyond her modest level, and the superlative deportment therein of the well-born.

"Not at all!" she replied, with her best affability. "But will they let you come in again without paying?"

"Oh, I'll risk that," he whispered, smiling superiorly.

Then he went, leaving the reticule, and she was alone.

She rearranged the reticule on the seat by her side. The reticule being already perfectly secure, there was no need for her to touch it, but some nervous movement was necessary to her. Yet she was less self-conscious than she had been with Louis at her elbow. She felt, however, a very slight sense of peril—of the unreality of the plush fauteuil on which she sat, and those rows of vaguely discerned faces on her right; and the reality of distant phenomena such as Mrs. Maldon in bed. Notwithstanding her strange and ecstatic experiences with Louis Fores that night in the dark, romantic town, the problem of the lost money remained, or ought to have remained, as disturbing as ever. To ignore it was not to destroy it. She sat rather tight in her place, increasing her primness, and trying to show by her carriage that she was an adult in full control of all her wise faculties. She set her lips to judge the film with the cold impartiality of middle age, but they persisted in being the fresh, responsive, mobile lips of a young girl. They were saying noiselessly: "He will be back in a moment. And he will find me sitting here just as he left me. When I hear him coming I shan't turn my head to look. It will be better not."

The film showed a forest with a wooden house in the middle of it. Out of this house came a most adorable young woman, who leaped on to a glossy horse and galloped at a terrific rate, plunging down ravines, and then trotting fast over the crests of clearings. She came to a man who was boiling a kettle over a camp-fire, and slipped lithely from the horse, and the man, with a start of surprise, seized her pretty waist and kissed her passionately, in the midst of the immense forest whose every leaf was moving. And she returned his kiss without restraint. For they were betrothed. And Rachel imagined the free life of distant forests, where love was, and where slim girls rode mettlesome horses more easily than the girls of the Five Towns rode bicycles. She could not even ride a bicycle, had never had the opportunity to learn. The vision of emotional pleasures that in her narrow existence she had not dreamed of filled her with mild, delightful sorrow. She could conceive nothing more heavenly than to embrace one's true love in the recesses of a forest.... Then came crouching Indians.... And then she heard Louis Fores behind her. She had not meant to turn round, but when a hand was put heavily on her shoulder she turned quickly, resenting the contact.

"I should like a word with ye, if ye can spare a minute, young miss," whispered a voice as heavy as the hand. It was old Thomas Batchgrew's face and whiskers that she was looking up at in the gloom.

As if fascinated, she followed in terror those flaunting whiskers up the slope of the narrow isle to the back of the auditorium. Thomas Batchgrew seemed to be quite at home in the theatre; he wore no hat and there was a pen behind his ear. Never would she have set foot inside the Imperial de Luxe had she guessed that Thomas Batchgrew was concerned in it. She thought she had heard once, somewhere, that he had to do with cinemas in other parts of the country, but it would not have occurred to her to connect him with a picture-palace so near home. She was not alone in her ignorance of the councillor's share in the Imperial. Practically nobody had heard of it until that night, for Batchgrew had come into the new enterprise by the back door of a loan to its promoters, who were richer in ideas than in capital; and now, the harvest being ripe, he was arranging, by methods not unfamiliar to capitalists, to reap where he had not sown.

Shame and fear overcame Rachel. The crystal dream was shivered to dust. Awful apprehension, the expectancy of frightful events, succeeded to it. She perceived that since the very moment of quitting the house the dread of some disaster had been pursuing her; only she had refused to see it—she had found oblivion from it in the new and agitatingly sweet sensations which Louis Fores had procured for her. But now the real was definitely sifted out from the illusory. And nothing but her own daily existence, as she had always lived it, was real. The rest was a snare. There were no forests, no passionate love, no flying steeds, no splendid adorers—for her. She was Rachel Fleckring and none else.

Councillor Batchgrew turned to the left, and through a small hole in the painted wall Rachel saw a bright beam shooting out in the shape of a cone—forests, and the unreal denizens of forests shimmering across the entire auditorium to impinge on the screen! And she heard the steady rattle of a revolving machine. Then Batchgrew beckoned her into a very small, queerly shaped room furnished with a table and a chair and a single electric lamp that hung by a cord from a rough hook in the ceiling. A boy stood near the door holding three tin boxes one above another in his arms, and keeping the top one in position with his chin. These boxes were similar to that in which Louis' tickets had been dropped.

"Did you want your boxes, sir?" asked the boy.

"Put 'em down," Thomas Batchgrew growled.

The boy deposited them in haste on the table and hurried out.

"How is Mrs. Maldon?" demanded Mr. Batchgrew with curtness, after he had snorted and sniffed. He remained standing near to Rachel.

"Oh, she's very much better," said Rachel eagerly. "She was asleep when I left."

"Have ye left her by herself?" Mr. Batchgrew continued his inquiry. His voice was as offensive as thick dark glue.

"Of course not! Mrs. Tams is sitting up with her." Rachel meant her tone to be a dignified reproof to Thomas Batchgrew for daring to assume even the possibility of her having left Mrs. Maldon to solitude. But she did not succeed, because she could not manage her tone. She desired intensely to be the self-possessed, mature woman, sure of her position and of her sagacity; but she could be nothing save the absurd, guilty, stammering, blushing little girl, shifting her feet and looking everywhere except boldly into Thomas Batchgrew's horrid eyes.

"So it's Mrs. Tams as is sitting with her!"

Rachel could not help explaining—

"I had to come down town to do some shopping for Sunday. Somebody had to come. Mr. Fores had called in to ask after Mrs. Maldon, and so he walked down with me." Every word she said appeared intolerably foolish to her as she uttered it.

"And then he brought ye in here!" Batchgrew grimly completed the tale.

"We came in here for ten minutes or so, as I'd finished my shopping so quickly. Mr. Fores has just run across to the butcher's to get something that was forgotten."

Mr. Batchgrew coughed loosely and loudly. And beyond the cough, beyond the confines of the ugly little room which imprisoned her so close to old Batchgrew and his grotesque whiskers, Rachel could hear the harsh, quick laughter of the audience, and then faint music—far off.

"If young Fores was here," said Mr. Batchgrew brutally, "I should tell him straight as he might do better than to go gallivanting about the town until that there money's found."

He turned towards his boxes.

"I don't know what you mean, Mr. Batchgrew," said Rachel, tapping her foot and trying to be very dignified.

"And I'll tell ye another thing, young miss," Batchgrew went on. "Every minute as ye spend with young Fores ye'll regret. He's a bad lot, and ye may as well know it first as last. Ye ought to thank me for telling of ye, but ye won't."

"I really don't know what you mean, Mr. Batchgrew!" She could not invent another phrase.

"Ye know what I mean right enough, young miss!... If ye only came in for ten minutes yer time's up."

Rachel moved to leave.

"Hold on!" Batchgrew stopped her. There was a change in his voice.

"Look at me!" he commanded, but with the definite order was mingled some trace of cajolery.

She obeyed, quivering, her cheeks the colour of a tomato. In spite of all preoccupations, she distinctly noticed—and not without a curious tremor—that his features had taken on a boyish look. In the almost senile face she could see ambushed the face of the youth that Thomas Batchgrew had been perhaps half a century before.

"Ye're a fine wench," said he, with a note of careless but genuine admiration. "I'll not deny it. Don't ye go and throw yerself away. Keep out o' mischief."

Forgetting all but the last phrase, Rachel marched out of the room, unspeakably humiliated, wounded beyond any expression of her own. The cowardly, odious brute! The horrible ancient! What right had he?... What had she done that was wrong, that would not bear the fullest inquiry. The shopping was an absolute necessity. She was obliged to come out. Mrs. Maldon was better, and quietly sleeping. Mrs. Tarns was the most faithful and capable old person that was ever born. Hence she was justified in leaving the invalid. Louis Fores had offered to go with her. How could she refuse the offer? What reason could there be for refusing it? As for the cinema, who could object to the cinema? Certainly not Thomas Batchgrew! There was no hurry. And was she not an independent woman, earning her own living? Who on earth had the right to dictate to her? She was not a slave. Even a servant had an evening out once a week. She was sinless....

And yet while she was thus ardently defending herself she knew well that she had sinned against the supreme social law—the law of "the look of things." It was true that chance had worked against her. But common sense would have rendered chance powerless by giving it no opportunity to be malevolent. She was furious with Rachel Fleckring. That Rachel Fleckring, of all mortal girls, should have exposed herself to so dreadful, so unforgettable a humiliation was mortifying in the very highest degree. Her lips trembled. She was about to burst into a sob. But at this moment the rattle of the revolving machine behind the hole ceased, the theatre blazed from end to end with sudden light, the music resumed, and a number of variegated advertisements were weakly thrown on the screen. She set herself doggedly to walk back down the slope of the aisle, not daring to look ahead for Louis. She felt that every eye was fixed on her with base curiosity.... When, after the endless ordeal of the aisle, she reached her place, Louis was not there. And though she was glad, she took offence at his delay. Gathering up the reticule with a nervous sweep of the hand, she departed from the theatre, her eyes full of tears. And amid all the wild confusion in her brain one little thought flashed clear and was gone: the wastefulness of paying for a whole night's entertainment and then only getting ten minutes of it!

IV

She met Louis Fores high up Bycars Lane, about a hundred yards below Mrs. Maldon's house. She saw some one come out of the gate of the house, and heard the gate clang in the distance. For a moment she could not surely identify the figure, but as soon as Louis, approaching, and carrying his stick, grew unmistakable even in the darkness, all her agitation, which had been subsiding under the influence of physical exercise, rose again to its original fever.

"Ah!" said Louis, greeting her with a most deferential salute. "There you are. I was really beginning to wonder. I opened the front door, but there was no light and no sound, so I shut it again and came back. What happened to you?"

His ingenuous and delightful face, so confident, good-natured, and respectful, had exactly the same effect on her as before. At the sight of it Thomas Batchgrew's vague accusation against Louis was dismissed utterly as the rancorous malice of an evil old man. For the rest, she had never given it any real credit, having an immense trust in her own judgment. But she had no intention of letting Louis go free. As she had been put in the wrong, so must he be put in the wrong. This seemed to her only just. Besides, was he not wholly to blame? Also she remembered with strange clearness the admiration in the mien of the hated Batchgrew, and the memory gave her confidence.

She said, with an effort after chilly detachment—

"I couldn't wait in the cinema alone for ever."

He was perturbed.

"But I assure you," he said nicely, "I was as quick as ever I could be. Heath had put my stick in his back parlour to keep it safe for me, and it was quite a business finding it again. Why didn't you wait?... I say, I hope you weren't vexed at my leaving you."

"Of course I wasn't vexed," she answered, with heat. "Didn't I tell you I didn't mind? But if you want to know, old Batchgrew came along while you were gone and insulted me."

"Insulted you? How? What was he doing there?"

"How should I know what he was doing there? Better ask him questions like that! All I can tell you is that he came to me and called me into a room at the back—and—and—told me I'd no business to be there, nor you either, while Mrs. Maldon was ill in bed."

"Silly old fool! I hope you didn't take any notice of him."

"Yes, that's all very fine, that is! It's easy for you to talk like that. But—but—well, I suppose there's nothing more to be said!" She moved to one side; her anger was rising. She knew that it was rising. She was determined that it should rise. She did not care. She rather enjoyed the excitement. She smarted under her recent experience; she was deeply miserable; and yet, at the same time, standing there close to Louis in the rustling night, she was exultant as she certainly had never been exultant before.

She walked forward grimly. Louis turned and followed her.

"I'm most frightfully sorry," he said.

She replied fiercely—

"It isn't as if I didn't wait. I waited in the porch I don't know how long. Then of course I came home, as there was no sign of you."

"When I went back you weren't there; it must have been while you were with old Batch; so I naturally didn't stay. I just came straight up here. I was afraid you were vexed because I'd left you alone."

"Well, and if I was!" said Rachel, splendidly contradicting herself. "It's not a very nice thing for a girl to be left alone like that—*and all on account of a stick*!" There was a break in her voice.

Arrived at the gate, she pushed it open.

"Good-night," she snapped. "Please don't come in."

And within the gate she deliberately stared at him with an unforgiving gaze. The impartial lamp-post lighted the scene.

"Good-night," she repeated harshly. She was saying to herself: "He really does take it in the most beautiful way. I could do anything I liked with him."

"Good-night," said Louis, with strict punctilio.

When she got to the top of the steps she remembered that Louis had the latch-key. He was gone. She gave a wet sob and impulsively ran down the steps and opened the gate. Louis returned. She tried to speak and could not.

"I beg your pardon," said Louis. "Of course you want the key."

He handed her the key with a gesture that disconcertingly melted the rigour of all her limbs. She snatched at it, and plunged for the gate just as the tears rolled down her cheeks in a shower. The noise of the gate covered a fresh sob. She did not look back. Amid all her quite real distress she was proud and happy—proud because she was old enough and independent enough and audacious enough to quarrel with her lover, and happy because she had suddenly discovered life. And the soft darkness and the wind, and the faint sky reflections of distant furnace fires, and the sense of the road winding upward, and the very sense of the black mass of the house in front of her (dimly lighted at the upper floor) all made part of her mysterious happiness.

CHAPTER VIII
END AND BEGINNING

I

"Mrs. Tams!" said Mrs. Maldon, in a low, alarmed, and urgent voice.

The gas was turned down in the bedroom, and Mrs. Maldon, looking from her bed across the chamber, could only just distinguish the stout, vague form of the charwoman asleep in an arm-chair. The light from the street lamp was strong enough to throw faint shadows of the window-frames on the blinds. The sleeper did not stir.

Mrs. Maldon summoned again, more loudly—

"Mrs. Tams!"

And Mrs. Tams, starting out of another world, replied with deprecation—

"Hey, hey!" as if saying: "I am here. I am fully awake and observant. Please remain calm."

Mrs. Maldon said agitatedly—

"I've just heard the front door open. I'm sure whoever it was was trying not to make a noise. There! Can't you hear anything?"

"That I canna'!" said Mrs. Tams.

"No!" Mrs. Maldon protested, as Mrs. Tams approached the gas to raise it. "Don't touch the gas. If anybody's got in let them think we're asleep."

The mystery of the vanished money and the fear of assassins seemed suddenly to oppress the very air of the room. Mrs. Maldon was leaning on one elbow in her bed.

Mrs. Tams said to her in a whisper—

"I mun go see."

"Please don't!" Mrs. Maldon entreated.

"I mun go see," said Mrs. Tams.

She was afraid, but she conceived that she ought to examine the house, and no fear could have stopped her from going forth into the zone of danger.

The next moment she gave a short laugh, and said in her ordinary tone—

"Bless us! I shall be forgetting the nose on my face next. It's Miss Rachel coming in, of course."

"Miss Rachel coming in!" repeated Mrs. Maldon. "Has she been out? I was not aware. She said nothing—"

"Her came up a bit since, and said her had to do some shopping."

"Shopping! At this time of night!" murmured Mrs. Maldon.

Said Mrs. Tams laconically—

"To-morrow's Sunday—and pray God ye'll fancy a bite o' summat tasty."

While the two old women, equalized in rank by the fact of Mrs. Maldon's illness, by the sudden alarm, and by the darkness of the room, were thus conversing, sounds came from the pavement through the slightly open windows—voices, and the squeak of the gate roughly pushed open.

"That's Miss Rachel now," said Mrs. Tams.

"Then who was it came in before?" Mrs. Maldon demanded.

There was the tread of rapid feet on the stone steps, and then the gate squeaked again.

Mrs. Tams went to the window and pulled aside the blind.

"Aye!" she announced simply. "It's Miss Rachel and Mr. Fores."

Mrs. Maldon caught her breath.

"You didn't tell me she was out with Mr. Fores," said Mrs. Maldon, stiffly but weakly.

"It's first I knew of it," Mrs. Tams replied, still spying over the pavement. "He's given her th' key. There! He's gone."

Mrs. Maldon muttered—

"The key? What key?"

"Th' latch-key belike."

"I must speak to Miss Rachel," breathed Mrs. Maldon in a voice of extreme and painful apprehension.

The front door closing sent a vibration through the bedroom. Mrs. Tarns hesitated an instant, and then raised the gas. Mrs. Maldon lay with shut eyes on her left side and gave no sign of consciousness. Light footsteps could be heard on the stairs.

"I'll go see," said Mrs. Tams.

In the heart of the aged woman exanimate on the bed, and in the heart of the aging woman whose stout, coarse arm was still raised to the gas-tap, were the same sentiments of wonder, envy, and pity, aroused by the enigmatic actions of a younger generation going its perilous, instinctive ways to keep the race alive.

Mrs. Tarns lighted a benzolene hand-lamp at the gas, and silently left the bedroom. She still somewhat feared an unlawful invader, but the arrival of Rachel had reassured her. Preceded by the waving little flame, she passed Rachel's door, which was closed, and went downstairs. Every mysterious room on the ground floor was in order and empty. No sign of an invasion. Through the window of the kitchen she saw the fresh cutlets under a wire cover in the scullery; and on the kitchen table were the tin of pineapple and the tin of cocoa, with the reticule near by. All doors that ought to be fastened were fastened. She remounted the stairs and blew out the lamp on the threshold of the mistress's bedroom. And as she did so she could hear Rachel winding up her alarm-clock in quick jerks, and the light shone bright like a silver rod under Rachel's door.

"Her's gone reet to bed," said Mrs. Tams softly, by the bedside of Mrs. Maldon. "Ye've no cause for to worrit yerself. I've looked over th' house."

Mrs. Maldon was fast asleep.

Mrs. Tams lowered the gas and resumed her chair, and the street lamp once more threw the shadows of the window-frames on the blinds.

II

The next day Mrs. Tams, who had been appointed to sleep in the spare room, had to exist under the blight of Rachel's chill disapproval because she had not slept in the spare room—nor in any bed at all. The arrangement had been that Mrs. Tams should retire at 4 a.m., Rachel taking her place with Mrs. Maldon. Mrs. Tams had not retired at 4 a.m. because Rachel had not taken her place.

As a fact, Rachel had been wakened by a bang of the front door, at 10.30 a.m. only. Her first glance at the alarm-clock on her dressing-table was incredulous. And she refused absolutely to believe that the hour was so late. Yet the alarm-clock was giving its usual sturdy, noisy tick, and the sun was high. Then she refused to believe that the alarm had gone off, and in order to remain firm in her belief she refrained from any testing of the mechanism, which might—indeed, would—have proved that the alarm had in fact gone off. It became with her an article of dogma that on that particular morning, of all mornings, the very reliable alarm-clock had failed in its duty. The truth was that she had lain awake till nearly three o'clock, turning from side to side and thinking bitterly upon the imperfections of human nature, and had then fallen into a deep, invigorating sleep from which perhaps half a dozen alarm-clocks might not have roused her.

She arose full of health and anger, and in a few minutes she was out of the bedroom, for she had not fully undressed; like many women, when there was watching to be done, she loved to keep her armour on and to feel the exciting strain of the unusual in every movement. She fell on Mrs. Tams as Mrs. Tams was coming upstairs after letting out the doctor and refreshing herself with cocoa in the kitchen. A careless observer might have thought from their respective attitudes that it was Mrs. Tarns, and not Rachel, who had overslept herself. Rachel divided the blame between the alarm-clock and Mrs. Tams for not wakening her; indeed, she seemed to consider herself the victim of a conspiracy between Mrs. Tams and the alarm-clock. She explicitly blamed Mrs. Tams for allowing the doctor to come and go without her knowledge. Even the doctor did not get off scot-free, for he ought to have asked for Rachel and insisted on seeing her.

She examined Mrs. Tams about the invalid's health as a lawyer examines a hostile witness. And when Mrs. Tams said that the invalid had slept, and was sleeping, stertorously in an unaccountable manner, and hinted that the doctor was not undisturbed by the new symptom and meant to call again later on, Rachel's tight-lipped mien indicated that this might not have occurred if only Mrs. Tams had fulfilled her obvious duty of wakening Rachel. Though she was hungry, she scornfully repulsed the suggestion of breakfast. Mrs. Tams, thoroughly accustomed to such behaviour in the mighty, accepted it as she accepted the weather. But if she had had to live through the night again—after all, a quite tolerable night—she would still not have wakened Rachel at 4 a.m.

Rachel softened as the day passed. She ate a good dinner at one o'clock, with Mrs. Tams in the kitchen, one or the other mounting at short intervals to see if Mrs. Maldon had stirred. Then she changed into her second-best frock, in anticipation of the doctor's Sunday afternoon visit, strictly commanded

Mrs. Tams (but with relenting kindness in her voice) to go and lie down, and established herself neatly in the sick-room.

Though her breathing had become noiseless again, Mrs. Maldon still slept. She had wakened only once since the previous night. She lay calm and dignified in slumber—an old and devastated woman, with that disconcerting resemblance to a corpse shown by all aged people asleep, but yet with little sign of positive illness save the slight distortion of her features caused by the original attack. Rachel sat idle, prim, in vague reflection, at intervals smoothing her petticoat, or giving a faint cough, or gazing at the mild blue September sky. She might have been reading a book, but she was not by choice a reader. She had the rare capacity of merely existing. Her thoughts flitted to and fro, now resting on Mrs. Maldon with solemnity, now on Mrs. Tams with amused benevolence, now on old Batchgrew with lofty disgust, and now on Louis Fores with unquiet curiosity and delicious apprehension.

She gave a little shudder of fright and instantly controlled it—Mrs. Maldon, instead of being asleep, was looking at her. She rose and went to the bedside and stood over the sick woman, by the pillow, benignly, asking with her eyes what desire of the sufferer's she might fulfil. And Mrs. Maldon looked up at her with another benignity. And they both smiled.

"You've slept very well," said Rachel softly.

Mrs. Maldon, continuing to smile, gave a scarcely perceptible affirmative movement of the head.

"Will you have some of your Revalenta? I've only got to warm it, here. Everything's ready."

"Nothing, thank you, dear," said Mrs. Maldon, in a firm, matter-of-fact voice.

The doctor had left word that food was not to be forced on her.

"Do you feel better?"

Mrs. Maldon answered, in a peculiar tone—

"My dear, I shall never feel any better than I do now."

"Oh, you mustn't talk like that!" said Rachel in gay protest.

"I want to talk to you, Rachel," said Mrs. Maldon, once more reassuringly matter-of-fact. "Sit down there."

Rachel obediently perched herself on the bed, and bent her head. And her face, which was now much closer to Mrs. Maldon's, expressed the gravity which Mrs. Maldon would wish, and also the affectionate condescension of youth towards age, and of health towards infirmity. And as almost unconsciously she exulted in her own youth, and strength, delicate little poniards of tragic grief for Mrs. Maldon's helpless and withered senility seemed to stab through that personal pride. The shiny, veined right hand of the old woman emerged from under the bedclothes and closed with hot, fragile grasp on Rachel's hand.

Within the impeccable orderliness of the bedroom was silence; and beyond was the vast Sunday afternoon silence of the district, producing the sensation of surcease, re-creating the impressive illusion of religion even out of the brutish irreligion that was bewailed from pulpits to empty pews in all the temples of all the Five Towns. Only the smoke waving slowly through the clean-washed sky from a few high chimneys over miles of deserted manufactories made a link between Saturday and Monday.

"I've something I want to say to you," said Mrs. Maldon, in that deceptive matter-of-fact voice. "I wanted to tell you yesterday afternoon, but I couldn't. And then again last night, but I went off to sleep."

"Yes?" murmured Rachel, duped by Mrs. Maldon's manner into perfect security. She was thinking: "What's the poor old thing got into her head now? Is it something fresh about the money?"

"It's about yourself," said Mrs. Maldon.

Rachel exclaimed impulsively—

"What about me?"

She could feel a faint vibration in Mrs. Maldon's hand.

"I want you not to see so much of Louis."

Rachel was shocked and insulted. She straightened her spine and threw back her head sharply. But she dared not by force withdraw her hand from Mrs. Maldon's. Moreover, Mrs. Maldon's clasp tightened almost convulsively.

"I suppose Mr. Batchgrew's been up here telling tales while I was asleep," Rachel expostulated, hotly and her demeanour was at once pouting, sulky, and righteously offended.

Mrs. Maldon was puzzled.

"This morning, do you mean, dear?" she asked.

Tears stood in Rachel's eyes. She could not speak, but she nodded her head. And then another sentence burst from her full breast: "And you told Mrs. Tams she wasn't to tell me Mr. Batchgrew'd called!"

"I've not seen or heard anything of Mr. Batchgrew," said Mrs. Maldon. "But I did hear you and Louis talking outside last night."

The information startled Rachel.

"Well, and what if you did, Mrs. Maldon?" she defended herself. Her foot tapped on the floor. She was obliged to defend herself, and with care. Mrs. Maldon's tranquillity, self-control, immense age and experience, superior deportment, extreme weakness, and the respect which she inspired, compelled the girl to intrench warily, instead of carrying off the scene in one stormy outburst of resentment as theoretically she might have done.

Mrs. Maldon said, cajolingly, flatteringly—

"My dear, do be your sensible self and listen to me."

It then occurred to Rachel that during the last day or so (the period seemed infinitely longer) she had been losing, not her common sense, but her immediate command of that faculty, of which she was, privately, very proud. And she braced her being, reaching up towards her own conception of herself, towards the old invulnerable Rachel Louisa Fleckring. At any cost she must keep her reputation for common sense with Mrs. Maldon.

And so she set a watch on her gestures, and moderated her voice, secretly yielding to the benevolence of the old lady, and said, in the tone of a wise and kind woman of the world and an incarnation of profound sagacity—

"What do I see of Mr. Fores, Mrs. Maldon? I see nothing of Mr. Fores, or hardly. I'm your lady help, and he's your nephew—at least, he's your great-nephew, and it's your house he comes to. I can't help being in the house, can I? If you're thinking about last night, well, Mr. Fores called to see how you were getting on, and I was just going out to do some shopping. He walked down with me. I suppose I needn't tell you I didn't ask him to walk down with me. He asked me. I couldn't hardly say no, could I? And there were some parcels and he walked back with me."

She felt so wise and so clever and the narrative seemed so entirely natural, proper, and inevitable that she was tempted to continue—

"And supposing we *did* go into a cinematograph for a minute or two— what then?"

But she had no courage for the confession. As a wise woman she perceived the advisability of letting well alone. Moreover, she hated confessions, remorse, and gnashing of teeth.

And Mrs. Maldon regarded her worldly and mature air, with its touch of polite condescension, as both comic and tragic, and thought sadly of all the girl would have to go through before the air of mature worldliness which she was now affecting could become natural to her.

"My dear," said Mrs. Maldon, "I have perfect confidence in you." It was not quite true, because Rachel's protest as to Mr. Batchgrew, seeming to point to strange concealed incidents, had most certainly impaired the perfection of Mrs. Maiden's confidence in Rachel.

Rachel considered that she ought to pursue her advantage, and in a voice light and yet firm, good-natured and yet restive, she said—

"I really don't think anybody has the right to talk to me about Mr. Fores.... No, truly I don't."

"You mustn't misunderstand me, Rachel," Mrs. Maldon replied, and her other hand crept out, and stroked Rachel's captive hand. "I am only saying to you what it is my duty to say to you—or to any other young woman that comes to live in my house. You're a young woman, and Louis is a young man. I'm making no complaint. But it's my duty to warn you against my nephew."

"But, Mrs. Maldon, I didn't know either him or you a month ago!"

Mrs. Maldon, ignoring the interruption, proceeded quietly—

"My nephew is not to be trusted."

Her aged face slowly flushed as in that single brief sentence she overthrew the grand principle of a lifetime. She who never spoke ill of anybody had spoken ill of one of her own family.

"But—" Rachel stopped. She was frightened by the appearance of the flush on those devastated yellow cheeks, and by a quiver in the feeble voice and in the clasping hand. She could divine the ordeal which Mrs. Maldon had set herself and through which she had passed. Mrs. Maldon carried conviction, and in so doing she inspired awe. And on the top of all Rachel felt profoundly and exquisitely flattered by the immolation of Mrs. Maiden's pride.

"The money—it has something to do with that!" thought Rachel.

"My nephew is not to be trusted," said Mrs. Maldon again. "I know all his good points. But the woman who married him would suffer horribly—horribly!"

"I'm so sorry you've had to say this," said Rachel, very kindly. "But I assure you that there's nothing at all, nothing whatever, between Mr. Fores and me." And in that instant she genuinely believed that there was not. She accepted Mrs. Maldon's estimate of Louis. And further, and perhaps illogically, she had the feeling of having escaped from a fatal danger. She expected Mrs. Maldon to agree eagerly that there was nothing between herself and Louis, and to reiterate her perfect confidence. But, instead, Mrs. Maldon, apparently treating Rachel's assurance as negligible, continued with an added solemnity—

"I shall only live a little while longer—a very little while." The contrast between this and her buoyant announcement on the previous day that she was not going to die just yet was highly disturbing, but Rachel could not protest or even speak. "A very little while!" repeated Mrs. Maldon reflectively. "I've not known you long—as you say—Rachel. But I've never seen a girl I liked more, if you don't mind me telling you. I've never seen a girl I thought better of. And I don't think I could die in peace if I thought Louis was going to cause you any trouble after I'm gone. No, I couldn't die in peace if I thought that."

And Rachel, intimately moved, thought: "She has saved me from something dreadful!" (Without trying to realize precisely from what.) "How splendid she is!"

And she cast out from her mind all the multitudinous images of Louis Fores that were there. And, full of affection, and flattered pride and gratitude and childlike admiration, she bent down and rewarded the old woman who had so confided in her with a priceless girlish kiss. And she had the sensation of beginning a new life.

III

And yet, a few moments later, when Mrs. Maldon faintly murmured, "Some one at the front door," Rachel grew at once uneasy, and the new life seemed an illusion—either too fine to be true or too leaden to be desired; and she was swaying amid uncertainties. Perhaps Louis was at the front door. He had not yet called; but surely he was bound to call some time during the day! Of the dozen different Rachels in Rachel, one adventurously hoped that he would come, and another feared that he would come; one ruled him sharply out of the catalogue of right-minded persons, and another was ready passionately to defend him.

"I think not," said Rachel.

"Yes, dear; I heard some one," Mrs. Maldon insisted.

Mrs. Maldon, long practised in reconstructing the life of the street from trifling hints of sound heard in bed, was not mistaken. Rachel, opening the door of the bedroom, caught the last tinkling of the front-door bell below. On the other side of the front door somebody was standing—Louis Fores, or another!

"It may be the doctor," she said brightly, as she left the bedroom. The coward in her wanted it to be the doctor. But, descending the stairs, she could see plainly through the glass that Louis himself was at the front door. The Rachel that feared was instantly uppermost in her. She was conscious of dread. From the breathless sinking within her bosom the stairs might have been the deck of a steamer pitching in a heavy sea.

She thought—

"Here is the Louis to whom I am indifferent. There is nothing between us, really. But shall I have strength to open the door to him?"

She opened the door, with the feeling that the act was tremendous and irrevocable.

The street, in the Sabbatic sunshine, was as calm as at midnight. Louis Fores, stiff and constrained, stood strangely against the background of it. The unusualness of his demeanour, which was plain to the merest glance, increased Rachel's agitation. It appeared to Rachel that the two of them faced each other like wary enemies. She tried to examine his face in the light of Mrs. Maldon's warning, as though it were the face of a stranger; but without much success.

"Is auntie well enough for me to see her?" asked Louis, without greeting or preliminary of any sort. His voice was imperfectly under control.

Rachel replied curtly—

"I dare say she is."

To herself she said—

"Of course if he's going to sulk about last night—well, he must sulk. Really and truly he got much less than he deserved. He had no business at all to have suggested me going to the cinematograph with him. The longer he sulks the better I shall be pleased."

And in fact she was relieved at his sullenness. She tossed her proud head, but with primness. And she fervently credited to the full Mrs. Maldon's solemn insinuations against the disturber.

Louis hesitated a second, then stepped in. Rachel marched processionally upstairs, and with the detachment of a footman announced to Mrs. Maldon that Mr. Fores waited below. "Oh, please bring him up," said Mrs. Maldon, with a mild and casual benevolence that surprised the girl; for Rachel, in the righteous ferocity of her years, vaguely thought that an adverse moral verdict ought to be swiftly followed by something in the nature of annihilation.

"Will you please come up," she invited Louis, from the head of the stairs, adding privately—"I can be as stiff as you can—and stiffer. How mistaken I was in you!"

She preceded him into the bedroom, and then with ostentatious formality left aunt and nephew together. Nobody should ever say any more that she encouraged the attentions of Louis Fores.

"What is the matter, dear?" Mrs. Maldon inquired from her bed, perceiving the signs of emotion on Louis' face.

"Has Mr. Batchgrew been here yet?" Louis demanded.

"No. Is he coming?"

"Yes, he's just been to my digs. Came in his car. Auntie, do you know that he's accusing me of stealing your money—and—and—all sorts of things! I don't want to hide anything from you. It's true I was with Rachel at the cinematograph last night, but—"

Mrs. Maldon raised her enfeebled, shaking hand.

"Louis!" she entreated. His troubled, ingenuous face seemed to torture her.

"I know it's a shame to bother you, auntie. But what was I to do? He's coming up here. I only want to tell you I've not got your money. I've not stolen it. I'm absolutely innocent—absolutely. And I'll swear it on anything you like." His voice almost broke under the strain of its own earnestness. His plaintive eyes invoked justice and protection. Who could have doubted that he was sincere in this passionate, wistful protestation of innocence?

"Louis!" Mrs. Maldon entreated again, committing herself to naught, taking no side, but finding shelter beneath the enigmatic, appealing repetition of his name. It was the final triumph of age over crude youth. "Louis!"

Rachel stood expectant and watchful in the kitchen. She was now filled with dread. She wanted to go up and waken Mrs. Tams, but was too proud. The thought had come into her mind: "His coming like this has something to do with the money. Perhaps he wasn't sulking with me after all. Perhaps ..." But what it was that she dreaded she could not have defined. And then she caught the sound of an approaching automobile. The car threw its shadow across the glazed front door, which she commanded from the kitchen, and stopped. And the front-door bell rang uncannily over her head. She opened the door to Councillor Batchgrew, whose breathing was irregular and rapid.

"Has Louis Fores been here?" Batchgrew asked.

"He's upstairs now with Mrs. Maldon."

Without warning, Thomas Batchgrew strode into the house and straight upstairs. His long whiskers sailed round the turn of the stairs and disappeared. Rachel was somewhat discomfited, and very resentful. But her dread was not thereby diminished. "They'll kill the old lady between them if they don't take care," she thought.

The next instant Louis appeared at the head of the stairs. With astounding celerity Rachel slipped into the parlour. She could not bear to encounter him in the lobby—it was too narrow. She heard Louis come down the stairs, saw him take his hat from the oak chest and heard him open the front gate. In the lobby he had looked neither to right nor left. "How do, Ernest!" she heard him greet the amateur chauffeur-in-chief of the Batchgrew family. His footfalls on the pavement died away into the general silence of the street. Overhead she could hear old Batchgrew walking to and fro. Without reflection she went upstairs and hovered near the door of Mrs. Maldon's bedroom. She said to herself that she was not eavesdropping. She listened, while pretending not to listen, but there was no sign of conversation within the room. And then she very distinctly heard old Batchgrew exclaim—

"And they go gallivanting off together to the cinema!"

Upon which ensued another silence.

Rachel flushed with shame, fury, and apprehension. She hated Batchgrew, and Louis, and all gross masculine invaders.

The mysterious silence within the room persisted. And then old Batchgrew violently opened the door and glared at Rachel. He showed no surprise at seeing her there on the landing.

"Ye'd better keep an eye on missis," he said gruffly. "She's gone to sleep seemingly."

And with no other word he departed.

Before the car had given its warning hoot Rachel was at Mrs. Maldon's side. The old lady lay in all tranquillity on her left arm. She was indeed asleep, or she was in a stupor, and the peculiar stertorous noise of her breathing had recommenced.

Rachel's vague dread vanished as she gazed at the worn features, and gave place to a new and definite fright.

"They have killed her!" she muttered.

And she ran into the next room and called Mrs. Tams.

"Who's below?" asked Mrs. Tarns, as, wide awake, she came out on to the landing.

"Nobody," said Rachel. "They've gone."

But the doctor was below. Mr. Batchgrew had left the front door open.

"What a good thing!" cried Rachel.

In the bedroom Dr. Yardley, speaking with normal loudness, just as though Mrs. Maldon had not been present, said to Rachel —

"I expected this this morning. There's nothing to be done. If you try to give her food she'll only get it into the lung. It's very improbable that she'll regain consciousness."

"But are you sure, doctor?" Rachel asked.

The doctor answered grimly —

"No, I'm not — I'm never sure. She *may* recover."

"She's been rather disturbed this afternoon."

The doctor lifted his shoulders.

"That's got nothing to do with it," said he. "As I told you, she's had an embolus in one artery of the brain. It lessened at first for a bit — they do sometimes — and now it's enlarging, that's all. Nothing external could affect it either way."

"But how long — ?" asked Rachel, recoiling.

V

Her chief sensation that evening was that she was alone, for Mrs. Tams was not a companion, but a slave. She was alone with a grave and strange responsibility, which she could not evade. Indeed, events had occurred in such a manner as to make her responsibility seem natural and inevitable, to give it the sanction of the most correct convention. Between 4.30 and 6 in the afternoon four separate calls of inquiry had been made at the house, thus demonstrating Mrs. Maldon's status in the town. One lady had left a fine bunch of grapes. To all these visitors Rachel had said the same things, namely, that Mrs. Maldon had been better on the Saturday, but was worse; that the case was very serious; that the doctor had been twice that day and was coming again, that Councillor Batchgrew was fully informed and had seen the patient; that Mr. Louis Fores, Mrs. Maldon's only near relative in England, was constantly in and out; that she herself had the assistance of Mrs. Tams, who was thoroughly capable, and that while she was much obliged for offers of help, she could think of no way of utilizing them.

So that when the door closed on the last of the callers, Rachel, who a month earlier had never even seen Mrs. Maldon, was left in sole rightful charge of the dying-bed. And there was no escape for her. She could not telegraph—the day being Sunday. Moreover, except Thomas Batchgrew, there was nobody to whom she might telegraph. And she did not want Mr. Batchgrew. Though Mr. Batchgrew certainly had not guessed the relapse, she felt no desire whatever to let him have news. She hated his blundering intrusions; and in spite of the doctor's statements she would insist to herself that he and Louis between them had somehow brought about the change in Mrs. Maldon. Of course she might fetch Louis. She did not know his exact address, but he could be discovered. At any rate, Mrs. Tams might be sent for him. But she could not bring herself to make any advance towards Louis.

At a little after six o'clock, when the rare chapel-goers had ceased to pass, and the still rarer church-goers were beginning to respond to distant bells, Mrs. Tams informed her that tea was ready for her in the parlour, and she descended and took tea, utterly alone. Mrs. Tams had lighted the fire, and had moved the table comfortably towards the fire—act of astounding initiative and courage, in itself a dramatic proof that Mrs. Maldon no longer reigned at Bycars. Tea finished, Rachel returned to the sick-room, where there was nothing whatever to do except watch the minutes recede. She thought of her father and brother in America.

Then Mrs. Tams, who had been clearing away the tea-things, came into the bedroom and said—

"Here's Mr. Fores, miss."

Rachel started.

"Mr. Fores! What does he want?" she asked querulously.

Mrs. Tams preserved her blandness.

"He asked for you, miss."

"Didn't he ask how Mrs. Maldon is?"

"No, miss."

"Well, I don't want to see him. You might run down and tell him what the doctor said, Mrs. Tams." She tried to make her voice casually persuasive.

"Shall I, miss?" said Miss Tams doubtfully, and turned to the door.

Rachel was again full of fear and resentment. Louis had committed the infamy of luring her into the cinematograph. It was through him that she had "got herself talked about." Mrs. Maldon's last words had been a warning against him. He and Mr. Batchgrew had desecrated the sick-room with their mysterious visitations. And now Louis was come again. From what catastrophes had not Mrs. Maldon's warning saved her!

"Here! I'll go," said Rachel, in a sudden resolve.

"I'm glad on it," said Mrs. Tams simply.

In the parlour Louis stood in front of the fire. Although the blinds were drawn, the gas had not been lighted; but the fire and the powerful street lamp together sufficed to give clearness to every object in the room. The table had been restored to its proper situation. The gift of grapes ornamented the sideboard.

"Good-evening," said Rachel sullenly, as if pouting. She avoided looking at Louis, and sat down on the Chesterfield.

Louis broke forth in a cascade of words—

"I say, I'm most awfully sorry. I hadn't the faintest notion this afternoon she was any worse—not the faintest. Otherwise I shouldn't have dreamt—I met the doctor just now in Moorthorne Road, and he told me."

"What did he tell you?" asked Rachel, still with averted head, picking at her frock.

"Well, he gave me to understand there's very little hope, and nothing to be done. If I'd had the faintest notion—"

"You needn't worry about that," said Rachel. "Your coming made no difference. The doctor said so." And she asked herself why she should go out of her way to reassure Louis. It would serve him right to think that his brusque visit, with Mr. Batchgrew's, was the origin of the relapse.

"Is there any change?" Louis asked.

Rachel shook her head "No," she said. "We just have to sit and watch."

"Doctor's coming in again to-night, isn't he?"

Rachel nodded.

"It seems it's an embolus."

Rachel nodded once more. She had still no conception of what an embolus was; but she naturally assumed that Louis could define an embolus with exactitude.

"I say," said Louis, and his voice was suddenly charged with magical qualities of persuasion, entreaty, and sincerity—"I say, you might look at me."

She flushed, but she looked up at him. She might have sat straight and remarked: "Mr. Fores, what do you mean by talking to me like that?" But she raised her eyes and her crimson cheeks for one timid instant, and dropped them. His voice had overcome her. With a single phrase, with a mere inflection, he had changed the key of the interview. And the glance at him had exposed her to the appeal of his face, more powerful than ten thousand logical arguments and warnings. His face proved that he was a sympathetic, wistful, worried fellow-creature—and miraculously, uniquely handsome. His face in the twilight was the most romantic face that Rachel had ever seen. His gestures had a celestial charm.

He said—

"I know I ought to apologize for the way I came in this afternoon. I do. But if you knew what cause I had ...! Would you believe that old Batch had come to my place, and practically accused me of stealing the old lady's money—*stealing* it!"

"Never!" Rachel murmured.

"Yes, he did. The fact is, he knew jolly well he'd no business to have left it in the house that night, so he wanted to get out of it by making *me* suffer. You know he's always been down on me. Well, I came straight up here and I told auntie. Of course I couldn't make a fuss, with her ill in bed. So I simply told her I hadn't got her money and I hadn't stolen it, and I left it at that. I thought the less said the better. But I had to say that much. I wonder what Julian would have said if he'd been accused. I just wonder!" He repeated the word, queerly evocative: "Julian!"

"What did Mrs. Maldon say?" Rachel asked.

"Well, she didn't say much. She believed me, naturally. And then old Batch came. I wasn't going to have a regular scene with him up there, so I left. I thought that was the only dignified thing to do. I wanted to tell you, and I've told you. Don't you think it's a shame?"

Rachel answered passionately—

"I do."

She answered thus because she had a tremendous desire to answer thus. To herself she said: "Do I?... Yes, I do." Louis' eyes drew sympathy out of her. It seemed to her to be of the highest importance that those appealing eyes should not appeal in vain.

"Item, he made a fearful fuss about you and me being at the cinema last night."

"I should like to know what it's got to do with him!" said Rachel, almost savagely. The word "item" puzzled her. Not understanding it, she thought she had misheard.

"That's what I thought, too," said Louis, and added, very gravely: "At the same time I'm really awfully sorry. Perhaps I oughtn't to have asked you. It was my fault. But old Batch would make the worst of anything."

Rachel replied with feverish conviction—

"Mr. Batchgrew ought to be ashamed. You weren't to blame, and I won't hear of it!"

Louis started forward with a sudden movement of the left arm.

"You're magnificent," he said, with emotion.

Rachel trembled, and shut her eyes. She heard his voice again, closer to her, repeating with even greater emotion: "You're magnificent." Tears were in her eyes. Through them she looked at him. And his form was so graceful, his face so nice, so exquisitely kind and lovable and loving, that her admiration became intense, even to the point of pain. She thought of Batchgrew, not with hate, but with pity. He was a monster, but he could not help it. He alone was responsible for all slanders against Louis. He alone had put Mrs. Maldon against Louis. Louis was obviously the most innocent of beings. Mrs. Maiden's warning, "The woman who married him would suffer horribly," was manifestly absurd. "Suffer horribly"—what a stinging phrase, like a needle broken in a wound! She felt tired and weak, above all tired of loneliness.

His hand was on hers. She trembled anew. She was not Rachel, but some new embodiment of surrender and acquiescence. And the change was delicious, fearful.... She thought: "I could die for him." She forgot that a few minutes before she had been steeling herself against him. She wanted him to kiss her, and waited an eternity. And when he had kissed her, and she was in a maze of rapture, a tiny idea shaped itself clearly in her mind for an instant: "This is wrong. But I don't care. He is mine"—and then melted like a cloud in a burning sky. And a sense of the miraculousness of destiny overcame her. In two days had happened enough for two years. It was staggering to think that only two days earlier she had been dreaming of him as of a star. Could so much, indeed, happen in two days? She imagined blissfully, in her ignorance of human experience, that her case was without precedent. Nay, her case appalled her in the rapidity of its development! And was thereby the more thrilling! She thought again: "Yes, I could die for him—and I would!" He was still the star, but—such was the miracle—she clasped him.

They heard Mrs. Tams knocking at the door. Nothing would ever cure the charwoman's habit of knocking before entering. Rachel arose from the sofa as out of a bush of blossoms. And in the artless, honest glance of her virginity and her simplicity, her eyes seemed to say to Mrs. Tams: "Behold the phoenix among men! He is to be my husband." Her pride in the strange, wondrous, incredible state of being affianced was tremendous, to the tragic point.

"Can ye hear, begging yer pardon?" said Mrs. Tams, pointing through the open door and upward. "Her's just begun to breathe o' that'n [like that]."

The loud, stertorous sound of Mrs. Maldon unconsciously drawing the final breaths of life filled the whole house. Louis and Rachel glanced at each other, scared, shamed, even horrified, to discover that the vast pendulum of the universe was still solemnly ticking through their ecstasy.

"I'm coming," said Rachel.

CHAPTER IX
THE MARRIED WOMAN

I

Wonderful things happen. If anybody had foretold to Mrs. Tams that in her fifty-eighth year she would accede to the honourable order of the starched white cap, Mrs. Tams could not have credited the prophecy. But there she stood, in the lobby of the house at Bycars, frocked in black, with the strings of a plain but fine white apron stretched round her stoutness, and the cap crowning her grey hair. It was Louis who had insisted on the cap, which Rachel had thought unnecessary and even snobbish, and which Mrs. Tams had nervously deprecated. Not without pleasure, however, had both women yielded to his indeed unanswerable argument: "You can't possibly have a servant opening the door without a cap. It's unthinkable."

Thus in her latter years of grandmotherhood had Mrs. Tams cast off the sackcloth of the charwoman and become a glorious domestic servant, with a room of her own in the house, and no responsibilities beyond the house, and no right to leave the house save once a week, when she visited younger generations, who still took from her and gave nothing back. She owed the advancement to Rachel, who, quite unused to engaging servants, and alarmed by harrowing stories of the futility of registry offices and advertisements, had seen in Mrs. Tams the comfortable solution of a fearful problem. Louis would have preferred a younger, slimmer, nattier, fluffier creature than Mrs. Tams, but was ready to be convinced that such as he wanted lived only in his fancy. Moreover, he liked Mrs. Tams, and would occasionally flatter her by a smack on the shoulder.

So in the April dusk Mrs. Tams stood in the windy lobby, and was full of vanity and the pride of life. She gazed forth in disdain at the little crowd of inquisitive idlers and infants that remained obstinately on the pavement hoping against hope that the afternoon's marvellous series of social phenomena was not over. She scorned the slatternly, stupid little crowd for its lack of manners. Yet she ought to have known, and she did know as well as any one, that though in Bursley itself people will pretend out of politeness that nothing unusual is afoot when something unusual most obviously *is* afoot, in the small suburbs of Bursley, such as Bycars, no human or divine power can prevent the populace from loosing its starved curiosity openly upon no matter what spectacle that may differ from the ordinary. Alas! Mrs. Tams in the past had often behaved even as the simple members of that crowd. Nevertheless, all ceremonies being over, she shut the front door with haughtiness, feeling glad that she was not as others are. And further, she was swollen and consequential because, without counting persons named Batchgrew, two visitors had come in a motor, and because at one supreme moment no less than two motors (including a Batchgrew motor) had been waiting together at the curb in front of her cleaned steps. Who could have foreseen this arrant snobbishness in the excellent child of nature, Mrs. Tams?

A far worse example of spiritual iniquity sat lolling on the Chesterfield in the parlour. Ignorance and simplicity and a menial imitativeness might be an excuse for Mrs. Tams; but not for Rachel, the mistress, the omniscient, the all-powerful, the giver of good, who could make and unmake with a nod. Rachel sitting gorgeous on the Chesterfield amid an enormous twilit welter and litter of disarranged chairs and tables; empty teapots, cups, jugs, and glasses; dishes of fragmentary remains of cake and chocolate; plates smeared with roseate ham, sticky teaspoons, loaded ash-trays, and a large general crumby mess—Rachel, the downright, the contemner of silly social prejudices and all nonsense, was actually puffed up because she had a servant in a cap and because automobiles had deposited elegant girls at her door and whirled them off again. And she would have denied it and yet was not ashamed.

The sole extenuation of Rachel's base worldliness was that during the previous six months she had almost continuously had the sensations of a person crossing Niagara on a tight-rope, and that now, on this very day, she had leaped to firm ground and was accordingly exultant. After Mrs. Maldon's death she had felt somehow guilty of disloyalty; she passionately regretted having had no opportunity to assure the old lady that her suspicions about Louis were wrong and cruel, and to prove to her in some mysterious way the deep rightness of the betrothal. She blushed only for the moment of her betrothal. She had solemnly bound Louis to keep the betrothal secret until Christmas. She had laid upon both of them a self-denying ordinance as to meeting. The funeral over, she was without a home. She wished to find another situation; Louis would not hear of it. She contemplated a visit to her father and brother in America. In response to a letter, her brother sent her the exact amount of the steerage fare, and, ready to accept it, she was astounded at Louis' fury against her brother and at the accent with which he had spit out the word "steerage." Her brother and father had gone steerage. However, she gave way to Louis, chiefly because she could not bear to leave him even for a couple of months. She was lodging at Knype, at a total normal expense of ten shillings a week. She possessed over fifty pounds—enough to keep her for six months and to purchase a trousseau, and not one penny would she deign to receive from her affianced.

The disclosure of Mrs. Maldon's will increased the delicacy of her situation. Mrs. Maldon had left the whole of her property in equal shares to Louis and Julian absolutely. There were others who by blood had an equal claim upon her with these two, but the rest had been mere names to her, and she had characteristically risen above the conventionalism of heredity. Mr. Batchgrew, the executor, was able to announce that in spite of losses the heirs would get over three thousand five hundred pounds apiece. Hence it followed that Rachel would be marrying for money as well as for position! She trembled when the engagement was at length announced. And when Louis, after consultation with Mr. Batchgrew, pointed out that it would be advantageous not merely to the estate as a whole, but to himself and to her, if he took over the house at Bycars and its contents at a valuation and made it their married home, she at first declined utterly. The scheme seemed sacrilegious to her. How could she dare to be happy in that house where Mrs. Maldon had died, in that house which was so intimately Mrs. Maldon's? But the manifold excellences of the scheme, appealing strongly to her common sense, overcame her scruples. The dead are dead; the living must live, and the living must not be morbid; it would be absurd to turn into a pious monument every house which death has emptied; Mrs. Maldon, had she known all the circumstances, would have been only too pleased, etc., etc. The affair was settled, and grew into public knowledge.

Rachel had to emerge upon the world as an engaged girl. Left to herself she would have shunned all formalities; but Louis, bred up in Barnes, knew what was due to society. Naught was omitted. Louis' persuasiveness could not be withstood. Withal, he was so right. And though Rachel in one part of her mind had a contempt for "fuss," in another she liked it and was half ashamed of liking it. Further, her common sense, of which she was still proud, told her that the delicacy of her situation demanded "fuss," and would be much assuaged thereby. And finally, the whole thing, being miraculous, romantic, and incredible, had the quality of a dream through which she lived in a dazed nonchalance. Could it be true that she had resided with Mrs. Maldon only for a month? Could it be true that her courtship had lasted only two days—or at most, three? Never, she thought, had a sensible, quiet girl ridden such a whirlwind before in the entire history of the world. Could Louis be as foolishly fond of her as he seemed? Was she truly to be married? "I shan't have a single wedding-present," she had said. Then wedding-presents began to come. "Are we married?" she had said, when they were married and in the conventional clothes in the conventional vehicle. After that she soon did realize that the wondrous and the unutterable had happened to her too. And she swung over to the other extreme: instead of doubting the reality of her own experiences, she was convinced that her experiences were more real than those of any other created girl, and hence she felt a slight condescension towards all the rest. "I am a married woman," she reflected at intervals, with intense momentary pride. And her fits of confusion in public would end in recurrences of this strange, proud feeling.

Then she had to face the return to Bursley, and, later, the At Home which Louis propounded as a matter of course, and which she knew to be inevitable. The house was her toy, and Mrs. Tams was her toy. But the glee of playing with toys had been overshadowed for days by the delicious dread of the At Home. "It will be the first caller that will kill me," she had said. "But will anybody really come?" And the first caller had called. And, finding herself still alive, she had become radiant, and often during the afternoon had forgotten to be clumsy. The success of the At Home was prodigious, startling. Now and then when the room was full, and people without chairs perched on the end of the Chesterfield, she had whispered to her secret heart in a tiny, tiny voice: "These are my guests. They all treat me with special deference. I am the hostess. *I am Mrs. Fores.*" The Batchgrew clan was well represented, no doubt by order from authority, Mrs. Yardley came, in surprising stylishness. Visitors arrived from Knype. Miss Malkin came and atoned for her historic glance in the shop. But the dazzlers were sundry male friends of Louis, with Kensingtonian accents, strange phrases, and assurance in the handling of teacups and the choosing of cake.... One by one and two by two they had departed, and at last Rachel, with a mind as it were breathless from rapid flittings to and fro, was seated alone on the sofa.

She was richly dressed in a dark blue taffeta dress that gave brilliance to her tawny hair. Perhaps she was over-richly dressed, for, like many girls who as a rule are not very interested in clothes, she was too interested in them at times, and inexperienced taste was apt to mislead her into an unfitness. Also her figure was too stiff and sturdy to favour elegance. But on this occasion the general effect of her was notably picturesque, and her face and hair, and the expression of her pose, atoned in their charm for the shortcomings and the luxuriance of the frock. She was no more the Rachel that Mrs. Maldon had known and that Louis had first kissed. Her glance had altered, and her gestures. She would ask herself, could it be true that she was a married woman? But her glance and gestures announced it true at every instant. A new languor and a new confidence had transformed the girl. Her body had been modified and her soul at once chastened and fired. Fresh in her memory was endless matter for meditation. And on the sofa, in a negligent attitude of repose, with shameless eyes gazing far into the caverns of the fire, and an unreadable faint smile on her face, she meditated. And she was the most seductive, tantalizing, self-contradictory object for study in the whole of Bursley. She had never been so interesting as in this brief period, and she might never be so interesting again.

Mrs. Tams entered. With her voice Mrs. Tams said, "Shall I begin to clear all these things away, *mam*?" But with her self-conscious eyes Mrs. Tams said to the self-conscious eyes of Rachel, "What a staggering world we live in, don't we?"

II

Rachel sprang from the Chesterfield, smoothed down her frock, shook her hair, and then ran upstairs to the large front bedroom, where Louis, to whom the house was just as much a toy as to Rachel, was about to knock a nail into a wall. Out of breath, she stood close to him very happily. The At Home was over. She was now definitely received as a married woman in a town full of married women and girls waiting to be married women. She had passed successfully through a trying and exhausting experience; the nervous tension was slackened. And therefore it might be expected that she would have a sense of reaction, the vague melancholy which is produced when that which has long been seen before is suddenly seen behind. But it was not so in the smallest degree. Every moment of her existence equally was thrilling and happy. One piquant joy was succeeded immediately by another as piquant. To Rachel it was not in essence more exciting to officiate at an At Home than to watch Louis drive a nail into a wall.

The man winked at her in the dusk; she winked back, and put her hand intimately on his shoulder. She thought, "I am safe with him now in the house." The feeling of solitude with him, of being barricaded against the world and at the mercy of Louis alone, was exquisite to her. Then Louis raised himself on his toes, and raised his left arm with the nail as high as he could, and stuck the point of the nail against a pencil-mark on the wall. Then he raised the right hand with the hammer; but the mark was just too high to be efficiently reached by both hands simultaneously. Louis might have stood on a chair. This simple device, however, was too simple for them.

Rachel said—

"Shall I stand on a chair and hold the nail for you?" Louis murmured—

"Brainy little thing! Never at a loss!"

She skipped on to a chair and held the nail. Towering thus above him, she looked down on her husband and thought: "This man is mine alone, and he is all mine." And in Rachel's fancy the thought itself seemed to caress Louis from head to foot.

"Supposing I catch you one?" said Louis, as he prepared to strike.

"I don't care," said Rachel.

And the fact was that really she would have liked him to hit her finger instead of the nail—not too hard, but still smartly. She would have taken pleasure in the pain: such was the perversity of the young wife. But Louis hit the nail infallibly every time.

He took up a picture which had been lying against the wall in a dark corner, and thrust the twisting wire of it over the nail.

Rachel, when in the deepening darkness she had peered into the frame, exclaimed, pouting—

"Oh, darling, you aren't going to hang that here, are you? It's so old-fashioned. You said it was old-fashioned yourself. I did want that thing that came this morning to be put somewhere here. Why can't you stick this in the spare room?... Unless, of course, you *prefer*...." She was being deferential to the art-expert in him, as well as to the husband.

"Not in the least!" said Louis, acquiescent, and unhooked the picture.

Taste changes. The rejected of Rachel was a water-colour by the late Athelstan Maldon, adored by Mrs. Maldon. Already it had been degraded from the parlour to the bedroom, and now it was to be pushed away like a shame into obscurity. It was a view of the celebrated Vale of Llangollen, finicking, tight, and hard in manner, but with a certain sentiment and modest skill. The way in which the initials "A.M." had been hidden amid the foreground foliage in the left-hand corner disclosed enough of the painter's quiet and proud temperament to show that he "took after" his mother. Yet a few more years, and the careless observer would miss those initials altogether and would be contemptuously inquiring, "Who did this old daub, I wonder?" And nobody would know who did the old daub, or that the old daub for thirty years had been an altar for undying affection, and also a distinguished specimen—admired by a whole generation of townsfolk—of the art of water-colour.

And the fate of Athelstan's sketch was symptomatic. Mrs. Maiden's house had been considered perfect, up to the time of her death. Rachel had at first been even intimidated by it; Louis had sincerely praised it. And indeed its perfection was an axiom of drawing-room conversation. But as soon as Louis and Rachel began to look on the house with the eye of inhabitants, the axiom fell to a dogma, and the dogma was exploded. The dreadful truth came out that Mrs. Maldon had shown a strange indifference to certain aspects of convenience, and that, in short, she must have been a peculiar old lady with ideas of her own. Louis proved unanswerably that in the hitherto faultless parlour the furniture was ill arranged, and suddenly the sideboard and the Chesterfield had changed places, and all concerned had marvelled that Mrs. Maldon had for so long kept the Chesterfield where so obviously the sideboard ought to have been, and the sideboard where so obviously the Chesterfield ought to have been.

And still graver matters had come to light. The house had an attic floor, which was unused and the scene of no activity except spring cleaning. A previous owner, infected by the virus of modernity, had put a bath into one of the attics. Now Mrs. Maldon, as experiments disclosed, had actually had the water cut off from the bath. Eyebrows were lifted at the revelation of this caprice. The restoration of the supply of water and the installing of a geyser were the only expenditures which thrifty Rachel had sanctioned in the way of rejuvenating the house. Rachel had decided that the house must, at any rate for the present, be "made to do." That such a decision should be necessary astonished Rachel; and Mrs. Maldon would have been more than astonished to learn that the lady help, by fortitude and determination, was making her perfect house "do." As regards the household inventory, Rachel had been obliged to admit exceptions to her rule of endurance. Perhaps her main reason for agreeing to live in the house had been that there would be no linen to buy. But truly Mrs. Maldon's notion of what constituted a sufficiency of—for example—towels, was quite too inadequate. Louis protested that he could comfortably use all Mrs. Maldon's towels in half a day. More towels had to be obtained. There were other shortages, but some of them were set right by means of veiled indications to prospective givers of gifts.

"You mean that 'Garden of the Hesperides' affair for up here, do you?" said Louis.

Rachel gazed round the bedchamber. A memory of what it had been shot painfully through her mind. For the room was profoundly changed in character. Two narrow bedsteads given by Thomas Batchgrew, and described by Mrs. Tarns, in a moment of daring, as "flighty," had taken the place of Mrs. Maldon's bedstead, which was now in the spare room, the spare-room bedstead having been allotted to Mrs. Tams, and Rachel's old bedstead sold. Bright crocheted and embroidered wedding-presents enlivened the pale tones of the room. The wardrobe, washstand, dressing-table, chairs, carpet, and ottoman remained. But there were razors on the washstand and boot-trees under it; the wardrobe had been emptied, and filled on strange principles with strange raiment; and the Maldon family Bible, instead of being on the ottoman, was in the ottoman—so as to be out of the dust.

"Perhaps we may as well keep that here, after all," said Rachel, indicating Athelsan's water-colour. Her voice was soft. She remembered that the name of Mrs. Maldon, only a little while since a major notability of Bursley and the very mirror of virtuous renown, had been mentioned but once, and even then apologetically, during the afternoon.

Louis asked, sharply—

"Why, if you don't care for it? *I* don't."

"Well—" said Rachel. "As you like, then, dearest."

Louis walked out of the room with the water-colour, and in a moment returned with a photogravure of Lord Leighton's "The Garden of the Hesperides," in a coquettish gold frame—a gift newly arrived from Louis' connections in the United States. The marmoreal and academic work seemed wonderfully warm and original in that room at Bycars. Rachel really admired it, and admired herself for admiring it. But when Louis had hung it and flicked it into exact perpendicularity, and they had both exclaimed upon its brilliant effect even in the dusk, Rachel saw it also with the eyes of Mrs. Maldon, and wondered what Mrs. Maldon would have thought of it opposite her bed, and knew what Mrs. Maldon would have thought of it.

And then, the job being done and the progress of civilization assured, Louis murmured in a new appealing voice—

"I say, Louise!"

"Louise" was perhaps his most happy invention, and the best proof that Louis was Louis. Upon hearing that her full Christian names were Rachel Louisa, he had instantly said—"I shall call you Louise." Rachel was ravished, Louisa is a vulgar name—at least it is vulgar in the Five Towns, where every second general servant bears it. But Louise was full of romance, distinction, and beauty. And it was the perfect complement to Louis. Louis and Louise—ideal coincidence! "But nobody except me is to call you Louise," he had added. And thus completed her bliss.

"What?" she encouraged him amorously.

"Suppose we go to Llandudno on Saturday for the week-end?"

His tone was gay, gentle, innocent, persuasive. Yet the words stabbed her and her head swam.

"But why?" she asked, controlling her utterance.

"Oh, well! Be rather a lark, wouldn't it?" It was when he talked in this strain that the inconvenient voice of sagacity within her would question for one agonizing instant whether she was more secure as the proud, splendid wife of Louis Fores than she had been as a mere lady help. And the same insistent voice would repeat the warnings which she had had from Mrs. Maldon and from Thomas Batchgrew, and would remind her of what she herself had said to herself when Louis first kissed her—"This is wrong. But I don't care. He is mine."

Upon hearing of his inheritance from Mrs. Maldon, Louis was for throwing up immediately his situation at Horrocleave's. Rachel had dissuaded him from such irresponsible madness. She had prevented him from running into a hundred expenses during their engagement and in connection with the house. And he had in the end enthusiastically praised her common sense. But that very morning at the midday meal he had surprised her by announcing that on account of the reception he should not go to the works at all in the afternoon, though he had omitted to warn Horrocleave. Ultimately she had managed, by guile, to dispatch him to the works for two hours. And now in the evening he was alarming her afresh. Why go to Llandudno? What point was there in rushing off to Llandudno, and scattering in three days more money than they could save in three weeks? He frightened her ingrained prudence, and her alarm was only increased by his obvious failure to realize the terrible defect in himself. (For to her it was terrible.) The joyous scheme of an excursion to Llandudno had suddenly crossed his mind, exciting the appetite for pleasure. Hence the appetite must be immediately indulged!... Rachel had been brought up otherwise. And as a direct result of Louis' irresponsible suggestion she had a vision of the house with county-court bailiffs lodged in the kitchen.... She had only to say—"Yes, let's go," and they would be off on the absurd and wicked expedition.

"I'd really rather not," she said, smiling, but serious.

"All serene. But, anyhow, next week's Easter, and we shall have to go somewhere then, you know."

She put her hands on his shoulders and looked close at him, knowing that she must use her power and that the heavy dusk would help her.

"Why?" she asked again. "I'd much sooner stay here at Easter. Truly I would!... With you!"

The episode ended with an embrace. She had won.

"Very well! Very well!" said Louis. "Easter in the coal-cellar if you like. I'm on for anything."

"But don't you *see*, dearest?" she said.

And he imitated her emphasis, full of teasing good humour—

"Yes, I *see*, dearest."

She breathed relief, and asked—

"Are you going to give me my bicycle lesson?"

III

Louis had borrowed a bicycle for Rachel to ruin while learning to ride. He said that a friend had lent it to him—a man in Hanbridge whose mother had given up riding on account of stoutness—but who exactly this friend was Rachel knew not, Louis' information being characteristically sketchy and incomplete; and with his air of candour and good humour he had a strange way of warding off questions; so that already Rachel had grown used to a phrase which she would utter only in her mind, "I don't like to ask him—"

It pleased Louis to ride this bicycle out of the back yard, down the sloping entry, and then steer it through another narrow gateway, across the pavement, and let it solemnly bump, first with the front wheel and then with the back wheel, from the pavement into the road. During this feat he stood on the pedals. He turned the machine up Bycars Lane, and steadily climbed the steep at Rachel's walking pace. And Rachel, hurrying by his side, watched in the obscurity the play of his ankles as he put into practice the principles of pedalling which he had preached. He was a graceful rider; every movement was natural and elegant. Rachel considered him to be the most graceful cyclist that ever was. She was fascinated by the revolutions of his feet.

She felt ecstatically happy. The episode of his caprice for the seaside was absolutely forgotten; after all, she asked for nothing more than possession of him, and she had that, though indeed it seemed too marvellous to be true. The bicycle lesson was her hour of magic; and more so on this night than on previous nights.

"I must change my dress," she had said. "I can't go in this one."

"Quick, then!"

His impatience could not wait. He had helped her. He undid hooks, and fastened others.... The rich blue frock lay across the bed and looked lovely on the ivory-coloured counterpane. It seemed indeed to be a part of that in her which was Louise. Then she was in a short skirt which she had devised herself, and he was pushing her out of the room, his hand on her back. And she had feigned reluctance, resisting his pressure, while laughing with gleeful eagerness to be gone. No delay had been allowed. As they passed through the kitchen, not one instant for parley with Mrs. Tams as to the domestic organization of the evening! He was still pushing her.... Thus she had had to confide her precious house and its innumerable treasures to Mrs. Tams. And in this surrender to Louis' whim there was a fearful joy.

When Louis turned at last into Park Road, and stepped from between the wheels, she exclaimed, a little breathless from quick walking level with him up the hill—

"I can't bear to see you ride so well. Oh!" She crunched her teeth with a loving, cruel gesture. "I should like to hurt you frightfully!"

"What for?"

"Because I shall never, never be able to ride as well as you do!"

He winked.

"Here! Take hold."

"I'm not ready! I'm not ready!" she cried.

But he loosed the machine, and she was obliged to seize it as it fell. That was his teasing.

Park Road had been the scene of the lesson for three nights. It was level, and it was unfrequented. "And the doctor's handy in case you break your neck," Louis had said. Dr. Yardley's red lamp shone amicably among yellow lights, and its ray with theirs was lost in the mysterious obscurities of the closed park. Not only was it socially advisable for Rachel to study the perverse nature of the bicycle at night—for not to know how to ride the bicycle was as shameful as not to know how to read and write—but she preferred the night for the romantic feeling of being alone with Louis, in the dark and above the glow of the town. She loved the sharp night wind on her cheek, and the faint clandestine rustling of the low evergreens within the park palisade, and the invisible and almost tangible soft sky, revealed round the horizon by gleams of fire. She had longed to ride the bicycle as some girls long to follow the hunt or to steer an automobile or a yacht. And now her ambition was being attained amid all circumstances of bliss.

And yet she would shrink from beginning the lesson.

"The lamp! You've forgotten to light the lamp!" she said.

"Get on," said he.

"But suppose a policeman comes?"

"Suppose you get on and start! Do you think I don't know you? Policemen are my affair. Besides, all nice policemen are in bed.... Don't be afraid. It isn't alive. I've got hold of the thing. Sit well down. No! There are only two pedals. You seem to think there are about nineteen. Right! No, no, *no*! Don't—do not—cling to those blooming handle-bars as if you were in a storm at sea. Be a nice little cat in front of the fire—all your muscles loose. Now! Are you ready?"

"Yes," she murmured, with teeth set and dilated eyes staring ahead at the hideous dangers of Park Road.

He impelled. The pedals went round. The machine slid terribly forward.

And in a moment Louis said, mischievously—

"I told you you'd have to go alone to-night. There you are!"

His footsteps ceased.

"Louis!" she cried, sharply and yet sadly upbraiding his unspeakable treason. Her fingers gripped convulsively the handle-bars. She was moving alone. It was inconceivably awful and delightful. She was on the back of a wild pony in the forest. The miracle of equilibrium was being accomplished. The impossible was done, and at the first attempt. She thought very clearly how wondrous was life, and how perfectly happy fate had made her. And then she was lying in a tangle amid dozens of complex wheels, chains, and bars.

"Hurt?" shouted Louis, as he ran up.

She laughed and said "No," and sat up stiffly, full of secret dolours. Yet he knew and she knew that the accidents of the previous two nights had covered her limbs with blue discolorations, and that the latest fall was more severe than any previous one. Her courage enchanted Louis and filled him with a sense of security. She was not graceful in these exercises. Her ankles were thick and clumsy. Not merely had she no natural aptitude for physical feats—apparently she was not lissom, nor elegant in motion. But what courage! What calm, bright endurance! What stoicism! Most girls would have reproached him for betraying them to destruction, would have pouted, complained, demanded petting and apologies. But not she! She was like a man. And when he helped her to pick herself up he noticed that after all she was both lissom and agile, and exquisitely, disturbingly girlish in her short dusty skirt; and that she did trust him and depend on him. And he realized that he was safe for life with her. She was created for him.

Work was resumed.

"Now don't let go of me till I tell you," she enjoined lightly.

"I won't," he answered. And it seemed to him that his loyalty to her expanded and filled all his soul.

Later, as she approached the other end of Park Road, near Moorthorne Road, a tram-car hurled itself suddenly down Moorthorne Road and overthrew her. It is true that the tram-car was never less than twenty yards away from her. But even at twenty yards it could overthrow. Rachel sat dazed in the road, and her voice was uncertain as she told Louis to examine the bicycle. One of the pedals was bent, and prevented the back wheel from making a complete revolution.

"It's nothing," said Louis. "I'll have it right in the morning."

"Who's that?" Rachel, who had risen, gasping, turned to him excitedly as he was bending over the bicycle. Conscious that somebody had been standing at the corner of the street, he glanced up. A figure was moving quickly down Moorthorne Road in the direction of the station.

"I dun'no," said he.

"It's not Julian, is it?"

In a peculiar tone Louis replied—

"Looks like him, doesn't it?" And then impulsively he yelled "Hi!"

The figure kept on its way.

"Seeing that the inimitable Julian's still in South Africa, it can't very well be him. And, anyhow, I'm not going to run after him."

"No, of course it can't," Rachel assented.

Presently the returning procession was re-formed. Louis pushed the bicycle on its front wheel, and Rachel tried to help him to support the weight of the suspended part. He had attempted in vain to take the pedal off the crank.

"It's perhaps a good thing you fell just then," said Louis. "Because old Batch is coming in to-night, and we'd better not be late."

"But you never told me!"

"Didn't I? I forgot," he said blandly.

"Oh, Louis!... He's not coming for supper, I hope?"

"My child, if there's a chance of a free meal, old Batch will be on the spot."

The unaccustomed housewife foretold her approaching shame, and proclaimed Louis to be the author of it. She began to quicken her steps.

"You certainly ought to have let me know sooner, dearest," she said seriously. "You really are terrible."

Hard knocks had not hurt her. But she was hurt now. And Louis' smile was very constrained. Her grave manner of saying "dearest" had disquieted him.

CHAPTER X
THE CHASM

I

It is true that Rachel held Councillor Thomas Batchgrew in hatred, that she had never pardoned him for the insult which he had put upon her in the Imperial Cinema de Luxe; and that, indeed, she could never pardon him for simply being Thomas Batchgrew. Nevertheless, there was that evening in her heart a little softening towards him. The fact was that the councillor had been flattering her. She would have denied warmly that she was susceptible to flattery; even if authoritatively informed that no human being whatever is unsusceptible to flattery, she would still have protested that she at any rate was, for, like numerous young and inexperienced women, she had persuaded herself that she was the one exception to various otherwise universal rules.

It remained that Thomas Batchgrew had been flattering her. On arrival he had greeted her with that tinge of deference which from an old man never fails to thrill a girl. Rachel's pride as a young married woman was tigerishly alert and hungry that evening. Thomas Batchgrew, little by little, tamed and fed it very judiciously at intervals, until at length it seemed to purr content around him like a cat. The phenomenon was remarkable, and the more so in that Rachel was convinced that, whereas she was as critical and inimical as ever, old Batchgrew had slightly improved. He behaved "heartily," and everybody appreciates such behaviour in the Five Towns. He was by nature far too insensitive to notice that the married lovers were treating each other with that finished courtesy which is the symptom of a tiff or of a misunderstanding. And the married lovers, noticing that he noticed nothing, were soon encouraged to make peace; and by means of certain tones and gestures peace was declared in the very presence of the unperceiving old brute, which was peculiarly delightful to the contracting parties.

Rachel had less difficulty with the supper than she feared, whereby also her good-humour was fostered. With half a cold leg of mutton, some cheeses, and the magnificent fancy remains of an At Home tea, arrayed with the d'oyleys and embroidered cloths which brides always richly receive in the Five Towns, a most handsome and impressive supper can be concocted. Rachel was astonished at the splendour of her own table. Mr. Batchgrew treated this supper with unsurpassable tact. The adjectives he applied to it were short and emphatic and spoken with a full mouth. He ate the supper; he kept on eating it; he passed his plate with alacrity; he refused naught. And as the meal neared its end he emitted those natural inarticulate noises from his throat which in Persia are a sign of high breeding. Useless for Rachel in her heart to call him a glutton—his attitude towards her supper was impeccable.

And now the solid part of the supper was over. One extremity of the Chesterfield had been drawn closer to the fire—an operation easily possible in its new advantageous position—and Louis as master of the house had mended the fire after his own method, and Rachel sat upright (somewhat in the manner of Mrs. Maldon) in the arm-chair opposite Mr. Batchgrew, extended half-reclining on the Chesterfield. And Mrs. Tams entered with coffee.

"You'll have coffee, Mr. Batchgrew?" said the hostess.

"Nay, missis! I canna' sleep after it."

Secretly enchanted by the sweet word "missis," Rachel was nevertheless piqued by this refusal.

"Oh, but you must have some of Louise's coffee," said Louis, standing negligently in front of the fire.

Already, though under a month old as a husband, Louis, following the eternal example of good husbands, had acquired the sure belief that his wife could achieve a higher degree of excellence in certain affairs than any other wife in the world. He had selected coffee as Rachel's speciality.

"Louise's?" repeated old Batchgrew, puzzled, in his heavy voice.

Rachel flushed and smiled.

"He calls me Louise, you know," said she.

"Calls you Louise, does he?" Batchgrew muttered indifferently. But he took a cup of coffee, stirred part of its contents into the saucer and on to the Chesterfield, and began to sup the remainder with a prodigious splutter of ingurgitation.

"And you must have a cigarette, too," Louis carelessly insisted. And Mr. Batchgrew agreed, though it was notorious that he only smoked once in a blue moon, because all tobacco was apt to be too strong for him.

"You can clear away," Rachel whispered, in the frigid tones of one accustomed to command cohorts of servants in the luxury of historic castles.

"Yes, ma'am," Mrs. Tams whispered back nervously, proud as a major-domo, though with less than a major-domo's aplomb.

No pride, however, could have outclassed Rachel's. She had had a full day, and the evening was the crown of the day, because in the evening she was entertaining privately for the first time. She was the one lady of the party; for these two men she represented woman, and they were her men. They depended on her for their physical well-being, and not in vain. She was the hostess; hers to command; hers the complex responsibility of the house. She had begun supper with painful timidity, but the timidity had now nearly vanished in the flush of social success. Critical as only a young wife can be, she was excellently well satisfied with Louis' performance in the role of host. She grew more than ever sure that there was only one Louis. See him manipulate a cigarette—it was the perfection of worldliness and agreeable, sensuous grace! See him hold a match to Mr. Batchgrew's cigarette!

Now Mr. Batchgrew smoked a cigarette clumsily. He seemed not to be able to decide whether a cigarette was something to smoke or something to eat. Mr. Batchgrew was more ungainly than ever, stretched in his characteristic attitude at an angle of forty-five degrees; his long whiskers were more absurdly than ever like two tails of a wire-haired white dog; his voice more coarsely than ever rolled about the room like undignified thunder. He was an old, old man, and a sinister. It was precisely his age that caressed Rachel's pride. That any man so old should have come to her house for supper, should be treating her as an equal and with the directness of allusion in conversation due to a married woman but improper to a young girl—this was very sweet to Rachel. The subdued stir made by Mrs. Tams in clearing the table was for Rachel a delicious background to the scene. The one flaw in it was her short skirt, which she had not had time to change. Louis had protested that it was entirely in order, and indeed admirably coquettish, but Rachel would have preferred a long train of soft drapery disposed with art round the front of her chair.

"What you want here is electricity," said Thomas Batchgrew, gazing at the incandescent gas; he could never miss a chance, and was never discouraged in the pursuit of his own advantage.

"You think so?" murmured Louis genially.

"I could put ye in summat as 'u'd—;"

Rachel broke in a clear, calm decision—

"I don't think we shall have any electricity just yet."

The gesture of the economical wife in her was so final that old Batchgrew raised his eyebrows with a grin at Louis, and Louis humorously drew down the corners of his mouth in response. It was as if they had both said, in awe—

"She has spoken!"

And Rachel, still further flattered and happy, was obliged to smile.

When Mrs. Tams had made her last tiptoe journey from the room and closed the door with due silent respect upon those great ones, the expression of Thomas Batchgrew's face changed somewhat; he looked round, as though for spies, and then drew a packet of papers from his pocket. And the expression of the other two faces changed also. For the true purpose of the executor's visit was now to be made formally manifest.

"Now about this statement of account—*re* Elizabeth Maldon, deceased," he growled deeply.

"By the way," Louis interrupted him. "Is Julian back?"

"Julian back? Not as I know of," said Mr. Batchgrew aggressively. "Why?"

"We thought we saw him walking down Moorthorne Road to-night."

"Yes," said Rachel. "We both thought we saw him."

"Happen he is if he aeroplaned it!" said Batchgrew, and fumbled nervously with the papers.

"It couldn't have been Julian," said Louis, confidently, to Rachel.

"No, it couldn't," said Rachel.

But neither conjured away the secret uneasiness of the other. And as for Rachel, she knew that all through the evening she had, inexplicably, been disturbed by an apprehension that Julian, after his long and strange sojourn in South Africa, had returned to the district. Why the possible advent of Julian should disconcert her, she thought she could not divine. Mr. Batchgrew's demeanour as he answered Louis' question mysteriously increased her apprehension. At one moment she said to herself, "Of course it wasn't Julian." At the next, "I'm quite sure I couldn't be mistaken." At the next, "And supposing it was Julian—what of it?"

II

When Batchgrew and Louis, sitting side by side on the Chesterfield, began to turn over documents and peer into columns, and carry the finger horizontally across sheets of paper in search of figures, Rachel tactfully withdrew, not from the room, but from the conversation, it being her proper role to pretend that she did not and could not understand the complicated details which they were discussing. She expected some rather dazzling revelation of men's trained methods at this "business interview" (as Louis had announced it), for her brother and father had never allowed her the slightest knowledge of their daily affairs. But she was disappointed. She thought that both the men were somewhat absurdly and self-consciously trying to be solemn and learned. Louis beyond doubt was self-conscious— acting as it were to impress his wife—and Batchgrew's efforts to be hearty and youthful with the young roused her private ridicule.

Moreover, nothing fresh emerged from the interview. She had known all of it before from Louis. Batchgrew was merely repeating and resuming. And Louis was listening with politeness to recitals with which he was quite familiar. In words almost identical with those already reported to her by Louis, Batchgrew insisted on the honesty and efficiency of the valuer in Hanbridge, a lifelong friend of his own, who had for a specially low fee put a price on the house at Bycars and its contents for the purpose of a division between Louis and Julian. And now, as previously with Louis, Rachel failed to comprehend how the valuer, if he had been favourably disposed towards Louis, as Batchgrew averred, could at the same time have behaved honestly towards Julian. But neither Louis nor Batchgrew seemed to realize the point. They both apparently flattered themselves with much simplicity upon the partiality of the lifelong friend and valuer for Louis, without perceiving the logical deduction that if he was partial he was a rascal. Further, Thomas Batchgrew "rubbed Rachel the wrong way" by subtly emphasizing his own marvellous abilities as a trustee and executor, and by assuring Louis repeatedly that all conceivable books of account, correspondence, and documents were open for his inspection at any time. Batchgrew, in Rachel's opinion, might as well have said, "You naturally suspect me of being a knave, but I can prove to you that you are wrong."

Finally, they came to the grand total of Louis' inheritance, which Rachel had known by heart for several days past; yet Batchgrew rolled it out as a piece of tremendous news, and immediately afterwards hinted that the sum represented less than the true worth of Louis' inheritance, and that he, Batchgrew, as well as his lifelong friend the valuer, had been influenced by a partiality for Louis. For example, he had contrived to put all the house property, except the house at Bycars, into Julian's share; which was extremely advantageous for Louis because the federation of the Five Towns into one borough had rendered property values the most capricious and least calculable of all worldly possessions.... And Louis tried to smile knowingly at the knowing trustee and executor with his amiable partiality for one legatee as against the other. Louis' share, beyond the Bycars house, was in the gilt-edged stock of limited companies which sold water and other necessaries of life to the public on their own terms.

Rachel left the pair for a moment, and returned from upstairs with a grey jacket of Louis' from which she had to unstitch the black *crêpe* armlet announcing to the world Louis' grief for his dead great-aunt; the period of mourning was long over, and it would not have been quite nice for Louis to continue announcing his grief.

As she came back into the room she heard the word "debentures," and that single word changed her mood instantly from bland feminine toleration to porcupinish defensiveness. She did not, as a fact, know what debentures were. She could not for a fortune have defined the difference between a debenture and a share. She only knew that debentures were connected with "limited companies"—not waterworks companies, which she classed with the Bank of England—but just any limited companies, which were in her mind a bottomless pit for the savings of the foolish. She had an idea that a debenture was, if anything, more fatal than a share. She was, of course, quite wrong, according to general principles; but, unfortunately, women, as all men sooner or later learn, have a disconcerting habit of being right in the wrong way for the wrong reasons. In a single moment, without justification, she had in her heart declared war on all debentures. And as soon as she gathered that Thomas Batchgrew was suggesting to Louis the exchange of waterworks stock for seven per cent. debentures in the United Midland Cinemas Corporation, Limited, she became more than ever convinced that her instinct about debentures was but too correct. She sat down primly, and detached the armlet, and removed all the bits of black cotton from the sleeve, and never raised her head nor offered a remark, but she was furious—furious to protect her husband against sharks and against himself.

The conduct and demeanour of Thomas Batchgrew were now explained. His visit, his flattery, his heartiness, his youthfulness, all had a motive. He had safeguarded Louis' interests under the will in order to rob him afterwards as a cinematograph speculator. The thing was as clear as daylight. And yet Louis did not seem to see it. Louis listened to Batchgrew's ingenious arguments with naïve interest and was obviously impressed. When Batchgrew called him "a business man as smart as they make 'em," and then proved that the money so invested would be as safe as in a stocking, Louis agreed with a great air of acumen that certainly it would. When Batchgrew pointed out that, under the proposed new investment, Louis would be receiving in income thirty or thirty-five shillings for every pound under the old investments, Louis' eye glistened—positively glistened! Rachel trembled. She saw her husband beggared, and there was nothing that frightened her more than the prospect of Louis without a reserve of private income. She did not argue the position—she simply knew that Louis without sure resources behind him would be a very dangerous and uncertain Louis, perhaps a tragic Louis. She frankly admitted this to herself. And old Batchgrew went on talking and inveigling until Rachel was ready to believe that the device of debentures had been originally invented by Thomas Batchgrew himself with felonious intent.

An automobile hooted in the street.

"Well, ye'll think it over," said Thomas Batchgrew.

"Oh I *will*!" said Louis eagerly.

And Rachel asked herself, almost shaking—"Is it possible that he is such a simpleton?"

"Only I must know by Tuesday," said Thomas Batchgrew. "I thought I'd give ye th' chance, but I can't keep it open later than Tuesday."

"Thanks, awfully," said Louis. "I'm very much obliged for the offer. I'll let you know—before Tuesday."

Rachel frowned as she folded up the jacket. If, however, the two men could have seen into her mind they would have perceived symptoms of danger more agitating than one little frown.

"Of course," said Thomas Batchgrew easily, with a short laugh, in the lobby, "if it hadna been for *her* making away with that nine hundred and sixty-odd pound, you'd ha' had a round sum o' thousands to invest. I've been thinking o'er that matter, and all I can see for it is as her must ha' thrown th' money into th' fire in mistake for th' envelope, or with th' envelope. That's all as I can see for it."

Louis flushed slightly as he slapped his thigh.

"Never thought of that!" he cried. "It very probably *was* that. Strange it never occurred to me!"

Rachel said nothing. She had extreme difficulty in keeping control of herself while old Batchgrew, with numerous senile precautions, took his slow departure. She forgot that she was a hostess and a woman of the world.

III

"Hello! What's that?" Rachel asked, in a self-conscious voice, when they were in the parlour again.

Louis had almost surreptitiously taken an envelope from his pocket, and was extracting a paper from it.

On finding themselves alone they had not followed their usual custom of bursting into comment, favourable or unfavourable, on the departed—a practice due more to a desire to rouse and enjoy each other's individualities than to a genuine interest in the third person. Nor had they impulsively or deliberately kissed, as they were liable to do after release from a spell of worldliness. On the contrary, both were still constrained, as if the third person was still with them. The fact was that there were two other persons in the room, darkly discerned by Louis and Rachel—namely, a different, inimical Rachel and a different, inimical Louis. All four, the seen and the half-seen, walked stealthily, like rival beasts in the edge of the jungle.

"Oh!" said Louis with an air of nonchalance. "It came by the last post while old Batch was here, and I just shoved it into my pocket."

The arrivals of the post were always interesting to them, for during the weeks after marriage letters are apt to be more numerous than usual, and to contain delicate and enchanting surprises. Both of them were always strictly ceremonious in the handling of each other's letters, and yet both deprecated this ceremoniousness in the beloved. Louis urged Rachel to open his letters without scruple, and Rachel did the same to Louis. But both—Louis by chivalry and Rachel by pride—were prevented from acting on the invitation. The envelope in Louis' hand did not contain a letter, but only a circular. The fact that the flap of the envelope was unsealed and the stamp a mere halfpenny ought rightly to have deprived the packet of all significance as a subject of curiosity. Nevertheless, the different, inimical Rachel, probably out of sheer perversity, went up to Louis and looked over his shoulder as he read the communication, which was a printed circular, somewhat yellowed, with blanks neatly filled in, and the whole neatly signed by a churchwarden, informing Louis that his application for sittings at St. Luke's Church (commonly called the Old Church) had been granted. It is to be noted that, though applications for sittings in the Old Church were not overwhelmingly frequent, and might indeed very easily have been coped with by means of autograph replies, the authorities had a sufficient sense of dignity always to circularize the applicants.

This document, harmless enough, and surely a proof of laudable aspirations in Louis, gravely displeased the different, inimical Rachel, and was used by her for bellicose purposes.

"So that's it, is it?" she said ominously.

"But wasn't it understood that we were to go to the Old Church?" said the other Louis, full of ingenious innocence.

"Oh! Was it?"

"Didn't I mention it?"

"I don't remember."

"I'm sure I did."

The truth was that Louis had once casually remarked that he supposed they would attend the Old Church. Rachel would have joyously attended any church or any chapel with him. At Knype she had irregularly attended the Bethesda Chapel—sometimes (in the evenings) with her father, oftener alone, never with her brother. During her brief employment with Mrs. Maldon she had been only once to a place of worship, the new chapel in Moorthorne Road, which was the nearest to Bycars and had therefore been favoured by Mrs. Maldon when her limbs were stiff. In the abstract she approved of religious rites. Theologically her ignorance was such that she could not have distinguished between the tenets of church and the tenets of chapel, and this ignorance she shared with the large majority of the serious inhabitants of the Five Towns. Why, then, should she have "pulled a face" (as the saying down there is) at the Old Parish Church?

One reason, which would have applied equally to church or chapel, was that she was disconcerted and even alarmed by Louis' manifest tendency to settle down into utter correctness. Louis had hitherto been a devotee of joy—never as a bachelor had he done aught to increase the labour of churchwardens—and it was somehow as a devotee of joy that Rachel had married him. Rachel had been settled down all her life, and naturally desired and expected that an unsettling process should now occur in her career. It seemed to her that in mere decency Louis might have allowed at any rate a year or two to pass before occupying himself so stringently with her eternal welfare. She belonged to the middle class (intermediate between the industrial and the aristocratic employing) which is responsible for the Five Towns' reputation for joylessness, the class which sticks its chin out and gets things done (however queer the things done may be), the class which keeps the district together and maintains its solidity, the class which is ashamed of nothing but idleness, frank enjoyment, and the caprice of the moment. (Its idiomatic phrase for expressing the experience of gladness, "I sang 'O be joyful,'" alone demonstrates its unwillingness to rejoice.) She had espoused the hedonistic class (always secretly envied by the other), and Louis' behaviour as a member of that class had already begun to disappoint her. Was it fair of him to say in his conduct: "The fun is over. We must be strictly conventional now"? His costly caprices for Llandudno and the pleasures of idleness were quite beside the point.

Another reason for her objection to Louis' overtures to the Old Church was that they increased her suspicion of his snobbishness. No person nourished from infancy in chapel can bring himself to believe that the chief motive of church-goers is not the snobbish motive of social propriety. And dissenters are so convinced that, if chapel means salvation in the next world, church means salvation in this, that to this day, regardless of the feelings of their pastors, they will go to church once in their lives—to get married. At any rate, Rachel was positively sure that no anxiety about his own soul or about hers had led Louis to join the Old Church.

"Have you been confirmed?" she asked.

"Yes, of course," Louis replied politely.

She did not like that "of course."

"Shall I have to be?"

"I don't know."

"Well," said she, "I can tell you one thing—I shan't be."

IV

Rachel went on—

"You aren't really going to throw your money away on those debenture things of Mr. Batchgrew's, are you?"

Louis now knew the worst, and he had been suspecting it. Rachel's tone fully displayed her sentiments, and completed the disclosure that "the little thing" was angry and aggressive. (In his mind Louis regarded her at moments, as "the little thing.") But his own politeness was so profoundly rooted that practically no phenomenon of rudeness could overthrow it.

"No," he said, "I'm not going to 'throw my money away' on them."

"That's all right, then," she said, affecting not to perceive his drift. "I thought you were."

"But I propose to put my money into them, subject to anything you, as a financial expert, may have to say."

Nervously she had gone to the window and was pretending to straighten a blind.

"I don't think you need to make fun of me," she said. "You think I don't notice when you make fun of me. But I do—always."

"Look here, young 'un," Louis suddenly began to cajole, very winningly.

"I'm about as old as you are," said she, "and perhaps in some ways a bit older. And I must say I really wonder at you being ready to help Mr. Batchgrew after the way he insulted me in the cinema."

"Insulted you in the cinema!" Louis cried, genuinely startled, and then somewhat hurt because Rachel argued like a woman instead of like a man. In reflecting upon the excellences of Rachel he had often said to himself that her unique charm consisted in the fact that she combined the attractiveness of woman with the powerful commonsense of man. In common with a whole enthusiastic army of young husbands he had been convinced that his wife was the one female creature on earth to whom you could talk as you would to a male. "Oh!" he murmured.

"Have you forgotten it, then?" she asked coldly. To herself she was saying: "Why am I behaving like this? After all, he's done no harm yet." But she had set out, and she must continue, driven by the terrible fear of what he might do. She stared at the blind. Through a slit of window at one side of it she could see the lamp-post and the iron kerb of the pavement.

"But that's all over long ago," he protested amiably. "Just look how friendly you were with him yourself over supper! Besides—"

"Besides what? I wasn't friendly. I was only polite. I had to be. Nobody's called Mr. Batchgrew worse names than you have. But you forget. Only I don't forget. There's lots of things I don't forget, although I don't make a song about them. I shan't forget in a hurry how you let go of my bike without telling me and I fell all over the road. I know I'm lots more black and blue even than I was."

If Rachel would but have argued according to his rules of debate, Louis was confident that he could have conducted the affair to a proper issue. But she would not. What could he say? In a flash he saw a vista of, say, forty years of conjugal argument with a woman incapable of reason, and trembled. Then he looked again, and saw the lines of Rachel's figure in her delightful short skirt and was reassured. But still he did not know what to say. Rachel spared him further cogitation on that particular aspect of the question by turning round and exclaiming, passionately, with a break in her voice—

"Can't you see that he'll swindle you out of the money?"

It seemed to her that the security of their whole future depended on her firmness and strong sagacity at that moment. She felt herself to be very wise and also, happily, very vigorous. But at the same time she was afflicted by a kind of despair at the thought that Louis had indeed been, and still was, ready to commit the disastrous folly of confiding money to Thomas Batchgrew for investment. And as Louis had had a flashing vision of the future, so did Rachel now have such a vision. But hers was more terrible than his. Louis foresaw merely vexation. Rachel foresaw ruin doubtfully staved off by eternal vigilance on her part and by nothing else—an instant's sleepiness, and they might be in the gutter and she the wife of a ne'er-do-well. She perceived that she must be reconciled to a future in which the strain of intense vigilance could never once be relaxed. Strange that a creature so young and healthy and in love should be so pessimistic, but thus it was! She remembered in in spite of herself the warnings against Louis which she had been compelled to listen to in the previous year.

"Odd, of course!" said Louis. "But I can't exactly see how he'll swindle me out of the money! A debenture is a debenture."

"Is it?"

"Do you know what a debenture is, my child?"

"I don't need to know what a debenture is, when Mr. Batchgrew's mixed up in it."

Louis suppressed a sigh. He first thought of trying to explain to her just what a debenture was. Then he abandoned the enterprise as too complicated, and also as futile. Though he should prove to her that a debenture combined the safety of the Bank of England with the brilliance of a successful gambling transaction, she would not budge. He was acquiring valuable and painful knowledge concerning women every second. He grew sad, not simply with the weight of this new knowledge, but more because, though he had envisaged certain difficulties of married existence, he had not envisaged this difficulty. He had not dreamed that a wife would demand a share, and demand it furiously, in the control of his business affairs. He had sincerely imagined that wives listened with much respect and little comprehension when business was on the carpet, content to murmur soothingly from time to time, "Just as you think best, dear." Life had unpleasantly astonished him.

It was on the tip of his tongue to say to Rachel, with steadying facetiousness—

"You mustn't forget that I know a bit about these things, having spent years of my young life in a bank."

But a vague instinct told him that to draw attention to his career in the bank might be unwise—at any rate, in principle.

"Can't you see," Rachel charged again, "that Mr. Batchgrew has only been flattering you all this time so as to get hold of your money? And wasn't it just like him to begin again harping on the electricity?>"

"Flattering me?"

"Well, he couldn't bear you before—if you'd only heard the things he used to say!—and now he simply licks your boots."

"What things did he say?" Louis asked, disturbed.

"Oh, never mind!"

Louis became rather glum and obstinate.

"The money will be perfectly safe," he insisted, "and our income pretty nearly doubled. I suppose I ought to know more about these things than you."

"What's the use of income being doubled if you lose the capital?" Rachel snapped, now taking a horrid, perverse pleasure in the perilous altercation. "And if it's so safe why is he ready to give you so much interest?"

The worst of women, Louis reflected, is that in the midst of a silly argument that you can shatter in ten words they will by a fluke insert some awkward piece of genuine ratiocination, the answer to which must necessarily be lengthy and ineffective.

"It's no good arguing," he said pleasantly, and then repeated, "I ought to know more about these things than you."

Rachel raised her voice in exasperation—

"I don't see it, I don't see it at all. If it hadn't been for me you'd have thrown up your situation—and a nice state of affairs there would have been then! And how much money would you have wasted on holidays and so on and so on if I hadn't stopped you, I should like to know!"

Louis was still more astonished. Indeed, he was rather nettled. His urbanity was unimpaired, but he permitted himself a slight acidity of tone as he retorted with gentle malice—

"Well, you can't help the colour of your hair. So I'll keep my nerve."

"I didn't expect to be insulted!" cried Rachel, flushing far redder than that rich hair of hers, and paced pompously out of the room, her face working violently. The door was ajar. She passed Mrs. Tams on the stairs, blindly, with lowered head.

V

In the conjugal bedroom, full of gas-glare and shadows, there were two old women. One was Mrs. Tams, ministering; the other was Rachel Fores, once and not long ago the beloved and courted girlish Louise of a chevalier, now aged by all the sorrow of the world. She lay in bed—in her bed nearest the fireplace and farthest from the door.

She had undressed herself with every accustomed ceremony, arranging each article of attire, including the fine frock left on the bed, carefully in its place, as is meet in a chamber where tidiness depends on the loyal cooperation of two persons, but through her tears. She had slipped sobbing into bed. The other bed was empty, and its emptiness seemed sinister to her. Would it ever be occupied again? Impossible that it should ever be occupied again! Its rightful occupant was immeasurably far off, along miles of passages, down leagues of stairs, separated by impregnable doors, in another universe, the universe of the ground floor. Of course she might have sprung up, put on her enchanting dressing-gown, tripped down a few steps in a moment of time, and peeped in at the parlour door—just peeped in, in that magic ribboned peignoir, and glanced—and the whole planet would have been reborn. But she could not. If the salvation of the human race had depended on it, she could not—partly because she was a native of the Five Towns, where such things are not done, and no doubt partly because she was just herself.

She was now more grieved than angry with Louis. He had been wrong; he was a foolish, unreliable boy—but he was a boy. Whereas she was his mother, and ought to have known better. Yes, she had become his mother in the interval. For herself she experienced both pity and anger. What angered her was her clumsiness. Why had she lost her temper and her head? She saw clearly how she might have brought him round to her view with a soft phrase, a peculiar inflection, a tiny appeal, a caress, a mere dimpling of the cheek. She saw him revolving on her little finger.... She knew all things now because she was so old. And then suddenly she was bathing luxuriously in self-pity, and young and imperious, and violently resentful of the insult which he had put upon her—an insult which recalled the half-forgotten humiliations of her school-days, when loutish girls had baptized her with the name of a vegetable.... And then, again suddenly, she deeply desired that Louis should come upstairs and bully her.

She attached a superstitious and terrible importance to the tragical episode in the parlour because it was their first quarrel as husband and wife. True, she had stormed at him before their engagement, but even then he had kept intact his respect for her, whereas now, a husband, he had shamed her. The breach, she knew, could never be closed. She had only to glance at the empty bed to be sure that it was eternal. It had been made slowly yet swiftly; and it was complete and unbridgable ere she had realized its existence. When she contrasted the idyllic afternoon with the tragedy of the night, she was astounded by the swiftness of the change. The catastrophe lay, not in the threatened loss of vast sums of money and consequent ruin—that had diminished to insignificance!—but in the breach.

And then Mrs. Tams had inserted herself in the bedroom. Mrs. Tams knew or guessed everything. And she would not pretend that she did not; and Rachel would not pretend—did not even care to pretend, for Mrs. Tams was so unimportant that nobody minded her. Mrs. Tams had heard and seen. She commiserated. She stroked timidly with her gnarled hand the short, fragile sleeve of the nightgown, whereat Rachel sobbed afresh, with more plenteous tears, and tried to articulate a word, and could not till the third attempt. The word was "handkerchief." She was not weeping in comfort. Mrs. Tams was aware of the right drawer and drew from it a little white thing—yet not so little, for Rachel was Rachel!—and shook out its quadrangular folds, and it seemed beautiful in the gaslight; and Rachel took it and sobbed "Thank you."

Mrs. Tams rose higher than even a general servant; she was the soubrette, the confidential maid, the very echo of the young and haughty mistress, leagued with the worshipped creature against the wickedness and wile of a whole sex. Mrs. Tams had no illusions save the sublime illusion that her mistress was an angel and a martyr. Mrs. Tams had been married, and she had seen a daughter married. She was an authority on first quarrels and could and did tell tales of first quarrels—tales in which the husband, while admittedly an utterly callous monster, had at the same time somehow some leaven of decency. Soon she was launched in the epic recital of the birth and death of a grandchild; Rachel, being a married women like the rest, could properly listen to every interesting and recondite detail. Rachel sobbed and sympathized with the classic tale. And both women, as it was unrolled, kept well in their minds the vision of the vile man, mysterious and implacable, alone in the parlour. Occasionally Mrs. Tams listened for a footstep, ready discreetly to withdraw at the slightest symptom on the stairs. Once when she did this, Rachel murmured, weakly, "He won't—" and then lapsed into new weeping. And after a little time Mrs. Tams departed.

VI

Mrs. Tams had decided to undertake an enterprise involving extreme gallantry—surpassing the physical. She went downstairs and stood outside the parlour door, which was not quite shut. Within the parlour, or throne-room, existed a beautiful and superior being, full of grace and authority, who belonged to a race quite different from her own, who was beyond her comprehension, who commanded her and kept her alive and paid money to her, who accepted her devotion casually as a right, who treated her as a soft cushion between himself and the drift and inconvenience of the world, and who occasionally, as a supreme favour, caught her a smart slap on the back, which flattered her to excess. She went into the throne-room if she was called thither, or if she had cleansing or tidying work there; she spoke to the superior being if he spoke to her. But she had never till then conceived the breath-taking scheme of entering the throne-room for a purpose of her own, and addressing the superior being without an invitation to do so.

Nevertheless, since by long practice she was courageous, she meant to execute the scheme. And she began by knocking at the door. Although Rachel had seriously warned her that for a domestic servant to knock at the parlour door was a grave sin, she simply could not help knocking. Not to knock seemed to her wantonly sacrilegious. Thus she knocked, and a voice told her to come in.

There was the superior being, his back to the fire and his legs apart—formidable!

She curtsied—another sin according to the new code. Then she discovered that she was inarticulate.

"Well?"

Words burst from her—

"Her's crying her eyes out up yon, mester."

And Mrs. Tams also snivelled.

The superior being frowned and said testily, yet not without a touch of careless toleration—

"Oh, get away, you silly old fool of a woman!"

Mrs. Tarns got away, not entirely ill-content.

In the lobby she heard an unusual rapping on the glass of the front door, and sharply opened it to inform the late disturber that there existed a bell and a knocker for respectable people. A shabby youth gave her a note for "Louis Fores, Esq.," and said that there was an answer. So that she was forced to renew the enterprise of entering the throne-room.

In another couple of minutes Louis was running upstairs. His wife heard him, and shook in bed from excitement at the crisis which approached. But she could never have divined the nature of the phenomenon by which the unbridgable breach was about to be closed.

"Louise!"

"Yes," she whimpered. Then she ventured to spy at his face through an interstice of the bedclothes, and saw thereon a most queer, white expression.

"Some one's just brought this. Read it."

He gave her the note, and she deciphered it as well as she could—

> DEAR Louis,—If you aren't gone to bed I want to see you to-night about that missing money of aunt's. I've something I must tell you and Rachel. I'm at the "Three Tuns."
>
> JULIAN MALDON.

"But what does he mean?" demanded Rachel, roused from her heavy mood of self-pity.

"I don't know."

"But what can he mean?" she insisted.

"Haven't a notion."

"But he must mean something!"

Louis asked—

"Well, what should *you* say he means?"

"How very strange!" Rachel murmured, not attempting to answer the question. "And the 'Three Tuns'! Why does he write from the 'Three Tuns'? What's he doing at the 'Three Tuns'? Isn't it a very low public-house? And everybody thought he was still in South Africa!... I suppose, then, it *must* have been him that we saw to-night."

"You may bet it was."

"Then why didn't he come straight here? That's what I want to know. He couldn't have called before we got here, because if he had Mrs. Tams would have told us."

Louis nodded.

"Didn't you think Mr. Batchgrew looked very *queer* when you mentioned Julian to-night?" Rachel continued to express her curiosity and wonder.

"No. I didn't notice anything particular," Louis replied vaguely.

Throughout the conversation his manner was self-conscious. Rachel observed it, while feigning the contrary, and in her turn grew uneasy and even self-conscious also. Further, she had the feeling that Louis was depending upon her for support, and perhaps for initiative. His glance, though furtive, had the appealing quality which rendered him sometimes so exquisitely wistful to her. As he stood over her by the bed, he made a peculiar compound of the negligent, dominant masculine and the clinging feminine.

"And why didn't he let anybody know of his return?" Rachel went on.

Louis, veering towards the masculine, clenched the immediate point—

"The question before the meeting is," he smiled demurely, "what answer am I to send?"

"I suppose you must see him to-night."

"Nothing else for it, is there? Well, I'll scribble him a bit of a note."

"But I shan't see him, Louis."

"No?"

In an instant Rachel thought to herself: "He doesn't want me to see him."

Aloud she said: "I should have to dress myself all over again. Besides, I'm not fit to be seen."

She was referring, without any apparent sort of shame, to the redness of her eyes.

"Well, I'll see him by myself, then."

Louis turned to leave the bedroom. Whereat Rachel was very disconcerted and disappointed. Although the startling note from Julian had alarmed her and excited in her profound apprehensions whose very nature she would scarcely admit to herself, the main occupation of her mind was still her own quarrel with Louis. The quarrel was now over, for they had conversed in quite sincere tones of friendliness, but she had desired and expected an overt, tangible proof and symbol of peace. That proof and symbol was a kiss.

Louis was at the door ... he was beyond the door ... she was lost.

"Louis!" she cried.

He put his face in at the door.

"Will you just pass me my hand-mirror. It's on the dressing-table."

Louis was thrilled by this simple request. The hand-mirror had arrived in the house as a wedding-present. It was backed with tortoise-shell, and seemingly the one thing that had reconciled Rachel the downright to the possession of a hand-mirror was the fact that the tortoise-shell was real tortoise-shell. She had "made out" that a hand-mirror was too frivolous an object for the dressing-table of a serious Five Towns woman. She had always referred to it as "the" hand-mirror—as though disdaining special ownership. She had derided it once by using it in front of Louis with the mimic foolish graces of an empty-headed doll. And now she was asking for it because she wanted it; and she had said "my" hand-mirror!

This revelation of the odalisque in his Rachel enchanted Louis, and incidentally it also enchanted Rachel. She had employed a desperate remedy, and the result on both of them filled her with a most surprising gladness. Louis judged it to be deliciously right that Rachel should be anxious to know whether her weeping had indeed made her into an object improper for the beholding of the male eye, and Rachel to her astonishment shared his opinion. She was "vain," and they were both well content. In taking it she touched his hand. He bent and kissed her. Each of them was ravaged by formidable fears for the future, tremendously disturbed in secret by the mysterious word from Julian; and yet that kiss stood unique among their kisses, and in their simplicity they knew not why. And as they kissed they hated Julian, and the past, and the whole world, for thus coming between them and deranging their love. They would, had it been possible, have sold all the future for tranquillity in that moment.

VII

Going downstairs, Louis found Mrs. Tarns standing in the back part of the lobby between the parlour door and the kitchen; obviously she had stationed herself there in order to keep watch on the messenger from the "Three Tuns." As the master of the house approached with dignity the foot of the stairs, the messenger stirred, and in the classic manner of messengers fingered uneasily his hat. The fingers were dirty. The hat was dirty and shabby. It had been somebody else's hat before coming into the possession of the messenger. The same applied to his jacket and trousers. The jacket was well cut, but green; the trousers, with their ragged, muddy edges, yet betrayed a pattern of distinction. Round his neck the messenger wore a thin muffler, and on his feet an exhausted pair of tennis-shoes. These noiseless shoes accentuated and confirmed the stealthy glance of his eyes. Except for an unshaven chin, and the confidence-destroying quality that lurked subtly in his aspect, he was not repulsive to look upon. His features were delicate enough, his restless mouth was even pretty, and his carriage graceful. He had little of the coarseness of industrialism—probably because he was not industrial. His age was about twenty, and he might have sold *Signals* in the street, or run illegal errands for street-bookmakers. At any rate, it was certain that he was not above earning a chance copper from a customer of the "Three Tuns." His clear destiny was never to inspire respect or trust, nor to live regularly (save conceivably in prison), nor to do any honest daily labour. And if he did not know this, he felt it. All his movements were those of an outcast who both feared and execrated the organism that was rejecting him.

Louis, elegant, self-possessed, and superior, passed into the parlour exactly as if the messenger had been invisible. He was separated from the messenger by an immeasurable social prestige. He was raised to such an altitude above the messenger that he positively could not see the messenger with the naked eye. And yet for one fraction of a second he had the illusion of being so intimately akin to the messenger that a mere nothing might have pushed him into those vile clothes and endowed him with that furtive look and that sinister aspect of a helot. For one infinitesimal instant he was the messenger; and shuddered. Then the illusion as swiftly faded, and—such being Louis' happy temperament—was forgotten. He disappeared into the parlour, took a piece of paper and an envelope from the small writing-table behind Rachel's chair, and wrote a short note to Julian—a note from which facetiousness was not absent—inviting him to come at once. He rang the bell. Mrs. Tams entered, full of felicity because the great altercation was over and concord established.

"Give this to that chap," said Louis, casually imperative, holding out the note but scarcely glancing at Mrs. Tams.

"Yes, sir," said Mrs. Tarns with humble eagerness, content to be a very minor tool in the hidden designs of the exalted.

"And then you can go to bed."

"Oh! It's of no consequence, I'm sure, sir," Mrs. Tams answered.

Louis heard her say importantly and condescendingly to the messenger—

"Here ye are, young man."

She shut the front door as though much relieved to get such a source of peril and infection out of the respectable house.

Immediately afterwards strange things happened to Louis in the parlour. He had intended to return at once to his wife in order to continue the vague, staggered conversation about Julian's thunderbolt. But he discovered that he could not persuade himself to rejoin Rachel. A self-consciousness, growing every moment more acute and troublesome, prevented him from so doing. He was afraid that he could not discuss the vanished money without blushing, and it happened rarely that he lost control of his features, which indeed he could as a rule mould to the expression of a cherub whenever desirable. So he sat down in a chair, the first chair to hand, any chair, and began to reflect. Of course he was safe. The greatest saint on earth could not have been safer than he was from conviction of a crime. He might be suspected, but nothing could possibly be proved against him. Moreover, despite his self-consciousness, he felt innocent; he really did feel innocent, and even ill-used. The money had forced itself upon him in an inexcusable way; he was convinced that he had never meant to misappropriate it; assuredly he had received not a halfpenny of benefit from it. The fault was entirely the old lady's. Yes, he was innocent and he was safe.

Nevertheless, he did not at all like the resuscitation of the affair. The affair had been buried. How characteristic of the inconvenient Julian to rush in from South Africa and dig it up! Everybody concerned had decided that the old lady on the night of her attack had not been responsible for her actions. She had annihilated the money—whether by fire, as Batchgrew had lately suggested, or otherwise, did not matter. Or, if she had not annihilated the money, she had "done something" with it—something unknown and unknowable. Such was the acceptable theory, in which Louis heartily concurred. The loss was his—at least half the loss was his—and others had no right to complain. But Julian was without discretion. Within twenty-four hours Julian might well set the whole district talking.

Louis was dimly aware that the district already had talked, but he was not aware to what extent it had talked. Neither he nor anybody else was aware how the secret had escaped out of the house. Mrs. Tarns would have died rather than breathe a word. Rachel, naturally, had said naught; nor had Louis. Old Batchgrew had decided that his highest interest also was to say naught, and he had informed none save Julian. Julian might have set the secret free in South Africa, but in a highly distorted form it had been current in certain strata of Five Towns society long before it could have returned from South Africa. The rough, commonsense verdict of those select few who had winded the secret was simply that "there had been some hanky-panky," and that beyond doubt Louis was "at the bottom of it," but that it had little importance, as Mrs. Maldon was dead, poor thing. As for Julian, "a rough customer, though honest as the day," he was reckoned to be capable of protecting his own interests.

And then, amid all his apprehensions, a new hope sprouted in Louis' mind. Perhaps Julian was acquainted with some fact that might lead to the recovery of a part of the money. Had Louis not always held that the pile of notes which had penetrated into his pocket did not represent the whole of the nine hundred and sixty-five pounds? Conceivably it represented about half of the total, in which case a further sum of, say, two hundred and fifty pounds might be coming to Louis. Already he was treating this two hundred and fifty pounds as a windfall, and wondering in what most pleasant ways he could employ it!... But with what kind of fact could Julian be acquainted?... Had Julian been dishonest? Louis would have liked to think Julian dishonest, but he could not. Then what ...?

He heard movements above. And the front gate creaked. As if a spring had been loosed, he jumped from the chair and ran upstairs—away from the arriving Julian and towards his wife. Rachel was just getting up.

"Don't trouble," he said. "I'll see him. I'll deal with him. Much better for you to stay in bed."

He perceived that he did not want Rachel to hear what Julian had to say until after he had heard it himself.

Rachel hesitated.

"Do you think so?... What have you been doing? I thought you were coming up again at once."

"I had one or two little things—"

A terrific knock resounded on the front door.

"There he is!" Louis muttered, as it were aghast.

CHAPTER XI
JULIAN'S DOCUMENT

I

Julian Maldon faced Louis in the parlour. Louis had conducted him there without the assistance of Mrs. Tams, who had been not merely advised, but commanded, to go to bed. Julian had entered the house like an exasperated enemy—glum, suspicious, and ferocious. His mien seemed to say: "You wanted me to come, and I've come. But mind you don't drive me to extremities." Impossible to guess from his grim face that he had asked permission to come! Nevertheless he had shaken Louis' hand with a ferocious sincerity which Louis felt keenly the next morning. He was the same Julian except that he had grown a brown beard. He had exactly the same short, thick-set figure, and the same defiant stare. South Africa had not changed him. No experience could change him. He would have returned from ten years at the North Pole or at the Equator, with savages or with uncompromising intellectuals, just the same Julian. He was one of those beings who are violently themselves all the time. By some characteristic social clumsiness he had omitted to remove his overcoat in the lobby. And now, in the parlour, he could not get it off. As a man seated, engaged in conversation by a woman standing, forgets to rise at once and then cannot rise, finding himself glued to the chair, so was Julian with his overcoat; to take it off he would have had to flay himself alive.

"Won't you take off your overcoat?" Louis suggested.

"No."

With his instinctive politeness Louis turned to improve the fire. And as he poked among the coals he said, in the way of amiable conversation—

"How's South Africa?"

"All right," replied Julian, who hated to impart his sensations. If Julian had witnessed Napoleon's retreat from Moscow he would have come to the Five Towns and, if questioned—not otherwise—would have said that it was all right.

Louis, however, suspected that his brevity was due to Julian's resentment of any inquisitiveness concerning his doings in South Africa; and he therefore at once abandoned South Africa as a subject of talk, though he was rather curious to know what, indeed, Julian had been about in South Africa for six mortal months. Nobody in the Five Towns knew for certain what Julian had been about in South Africa. It was understood that he had gone there as a commercial traveller for his own wares, when his business was in a highly unsatisfactory condition, and that he had meant to stay for only a month. The excursion had been deemed somewhat mad, but not more mad than sundry other deeds of Julian. Then Julian's manager, Foulger, had (it appeared) received authority to assume responsible charge of the manufactory until further notice. From that moment the business had prospered: a result at which nobody was surprised, because Foulger was notoriously a "good man" who had hitherto been baulked in his ideas by an obstinate young employer.

In a community of stiff-necked employers, Julian already held a high place for the quality of being stiff-necked. Jim Horrocleave, for example, had a queer, murderous manner with customers and with "hands," but Horrocleave was friendly towards scientific ideas in the earthenware industry, and had even given half a guinea to the fund for encouraging technical education in the district. Whereas Julian Maldon not only terrorized customers and work-people (the latter nevertheless had a sort of liking for him), but was bitingly scornful of "cranky chemists," or "Germans," as he called the scientific educated experts. He was the pure essence of the British manufacturer. He refused to make what the market wanted, unless the market happened to want what he wanted to make. He hated to understand the reasons underlying the processes of manufacture, or to do anything which had not been regularly done for at least fifty years. And he accepted orders like insults. The wonder was, not that he did so little business, but that he did so much. Still, people did respect him. His aunt Maldon, with her skilled habit of finding good points in mankind, had thought that he must be remarkably intelligent because he was so rude.

Beyond a vague rumour that Julian had established a general pottery agency in Cape Town with favourable prospects, no further news of him had reached England. But of course it was admitted that his inheritance had definitely saved the business, and also much improved his situation in the eyes of the community ... And now he had achieved a reappearance which in mysteriousness excelled even his absence.

"So you see we're installed here," said Louis, when he had finished with the fire.

"Aye!" muttered Julian dryly, and shut his lips.

Louis tried no more conversational openings. He was afraid. He waited for Julian's initiative as for an earthquake; for he knew now at the roots of his soul that the phrasing of the note was misleading, and that Julian had come to charge him with having misappropriated the sum of nine hundred and sixty-five pounds. He had, in reality, surmised as much on first reading the note, but somehow he had managed to put away the surmise as absurd and incredible.

After a formidable silence Julian said savagely—

"Look here. I've got something to tell you. I've written it all down, and I thought to send it ye by post. But after I'd written it I said to myself I'd tell it ye face to face or I'd die for it. And so here I am."

"Oh!" Louis murmured. He would have liked to be genially facetious, but his mouth was dried up. He could not ask any questions. He waited.

"Where's missis?" Julian demanded.

Louis started, not instantly comprehending.

"Rachel? She's—she's in bed. She'd gone to bed before you sent round."

"Well, I'll thank ye to get her up, then!" Julian pronounced. "She's got to hear this at first hand, not at second." His gaze expressed a frank distrust of Louis.

"But—"

At this moment Rachel came into the parlour, apparently fully dressed. Her eyes were red, but her self-control was complete.

Julian glared at Louis as at a trapped liar.

"I thought ye said she was in bed."

"She was," said Louis. He could find nothing to say to his wife.

Rachel nonchalantly held out her hand.

"So you've come," she said.

"Aye!" said Julian gruffly, and served Rachel's hand as he had served Louis'.

She winced without concealment.

"Was it you we saw going down Moorthorne Road to-night?" she asked.

"It was," said Julian, looking at the carpet.

"Well, why didn't you come in then?"

"I couldn't make up my mind, if you must know."

"Aren't you going to sit down?"

Julian sat down.

Louis reflected that women were astonishing and incalculable, and the discovery seemed to him original, even profound. Imagine her tackling Julian in this fashion, with no preliminaries! She might have seen Julian last only on the previous day! The odalisque had vanished in this chill and matter-of-fact housewife.

"And why were you at the 'Three Tuns'?" she went on.

Julian replied with extraordinary bitterness—

"I was at the 'Three Tuns' because I was at the 'Three Tuns.'"

"I see you've grown a beard," said Rachel.

"Happen I have," said Julian. "But what I say is, I've got something to tell you two. I've written it all down and I thought to post it to ye. But after I'd written it I says to myself, 'I'll tell 'em face to face or I'll die for it.'"

"Is it about that money?" Rachel inquired.

"Aye!"

"Then Mr. Batchgrew did write and tell you about it. Won't you take that great, thick overcoat off?"

Julian jumped up as if in fury, pulled off the overcoat with violent gestures, and threw in on the Chesterfield. Then he sat down again, and, sticking out his chin, stared inimically at Louis.

Louis' throat was now so tight that he was nervously obliged to make the motion of swallowing. He could look neither at Rachel nor at Julian. He was nonplussed. He knew not what to expect nor what he feared. He could not even be sure that what he feared was an accusation. "I am safe. I am safe," he tried to repeat to himself, deeply convinced, nevertheless, against his reason, that he was not safe. The whole scene, every aspect of it, baffled and inexpressibly dismayed him.

Julian still stared, with mouth open, threatening. Then he slapped his knee.

"Nay!" said he. "I shall read it to ye." And he drew some sheets of foolscap from his pocket. He opened the sheets, and frowned at them, and coughed. "Nay!" said he. "There's nothing else for it. I must smoke."

And he produced a charred pipe which might or might not have been the gift of Mrs. Maldon, filled it, struck a match on his boot, and turbulently puffed outrageous quantities of smoke. Louis, with singular courage, lit a cigarette, which gave him a little ease of demeanour, if not confidence.

II

And then at length Julian began to read—

"'Before I went to South Africa last autumn I found myself in considerable business difficulties. The causes of said difficulties were bad trade, unfair competition, and price-cutting at home and abroad, especially in Germany, and the modern spirit of unrest among the working-classes making it impossible for an employer to be master on his own works. I was not insolvent, but I needed capital, the life-blood of industry. In justice to myself I ought to explain that my visit to South Africa was very carefully planned and thought out. I had a good reason to believe that a lot of business in door-furniture could be done there, and that I could obtain some capital from a customer in Durban. I point this out merely because trade rivals have tried to throw ridicule upon me for going out to South Africa when I did. I must ask you to read carefully'—you see, this was a letter to you," he interjected—"read carefully all that I say. I will now proceed."

"'When I came to Aunt Maldon's the night before I left for South Africa I wanted a wash, and I went into the back room—I mean the room behind the parlour—and took off my coat preparatory to going into the scullery to perform my ablutions. While in the back room I noticed that the picture nearest the cupboard opposite the door was hung very crooked. When I came back to put my coat on again after washing, my eye again caught the picture. There was a chair almost beneath it. I got on the chair and put the picture into an horizontal position. While I was standing on the chair I could see on the top of the cupboard, where something white struck my attention. It was behind the cornice of the cupboard, but I could see it. I took it off the top of the cupboard and carefully scrutinized it by the gas, which, as you know, is at the corner of the fireplace, close to the cupboard. It was a roll consisting of Bank of England notes, to the value of four hundred and fifty pounds. I counted them at once, while I was standing on the chair. I then put them in the pocket of my coat which I had already put on. I wish to point out that if the chair had not been under the picture I should in all human probability not have attempted to straighten the picture. Also—'"

"But surely, Julian," Louis interrupted him, in a constrained voice, "you could have reached the picture without standing on the chair?" He interrupted solely from a tremendous desire for speech. It would have been impossible for him to remain silent. He had to speak or perish.

"I couldn't," Julian denied vehemently. "The picture's practically as high as the top of the cupboard—or was."

"And could *you* see on to the top of the cupboard from a chair?" Louis, with a peculiar gaze, was apparently estimating Julian's total height from the ground when raised on a chair.

Julian dashed down the papers.

"Here! Come and look for yourself!" he exclaimed with furious pugnacity. "Come and look." He jumped up and moved towards the door.

Rachel and Louis followed him obediently. In the back room it was he who struck a match and lighted the gas.

"You've shifted the picture!" he cried, as soon as the room was illuminated.

"Yes, we have," Louis admitted.

"But there's where it was!" Julian almost shouted, pointing. "You can't deny it! There's the marks. Are they as high as the top of the cupboard, or aren't they?" Then he dragged along a chair to the cupboard and stood on it, puffing at his pipe. "Can I see on to the top of the cupboard or can't I?" he demanded. Obviously he could see on to the top of the cupboard.

"I didn't think the top was so low," said Louis.

"Well, you shouldn't contradict," Julian chastised him.

"It's just as your great-aunt said," put in Rachel, in a meditative tone. "I remember she told us she pushed a chair forward with her knee. I dare say in getting on to the chair she knocked her elbow or something against the picture, and no doubt she left the chair more or less where she'd pushed it. That would be it."

"Did she say that to you?" Louis questioned Rachel.

"It doesn't matter much what she said," Julian growled. "That's how it *was*, anyway. I'm telling you. I'm not here to listen to theories."

"Well," said Louis amiably, "you put the notes into your pocket. What then?"

Julian removed his pipe from his mouth.

"What then? I walked off with 'em."

"But you don't mean to tell us you meant—to appropriate them, Julian? You don't mean that!" Louis spoke reassuringly, good-naturedly, and with a slight superiority.

"No, I don't. I don't mean I appropriated 'em." Julian's voice rose defiantly. "I mean I stole them.... I stole them, and what's more, I meant to steal them. And so there ye are! But come back to the parlour. I must finish my reading."

He strode away into the parlour, and the other two had no alternative but to follow him. They followed him like guilty things; for the manner of his confession was such as apparently to put his hearers, more than himself, in the wrong. He confessed as one who accuses.

"Sit down," said he, in the parlour.

"But surely," Louis protested, "if you're serious—"

"If I'm serious, man! Do you take me for a bally mountebank? Do you suppose I'm doing this for fun?"

"Well," said Louis, "if you *are* serious, you needn't tell us any more. We know, and that's enough, isn't it?"

Julian replied curtly, "You've got to hear me out."

And picking up his document from the floor, he resumed the perusal.

"'Also, if the gas hadn't been where it is, I should not have noticed anything on the top of the cupboard. I took the notes because I was badly in need of money, and also because I was angry at money being left like that on the tops of cupboards. I had no idea Aunt Maldon was such a foolish woman.'"

Louis interjected soothingly: "But you only meant to teach the old lady a lesson and give the notes back."

"I didn't," said Julian, again extremely irritated. "Can't ye understand plain English? I say I stole the money, and I meant to steal it. Don't let me have to tell ye that any more. I'll go on: 'The sight of the notes was too sore a temptation for me, and I yielded to it. And all the more shame to me, for I had considered myself an honest man up to that very hour. I never thought about the consequences to my Aunt Maldon, nor how I was going to get rid of the notes. I wanted money bad, and I took it. As soon as I'd left the house I was stricken with remorse. I could not decide what to do. The fact is I had no time to reflect until I was on the steamer, and it was then too late. Upon arriving at Cape Town I found the cable stating that Aunt Maldon was dead. I draw a veil over my state of mind, which, however, does not concern you. I ought to have returned to England at once, but I could not. I might have sent to Batchgrew and told him to take half of four hundred and fifty pounds off my share of Aunt Maldon's estate and put it into yours. But that would not have helped my conscience. I had it on my conscience, as it might have been on my stomach. I tried religion, but it was no good to me. It was between a prayer-meeting and an experience-meeting at Durban that I used part of the ill-gotten money. I had not touched it till then. But two days later I got back the very note that I'd spent. A prey to remorse, I wandered from town to town, trying to do business.'"

III

Rachel stood up.

"Julian!"

It was the first time in her life that she had called him by his Christian name.

"What?"

"Give me that." As he hesitated, she added, "I want it."

He handed her the written confession.

"I simply can't bear to hear you reading it," said Rachel passionately. "All about a prey to remorse and so on and so on! Why do you want to confess? Why couldn't you have paid back the money and have done with it, instead of all this fuss?"

"I must finish it now I've begun," Julian insisted sullenly.

"You'll do no such thing—not in my house."

And, repeating pleasurably the phrase "not in *my* house," Rachel stuck the confession into the fire, and feverishly forced it into the red coals with lunges of the poker. When she turned away from the fire she was flushing scarlet. Julian stood close by her on the hearth-rug.

"You don't understand," he said, with half-fearful resentment. "I had to punish myself. I doubt I'm not a religious man, but I had to punish myself. There's nobody in the world as I should hate confessing to as much as Louis here, and so I said to myself, I said, 'I'll confess to Louis.' I've been wandering about all the evening trying to bring myself to do it…. Well, I've done it."

His voice trembled, and though the vibration in it was almost imperceptible, it was sufficient to nullify the ridiculousness of Julian's demeanour as a wearer of sackcloth, and to bring a sudden lump into Rachel's throat. The comical absurdity of his bellicose pride because he had accomplished something which he had sworn to accomplish was extinguished by the absolutely painful sincerity of his final words, which seemed somehow to damage the reputation of Louis. Rachel could feel her emotion increasing, but she could not have defined what her emotion was. She knew not what to do. She was in the midst of a new and intense experience, which left her helpless. All she was clearly conscious of was an unrepentant voice in her heart repeating the phrase: "I don't care! I'm glad I stuck it in the fire! I don't care! I'm glad I stuck it in the fire." She waited for the next development. They were all waiting, aware that individual forces had been loosed, but unable to divine their resultant, and afraid of that resultant. Rachel glanced furtively at Louis. His face had an uneasy, stiff smile.

With an aggrieved air Julian knocked the ashes out of his pipe.

"Anyhow," said Louis at length, "this accounts for four hundred and fifty out of nine sixty-five. What we have to find out now, all of us, is what happened to the balance."

"I don't care a fig about the balance," said Julian impetuously. "I've said what I had to say and that's enough for me."

And he did not, in fact, care a fig about the balance. And if the balance had been five thousand odd instead of five hundred odd, he still probably would not have cared. Further, he privately considered that nobody else ought to care about the balance, either, having regard to the supreme moral importance to himself of the four hundred and fifty.

"Have you said anything to Mr. Batchgrew?" Louis asked, trying to adopt a casual tone, and to keep out of his voice the relief and joy which were gradually taking possession of his soul. The upshot of Julian's visit was so amazingly different from the apprehension of it that he could have danced in his glee.

"Not I!" Julian answered ferociously. "The old robber has been writing me, wanting me to put money into some cinema swindle or other. I gave him a bit of my mind."

"He was trying the same here," said Rachel. The words popped by themselves out of her mouth, and she instantly regretted them. However, Louis seemed to be unconscious of the implied reproach on a subject presumably still highly delicate.

"But you can tell him, if you've a mind," Julian went on challengingly.

"We shan't do any such thing," said Rachel, words again popping by themselves out of her mouth. But this time she put herself right by adding, "Shall we, Louis?"

"Of course not," Louis agreed very amiably.

Rachel began to feel sympathetic towards the thief. She thought: "How strange to have some one close to me, and talking quite naturally, who has stolen such a lot of money and might be in prison for it—a convict!" Nevertheless, the thief seemed to be remarkably like ordinary people.

"Oh!" Julian ejaculated. "Well, here's the notes." He drew a lot of notes from a pocket-book and banged them down on the table. "Four hundred and fifty. The identical notes. Count 'em." He glared afresh, and with even increased virulence.

"That's all right," said Louis. "That's all right. Besides, we only want half of them."

Sundry sheets of the confession, which had not previously caught fire, suddenly blazed up with a roar in the grate, and all looked momentarily at the flare.

"You've *got* to have it all!" said Julian, flushing.

"My dear fellow," Louis repeated, "we shall only take half. The other half's yours."

"As God sees me," Julian urged, "I'll never take a penny of that money! Here—"

He snatched up all the notes and dashed wrathfully out of the parlour. Rachel followed quickly. He went to the back room, where the gas had been left burning high, sprang on to a chair in front of the cupboard, and deposited the notes on the top of the cupboard, in the very place from which he had originally taken them.

"There!" he exclaimed, jumping down from the chair. The symbolism of the action appeared to tranquillize him.

IV

For a moment Rachel, as a newly constituted housewife to whom every square foot of furniture surface had its own peculiar importance, was enraged to see Julian's heavy and dirty boots again on the seat of her unprotected chair. But the sense of hurt passed like a spasm as her eyes caught Julian's. They were alone together in the back room and not far from each other. And in the man's eyes she no longer saw the savage Julian, but an intensely suffering creature, a creature martyrized by destiny. She saw the real Julian glancing out in torment at the world through those eyes. The effect of the vibration in Julian's voice a few minutes earlier was redoubled. Her emotion nearly overcame her. She desired very much to succour Julian, and was aware of a more distinct feeling of impatience against Louis.

She thought Julian had been magnificently heroic, and all his faults of demeanour were counted to him for excellences. He had been a thief; but the significance of the word "thief" was indeed completely altered for her. She had hitherto envisaged thieves as rascals in handcuffs bandied along the streets by policemen at the head of a procession of urchins—dreadful rascals! But now a thief was just a young man like other young men—only he had happened to see some bank-notes lying about and had put them in his pocket and then had felt very sorry for what he had done. There was no crime in what he had done ... was there? She pictured Julian's pilgrimage through South Africa, all alone. She pictured his existence at Knype, all alone; and his very ferocity rendered him the more wistful and pathetic in her sight. She was sure that his mother and sisters had never understood him; and she did not think it quite proper on their part to have gone permanently to America, leaving him solitary in England, as they had done. She perceived that she herself was the one person in the world capable of understanding Julian, the one person who could look after him, influence him, keep him straight, civilize him, and impart some charm to his life. And she was glad that she had the status of a married woman, because without that she would have been helpless.

Julian sat down, or sank, on to the chair.

"I'm very sorry I spoke like that to you in the other room—I mean about what you'd written," she said. "I suppose I ought not to have burnt it."

She spoke in this manner because to apologize to him gave her a curious pleasure.

"That's nothing," he answered, with the quietness of fatigue. "I dare say you were right enough. Anyhow, ye'll never see me again."

She exclaimed, kindly protesting—

"Why not, I should like to know?"

"You won't want me here as a visitor, after all this." He faintly sneered.

"I shall," she insisted.

"Louis won't."

She replied: "You must come and see me. I shall expect you to. I must tell you," she added confidentially, in a lower tone, "I think you've been splendid to-night. I'm sure I respect you much more than I did before—and you can take it how you like!"

"Nay! Nay!" he murmured deprecatingly. All the harshness had melted out of his voice.

Then he stood up.

"I'd better hook it," he said briefly. "Will you get me my overcoat, missis."

She comprehended that he wished to avoid speaking to Louis again that night, and, nodding, went at once to the parlour and brought away the overcoat.

"He's going," she muttered hastily to Louis, who was standing near the fire. Leaving the parlour, she drew the door to behind her.

She helped Julian with his overcoat and preceded him to the front door. She held out her hand to be tortured afresh, and suffered the grip of the vice with a steady smile.

"Now don't forget," she whispered.

Julian seemed to try to speak and to fail.... He was gone. She carefully closed and bolted the door.

V

Louis had not followed Julian and Rachel into the back room because he felt the force of an instinct to be alone with his secret satisfaction. In those moments it irked him to be observed, and especially to be observed by Rachel, not to mention Julian. He was glad for several reasons — on account of his relief, on account of the windfall of money, and perhaps most of all on account of the discovery that he was not the only thief in the family. The bizarre coincidence which had divided the crime about equally between himself and Julian amused him. His case and Julian's were on a level. Nevertheless, he somewhat despised Julian, patronized him, condescended to him. He could not help thinking that Julian was, after all, a greater sinner than himself. Never again could Julian look him (Louis) in the face as if nothing had happened. The blundering Julian was marked for life, by his own violent, unreasonable hand. Julian was a fool.

Rachel entered rather solemnly.

"Has he really gone?" Louis asked. Rachel did not care for her husband's tone, which was too frivolous for her. She was shocked to find that Louis had not been profoundly impressed by the events of the night.

"Yes," she said.

"What's he done with the money?"

"He's left it in the other room." She would not disclose to Louis that Julian had restored the notes to the top of the cupboard, because she was afraid that he might treat the symbolic act with levity.

"All of it?"

"Yes. I'll bring it you."

She did so. Louis counted the notes and casually put them in his breast pocket.

"Oddest chap I ever came across!" he observed, smiling.

"But aren't you sorry for him?" Rachel demanded.

"Yes," said Louis airily. "I shall insist on his taking half, naturally."

"I'm going to bed," said Rachel. "You'll see all the lights out."

She offered her face and kissed him tepidly.

"What's come over the kid?" Louis asked himself, somewhat disconcerted, when she had gone.

He remained smoking, purposeless, in the parlour until all sounds had ceased overhead in the bedroom. Then he extinguished the gas in the parlour, in the back room, in the kitchen, and finally in the lobby, and went upstairs by the light of the street lamp. In the bedroom Rachel lay in bed, her eyes closed. She did not stir at his entrance. He locked the bank-notes in a drawer of the dressing-table, undressed with his usual elaborate care, approached Rachel's bed and gazed at her unresponsive form, turned down the gas to a pinpoint, and got into bed himself. Not the slightest sound could be heard anywhere, either in or out of the house, save the faint breathing of Rachel. And after a few moments Louis no longer heard even that. In the darkness the mystery of the human being next him began somehow to be disquieting. He was capable of imagining that he lay in the room with an utter stranger. Then he fell asleep.

CHAPTER XII
RUNAWAY HORSES

I

Rachel, according to her own impression the next morning, had no sleep during that night. The striking of the hall clock could not be heard in the bedroom with the door closed, but it could be felt as a faint, distinct concussion; and she had thus noted every hour, except four o'clock, when daylight had come and the street lamp had been put out. She had deliberately feigned sleep as Louis entered the room, and had maintained the soft, regular breathing of a sleeper until long after he was in bed. She did not wish to talk; she could not have talked with any safety.

Her brain was occupied much by the strange and emotional episode of Julian's confession, but still more by the situation of her husband in the affair. Julian's story had precisely corroborated one part of Mrs. Maldon's account of her actions on the evening when the bank-notes had disappeared. Little by little that recital of Mrs. Maldon's had been discredited, and at length cast aside as no more important than the delirium of a dying creature; it was an inconvenient story, and would only fit in with the alternative theories that money had wings and could fly on its own account, or that there had been thieves in the house. Far easier to assume that Mrs. Maldon in some lapse had unwittingly done away with the notes! But Mrs. Maldon was now suddenly reinstated as a witness. And if one part of her evidence was true, why should not the other part be true? Her story was that she had put the remainder of the bank-notes on the chair on the landing, and then (she thought) in the wardrobe. Rachel recalled clearly all that she had seen and all that she had been told. She remembered once more the warnings that had been addressed to her. She lived the evening and the night of the theft over again, many times, monotonously, and with increasing woe and agitation.

Then with the greenish dawn, that the blinds let into the room, came some refreshment and new health to the brain, but the trend of her ideas was not modified. She lay on her side and watched the unconscious Louis for immense periods, and occasionally tears filled her eyes. The changes in her existence seemed so swift and so tremendous as to transcend belief. Was it conceivable that only twelve hours earlier she had been ecstatically happy? In twelve hours—in six hours—she had aged twenty years, and she now saw the Rachel of the reception and of the bicycle lesson as a young girl, touchingly ingenuous, with no more notion of danger than a baby.

At six o'clock she arose. Already she had formed the habit of arising before Louis, and had reconciled herself to the fact that Louis had to be forced out of bed. Happily, his feet once on the floor, he became immediately manageable. Already she was the conscience and time-keeper of the house. She could dress herself noiselessly; in a week she had perfected all her little devices for avoiding noise and saving time. She finally left the room neat, prim, with lips set to a thousand responsibilities. She had a peculiar sensation of tight elastic about her eyes, but she felt no fatigue, and she did not yawn. Mrs. Tams, who had just descended, found her taciturn and exacting. She would have every household task performed precisely in her own way, without compromise. And it appeared that the house, which had the air of being in perfect order, was not in order at all, that indeed the processes of organization had, in young Mrs. Fores' opinion, scarcely yet begun. It appeared that there was no smallest part or corner of the house as to which young Mrs. Fores had not got very definite ideas and plans. The individuality of Mrs. Tams was to have scope nowhere. But after all, this seemed quite natural to Mrs. Tams.

When Rachel went back to the bedroom, about 7.30, to get Louis by ruthlessness and guile out of bed, she was surprised to discover that he had already gone up to the bathroom. She guessed, with vague alarm, from this symptom that he had a new and very powerful interest in life. He came to breakfast at three minutes to eight, three minutes before it was served. When she entered the parlour in the wake of Mrs. Tams he kissed her with gay fervour. She permitted herself to be kissed. Her unresponsiveness, though not marked, disconcerted him and somewhat dashed his mood. Whereupon Rachel, by the reassurance of her voice, set about to convince him that he had been mistaken in deeming her unresponsive. So that he wavered between two moods.

As she sat behind the tray, amid the exquisite odours of fresh coffee and Ted Malkin's bacon (for she had forgiven Miss Malkin), behaving like a staid wife of old standing, she well knew that she was a mystery for Louis. She was the source of his physical comfort, the origin of the celestial change in his life which had caused him to admit fully that to live in digs was "a rotten game"; but she was also, that morning, a most sinister mystery. Her behaviour was faultless. He could seize on no definite detail that should properly disturb him; only she had woven a veil between herself and him. Still, his liveliness scarcely abated.

"Do you know what I'm going to do this very day as ever is?" he asked.

"What is it?"

"I'm going to buy you a bike. I've had enough of that old crock I borrowed for you. I shall return it and come back with a new 'un. And I know the precise bike that I shall come back with. It's at Bostock's at Hanbridge. They've just opened a new cycle department."

"Oh, Louis!" she protested.

His scheme for spending money on her flattered her. But nevertheless it was a scheme for spending money. Two hundred and twenty-five pounds had dropped into his lap, and he must needs begin instantly to dissipate it. He could not keep it. That was Louis! She refused to see that the purchase of a bicycle was the logical consequence of her lessons. She desired to believe that by some miracle at some future date she could possess a bicycle without a bicycle being bought—and in the meantime was there not the borrowed machine?

Suddenly she yawned.

"Didn't you sleep well?" he demanded.

"Not very."

"Oh!"

She could almost see into the interior of his brain, where he was persuading himself that fatigue alone was the explanation of her peculiar demeanour, and rejoicing that the mystery was, after all, neither a mystery nor sinister.

"I say," he began between two puffs of a cigarette after breakfast, "I shall send back half of that money to Julian. I'll send the notes by registered post."

"Shall you?"

"Yes. Don't you think he'll keep them?"

"Supposing I was to take them over to him myself—and insist?" she suggested.

"It's a notion. When?"

"Well, on Saturday afternoon. He'll be at home probably then."

"All right," Louis agreed. "I'll give you the money later on."

Nothing more was said as to the Julian episode. It seemed that husband and wife were equally determined not to discuss it merely for the sake of discussing it.

Shortly after half-past eight Louis was preparing the borrowed bicycle and his own in the back yard.

"I shall ride mine and tow the crock," said he, looking up at Rachel as he screwed a valve. She had come into the yard in order to show a polite curiosity in his doings.

"Isn't it dangerous?"

"Are you dangerous?" he laughed.

"But when shall you go?"

"Now."

"Shan't you be late at the works?"

"Well, if I'm late at the beautiful works I shall be late at the beautiful works. Those who don't like it will have to lump it."

Once more, it was the consciousness of a loose, entirely available two hundred and twenty-five pounds that was making him restive under the yoke of regular employment. For a row of pins, that morning, he would have given Jim Horrocleave a week's notice, or even the amount of a week's wages in lieu of notice! Rachel sighed, but within herself.

In another minute he was elegantly flying down Bycars Lane, guiding his own bicycle with his right hand and the crock with his left hand. The feat appeared miraculous to Rachel, who watched from the bow-window of the parlour. Beyond question he made a fine figure. And it was for her that he was flying to Hanbridge! She turned away to her domesticity.

II

It seemed to her that he had scarcely been gone ten minutes when one of the glorious taxicabs which had recently usurped the stand of the historic fly under the Town Hall porch drew up at the front door, and Louis got out of it. The sound of his voice was the first intimation to Rachel that it was

Louis who was arriving. He shouted at the cabman as he paid the fare. The window of the parlour was open and the curtains pinned up. She ran to the window, and immediately saw that Louis' head was bandaged. Then she ran to the door. He was climbing rather stiffly up the steps.

"All right! All right!" he shouted at her. "A spill. Nothing of the least importance. But both the jiggers are pretty well converted into old iron. I tell you it's all *right*! Shut the door."

He bumped down on the oak chest, and took a long breath.

"But you are frightfully hurt!" she exclaimed. She could not properly see his face for the bandages.

Mrs. Tams appeared. Rachel murmured to her in a flash—

"Go out the back way and fetch Dr. Yardley at once."

She felt herself absolutely calm. What puzzled her was Louis' shouting. Then she understood he was shouting from mere excitement and did not realize that he shouted.

"No need for any doctor! Quite simple!" he called out.

But Rachel gave a word confirming the original order to Mrs. Tams, who disappeared.

"First thing I knew I was the centre of an admiring audience, and fat Mrs. Heath, in her white apron and the steel hanging by her side, was washing my face with a sponge and a basin of water, and Heath stood by with brandy. It was nearly opposite their shop. People in the tram had a rare view of me."

"But was it the tram-car you ran into?" Rachel asked eagerly.

He replied with momentary annoyance—

"Tram-car! Of course it wasn't the tram-car. Moreover, I didn't run into anything. Two horses ran into me. I was coming down past the Shambles into Duck Bank—very slowly, because I could hear a tram coming along from the market-place—and just as I got past the Shambles and could see along the market-place, I saw a lad on a cart-horse and leading another horse. No stirrups, no saddle. He'd no more control over either horse than a baby over an elephant. Not a bit more. Both horses were running away. The horse he was supposed to be leading was galloping first. They were passing the tram at a fine rate."

"But how far were they off you?"

"About ten yards. I said to myself, 'If that chap doesn't look out he'll be all over me in two seconds.' I turned as sharp as I could away to the left. I could have turned sharper if I'd had your bicycle in my right hand instead of my left. But it wouldn't have made any difference. The first horse simply made straight for me. There was about a mile of space for him between me and the tram, but he wouldn't look at it. He wanted me, and he had me. They both had me. I never felt the actual shock. Curious, that! I'm told one horse put his foot clean through the back wheel of my bike. Then he was stopped by the front palings of the Conservative Club. Oh! a pretty smash! The other horse and the boy thereon finished half-way up Moorthorne Road. He could stick on, no mistake, that kid could. Midland Railway horses. Whoppers. Either being taken to the vets' or brought from the vet's—I don't know. I forget."

Rachel put her hand on his arm.

"Do come into the parlour and have the easy-chair."

"I'll come—I'll come," he said, with the same annoyance. "Give us a chance." His voice was now a little less noisy.

"But you might have been killed!"

"You bet I might! Eight hoofs all over me! One tap from any of the eight would have settled yours sincerely."

"Louis!" She spoke firmly. "You must come into the parlour. Now come along, do, and sit down and let me look at your face." She removed his hat, which was perched rather insecurely on the top of the bandages. "Who was it looked after you?"

"Well," he hesitated, following her into the parlour, "it seems to have been chiefly Mrs. Heath."

"But didn't they take you to a chemist's? Isn't there a chemist's handy?"

"The great Greene had one of his bilious attacks and was in bed, it appears. And the great Greene's assistant is only just out of petticoats, I believe. However, everybody acted for the best, and here I am. And if you ask me, I think I've come out of it rather well."

He dropped heavily on to the Chesterfield. What she could see of his cheeks was very pale.

"Open the window," he murmured. "It's frightfully stuffy here."

"The window is open," she said. In fact, a noticeable draught blew through the room. "I'll open it a bit more."

Before doing so she lifted his feet on to the Chesterfield.

"That's better. That's better," he breathed.

When, a moment later, she returned to him with a glass of water which she had brought from the kitchen, spilling drops of it along the whole length of the passage, he smiled at her and then winked.

It was the wink that seemed pathetic to her. She had maintained her laudable calm until he winked, and then her throat tightened.

"He may have some dreadful internal injury," she thought. "You never know. I may be a widow soon. And every one will say, 'How young she is to be a widow!' It will make me blush. But such things can't happen to me. No, he's all right. He came up here alone. They'd never have let him come up here alone if he hadn't been all right. Besides, he can walk. How silly I am!"

She bent down and kissed him passionately.

"I must have those bandages off, dearest," she whispered. "I suppose to-morrow I'd better return them to Mrs. Heath."

He muttered: "She said she always kept linen for bandages in the shop because they so often cut themselves. Now, I used to think in my innocence that butchers never cut themselves."

Very gently and intently Rachel unfastened two safety-pins that were hidden in Louis' untidy hair. Then she began to unwind a long strip of linen. It stuck to a portion of the cheek close to the ear. Louis winced. The inner folds of the linen were discoloured. Rachel had a glimpse of a wound....

"Go on!" Louis urged. "Get at it, child!"

"No," she said. "I think I shall leave it just as it is for the doctor to deal with. Shall you mind if I leave you for a minute? I must get some warm water and things ready against the doctor comes."

He retorted facetiously: "Oh! Do what you like! Work your will on me.... Doctor! Any one 'ud think I was badly injured. Why, you cuckoo, it's only skin wounds!"

"But doesn't it *hurt*?"

"Depends what you call hurt. It ain't a picnic."

"I think you're awfully brave," she said simply.

At the door she stopped and gazed at him, undecided.

"Louis," she said in a motherly tone, "I should like you to go to bed. I really should. You ought to, I'm sure."

"Well, I shan't," he replied.

"But please! To please me! You can get up again."

"Oh, go to blazes!" he cried resentfully. "What in thunder should I go to bed for, I should like to know? Have a little sense, do!" He shut his eyes.

He had never till then spoken to her so roughly.

"Very well," she agreed, with soothing acquiescence. His outburst had not irritated her in the slightest degree.

In the kitchen, as she bent over the kettle and the fire, each object was surrounded by a sort of halo, like the moon in damp weather. She brushed her hand across her eyes, contemptuous of herself. Then she ran lightly upstairs and searched out an old linen garment and tore the seams of it apart. She crept back to the parlour and peeped in. Louis had not moved on the sofa. His eyes were still closed. After a few seconds, he said, without stirring—

"I've not yet passed away. I can see you."

She responded with a little laugh, somewhat forced.

After an insupportable delay Mrs. Tams reappeared, out of breath. Dr. Yardley had just gone out, but he was expected back very soon and would then be sent down instantly.

Mrs. Tams, quite forgetful of etiquette, followed Rachel, unasked, into the parlour.

"What?" said Louis loudly. "Two of you! Isn't one enough?"

Mrs. Tams vanished.

"Heath took charge of the bikes," Louis murmured, as if to the ceiling.

Over half an hour elapsed before the gate creaked.

"There he is!" Rachel exclaimed happily. After having conceived a hundred different tragic sequels to the accident, she was lifted by the mere creak of the gate into a condition of pure optimism, and she realized what a capacity she had for secretly being a ninny in an unexpected crisis. But she thought with satisfaction: "Anyhow, I don't show it. That's one good thing!" She was now prepared to take oath that she had not for one moment been *really* anxious about Louis. Her demeanour, as she stated the case to the doctor, was a masterpiece of tranquil unconcern.

III

Dr. Yardley said that he was in a hurry—that, in fact, he ought to have been quite elsewhere at the time. He was preoccupied, and showed no sympathy with the innocent cyclist who had escaped the fatal menace of hoofs. When Rachel offered him the torn linen, he silently disdained it, and, opening a small bag which he had brought with him, produced therefrom a roll of cotton-wool in blue paper, and a considerable quantity of sticking-plaster on a brass reel. He accepted, however, Rachel's warm water.

"You might get me some Condy's Fluid," he said shortly.

She had none! It was a terrible lapse for a capable housewife.

Dr. Yardley raised his eyebrows: "No Condy's Fluid in the house!"

She was condemned.

"I do happen to have a couple of tablets of Chinosol," he said, "but I wanted to keep them in reserve for later in the day."

He threw two yellow tablets into the basin of water.

Then he laid Louis flat on the sofa, asked him a few questions, and sounded him in various parts. And at length he slowly, but firmly, drew off Mrs. Heath's bandages, and displayed Louis' head to the light.

"Hm!" he exclaimed.

Rachel restrained herself from any sound. But the spectacle was ghastly. The one particle of comfort in the dreadful matter was that Louis could not see himself.

Thenceforward Dr. Yardley seemed to forget that he ought to have been elsewhere. Working with extraordinary deliberation, he coaxed out of Louis' flesh sundry tiny stones and many fragments of mud, straightened twisted bits of skin, and he removed other pieces entirely. He murmured, "Hm!" at intervals. He expressed a brief criticism of the performance of Mrs. Heath, as distinguished from her intentions. He also opined that the great Greene might not perhaps have succeeded much better than Mrs. Heath, even if he had not been bilious. When the dressing was finished, the gruesome terror of Louis' appearance seemed to be much increased. The heroic sufferer rose and glanced at himself in the mirror, and gave a faint whistle.

"Oh! So that's what I look like, is it? Well, what price me as a victim of the Inquisition!" he remarked.

"I should advise you not to take exercise just now, young man," said the doctor. "D'you feel pretty well?"

"Pretty well," answered Louis, and sat down.

In the lobby the doctor, once more in a hurry, said to Rachel—

"Better get him quietly to bed. The wounds are not serious, but he's had a very severe shock."

"He's not marked for life, is he?" Rachel asked anxiously.

"I shouldn't think so," said the doctor, as if the point was a minor one. "Let him have some nourishment. You can begin with hot milk—but put some water to it," he added when he was half-way down the steps.

As Rachel re-entered the parlour she said to herself: "I shall just have to get him to bed somehow, whatever he says! If he's unpleasant he must *be* unpleasant, that's all."

And she hardened her heart. But immediately she saw him again, sitting forlornly in the chair, with the whole of the left side of his face criss-crossed in whitish-grey plaster, she was ready to cry over him and flatter his foolishest whim. She wanted to take him in her arms, if he would but have allowed her. She felt that she could have borne his weight for hours without moving, had he fallen asleep against her bosom.... Still, he must be got to bed. How negligent of the doctor not to have given the order himself!

Then Louis said: "I say! I think I may as well lie down!"

She was about to cry out, "Oh, you must!"

But she forbore. She became as wily as old Batchgrew.

"Do you think so?" she answered, doubtfully.

"I've nothing else particular on hand," he said.

She knew that he wanted to surrender without appearing to surrender.

"Well," she suggested, "will you lie down on the bed for a bit?"

"I think I will."

"And then I'll give you some hot milk."

She dared not help him to mount the stairs, but she walked close behind him.

"I was thinking," he said on the landing, "I'd stroll down and take stock of those bicycles later in the day. But perhaps I'm not fit to be seen."

She thought: "You won't stroll down later in the day—I shall see to that."

"By the way," he said, "you might send Mrs. Tams down to Horrocleave's to explain that I shan't give them my valuable assistance to-day.... Oh! Mrs. Tams"—the woman was just bustling out of the bedroom, duster in hand—"will you toddle down to the works and tell them I'm not coming?"

"Eh, mester!" breathed Mrs. Tams, looking at him. "It's a mercy it's no worse."

"Yes," Louis teased her, "but you go and look at the basin downstairs, Mrs. Tams. That'll give you food for thought."

Shaking her head, she smiled at Rachel, because the master had spirit enough to be humorous with her.

In the bedroom, Louis said, "I might be more comfortable if I took some of my clothes off."

Thereupon he abandoned himself to Rachel. She did as she pleased with him, and he never opposed. Seven bruises could be counted on his left side. He permitted himself to be formally and completely put to bed. He drank half a glass of hot milk, and then said that he could not possibly swallow any more. Everything had been done that ought to be done and that could be done. And Rachel kept assuring herself that there was not the least cause for anxiety. She also told herself that she had been a ninny once that morning, and that once was enough. Nevertheless, she remained apprehensive, and her apprehensions increased. It was Louis' unnatural manageableness that disturbed her.

And when, about three hours later, he murmured, "Old girl, I feel pretty bad."

"I knew it," she said to herself.

His complaint was like a sudden thunderclap in her ears, after long faint rumblings of a storm.

Towards tea-time she decided that she must send for the doctor again. Louis indeed demanded the doctor. He said that he was very ill. His bruised limbs and his damaged face caused him a certain amount of pain. It was not, however, the pain that frightened him, but a general and profound sensation of illness. He could describe no symptoms. There were indeed no symptoms save the ebbing of vitality. He said he had never in his life felt as he felt then. His appearance confirmed the statement. The look of his eyes was tragic. His hands were pale. His agonized voice was extremely distressing to listen to. The bandages heightened the whole sinister effect. Dusk shadowed the room. Rachel lit the gas and drew the blinds. But in a few moments Louis complained of the light, and she had to lower the jet.

The sounds of the return of Mrs. Tams could be heard below. Mrs. Tams had received instructions to bring the doctor back with her, but Rachel's ear caught no sign of the doctor. She went out to the head of the stairs. The doctor simply must be there. It was not conceivable that when summoned he should be "out" twice in one day, but so it was. Mrs. Tams, whispering darkly from the dim foot of the stairs, said that Mrs. Yardley hoped that he would be in shortly, but could not be sure.

"What am I to do?" thought Rachel. "This is a crisis. Everything depends on me. What shall I do? Shall I send for another doctor?" She decided to risk the chances and wait. It would be too absurd to have two doctors in the house. What would people say of her and of Louis, if the rumour ran that she had lost her head and filled the house with doctors when the case had no real gravity? People would say that she was very young and inexperienced, and a freshly married wife, and so on. And Rachel hated to be thought young or freshly married. Besides, another doctor might be "out" too. And further, the case could not be truly serious. Of course, if afterwards it did prove to be serious, she would never forgive herself.

"He'll be here soon," she said cheerfully, to Louis in the bedroom.

"If he isn't—" moaned Louis, and stopped.

She gave him some brandy, against his will. Then, taking his wrist to feel it, she felt his fingers close on her wrist, as if for aid. And she sat thus on the bed holding his hand in the gloom of the lowered gas.

IV

His weakness and his dependence on her gave her a feeling of kind superiority. And also her own physical well-being was such that she could not help condescending towards him. She cared for a trustful, helpless little dog. She thought a great deal about him; she longed ardently to be of assistance to him; she had an acute sense of her responsibility and her duty. Yet, notwithstanding all that, her brain was perhaps chiefly occupied with herself and her own attitude towards existence. She became mentally and imaginatively active to an intense degree. She marvelled at existence as she had never marvelled before, and while seeming suddenly to understand it better she was far more than ever baffled by it. Was it credible that the accident of a lad losing control of a horse could have such huge and awful consequences on two persons utterly unconnected with the lad? A few seconds sooner, a few seconds later—and naught would have occurred to Louis, but he must needs be at exactly a certain spot at exactly a certain instant, with the result that now she was in torture! If this, if that, if the other—Louis would have been well and gay at that very moment, instead of a broken organism humiliated on a bed and clinging to her like a despairing child.

The rapidity and variety of events in her life again startled her, and once more she went over them. The disappearance of the bank-notes was surely enough in itself. But on the top of that fell the miracle of her love affair. Her marriage was like a dream of romance to her, untrue, incredible. Then there was the terrific episode of Julian on the previous night. One would have supposed that after that the sensationalism of events would cease. But, no! The unforeseeable had now occurred, something which reduced all else to mere triviality.

And yet what had in fact occurred? Acquaintances, in recounting her story, would say that she had married her mistress's nephew, that there had been trouble between Louis and Julian about some bank-notes, and that Louis had had a bicycle accident. Naught more! A most ordinary chronicle! And if he died now, they would say that Louis had died within a month of the wedding and how sad it was! Husbands indubitably do die, young wives indubitably are transformed into widows—daily event, indeed!... She seemed to perceive the deep, hidden meaning of life. There were three Rachels in her—one who pitied Louis, one who pitied herself, and one who looked on and impartially comprehended. The last was scarcely unhappy— only fervently absorbed in the prodigious wonder of the hour.

"Can't you do anything?" Louis murmured.

"If Dr. Yardley doesn't come quick, I shall send for some other doctor," she said, with decision.

He sighed.

"Better send for a lawyer at the same time," he said.

"A lawyer?"

"Yes. You know I've not made my will."

"Oh, Louis! Please don't talk like that! I can't bear to hear you."

"You'll have to hear worse things than that," he said pettishly, loosing her hand. "I've got to have a solicitor here. Later on you'll probably be only too glad that I had enough common sense to send for a solicitor. Somebody must have a little common sense. I expect you'd better send for Lawton.... Oh! It's Friday afternoon—he'll have left early for his week-end golf, I bet." This last discovery seemed to exhaust his courage.

In another minute the doctor, cheerful and energetic, was actually in the room, and the gas brilliant. He gazed at an exanimate Louis, made a few inquiries and a few observations of his own, gave some brief instructions, and departed. The day was in truth one of his busy days.

He seemed surprised when Rachel softly called to him on the stairs.

"I suppose everything's all right, doctor?"

"Yes," said he casually. "He'll feel mighty queer for a few days. That's all."

"Then there's no danger?"

"Certainly not."

"But he thinks he's dying."

Dr. Yardley smiled carelessly.

"And do you?... He's no more dying than I am. That's only the effect of the shock. Didn't I tell you this morning? You probably won't be able to stop him just yet from thinking he's dying—it is a horrid feeling—but you needn't think so yourself, Mrs. Fores." He smiled.

"Oh, doctor," she burst out, "you don't know how you've relieved me!"

"You'll excuse me if I fly away," said Dr. Yardley calmly. "There's a crowd of insurance patients waiting for me at the surgery."

V

In the middle of the night Rachel was awakened by Louis' appeal. She was so profoundly asleep that for a few moments she could not recall what it was that had happened during the previous day to cause her anxiety.

After the visit of the doctor, Louis' moral condition had apparently improved. He had affected to be displeased by the doctor's air of treating his case as though it was deprived of all importance. He had said that the doctor had failed to grasp his case. He had stated broadly that in these days of State health insurance all doctors were too busy and too wealthy to be of assistance to private patients capable of paying their bills in the old gentlemanly fashion. But his remarks had not been without a touch of facetiousness in their wilful disgust. And the mere tone of his voice proved that he felt better. To justify his previous black pessimism he had of course been obliged to behave in a certain manner (well known among patients who have been taking themselves too seriously), and Rachel had understood and excused. She would have been ready, indeed, to excuse for worse extravagances than any that could have occurred to the fancy of a nature so polite and benevolent as that of Louis; for, in order to atone for her silly school-girlishness, she had made a compact with herself to be an angel and a serpent simultaneously for the entire remainder of her married life.

Then Mrs. Tams had come in, from errands of marketing, with a copy of the early special of the *Signal*, containing a description of the accident. Mrs. Tams had never before bought such a thing as a newspaper, but an acquaintance of hers who "stood the market" with tripe and chitterlings had told her that Mr. Fores was "in" the *Signal*, and accordingly she had bravely stopped a news-boy in the street and made the purchase. To Rachel she pointed out the paragraph with pride, and to please her and divert Louis, Rachel had introduced the newspaper into the bedroom. The item was headed: "Runaway Horses in Bursley Market-place. Providential Escape." It spoke of Mr. Louis Fores' remarkable skill and presence of mind in swerving away with two bicycles. It said that Mr. Louis Fores was an accomplished cyclist, and that after a severe shaking Mr. Louis Fores drove home in a taxicab "apparently little the worse, save for facial contusions, for his perilous adventure." Lastly, it said that a representative of the Midland Railway had "assured our representative that the horses were not the property of the Midland Railway." Louis had sardonically repeated the phrase "apparently little the worse," murmuring it with his eyes shut. He had said, "I wish they could see me." Still, he had made no further mention of sending for a solicitor. He had taken a little food and a little drink. He had asked Rachel when she meant to go to bed. And at length Rachel, having first arranged food for use in the night, and fixed a sheet of note-paper on the gas-bracket as a screen between the gas and Louis, had undressed and got into bed, and gone off into a heavy slumber with a mind comparatively free.

In response to his confusing summons, she stumbled to her peignoir and slipped it on.

"Yes, dear?" she spoke softly.

"I couldn't bear it any longer," said the voice of Louis. "I just had to waken you."

She raised the gas, and her eyes blinked as she stared at him. His bedclothes were horribly disarranged.

"Are you in pain?" she asked, smoothing the blankets.

"No. But I'm so ill. I—I don't want to frighten you—"

"The doctor said you'd feel ill. It's the shock, you know."

She stroked his hand. He did indubitably look very ill. His appearance of woe, despair, and dreadful apprehension was pitiable in the highest degree. With a gesture of intense weariness he declined food, nor could she persuade him to take anything whatever.

"You'll be ever so much better to-morrow. I'll sit up with you. You were bound to feel worse in the night."

"It's more than shock that I've got," he muttered. "I say, Rachel, it's all up with me. I *know* I'm done for. You'll have to do the best you can."

The notion shot through her head that possibly, after all, the doctor might have misjudged the case. Suppose Louis were to die in the night? Suppose the morning found her a widow? The world was full of the strangest happenings.... Then she was herself again and immovably cheerful in her secret heart. She thought: "I can go through worse nights than this. One night, some time in the future, either he will really be dying or I shall. This night is nothing." And she held his hand and sat in her old place on his bed. The room was chilly. She decided that in five minutes she would light the gas-stove, and also make some tea with the spirit-lamp. She would have tea whether he still refused or not. His watch on the night-table showed half-past two. In about an hour the dawn would be commencing. She felt that she had reserves of force against any contingency, against any nervous strain.

Then he said, "I say, Rachel."

He was too ill to call her "Louise."

"I shall make some tea soon," she answered.

He went on: "You remember about that missing money—I mean before auntie died. You remember—"

"Don't talk about that, dear," she interrupted him eagerly. "Why should you bother about that now?"

In one instant those apparently exhaustless reserves of moral force seemed to have ebbed away. She had imagined herself equal to any contingency, and now there loomed a contingency which made her quail.

"I've got to talk about that," he said in his weak and desperate voice. His bruised head was hollowed into the pillow, and he stared monotonously at the ceiling, upon which the paper screen of the gas threw a great trembling shadow. "That's why I wakened you. You don't know what the inside of my brain's like.... Why did you say to them you found the scullery door open that night? You know perfectly well it wasn't open."

She could scarcely speak.

"I—I—Louis don't talk about that now. You're too ill," she implored.

"I know why you said it."

"Be quiet!" she said sharply, and her voice broke.

But he continued in the same tone—

"You made up that tale about the scullery door because you guessed I'd collared the money and you wanted to save me from being suspected. Well, I did collar the money! Now I've told you!"

She burst into a sob, and her head dropped on to his body.

"Louis!" she cried passionately, amid her sobs. "Why ever did you tell me? You've ruined everything now. Everything!"

"I can't help that," said Louis, with a sort of obstinate and defiant weariness. "It was on my mind, and I just had to tell you. You don't seem to understand that I'm dying."

Rachel jumped up and sprang away from the bed.

"Of course you're not dying!" she reproached him. "How can you imagine such things?"

Her heart suddenly hardened against him—against his white-bandaged head and face, against his feeble voice of a beaten martyr. It seemed to her disgraceful that he, a strong male creature, should be lying there damaged, helpless, and under the foolish delusion that he was dying. She recalled with bitter gusto the tone in which the doctor had said, "He's no more dying than I am!" All her fears that the doctor might be wrong had vanished away. She now resented her husband's illness; as a nurse, when danger is over, will resent a patient's long convalescence, somehow charging it to him as a sin.

"I found the other half of the notes under the chair on the—" Louis began again.

"Please!" she objected with quick resounding violence, and raised a hand.

He said—

"You must listen."

She answered, passionately—

"I won't listen! I won't listen! And if you don't stop I shall leave the room! I shall leave you all alone!... Yes, I shall!" She moved a little towards the door.

His gloomy and shifty glance followed her, and there was a short silence.

"You needn't work yourself up into such a state," murmured Louis at length. "But I *should* like to know whether the scullery door was open or not, when you came downstairs that night?"

Rachel's glance fell. She blushed. The tears had ceased to drop from her eyes. She made no answer.

"You see," said Louis, with a half-sneering triumph, "I knew jolly well it wasn't open. So did old Batchgrew know, too."

She shut her lips together, went decisively to the mantelpiece, struck a match, and lit the stove. Like the patent gas-burner downstairs, the stove often had to be extinguished after the first lighting and lighted again with a second and different kind of explosion. And so it was now. She flung down the match pettishly into the hearth. Throughout the whole operation she sniffed convulsively, to prevent a new fit of sobbing. Her peignoir being very near to the purple-green flames that folded themselves round the asbestos of the stove, she reflected that the material was probably inflammable, and that a careless movement might cause it to be ignited. "And not a bad thing, either!" she said to herself. Then, without looking at all towards the bed, she lit the spirit-lamp in order to make tea. The sniffing continued, as she went through the familiar procedure.

The water would not boil, demonstrating the cruel truth of proverbs. She sat down and, gazing into the stove, now a rich red, ignored the saucepan. The dry heat from the stove burnt her ankles and face. Not a sound from the small saucepan, balanced on its tripod over the wavering blue flame of the spirit-lamp! At last, uncontrollably impatient, she lifted the teapot off the inverted lid of the saucepan, where she had placed it to warm, and peered into the saucepan. The water was cheerfully boiling! She made the tea, and sat down again to wait until it should be infused. She had to judge the minutes as well as she could, for she would not go across to the night-table to look at Louis' watch; her own was out of order, and so was the clock. She counted two hundred and fifty, and then, anticipating feverishly the tonic glow of the tea in her breast, she poured out a cup. Only colourless steaming water came forth from the pot. She had forgotten to put in the tea! Misfortune not unfamiliar to dazed makers of tea in the night! But to Rachel now the consequences of the omission seemed to amount to a tragedy. Had she the courage to begin the interminable weary process afresh? She was bound to begin it afresh. With her eyes obscured by tears, she put the water back into the saucepan and searched for the match-box. The water boiled almost immediately, and by so doing comforted her.

While waiting for the infusion, she realized little by little that for a few moments she must have been nearly hysterical, and she partially resumed possession of herself. The sniffing ceased, her vision cleared; she grew sardonic. All her chest was filled with cold lead. "This truly is the end," she thought. She had thought that Julian's confession must be the end of the violent experiences which had befallen her in Mrs. Malden's house. Then she had thought that Louis' accident must be the end. Each time she had been mistaken. But she could not be mistaken now. No conceivable event, however awful, could cap Louis' confession that he had thieved—and under such circumstances!

She did not drink the first cup of tea. No! She must needs carry it, spilling it, to Louis in bed. He was asleep, or he was in a condition that resembled sleep. Assuredly he was ill. He made a dreadful object in his bandages amid the disorder of the bed, upon which strong shadows fell from the gas and from the stove. No matter! If he was ill, he was ill. So much the worse for him! He was not dangerously ill. He was merely passing through a stress which had to be passed through. It would soon be over, and he would be the same eternal Louis that he had always been.

"Here!" she said.

He stirred, opened his eyes.

"Here's some tea!" she said coldly. "Drink it."

He gave a gesture of dissent. But it was useless. She had brewed the tea and had determined that he should drink a cup. Whether he desired it or loathed it was a question irrelevant. He was appointed to drink some tea, and she would not taste until he had drunk. This self-sacrifice was her perverse pleasure.

"Come!... Please don't make it any more awkward for me."

With her right arm she raised the pillow and his head on it. He drank, his sick lips curling awkwardly upon the rim of the cup, which she held for him. When he had drunk, she put the cup down on the night-table, and tidied his bed, as though he had been a naughty child. And then she left him, and drank tea slowly, savouringly, by herself in a chair near the dressing-table, out of the same cup.

VI

She had lied about the scullery door being open when she went downstairs on the night of the disappearance of the bank-notes. The scullery door had not been open. The lie was clumsy, futile, ill-considered. It had burst out of the impulsiveness and generosity of her nature. She had perceived that suspicion was falling, or might fall, upon Louis Fores, and the sudden lie had flashed forth to defend him. That she could ultimately be charged with having told the lie in order to screen herself from suspicion had never once occurred to her. And it did not even occur to her now as she sat perched uncomfortably on the chair in the night of desolation. She was now deeply ashamed of the lie—and she ought not to have been ashamed, for it was a lie magnanimous and fine; she might rather have taken pride in it. She was especially ashamed of her repetition of the lie on the following day to Thomas Batchgrew, and of her ingenious embroidery upon it. She hated to remember that she had wept violently in front of Thomas Batchgrew when he had charged her with having a secret about the loss of the notes. He must have well known that she was lying; he must have suspected her of some complicity; and if later he had affected to ignore all the awkward aspects of the episode it was only because he wished to remain on good terms with Louis for his own ends.

Had she herself all the time suspected Louis? In the harsh realism of the night hours she was not able positively to assert that she had never suspected him until after Julian's confession had made her think; but, on the other hand, she would not directly accuse herself of having previously suspected him. The worst that she could say was that she had been determined to believe him guiltless. She loved him; she had wanted his love; she would permit nothing to prevent their coming together; and so in her mind she had established his innocence apparently beyond any overthrowing. She might have allowed herself to surmise that in the early past he had been naughty, untrustworthy, even wicked—but that was different, that did not concern her. His innocence with regard to the bank-notes alone mattered. And she had been genuinely convinced of it. A few moments before he kissed her for the first time, she had been genuinely convinced of it. And after the betrothal her conviction became permanent. She tried to scorn now the passion which had blinded her. Mrs. Maldon, at any rate, must have known that he was connected with the disappearance of the notes. In the light of Louis' confession Rachel could see all that Mrs. Maldon was implying in that last conversation between them.

So that she might win him she had been ready to throttle every doubt of his honesty. But now the indubitable fact that he was a thief seemed utterly monstrous and insupportable. And, moreover, his crime was exceptionally cruel. Was it conceivable that he could so lightly cause so much distress of spirit to a woman so aged, defenceless, and kind? According to the doctor, the shock of the robbery had not been the originating cause of Mrs. Maldon's death; but it might have been; quite possibly it had hastened death.... Louis was not merely a thief; he was a dastardly thief.

But even that in her eyes did not touch the full height of his offence. The vilest quality in him was his capacity to seem innocent. She could recall the exact tone in which he had exclaimed: "Would you believe that old Batch practically accused me of stealing the old lady's money?... Don't you think it's a shame?" The recollection filled her with frigid anger. Her resentment of the long lie which he had lived in her presence since their betrothal was tremendous in its calm acrimony. A man who could behave as he had behaved would stop at nothing, would be capable of all.

She contrasted his conduct with the grim candour of Julian Maldon, whom she now admired. It was strange and dreadful that both the cousins should be thieves; the prevalence of thieves in that family gave her a shudder. But she could not judge Julian Maldon severely. He did not appear to her as a real thief. He had committed merely an indiscretion. It was his atonement that made her admire him. Though she hated confessions, though she had burnt his exasperating document, she nevertheless liked the manner of his atonement. Whereas she contemned Louis for having confessed.

"He thought he was dying and so he confessed!" she reflected with asperity. "He hadn't even the pluck to go through with what he had begun.... Ah! If I had committed a crime and once denied it, I would deny it with my last breath, and no torture should drag it out of me!"

And she thought: "I am punished. This is my punishment for letting myself be engaged while Mrs. Maldon was dying."

Often she had dismissed as childish the notion that she was to blame for accepting Louis just when she did. But now it returned full of power and overwhelmed her. And like a whipped child she remembered Mrs. Maldon's warning: "My nephew is not to be trusted. The woman who married him would suffer horribly." And she was the woman who had married him. It seemed to her that the warnings of the dying must of necessity prove to be valid.

Some mysterious phenomenon on the window-blind at her right hand attracted her attention, and she looked round, half startled. It was the dawn, furtive and inexorable. She had watched dawns, and she had watched them in that very bedroom. Only on the previous morning the dawn had met her smarting and wakeful eyes, and she had imagined that no dawn could be more profoundly sad!... And a little earlier still she had been desolating herself for hours because Louis was going to be careless about his investments, because he was unreliable and she would have to watch ceaselessly over his folly. She had imagined then that no greater catastrophe could overtake her than some material result of his folly!... What a trivial apprehension! What a child she had been!

In the excitement and alarm of his accident she had honestly forgotten her suspicions of him. That disconcerted her.

She rose from the chair, stiff. The stove, with its steady faint roar of imperfectly consumed gas, had thoroughly heated the room. In careful silence she put the tea-things together. Then she ventured to glance at Louis.

He was asleep. He had been restlessly asleep for a long time. She eyed him bitterly in his bandages. Only last night she had been tormented by that fear that his face might be marked for life. Again the trivial! What did it matter whether his face was marked for life or not?...

It did not occur to her to attempt to realize how intense must have been the spiritual tribulation which had forced him to confess. She knew that he was not dying, that he was in no danger whatever, and she was perfectly indifferent to the genuineness of his own conviction that he was dying. She simply thought: "He had to go through all that. If he fancied he was dying, can I help it?" ... Then she looked at her own empty bed. He reposed; he slept. But she did not repose nor sleep.

She drew aside one of the blinds, and as she did so she could feel the steady slight current of cold air entering the room from the window open at the top. The street seemed to be full of daylight. The dawn had been proceeding in its vast secrecy and was now accomplished. She drew up the blind slowly, and then the gas-flame over the dressing-table seemed so pale and futile that she extinguished it, from a sort of pity. In silence she pulled out the iron bolts in the window-sash that had been Mrs. Maldon's device for preventing burglars from opening further a window already open a little, thus combining security with good hygiene. Louis had laughed at these bolts, but Mrs. Maldon had so instilled their use into both Rachel and Mrs. Tams that to insert them at night was part of the unchangeable routine of the house. Rachel gently pushed up the lower sash and looked forth.

Bycars Lane, though free from mud, was everywhere heavily bedewed. The narrow pavement glistened. The roofs glistened. Drops of water hung on all the edges of the great gas-lamp beneath her, which was still defying the dawn. The few miserable trees and bushes on the vague lands beyond the lane were dripping with water. The sky was low and heavy, in scarcely distinguishable shades of purplish grey, and Bycars Pool, of which she had a glimpse, appeared in its smooth blackness to be not more wet than the rest of the scene. Nothing stirred. Not the tiniest branch stirred on the leafless trees, nor a leaf on a grey rhododendron-bush in a front garden below. Every window within sight had its blind drawn. No smoke rose from any house-chimney, and the distant industrial smoke on the horizon hung in the lower air, just under the clouds, undecided and torpid. The wet air was moveless, and yet she could feel it impinging with its cool, sharp humidity on her cheek.

The sensation of this contact was delicious. She was surrounded, not by the slatternly Five Towns landscape and by the wretchedness of the familiar bedroom, but by the unanswerable, intimidating, inspiring mystery of life itself. A man came hurrying with a pole out of the western vista of the lane, and stopped in front of the gas-lamp, and in an instant the flame was reduced to a little fat worm of blue, and the man passed swiftly up the lane, looking straight ahead with bent shoulders, and was gone. Never before had Rachel actually seen the lamp put out. Never before had she noticed, as she noticed now, that the lamp had a number, an identity—1054. The meek acquiescence of the lamp, and the man's preoccupied haste, seemed to bear some deep significance, which, however, she could not seize. But the aspect of the man afflicted her, she did not know why.

Then a number of other figures, in a long spasmodic procession, passed up the lane after the man, and were gone out of sight. Their heavy boots clacked on the pavement. They wore thick, dirty greyish-black clothes, but no overcoats; small tight caps in their hands, and dark kerchiefs round their necks: about thirty of them in all, colliers on their way to one of the pits on the Moorthorne ridge. They walked quickly, but they did not hurry as their forerunner hurried. Several of them smoked pipes. Though some walked in pairs, none spoke; none looked up or aside. With one man walked stolidly a young woman, her overskirt raised and pulled round her head from the back for a shawl; but even these two did not converse. The procession closed with one or two stragglers. Rachel had never seen these pilgrims before, but she had heard them; and Mrs. Maldon had been acquainted with all their footfalls. They were tragic to Rachel; they infected her with the most recondite horror of existence; they left tragedy floating behind them in the lane like an invisible but oppressive cloud. Their utterly incurious indifference to Rachel in her peignoir at the window was somehow harrowing.

The dank lane and vaporous, stagnant landscape were once more dead and silent, and would for a long time remain so, for though potters begin work early, colliers begin work much earlier, living in a world of customs of their own. At last a thin column of smoke issued magically from a chimney down to the left. Some woman was about; some woman's day had opened within that house. At the thought of that unseen woman in that unknown house Rachel could have cried. She could not remain at the window. She was unhappy; but it was not her woe that overcame her, for if she was unhappy, her unhappiness was nevertheless exquisite. It was the mere realization that men and women lived that rendered her emotions almost insupportable. She felt her youth. She thought, "I am only a girl, and yet my life is ruined already." And even that thought she hugged amorously as though it were beautiful. Amid the full disaster and regret, she was glad to be alive. She could not help exulting in the dreadful moment.

She closed the sash and began to dress, seldom glancing at Louis, who slept and dreamed and muttered. When she was dressed she looked carefully in the drawer where he deposited certain articles from his pockets, in order to find the bundle of notes left by Julian. In vain! Then she searched for his bunch of keys (which ultimately she found in one of his pockets) and unlocked his private drawer. The bundle of notes lay there. She removed it, and hid it away in one of her own secret places. After she had made preparations to get ready some invalid's food at short notice, she went downstairs.

VII

She went downstairs without any definite purpose—merely because activity of some kind was absolutely necessary to her. The clock in the lobby showed dimly a quarter past five. In the chilly twilit kitchen the green-lined silver-basket lay on the table in front of the window, placed there by a thoughtful and conscientious Mrs. Tams. On the previous morning Rachel had given very precise orders about the silver (as the workaday electro-plate was called), but owing to the astounding events of the day the orders had not been executed. Mrs. Tams had evidently determined to carry them out at an early hour.

Rachel opened a cupboard and drew forth the apparatus for cleaning. She was intensely fatigued, weary, and seemingly spiritless, but she began to clean the silver—at first with energy and then with serious application. She stood at the table, cleaning, as she had stood there when Louis came into her kitchen on the night of the robbery; and she thought of his visit and of her lost bliss, and the tears fell from her eyes on the newspaper which protected the whiteness of the scrubbed table. She would not think of the future; could not. She went on cleaning, and that silver had never been cleaned as she cleaned it then. She cleaned it with every attribute of herself, forgetting her fatigue. The tears dried on her cheek. The faithful, scrupulous work either drugged or solaced her. Just as she was finishing, Mrs. Tarns, with her immense bodice unfastened, came downstairs, apronless. The lobby clock struck six.

"Eh, missis!" breathed Mrs. Tams. "What's this?"

Rachel gave a nervous laugh.

"I was up. Mr. Fores was asleep, and I had to do something, so I thought—"

"Has he had a good night, ma'am?"

"Fair. Yes, pretty good. I must run up and see if he is awake."

Mrs. Tams saw the stains on Rachel's cheeks, but she could not mention them. Rachel had an impulse to fall on Mrs. Tams' enormous breast and weep. But the conventions of domesticity were far too strong for her also. Mrs. Tams was the general servant; what Louis occasionally called "the esteemed skivvy." Once Mrs. Tams had been wife, mother, grandmother, victim, slave, diplomatist, serpent, heroine. Once she had bent from morn till night under the terrific weight of a million perils and responsibilities. Once she could never be sure of her next meal, or the roof over her head, or her skin, or even her bones. Once she had been the last resource and refuge not merely of a house, but of half a street, and she had had a remedy for every ill, a balm for every wound. But now she was safe, out of harm's way. She had no responsibilities worth a rap. She had everything an old woman ought to desire. And yet the silly old woman felt a lack, as she impotently watched Rachel leave the kitchen. Perhaps she wanted her eye blacked, or the menace of a policeman, or a child down with diphtheria, to remind her that the world revolved.

CHAPTER XIII
DEAD-LOCK

I

Louis had wakened up a few minutes before Rachel returned to the bedroom from that most wonderfully conscientious spell of silver-cleaning. He was relieved to find himself alone. He was ill, perhaps very ill, but he felt unquestionably better than in the night. He was delivered from the appalling fear of death which had tortured and frightened him, and his thankfulness was intense; and yet at the same time he was aware of a sort of heroical sentimental regret that he was not, after all, dead; he would almost have preferred to die with grandeur, young, unfortunate, wept for by an inconsolable wife doomed to everlasting widowhood. He was ashamed of his bodily improvement, which rendered him uncomfortably self-conscious, for he had behaved as though dying when, as the event proved, he was not dying.

When Rachel came in, this self-consciousness grew terrible. And in his weakness, his constraint, his febrile perturbation which completely destroyed presence of mind, he feebly remarked—

"Did any one call yesterday to ask how I was?"

As soon as he had said it he knew that it was inept, and quite unsuitable to the role which he ought to play.

Rachel had gone straight to the dressing-table, apparently ignoring him, though she could not possibly have failed to notice that he was awake. She turned sharply and gazed at him with a look of inimical contempt that aggrieved and scarified him very acutely. Making no answer to his query, content solely to condemn it with her eyes as egotistic and vain, she said—

"I'm going to make you some food."

And then she curtly showed him her bent back, and over the foot of the bed he could see her preparations—preliminary stirring with a spoon, the placing of the bright tin saucepan on the lamp, the opening of the wick, seizing of the match-box.

As soon as the cooking was in train, she threw up the window wide and then came to the bed.

"I'll just put your bed to rights again," she remarked, and seized the pillow, waiting implacably for him to raise his head. He had to raise his head.

"I'm very ill," he moaned.

She replied in a tone of calm indifference—

"I know you are. But you'll soon be better. You're getting a little better every hour." And she finished arranging the bed, which was presently in a state of smooth geometrical correctness. He could find no fault with her efficiency, nor with her careful handling of his sensitive body. But the hard, the marmoreal cruelty of his wife's spirit exquisitely wounded his soul, which, after all, was at least as much in need of consolation as his body. He was positively daunted.

II

He had passed through dreadful moments in the early part of the night while Rachel slept. When he had realized that he was doomed—for the conviction that death was upon him had been absolutely sincere and final for a long time—he was panic-stricken, impressed, and strangely proud, all at once. But the panic was paramount. He was afraid, horribly afraid. His cowardice was ghastly, even to himself, shot through though it was by a peculiar appreciation of the grandiosity of his fate as a martyr to clumsy chance. He was reduced by it to the trembling repentant sinner, as the proud prisoner is reduced to abjection by prolonged and secret torture in Oriental prisons. He ranged in fright over the whole of his career, and was obliged to admit, and to admit with craven obsequiousness, that he had been a wicked man, obstinate in wickedness.

He remembered matters which had utterly vanished from his memory. He remembered, for example, the excellence of his moral aspirations when he had first thought of Rachel as a wife, and the firm, high resolves which were to be carried out if he married her. Forgotten! Forgotten! As soon as he had won her he had thought of nothing but self-indulgence, pleasure, capricious delights. His tailor still languished for money long justly due.

He had not even restored the defalcations in Horrocleave's petty cash. Of course it would have been difficult to restore a sum comparatively so large without causing suspicion. To restore it would have involved a long series of minute acts, alterations of alterations in the cash entries, and constant ingenuity in a hundred ways. But it ought to have been done, and might have been done. It might have been done. He admitted that candidly, fully, with despicable tremblings....

And the worst of all, naturally, was the theft from his aunt. Theft? Was it a theft? He had never before consented to define the affair as a theft; it had been a misfortune, an indiscretion. But now he was ready to call it a theft, in order to be on the safe side. For the sake of placating Omnipotence let it be deemed a theft, and even a mean theft, entailing dire consequences on a weak old woman! Let it be as bad as the severest judge chose to make it! He would not complain. He would accept the arraignment (though really he had not been so blameworthy, etc....). He knew that with all his sins he, possessed the virtues of good nature, kindness, and politeness. He was not wholly vile. In some ways he honestly considered himself a model to mankind.

And then he had recalled certain information received in childhood from authoritative persons about the merciful goodness of God. His childhood had been rather ceremoniously religious, for his step-uncle, the Lieutenant-General, was a great defender of Christianity as well as of the British Empire. The Lieutenant-General had even written a pamphlet against a ribald iconoclastic book published by the Rationalist Press Association, in which pamphlet he had made a sorry mess of Herbert Spencer. All the Lieutenant-General's relatives and near admirers went to church, and they all went to precisely the same kind of church, for no other kind would have served. Louis, however, had really liked going to church. There had once even been a mad suggestion that he should become a choir-boy, but the Lieutenant-General had naturally decided that it was not meet for a child of breeding to associate with plebeians in order to chant the praises of the Almighty.

Louis at his worst had never quite ceased to attend church, though he was under the impression that his religious views had broadened, if not entirely changed. Beneath the sudden heavy menace of death he discovered that his original views were, after all, the most authentic and the strongest. And he had much longed for converse with a clergyman, who would repeat to him the beautiful reassurances of his infancy. Even late in the afternoon, hours before the supreme crisis, he would have welcomed a clergyman, for he was already beginning to be afraid. He would have liked a clergyman to drop in by accident; he would have liked the first advances to come from the clergyman.

But he could not bring himself to suggest that the rector of St. Luke's, of whose flock he now formed part, should be sent for. He had demanded a lawyer, and that was as near to a clergyman as he could get. He had been balked of the lawyer. Further on in the evening, when his need was more acute and his mind full of frightful secret apprehensions, he was as far as ever from obtaining a clergyman. And he knew that, though his eternal welfare might somehow depend on the priest, he could never articulate to Rachel the words, "I should like to see a clergyman." It would seem too absurd to ask for a clergyman.... Strangeness of the human heart!

It was after Rachel had fallen asleep that the idea of confession had occurred to him as a means towards safety in the future life. The example of Julian had inspired him. He had despised Julian; he had patronized Julian; but in his extremity he had been ready to imitate him. He seemed to conceive that confession before death must be excellent for the soul. At any rate, it prevented one from going down to the tomb with a lie tacit on the lips. He was very ill, very weak, very intimidated. And he was very solitary and driven in on himself—not so much because Rachel had gone to sleep as because neither Rachel nor anybody else would believe that he was really dying. His spirit was absorbed in the gravest preoccupations that can trouble a man. His need of sympathy and succour was desperate. Thus he had wakened Rachel. At first she had been as sympathetic and consoling as he could desire. She had held his hand and sat on the bed. The momentary relief was wonderful. And he had been encouraged to confess.

He had prodded himself on to confession by the thought that Rachel must have known of his guilt all along—otherwise she would never have told that senseless lie about the scullery door being open. Hence his confession could not surprise her. She would receive it in the right, loving, wifely attitude, telling him that he was making too much of a little, that it was splendid of him to confess, and generally exonerating and rehabilitating him.

Then he had begun to confess. The horrible change in her tone as he came to the point had unnerved him. Her wild sobs when the confession was made completed his dismay. And then, afterwards, her incredible harshness and cruelty, her renewed refusal, flat and disdainful, to believe that he was dying—these things were the most wounding experience of his entire existence. As for her refusal to listen to the rest of his story, the important part, the exculpatory part—it was monstrously unjust. He had had an instant's satisfaction on beholding her confusion at being charged with the lie about the scullery door, but it was a transient advantage. He was so ill.... She had bullied him with the lacerating emphasis of her taciturn remarks.... And at last she had requested him not to make it any more awkward for *her*!...

III

When he had obediently taken the food and thanked her for it very nicely, he felt much better. The desire for a clergyman, or even for a lawyer, passed away from his mind; he forgot the majority of his sins and his aspirations, and the need for restoring the defalcations to Jim Horrocleave seemed considerably less urgent. Rachel stayed by him while he ate, but she would not meet his glance, and looked carefully at the window.

"As soon as I've tidied up the room, I'll just sponge your hands," said she. "The doctor will be here early. I suppose I mustn't touch your face."

Louis inquired—

"How do you know he'll be here early?"

"He said he should—because of the dressings, you know."

She went to work on the room, producing a duster from somewhere, and ringing for Mrs. Tams, who, however, was not permitted to enter. Louis hated these preparations for the doctor. He had never in his life been able to understand why women were always so absurdly afraid of the doctor's eye. As if the doctor would care! Moreover, the room was being tidied for the doctor, not for the invalid! The invalid didn't matter! When she came to him with a bowl of water, soap, and a towel, he loathed the womanish scheme of being washed in bed.

"I'll get up," he said. "I'm lots better." He had previously intended to feign extreme illness, but he forgot.

"Oh no, you won't," she replied coldly. "First you think you're dying, and then you think you're all right. You won't stir out of that bed till the doctor's been, at any rate."

And she lodged the bowl dangerously between his knees. He pretended to be contemptuous of her refusal to let him get up, but in fact he was glad of an excuse for not making good his boast. His previous statement that he was very ill was much nearer to the truth than the fine talking about being "lots better." If not very ill, he was, at any rate, more ill than he now thought he was, and eating had fatigued him. Nevertheless, he would wash his own hands. Rachel yielded to him in this detail with cynical indifference. She put the towel by the bowl, and left him to balance the bowl and keep the soap off the counterpane as best he could, while she rummaged in one of the drawers of the wardrobe—obviously for the simple sake of rummaging.

Her unwifeliness was astounding; it was so astounding that Louis did not all at once quite realize how dangerously he was wounded by it. He had seen that hard, contumelious mask on her face several times before; he had seen it, for instance, when she had been expressing her views on Councillor Batchgrew; but he had not conceived, in his absurd male confidence, that it would ever be directed against himself. He could not snatch the mask from her face, but he wondered how he might pierce it, and incidentally hurt her and make her cry softly. Ah! He had seen her in moods of softness which were celestial to him—surpassing all dreams of felicity!

The conviction of his own innocence and victimhood strengthened in him. Amid the morbid excitations of the fear of death, he had forgotten that in strict truth he had not stolen a penny from his great-aunt, that he was utterly innocent. He now vividly remembered that his sole intention in taking possession of the bank-notes had been to teach his great-aunt a valuable lesson about care in the guarding of money. Afterwards he had meant to put the notes back where he had found them; chance had prevented; he had consistently acted for the best in very sudden difficulties, and after all, in the result, it was not he who was responsible for the destruction of the notes, but Rachel.... True, that in the night his vision of the affair had been less favourable to himself, but in the night illness had vitiated his judgment, which was not strange, seeing the dreadful accident he had experienced.... He *might* have died, and where would Rachel have been then?... Was it not amazing that a young wife who had just escaped widowhood so narrowly could behave to a husband, a seriously sick husband, as Rachel was behaving to him?

He wished that he had not used the word "collar" in confessing to Rachel. It was equal to "steal." Its significance was undebatable. Yes, "collar" was a grave error of phrasing.

"I'm about done with this basin thing," he said, with all possible dignity, and asked for brushes of various sorts for the completion of his toilet. She served him slowly, coolly. Her intention was clear to act as a capable but frigid nurse—not as a wife. He saw that she thought herself the wife of a thief, and that she was determined not to be the wife of a thief. He could not bear it. The situation must be changed immediately, because his pride was bleeding to death.

"I say," he began, when she had taken away the towel and his tooth-powder.

"What?" Her tone challenged him.

"You wouldn't let me finish last night. I just wanted to tell you that I didn't—"

"I've no wish to hear another word." She stopped him, precisely as she had stopped him in the night. She was at the washstand.

"I should be obliged if you'd look at me when you speak to me," he reproached her manners. "It's only polite."

She turned to him with face flaming. They were both aware that his deportment was better than hers; and he perceived that the correction had abraded her susceptibility.

"I'll look at you all right," she answered, curtly and rather loudly.

He adopted a superior attitude.

"Of course I'm ill and weak," he said, "but even if I am I suppose I'm entitled to some consideration." He lay back on the pillow.

"I can't help your being ill," she answered. "It's not my fault. And if you're so ill and weak as all that, it seems to me the best thing you can do is to be quiet and not to talk, especially about—about that!"

"Well, perhaps you'll let me be the best judge of what I ought to talk about. Anyhow, I'm going to talk about it, and you're going to listen."

"I'm not."

"I say you're going to listen," he insisted, turning on his side towards her. "And why not? Why, what on earth did I say last night, after all, I should like to know?"

"You said you'd taken the other part of the money of Mrs. Maldon's—that's what you said. You thought you were dying, and so you told me."

"That's just what I want to explain. I'm going to explain it to you."

"No explanations for me, thanks!" she sneered, walking in the direction of the hearth. "I'd sooner hear anything, anything, than your explanations." She seemed to shudder.

He nerved himself.

"I tell you I *found* that money," he cried, recommencing.

"Well, good-bye," she said, moving to the door. "You don't seem to understand."

At the same moment there was a knock at the door.

"Come in, Mrs. Tarns," said Rachel calmly.

"She mustn't come in now," Louis protested.

"Come in, Mrs. Tams," Rachel repeated decisively.

And Mrs. Tams entered, curtsying towards the bed.

"What is it?" Rachel asked her.

"It's the greengrocer's cart, ma'am." The greengrocer usually did send round on Saturday mornings.

"I'll go down. Just clear up that washstand, will you?"

It was remarkable to Louis how chance would favour a woman in an altercation. But he had decided, even if somewhat hysterically, to submit to no more delay, and to end the altercation—and moreover, to end it in his own way.

"Rachel!" he called. Several times he called her name, more and more loudly. He ignored what was due to servants, to greengrocers, and to the dignity of employers. He kept on calling.

"Shall I fetch missis, sir?" Mrs. Tams suggested at length.

He nodded. Mrs. Tams departed, laden. Certainly the fat creature, from whom nothing could be hid by a younger generation, had divined that strife had supervened on illness, and that great destinies hung upon the issue. Neither Mrs. Tams nor Rachel returned to the bedroom. Louis began again to call for Rachel, and then to yell for her. He could feel that the effort was exhausting him, but he was determined to vanquish her.

IV

Without a sound she startlingly appeared in the room.

"What's the matter?" she inquired, with her irritating assumption of tranquillity.

"You know what's the matter."

"I wish you wouldn't scream like a baby," she said.

"You know I want to speak to you, and you're keeping out of the way on purpose."

Rachel said—

"Look here, Louis! Do you want me to leave the house altogether?"

He thought—

"What is she saying? We've only been married a few weeks. This is getting serious."

Aloud he answered—

"Of course I don't want you to leave the house."

"Well, then, don't say any more. Because if you do, I shall. I've heard all I want to hear. There are some things I can bear, and some I can't bear."

"If you don't listen—!" he exclaimed. "I'm warning you!"

She glanced at the thief in him, and at the coward penitent of the night, with the most desolating disdain, and left the room. That was her answer to his warning.

"All right, my girl! All right!" he said to himself, when she had gone, pulling together his self-esteem, his self-pity, and his masculinity. "You'll regret this. You see if you don't. As to leaving the house, we shall see who'll leave the house. Wait till I'm on my legs again. If there is to be a scandal, there shall be a scandal."

One thing was absolutely sure—he could not and would not endure her contumely, nor even her indifferent scorn. For him to live with it would be ridiculous as well as impossible. He was weak, but two facts gave him enormous strength. First, he loved her less than she loved him, and hence she was at a disadvantage. But supposing her passion for him was destroyed? Then the second fact came into play. He had money. He had thousands of pounds, loose, available! To such a nature as his the control of money gives a sense of everlasting security. Already he dreamt of freedom, of roaming the wide world, subject to no yoke but a bachelor's whim.

CHAPTER XIV
THE MARKET

I

Rachel thought she understood all Louis' mental processes. With the tragic self-confidence of the inexperienced wife, she was convinced that she had nothing to learn about the secret soul of the stranger to whom she had utterly surrendered herself, reserving from him naught of the maiden. Each fresh revelation of him she imagined to be final, completing her studies. In fact, it would have taken at least ten years of marriage to prove to her that a perception of ignorance is the summit of knowledge. She had not even realized that human nature is chiefly made up of illogical and absurd contradictions. Thus she left the house that Saturday morning gloomy, perhaps hopeless, certainly quite undecided as to the future, but serene, sure of her immediate position, and sure that Louis would act like Louis. She knew that she had the upper hand, both physically and morally. The doctor had called and done his work, and given a very reassuring report. She left Louis to Mrs. Tams, as was entirely justifiable, merely informing him that she had necessary errands, and even this information she gave through her veil, a demure contrivance which she had adapted for the first time on her honeymoon. It was his role to accept her august decisions.

The forenoon was better than the dawn. The sun had emerged; the moisture had nearly disappeared, except in the road; and the impulse of spring was moving in the trees and in the bodies of young women; the sky showed a virginal blue; the wandering clouds were milky and rounded, the breeze infinitely soft. It seemed to be in an earlier age that the dark colliers had silently climbed the steep of Bycars Lane amid the dankness and that the first column of smoke had risen forlornly from the chimney.

In spite of her desolated heart, and of her primness, Rachel stepped forward airily. She was going forth to an enormous event, namely, her first apparition in the shopping streets of the town on a Saturday morning as Mrs. Louis Fores, married woman. She might have postponed it, but into what future? Moreover, she was ashamed of being diffident about it. And, in the peculiar condition of her mind, she would have been ashamed to let a spiritual crisis, however appalling, interfere with the natural, obvious course of her duties. So far as the world was concerned, she was a happy married woman, who had to make her debut as a shopping housewife, and hence she was determined that her debut should be made.... And yet, possibly she might not have ventured away from the house at all, had she not felt that if she did not escape for a time from its unbreathable atmosphere into the liberty of the streets, she would stifle and expire. Wherever she put herself in the house she could not feel alone. In the streets she felt alone, even when saluting new acquaintances and being examined and probed by their critical stare. The sight of these acquaintances reminded her that she had a long list of calls to repay. And then the system of paying calls and repaying, and the whole system of society, seemed monstrously fanciful and unreal to her. There was only one reality. The solid bricks of the pavement suddenly trembled under her feet as though she were passing over a suspension-bridge. The enterprise of shopping became idiotic, humorous, incredibly silly in the face of that reality.

Nevertheless, the social system of Bursley, as exemplified in Wedgwood Street and the market-place, its principal shopping thoroughfares, was extremely alluring, bright, and invigorating that morning. It almost intoxicated, and had, indeed, a similar effect to that of a sparkling drink. Rachel had never shopped at large with her own money before. She had executed commissions for Mrs. Maldon. She had been an unpaid housekeeper to her father and brother. Now she was shopping as mistress of a house and of money. She owed an account of her outlay to nobody, not even to Louis. She recalled the humble and fantastic Saturday night when she had shopped with Louis as reticule-carrier ... centuries since. The swiftness and unforeseeableness of events frightened the girl masquerading as a wise, perfected woman. Her heart lay like a weight in her corsage for an instant, and the next instant she was in the bright system again, because she was so young.

Here and there in the streets, and in small groups in the chief shops, you saw prim ladies of every age, each with a gloved hand clasped over a purse. (But sometimes the purse lay safe under the coverlet of a perambulator.) These purses made all the ladies equal, for their contents were absolutely secret from all save the owners. All the ladies were spending, and the delight of spending was theirs. And in theory every purse was inexhaustible. At any rate, it was impossible to conceive a purse empty. The system wore the face of the ideal. Manners were proper to the utmost degree; they neatly marked the equality of the shoppers and the profound difference between the shoppers and the shopkeepers. All ladies were agreeable, all babies in perambulators were darlings. The homes thus represented by ladies and babies were clearly polite homes, where reigned suavity, tranquillity, affection, and plenty. Civilization was justified in Wedgwood Street and the market-place—and also, to some extent, in St. Luke's Square.... And Rachel was one of these ladies. Her gloved hand closed over a purse exactly in the style of the others. And her purse, regard being had to the inheritance of her husband, was supposed to hide vast sums; so much so that ladies who had descended from distant heights in pony-carts gazed upon her with the respect due to a rival. All welcomed her into the exclusive, correct little world—not only the shopkeepers but the buyers therein. She represented youthful love. Her life must be, and was, an idyll! True, she had no perambulator, but middle-aged ladies greeted her with wistfulness in their voices and in their eyes.

She smiled often as she told and retold the story of Louis' accident, and gave positive assurances that he was in no danger, and would not bear a scar. She blushed often. She was shyly happy in her unhappiness. The experience alternated between the unreal and the real. The extraordinary complexity of life was beginning to put its spell on her. She could not determine the relative values of the various facets of the experience.

When she had done the important parts of her business, she thought she would go into the covered market, which, having one entrance in the market-place and another in Wedgwood Street, connects the two thoroughfares. She had never been into the covered market because Mrs. Maldon had a prejudice against its wares. She went out of mere curiosity, just to enlarge her knowledge of her adopted town. The huge interior, with its glazed roof, was full of clatter, shouting, and the smell of innumerable varieties of cheese. She passed a second-hand bookstall without seeing it, and then discerned admirable potatoes at three-halfpence a peck less than she had been paying—and Mrs. Maldon was once more set down as an old lady with peculiarities. However, by the time Rachel had made a critical round of the entire place, with its birds in cages, popular songs at a penny, sweetstuffs, cheap cottons and woollens, bright tinware, colonial fleshmeat, sausage displays, and particularly its cheeses, Mrs. Maldon was already recovering her reputation as a woman whose death was an irreparable loss to the town.

As Rachel passed the negligible second-hand bookstall again, it was made visible to her by the fact that Councillor Thomas Batchgrew was just emerging from the shop behind it, with a large volume in his black-gloved hands. Thomas Batchgrew came out of the dark bookshop as a famous old actor, accustomed to decades of crude public worship, comes out of a fashionable restaurant into a fashionable thoroughfare. His satisfied and self-conscious countenance showed that he knew that nearly everybody in sight was or ought to be acquainted with his identity and his renown, and showed also that his pretence of being unaware of this tremendous and luscious fact was playful and not seriously meant to deceive a world of admirers. He was wearing a light tweed suit, with a fancy waistcoat and a hard, pale-grey hat. As he aged, his tendency to striking pale attire was becoming accentuated; at any rate, it had the advantage of harmonizing with his unique whiskers—those whiskers which differentiated him from all the rest of the human race in the Five Towns.

Rachel blushed, partly because he was suddenly so close to her, partly because she disapproved of the cunning expression on his red, seamed face and was afraid he might divine her thoughts, and partly because she recalled the violent things she had said against him to Louis. But as soon as Thomas Batchgrew caught sight of her the expression of his faced changed in an instant to one of benevolence and artless joy; the change in it was indeed dramatic.

And Rachel, pleased and flattered, said to herself, almost startled—

"He really admires me. And I do believe he always did."

And since admiration is a sweet drug, whether offered by a rascal or by the pure in heart, she forgot momentarily the horror of her domestic dilemma.

II

"Eh, lass!" Thomas Batchgrew was saying familiarly, after he had inquired about Louis, "I'm rare glad for thy sake it was no worse." His frank implication that he was glad only for her sake gratified and did not wound her as a wife.

The next moment he had dismissed the case of Louis and was displaying to her the volume which he carried. It was a folio Bible, printed by the Cornishman Tregorthy in the town of Bursley, within two hundred yards of where they were standing, in the earliest years of the nineteenth century—a bibliographical curiosity, as Thomas Batchgrew vaguely knew, for he wet his gloved thumb and, resting the book on one raised knee, roughly turned over several pages till he came to the title-page containing the word "Bursley," which he showed with pride to Rachel. Rachel, however, not being in the slightest degree a bibliophile, discerned no interest whatever in the title-page. She merely murmured with politeness, "Oh, yes! Bursley," while animadverting privately on the old man's odious trick of wetting his gloved thumb and leaving marks on the pages.

"The good old Book!" he said. "I've been after that volume for six months and more. I knew I should get it, but he's a stiff un—yon is," jerking his shoulder in the direction of the second-hand bookseller. Then he put the folio under his arm, delighted at the souvenir of having worsted somebody in a bargain, and repeated, "The good old Book!"

Rachel reflected—

"You unspeakable old sinner!"

Still, she liked his attitude towards herself. In addition to the book he insisted on carrying a small white parcel of hers which she had not put into the reticule. They climbed the steps out of the covered market and walked along the market-place together. And Rachel unmistakably did find pleasure in being seen thus with the great and powerful, if much criticized, Thomas Batchgrew, him to whom several times, less than a year earlier, she had scathingly referred as *that man*. His escort in the thoroughfare, and especially his demeanour towards herself, gave her a standing which she could otherwise scarcely have attained. Moreover, people might execrate him in private, but that he had conquered the esteem of their secret souls was well proved by their genuine eagerness to salute him as he walked sniffing along. He counted himself one of the seven prides of the district, and perhaps he was not far out.

"Come in a minute, lass," he said in a low, confidential voice, as they reached his branch shop, just beyond Malkin's. "I'll—" He paused.

A motor, apparently enormous, was buzzing motion-less in the wide entry by the side of the shop. It very slowly moved forward, crossed the footpath and half the street opposite the Town Hall, impeding a tram-car, and then curved backward into a position by the kerbstone. John's Ernest was at the steering-wheel. Councillor Batchgrew stood still with his mouth open to watch the manoeuvre.

"This is John's Ernest—my son John's eldest. Happen ye know him?" said Batchgrew to Rachel. "He's a good lad."

John's Ernest, a pleasant-featured young man of twenty-five, blushed and raised his hat. And Rachel also blushed as she nodded. It was astonishing that old Batchgrew could have a grandson with so honest a look on his face, but she had heard that son John, too, was very different from his father.

"Dunna go till I've seen thee," said Mr. Batchgrew to John's Ernest, and to Rachel, "Come in, Mrs. Fores."

John's Ernest silenced the car, and extricated himself with practised rapidity from the driver's seat.

"Where are ye going?" asked his grandfather.

"I'm going to lock the garage doors," said John's Ernest, with a humorous smile which seemed to add, "Unless you'd like them to be left open all Saturday afternoon." Rachel vividly remembered the playful, boyish voice which she had heard one night when the motor-car had called to take Mr. Batchgrew to Red Cow.

The councillor nodded.

In the small, untidy, disagreeable, malodorous shop, which in about half a century had scarcely altered its aspect, Thomas Batchgrew directed Rachel to a corner behind the counter and behind a partition, with a view of a fragment of the window. As she passed she saw one of the Batchgrew women (the wife of another grandson) and three little girls of various sizes flash in succession across an open doorway at the back. The granddaughter-in-law, who had an abode full of costly wedding-presents over the shop, had been one of her callers, but when they flashed across that doorway the Batchgrew women made a point of ignoring all phenomena in the shop.

"Has Louis decided about them debentures?" Thomas Batchgrew asked, still in a very low and confidential tone, as the two stood together in the corner. He had put the Book and the parcel down on a very ragged blotting-pad that lay on a chipped and ink-stained deal desk, and began to finger a yellow penholder. There was nobody else in the shop.

Rachel had foreseen his question.

She answered calmly: "Yes. He's quite decided that on the whole it'll be better if he doesn't put his money into debentures."

There was no foundation whatever for this statement; yet, in uttering the lie, she was clearly conscious of a feeling of lofty righteousness. She faced Thomas Batchgrew, though not with a tranquillity perfectly maintained, and she still enjoyed his appreciation of her, but she did not seem to care whether he guessed that she was lying or not.

"I'm sorry, lass!" he said simply, sniffing. "The lad's a fool. It isn't as if I've got to go hawking seven per cent. debentures to get rid of 'em—and in a concern like that, too! They'd never ha' been seven per cent if it hadna been for me. But it was you as I was thinking of when I offered 'em to Louis. I thought I should be doing ye a good turn."

The old man smiled amid his loud sniffs. He was too old to have retained any save an artistic interest in women. But an artistic interest in them he certainly had; and at an earlier period he had acquainted himself with life, as his eye showed. Rachel blushed a third time that morning, and more deeply than before. He was seriously nattering her now. Endearing qualities that had expired in him long ago seemed to be resuscitated and to animate his ruined features. Rachel dimly understood how it was that some woman had once married him and borne him a lot of children, and how it was that he had been so intimate and valued a friend of the revered husband of such a woman as Mrs. Maldon. She was, in the Five Towns phrase, "flustered." She almost believed what Thomas Batchgrew had said. She did believe it. She had misjudged him on the Thursday night when he spread the lure of the seven per cent. in front of Louis. At any rate, he assuredly did not care, personally, whether Louis accepted the debentures or not.

"However," the councillor went on, "he's got to know his own business best. And I don't know as it's any affair o' mine. But I was just thinking of you. When the husband has a good investment, th' wife generally comes in for something.... And what's more, it 'ud ha' stopped him from doing anything silly with his brass! *You* know."

"Yes," she murmured.

"I'm talking to ye because I've taken a fancy to ye," said the councillor. "I knew what you were the first time I set eyes on ye. Oh, I don't mind telling ye now—what harm is there in it? I'd a sort of a fancy as one day you and John's Ernest might ha' hit it off. I had it in my mind like."

A crude compliment, possibly in bad taste, possibly offensive; but Rachel was singularly moved by the revelation thus made. Before she could find a reply John's Ernest came into the shop, followed by an aproned assistant.

III

Then she was sitting by John's Ernest's side in the big motor-car, with her possessions at her feet. The enthronement had happened in a few moments. John's Ernest was going to Hanbridge.

"Ye can run Mrs. Fores up home on yer way," Thomas Batchgrew had suggested.

"But Bycars Lane is miles out of your way!" Rachel had cried.

Both men had smiled. "Won't make a couple of minutes' difference in the car," John's Ernest had modestly murmured.

She had been afraid to get into the automobile—afraid with a sort of stage-fright; afraid, as she might have been had she been called upon to sing at a concert in the Town Hall. She had imagined that all Bursley was gazing at her as she climbed into the car. Over the face of England automobiles are far more common than cuckoos, and yet for the majority, even of the proud and solvent middle class, they still remain as unattainable, as glitteringly wondrous, as a title. Rachel had never been in an automobile before; she had never hoped to be in an automobile. A few days earlier, and she had been regarding a bicycle as rather romantic! Louis had once mentioned a motor-cycle and side-carriage for herself, but she had rebuffed the idea with a shudder.

The whole town slid away behind her. The car was out of the market-place and crossing the top of Duck Bank, the scene of Louis' accident, before she had settled her skirts. She understood why the men had smiled at her; it was no more trouble for the car to go to Bycars than it would be for her to run upstairs. The swift movement of the car, silent and arrogant, and the occasional deep bass mysterious menace of its horn, and the grace of John's Ernest's gestures on the wheel as he curved the huge vehicle like a phantom round lumbering obstacles—these things fascinated and exalted her.

In spite of the horrible secret she carried all the time in her heart, she was somehow filled with an instinctive joy. And she began to perceive changes in her own perspective. The fine Louis, whom she had regarded as the summit of mankind, could never offer her an automobile; he existed entirely in a humbler world; he was, after all, a young man in a very small way of affairs. Batchgrew's automobile would swallow up, week by week, more than the whole of Louis' income. And further, John's Ernest by her side was invested with the mighty charm of one who easily and skilfully governs a vast and dangerous organism. All the glory of the inventors and perfecters of automobiles, and of manufacturing engineers, and of capitalists who could pay for their luxurious caprices, was centred in John's Ernest, merely because he directed and subjugated the energy of the miraculous machine.

And John's Ernest was so exquisitely modest and diffident, and yet had an almost permanent humorous smile. But the paramount expression on his face was honesty. She had never hitherto missed the expression of honesty on Louis' face, but she realized now that it was not there.... And she had been adjudged worthy of John's Ernest! The powerful of the world had had their eyes on her! Not Louis alone had noted her! Had Fate chosen, and had she herself chosen, that very motor-car might have been hers, and she at that instant riding in it as the mistress thereof! Strange thoughts, which intensely flattered and fostered her self-esteem. But she still had the horrible secret to carry with her.

When the car stopped in front of her gate, she forced open the door and jumped down with almost hysterical speed, said "Good-bye" and "Thank you" to John's Ernest, who becomingly blushed, and ran round the back of the car with her purchases. The car went on up the lane, the intention of John's Ernest being evident to proceed along Park Road and the Moorthorne ridge to Hanbridge rather than turn the car in the somewhat narrow lane. Rachel, instead of entering the house, thrust her parcels frantically on to the top step against the front door, and rushed down the steps again and down the lane. In a minute she was overtaking a man.

"Louis!" she cried.

From the car she had seen the incredible vision of Louis walking down the lane from the house. He and John's Ernest had not noticed each other, nor had Louis noticed that his wife was in the car.

Louis stopped now and looked back, hesitant.

There he was, with his plastered, pale face all streaked with greyish-white lines! Really Rachel had difficulty in believing her eyes. She had left him in bed, weak, broken; and he was there in the road fully dressed for the town and making for the town—a dreadful sight, but indubitably moving unaided on his own legs. It was simply monstrous! Fury leaped up in her. She had never heard of anything more monstrous. The thing was an absolute outrage on her nursing of him.

"Are you stark, staring mad?" she demanded.

He stood weakly regarding her. It was clear that he was already very enfeebled by his fantastic exertions.

"I wonder how much farther you would have gone without falling!" she said. "I'll thank you to come back this very instant!... This very instant!"

He had no strength to withstand her impetuous anger. His lower lip fell. He obeyed with some inarticulate words.

"And I should like to know what Mrs. Tams was doing!" said Rachel.

She neither guessed nor cared what was the intention of Louis' shocking, impossible escapade. She grasped his arm firmly. In ten minutes he was in bed again, under control, and Rachel was venting herself on Mrs. Tams, who took oath that she had been utterly unaware of the master's departure from the house.

CHAPTER XV
THE CHANGED MAN

I

Exactly a week passed, and Easter had come, before Rachel could set out upon an enterprise which she both longed and hated to perform. In the meantime the situation in the house remained stationary, except that after a relapse Louis' condition had gradually improved. She nursed him; he permitted himself to be nursed; she slept near him every night; no scene of irritation passed between them. But nothing was explained; even the fact that Rachel on the Saturday morning had overtaken Louis instead of meeting him—a detail which in secret considerably puzzled Louis, since it implied that his wife had been in the house when he left it—even this was not explained; as for the motor-car, Louis, absorbed, had scarcely noticed it, and Rachel did not mention it. She went on from one day into the next, proud, self-satisfied, sure of her strength and her position, indifferently scornful of Louis, and yet fatally stricken; she knew not in the least what was to be done, and so she waited for Destiny. Louis had to stop in bed for five days. His relapse worried Dr. Yardley, who, however, like many doctors, was kept in complete ignorance of the truth; Rachel was ashamed to confess that her husband had monstrously taken advantage of her absence to rise up and dress and go out; and Louis had said no word. On the Friday he was permitted to sit in a chair in the bedroom, and on Saturday he had the freedom of the house. It surprised Rachel that on the Saturday he had not dashed for the street, for after the exploit of the previous Saturday she was ready to expect anything. Had he done so she would not have interfered; he was really convalescent, and also the number of white stripes over his face and hair had diminished. In the afternoon he reclined on the Chesterfield to read, and fell asleep. Then it was that Rachel set out upon her enterprise. She said not a word to Louis, but instructed Mrs. Tams to inform the master, if he inquired, that she had gone over to Knype to see Mr. Maldon.

"Are you a friend of Mester Maldon's?" asked the grey-haired slattern who answered her summons at the door of Julian's lodgings in Granville

Street, Knype. There was a challenge in the woman's voice. Rachel accepted it at once.

"Yes, I am," she said, with decision.

"Well, I don't know as I want any o' Mester Maldon's friends here," said the landlady loudly. "Mester Maldon's done a flit from here, Mester Maldon has; and," coming out on to the pavement and pointing upward to a broken pane in the first-floor window, "that's a bit o' his fancy work afore he flitted!"

Rachel put her lips together.

"Can you give me his new address?"

"Can I give yer his new address? Pr'aps I can and pr'aps I canna, but I dunna see why I should waste my breath on Mester Maldon's friends—that I dunna! And I wunna!"

Rachel walked away. Before she reached the end of the frowsy street, whose meanness and monotony of tiny-bow-windows exemplified intensely the most deplorable characteristics of a district where brutish licence is decreasing, she was overtaken by a lanky girl in a pinafore.

"If ye please, miss, Mester Maldon's gone to live at 29 Birches Street, 'anbridge."

Having made this announcement, the girl ran off, with a short giggle.

Rachel, had to walk half a mile to reach the tram-route. This re-visiting of her native town, which she had quitted only a few weeks earlier, seemed to her like the sad resumption of an existence long forgotten. She was self-conscious and hoped that she would not encounter the curiosity of any of her Knype acquaintances. She felt easier when she was within the sheltering car and rumbling and jerking through the gloomy carnival of Easter Saturday afternoon in Knype and Cauldon on the way to Hanbridge.

After leaving the car in Crown Square, she had to climb through all the western quarter of Hanbridge to the very edge of the town, on the hummock that separates it from the Axe Moorlands. Birches Street, as she had guessed, was in the suburb known as Birches Pike. It ran right to the top of the hill, and the upper portion consisted of new cottage-houses in groups of two or three, with vacant lots between. Why should Julian have chosen Birches Street for residence, seeing that his business was in Knype? It was a repellent street; it was out even of the little world where sordidness is at any rate dignified by tradition and anaemic ideals can support each other in close companionship. It had neither a past nor a future. The steep end of it was an horizon of cloud. The April east wind blew the smoke of Hanbridge right across it.

In this east wind men in shirt-sleeves, and women with aprons over their heads, stood nonchalantly at cottage gates contemplating the vacuum of leisure. On two different parcels of land teams of shrieking boys were playing football, with piles of caps and jackets to serve as goal-posts. To the left, in a clough, was an enormous yellow marlpit, with pools of water in its depths, and gangways of planks along them, and a few overturned wheelbarrows lying here and there. A group of men drove at full speed up the street in a dogcart behind a sweating cob, stopped violently at the summit, and, taking watches from pockets, began to let pigeons out of baskets. The pigeons rose in wide circles and were lost in the vast dome of melancholy that hung over the district.

II

No. 29 was the second house from the top, new, and already in decay. It and its attached twin were named "Prospect Villas" in vermilion tiles on the yellowish-red bricks of the façade. Hot, and yet chilled by the wind, Rachel hesitated a moment at the gate, suddenly realizing the perils of her mission. And then she saw Julian Maldon standing in the bay-window of the ground floor; he was eating. Simultaneously he recognized her.

She thought, "I can't go back now."

He came sheepishly to the front door and asked her to walk in.

"Who'd have thought of seeing you?" he exclaimed. "You must take me as I am. I've only just moved in."

"I've been to your old address," she said, smiling, with an attempt at animation.

"A rare row I had there!" he murmured.

She understood, with a pang of compassion and yet with feminine disdain, the horrible thing that his daily existence was. No wonder he would never allow Mrs. Maldon to go and see him! The spectacle of his secret squalor would have desolated the old lady.

"Don't take any notice of all this," he said apologetically, as he preceded her into the room where she had seen him standing. "I'm not straight yet.... Not that it matters. By the way, take a seat, will you?"

Rachel courageously sat down.

Just as there were no curtains to the windows, so there was no carpet on the planked floor. A few pieces of new, cheap, ignoble furniture half filled the room. In one corner was a sofa-bedstead covered with an army blanket, in the middle a crimson-legged deal table, partly covered with a dirty cloth, and on the cloth were several apples, an orange, and a hunk of brown bread—his meal. Although he had only just "moved in," dust had had time to settle thickly on all the furniture. No pictures of any kind hid the huge sunflower that made the pattern of the wall-paper. In the hearth, which lacked a fender, a small fire was expiring.

"Ye see," said Julian, "I only eat when I'm hungry. It's a good plan. So I'm eating now. I've turned vegetarian. There's naught like it. I've chucked all that guzzling an swilling business. It's no good. I never touch a drop of liquor, nor a morsel of fleshmeat. Nor smoke, either. When you come to think of it, smoking's a disgusting habit."

Rachel said, pleasantly, "But you were smoking last week, surely?"

"Ah! But it's since then. I don't mind telling you. In fact, I meant to tell you, anyhow. I've turned over a new leaf. And it wasn't too soon. I've joined the Knype Ethical Society. So there you are!" His voice grew defiant and fierce, as in the past, and he proceeded with his meal.

Rachel knew nothing of the Knype Ethical Society, except that in spite of its name it was regarded with unfriendly suspicion by the respectable as an illicit rival of churches and chapels and a haunt of dubious characters who, under high-sounding mottoes, were engaged in the wicked scheme of setting class against class. She had accepted the general verdict on the Knype Ethical Society. And now she was confirmed in it. As she gazed at Julian Maldon in that dreadful interior, chewing apples and brown bread and sucking oranges, only when he felt hungry, she loathed the Knype Ethical Society. It was nothing to her that the Knype Ethical Society was responsible for a religious and majestic act in Julian Maldon—the act of turning over a new leaf.

"And why did you come up here?"

"Oh, various reasons!" said Julian, with a certain fictitious nonchalance, beneath which was all his old ferocious domination. "You see, I didn't get enough exercise before. Lived too close to the works. In fact, a silly existence. I saw it all plain enough as soon as I got back from South Africa.... Exercise! What you want is for your skin to act at least once every day. Don't you think so?" He seemed to be appealing to her for moral support in some revolutionary theory.

"Well—I'm sure I don't know."

Julian continued—

"If you ask me, I believe there are some people who never perspire from one year's end to another. Never! How can they expect to be well? How can they expect even to be clean? The pores, you know. I've been reading a lot about it. Well, I walk up here from Knype full speed every day. Everybody ought to do it. Then I have a bath."

"Oh! Is there a bathroom?"

"No, there isn't," he answered curtly. Then in a tone of apology: "But I manage. You see, I'm going to save. I was spending too much down there—furnished rooms. Here I took two rooms—this one and a kitchen—unfurnished; very much cheaper, of course. I've just fixed them up temporarily. Little by little they'll be improved. The woman upstairs comes in for half an hour in the morning and just cleans up when I'm gone."

"And does your cooking?"

"Not much!" said Julian bravely. "I do that myself. In the first place, I want very little cooking. Cooking's not natural. And what bit I do want—well, I have my own ideas about it, I've got a little pamphlet about rational eating and cooking. You might read it. Everybody ought to read it."

"I suppose all that sort of thing's very interesting," Rachel remarked at large, with politeness.

"It is," Julian said emphatically.

Neither of them felt the necessity of defining what was meant by "all that sort of thing." The phrase had been used with intention and was perfectly understood.

"But if you want to know what I really came up here for," Julian resumed, "I'll show you."

"Where?"

"Outside." And he repeated, "I'll show you."

III

She followed him as, bareheaded, he hurried out of the room into the street.

"Shan't you take cold without anything on your head in this wind?" she suggested mildly.

He would have snapped off the entire head of any other person who had ventured to make the suggestion. But he treated Rachel more gently because he happened to think that she was the only truly sensible and kind woman he had ever met in his life.

"No fear!" he muttered.

At the front gate he stopped and looked back at his bay-window.

"Now—curtains!" he said. "I won't have curtains. Blinds, at night, yes, if you like. But curtains! I never could see any use in curtains. Fallals! Keep the light out! Dust-traps!"

Rachel gazed at him. Despite his beard, he appeared to her as a big schoolboy, blundering about in the world, a sort of leviathan puppy in earnest. She liked him, on account of an occasional wistful expression in his eyes, and because she had been kind to him during his fearful visit to Bycars. She even admired him, for his cruel honesty and force. At the same time, he excited her compassion to an acute degree. As she gazed at him the tears were ready to start from her eyes. What she had seen, and what she had heard of the new existence which he was organizing for himself made her feel sick with pity. But mingled with her pity was a sharp disdain. The idea of Julian talking about cleanliness, dust-traps, and rationality gave her a desire to laugh and cry at once. All the stolid and yet wary conservatism of her character revolted against meals at odd hours, brown bread, apples, orange-sucking, action of the skin, male cooking, camp-beds, the frowsiness of casual charwomen, bare heads, and especially bare windows. If Rachel had been absolutely free to civilize Julian's life, she would have begun by measuring the bay-window.

She said firmly—

"I must say I don't agree with you about curtains."

His gestures of impatience were almost violent; but she would not flinch.

"Don't ye?"

"No."

"Straight?"

She nodded.

He drew breath. "Well, I'll get some—if it'll satisfy you."

His surrender was intensely dramatic to her. It filled her with happiness, with a consciousness of immense power. She thought: "I can influence him. I alone can influence him. Unless *I* look after him his existence will be dreadful—dreadful."

"You'd much better let me buy them for you." She smiled persuasively.

"Have it your own way!" he said gloomily. "Just come along up here."

He led her up to the top of the street.

"Ye'll see what I live up here for," he muttered as they approached the summit.

The other half of the world lay suddenly at their feet as they capped the brow, but it was obscured by mist and cloud. The ragged downward road was lost in the middle distance amid vaporous grey-greens and earthy browns.

"No go!" he exclaimed crossly. "Not clear enough! But on a fine day ye can see Axe and Axe Edge.... Finest view in the Five Towns."

The shrill cries of the footballers reached them.

"What a pity!" she sympathized eagerly. "I'm sure it must be splendid." His situation seemed extraordinarily tragic to her. His short hair, ruffled by the keen wind, was just like a boy's hair and somehow the sight of it touched her deeply.

He put his hands far into his pockets and drummed one foot on the ground.

"What brought ye up here?" he demanded, with his eyes on an invisible town of Axe.

She opened her hand-bag.

"I came to bring you this," she said, and offered him an envelope, which he took, wonderingly.

Then, when he had it in his hands, he said abruptly, angrily, "If it's that money, I won't take it."

"Yes you will."

"Has Louis sent ye?" This was the first mention of Louis, though he was well aware of the accident.

She shook her head.

"Well, let him keep his half, and you can keep mine."

"It's all there."

"How—all there?"

"All that you left the other night."

"But—but—" He seemed to be furious as he faced her.

Rachel went on—

"The other part of the missing money's been found ... Louis had it. So all this belongs to you. If some one hadn't told you it wouldn't have been fair."

She flushed slowly, trembling, but looking at him.

"Well!" Julian burst out with savage solemnity, "there's not many of your sort knocking about. By G— — there isn't!"

She walked quickly away from his passionate homage to her.

"Here!" he shouted, fingering the envelope.

But she kept on at a swift pace towards Hanbridge. About a quarter of a mile down the road the pigeon-flyer's dogcart stood empty outside a public-house.

CHAPTER XVI
THE LETTER

I

Rachel stood at her own front door and took off her glove in order more easily to manipulate the latch-key, which somehow, since coming into frequent use again, had never been the same manageable latch-key, but a cantankerous old thing, though still very bright. She opened the door quietly, and stepped inside quietly, lest by chance she might disturb Louis, the invalid—but also because she was a little afraid.

The most contradictory feelings can exist together in the mind. After the desolate discomfort of Julian Maldon's lodging and the spectacle of his clumsiness in the important affair of mere living, Rachel was conscious of a deep and proud happiness as she re-entered the efficient, cosy, and gracious organism of her own home. But simultaneously with this feeling of happiness she had a dreadful general apprehension that the organism might soon be destroyed, and a particular apprehension concerning her next interview with Louis, for at the next interview she would be under the necessity of telling him about her transaction with Julian. She had been absolutely determined upon that transaction. She had said to herself, "Whatever happens, I shall take that money to Julian and insist on his keeping all of it." She had, in fact, been very brave—indeed, audacious. Now the consequences were imminent, and they frightened her; she was less brave now. One awkward detail of the immediate future was that to tell Louis would be to reopen the entire question of the theft, which she had several times in the most abrupt and arrogant manner refused to discuss with him.

As soon as she had closed the front door she perceived that twilight was already obscuring the interior of the house. But she could plainly see that the parlour door was about two inches ajar, exactly as she had left it a couple of hours earlier. Probably Louis had not stirred. She listened vainly for a sign of life from him. Probably he was reading, for on rare occasions when he read a novel he would stick to the book with surprising pertinacity. At any rate, he would be too lofty to give any sign that he had heard her return. Under less sinister circumstances he might have yelled gaily: "I say, Rache!" for in a teasing mood he would sometimes prefer "Rache" to "Louise."

Rachel from the lobby could see the fire bright in the kitchen, and a trayful of things on the kitchen table ready to be brought into the parlour for high tea.

Mrs. Tams was out. It was not among Mrs. Tams's regular privileges to be out in the afternoon. But this was Easter Saturday—rather a special day—and, further, one of her daughters had gone away for Easter and left a child with one of her daughters-in-law, and Mrs. Tams had desired to witness some of the dealings of her daughter-in-law with her grandchild. Not without just pride had Mrs. Tams related the present circumstances to Rachel. In Mrs. Tams's young maturity parents who managed a day excursion to Blackpool in the year did well, and those who went away for four or five days at Knype Wakes in August were princes and plutocrats. But nowadays even a daughter of Mrs. Tams, not satisfied with a week at Knype Wakes, could take a week-end at Easter just like great folk such as Louis. Which proved that the community at large, or Mrs. Tams's family, had famously got up in the world. Rachel recalled Louis' suggestion, more than a week earlier, of a trip to Llandudno. The very planet itself had aged since then.

She looked at the clock. In twenty minutes Mrs. Tams would be back. She and Louis were alone together in the house. She might go straight into the parlour, and say, in as indifferent and ordinary a voice as she could assume: "I've just been over to Julian Maldon's to give him that money—all of it, you know," and thus get the affair finished before Mrs. Tams's reappearance. Louis was within a few feet of her, hidden only by the door which a push would cause to swing!... Yes, but she could not persuade herself to push the door! The door seemed to be protected from her hand by a mysterious spell which she dared not break. She was, indeed, overwhelmed by the simple but tremendous fact that Louis and herself were alone together in the darkening house. She decided, pretending to be quite calm: "I'll just run upstairs and take my things off first. There's no use in my seeming to be in a hurry."

In the bedroom she arranged her toilet for the evening, and established order in every corner of the chamber. Under the washstand lay the long row of Louis' boots and shoes, each pair in stretchers. She suddenly contrasted Julian's heavy and arrogant dowdiness with the nice dandyism of Louis. She could not help thinking that Julian would be a terrible person to live with.

This was the first thought favourable to Louis which had flitted through her mind for a long time. She dismissed it. Nothing in another man could be as terrible to live with as the defects of Louis. She set herself—she was obliged to set herself—high above Louis. The souvenir of the admiration of old Batchgrew and John's Ernest, the touching humility before her of Julian Maldon, once more inflated her self-esteem—it could not possibly have failed to do so. She knew that she was an extraordinary woman, and a prize.

Invigorated and reassured by these reflections, she descended proudly to the ground floor. And then, hesitating at the entrance to the parlour, she went into the kitchen and poked the fire. As the fire was in excellent condition there was no reason for this act except her diffidence at the prospect of an encounter with Louis. At last, having examined the tea-tray and invented other delays, she tightened her nerves and passed into the parlour to meet the man who seemed to be waiting for her like the danger of a catastrophe. He was not there. The parlour was empty. His book was lying on the Chesterfield.

She felt relieved. It was perhaps not very wise for him to have gone out for a walk, but if he chose to run risks, he was free to do so, for all she cared. In the meantime the interview was postponed; hence her craven relief. She lit the gas, but not by the same device as in Mrs. Maldon's day; and then she saw an envelope lying on the table. It was addressed in Louis' handwriting to "Mrs. Louis Fores." She was alone in the house. She felt sick. Why should he write a letter to her and leave it there on the table? She invented half a dozen harmless reasons for the letter, but none of them was the least convincing. The mere aspect of the letter frightened her horribly. There was no strength in her limbs. She tore the envelope in a daze.

The letter ran—

> Dear Rachel,—I have decided to leave England. I do not
> know how long I shall be away. I cannot and will not stand
> the life I have been leading with you this last week. I had a
> perfectly satisfactory explanation to give you, but you have
> most rudely refused to listen to it. So now I shall not give it.
> I shall write you as to my plans. I shall send you whatever
> money is necessary for you. By the way, I put four hundred
> and fifty pounds away in my private drawer. On looking for
> it this afternoon I see that you have taken it, without saying
> a word to me. You must account to me for this money. When
> you have done so we will settle how much I am to send

you. In the meantime you can draw from it for necessary expenses.

Yours,

L.F.

II

Rachel stared at the letter. It was the first letter she had seen written on the new note-paper, embossed with the address, "Bycars, Bursley." Louis would not have "Bycars Lane" on the note-paper, because "Bycars" alone was more vague and impressive; distant strangers might take it to be the name of a magnificent property. Her lips curled. She violently ripped the paper to bits and stuck them in the fire; a few fragments escaped and fluttered like snow on to the fender. She screwed up the envelope and flung it after the letter. Her face smarted and tingled as the blood rushed passionately to her head.

She thought, aghast: "Everything is over! He will never come back. He will never have enough moral force to come back. We haven't been married two months, and everything is over! And this is Easter Saturday! He wanted us to be at Llandudno or somewhere for Easter, and I shouldn't be at all surprised if he's gone there. Yes, he would be capable of that. And if it wasn't for the plaster on his face, he'd be capable of gallivanting on Llandudno pier this very night!"

She had no illusion as to him. She saw him as objectively as a god might have seen him.

And then she thought with fury: "Oh, what a fool I've been! What a little fool! Why didn't I listen to him? Why didn't I foresee?... No, I've *not* been a fool! I've not! I've not! What did I do wrong? Nothing! I couldn't have borne his explanations!... Explanations, indeed! I can imagine his explanations! Did he expect me to smile and kiss him after he'd told me he was a thief?"

And then she thought, in reference to his desertion: "It's not true! It can't be true!"

She wanted to read the letter again, so that perhaps she might read something into it that was hopeful. But to read it again was impossible. She tried to recall its exact terms, and could not. She could only remember with certainty that the final words were "Yours, L.F." Nevertheless, she knew that the thing was true; she knew by the weight within her breast and the horrible nausea that almost overcame her self-control.

She whispered, alone in the room—

"Yes, it's true! And it's happened to me!... He's gone!"

And not the ruin of her life, but the scandal of the affair, was the first matter that occupied her mind. She was too shaken yet to feel the full disaster. Her mind ran on little things. And just as once she had pictured herself self-conscious in the streets of Bursley as a young widow, so now she pictured herself in the far more appalling role of deserted wife. The scandal would be enormous. Nothing—no carefully invented fiction—would suffice to stifle it. She would never dare to show her face. She would be compelled to leave the district. And supposing a child came! Fears stabbed her. She felt tragically helpless as she stood there, facing a vision of future terrors. She had legal rights, of course. Her common sense told her that. She remembered also that she possessed a father and a brother in America. But no legal rights and no relatives would avail against the mere simple, negligent irresponsibility of Louis. In the end, she would have to rely on herself. All at once she recollected that she had promised to see after Julian's curtains.

She had almost no money. And how could the admiration of three men other than her husband (so enheartening a few minutes earlier) serve her in the crisis? No amount of masculine admiration could mitigate the crudity of the fact that she had almost no money. Louis' illness had interrupted the normal course of domestic finance—if, indeed, a course could be called normal which had scarcely begun. Louis had not been to the works. Hence he had received no salary. And how much salary was due to him, and whether he was paid weekly or monthly, she knew not. Neither did she know whether his inheritance actually had been paid over to him by Thomas Batchgrew.

What she knew was that she had received no house-keeping allowance for more than a week, and that her recent payments to tradesmen had been made from a very small remaining supply of her own prenuptial money. Economically she was as dependent on Louis as a dog, and not more so; she had the dog's right to go forth and pick up a living.... Of course Louis would send her money. Louis was a gentleman—he was not a cad. Yes, but he was a very careless gentleman. She was once again filled with the bitter realization of his extreme irresponsibility.

She heard a noise in the back lobby, and started. It was Mrs. Tams, returned. Mrs. Tams had a key of her own, of which she was proud — an affair of about four inches in length and weighing over a quarter of a pound. It fitted the scullery door, and was, indeed, the very key with which Rachel had embroidered her lie to Thomas Batchgrew on the day after the robbery. Mrs. Tams always took pleasure in entering the house from the rear, without a sound. She was now coming into the parlour with the tray for high tea. No wonder that Rachel started. Here was the first onset of the outer world.

Mrs. Tams came in, already perfectly transformed from a mother, mother-in-law, and grandmother into a parlour-maid with no human tie.

"Good-afternoon, Mrs. Tams."

"So ye've got back, ma'am!"

While Mrs. Tams laid the table, with many grunts and creakings of the solid iron in her stays, Rachel sat on a chair by the fire, trying to seem in a casual, dreamy mood, cogitating upon what she must say.

"Will mester be down for tea, ma'am?" asked Mrs. Tams, who had excusably assumed that Louis was upstairs.

And Rachel, forced now to defend, instead of attacking, blurted out —

"Oh! By the way, I was forgetting; Mr. Fores will not be in for tea."

Mrs. Tams, forgetting she was a parlour-maid, vociferated in amazement and protest —

"Not be in for tea, ma'am? And him as he is!" All her lately gathering suspicions were strengthened and multiplied.

Rachel had to continue as she had begun: "He's been called away on very urgent business. He simply had to go."

Mrs. Tams, intermitting her duties, stood still and gazed at Rachel.

"Was it far, ma'am, as he had for to go?"

A simple question, and yet how difficult to answer plausibly!

"Yes — rather."

"I suppose he'll be back to-night, ma'am?"

"Oh yes, of course!" replied Rachel, in absurd haste. "But if he isn't, I'm not to worry, he said. But he fully expects to be. We scarcely had time to talk, you see. He was getting ready when I came in."

"A telegram, ma'am, I suppose it was?"

"Yes.... That is, I don't know whether there was a telegram first, or not. But he was called for, you see. A cab. I couldn't have let him go off walking, not as he is."

Mrs. Tarns gave a gesture.

"I suppose I mun alter this 'ere table, then," said she, putting a cup and saucer back on the tray.

"Idiot! Idiot!" Rachel described herself to herself, when Mrs. Tams, very much troubled, had left the room. "'By the way, I was forgetting'— couldn't I have told her better than that? She's known for a week that there's been something wrong, and now she's certainly guessed there's something dreadfully wrong.... Just look at all the silly lies I've told already! What will it be like to-morrow—and Monday? I wonder what my face looked like while I was telling her!"

She rushed upstairs to discover what luggage Louis had taken with him. But apparently he had taken nothing whatever. The trunk, the valise, and the various bags were all stacked in the empty attic, exactly as she had placed them. He must have gone off in a moment, without any reflection or preparation.

And when Mrs. Tams served the solitary tea, Rachel was just as idiotic as before.

"By the way, Mrs. Tams," she began again, "did you happen to tell Mr. Fores where I'd gone this afternoon?... You see, we'd no opportunity to discuss anything," she added, striving once more after verisimilitude.

"Yes'm. I told him when I took him his early cup o' tea."

"Did he ask you?"

"Now ye puzzle me, ma'am! I couldn't swear to it to save my life. But I told him."

"What did he say?" Rachel tried to smile.

"He didna say aught."

Rachel remained alone, to objurgate Rachel. It was indeed only too obvious from Mrs. Tams's constrained and fussy demeanour that the old woman had divined the existence of serious trouble in the Fores household.

III

Some time after the empty ceremony of tea, Rachel sat in state in the parlour, dignified, self-controlled, pretending to sew, as she had pretended to eat and drink and, afterwards, to have an important enterprise of classifying and rearranging her possessions in the wardrobe upstairs. Let Mrs. Tams enter ever so unexpectedly, Rachel was a fit spectacle for her, with a new work-basket by her side on the table, and her feet primly on a footstool, quite in the style of the late Mrs. Maldon, and a serious and sagacious look on her face that the fire and the gas combined to illuminate. She did not actually sew, but the threaded needle was ready in her hand to move convincingly at a second's notice, for Mrs. Tams was of a restless and inquisitive disposition that night.

Apparently secure between the drawn blinds, the fire, the Chesterfield, and the sideboard, Rachel was nevertheless ranging wide among vast, desolate tracts of experience, and she was making singular discoveries. For example, it was not until she was alone in the parlour after tea that she discovered that during the whole of her interview with Julian Maldon in the afternoon she had never regarded him as a thief. And yet he was a thief—just as much as Louis! She had simply forgotten that he was a thief. He did not seem to be any the worse for being a thief. If he had shown the desire to explain to her by word of mouth the entire psychology of his theft, she would have listened with patience and sympathy; she would have encouraged him to rectitude. And yet Julian had no claim on her; he was not her husband; she did not love him. But because Louis was her husband, and had a claim on her, and had received all the proofs of her affection— therefore, she must be merciless for Louis! She perceived the inconsistency; she perceived it with painful clearness. She had the impartial logic of the self-accuser. At intervals the self-accuser was flagellated and put to flight by passionate reaction, but only to return stealthily and irresistibly....

She had been wrong to take the four hundred and fifty pounds without a word. True, Louis had somewhat casually authorized her to return half of the sum to Julian, but the half was not the whole. And in any case she ought to have told Louis of her project. There could be no doubt that, immediately upon Mrs. Tams's going out, Louis had looked for the four hundred and fifty pounds, and, in swift resentment at its disappearance, had determined to disappear also. He had been stung and stung again, past bearing (she argued) daily and hourly throughout the week, and the disappearance of the money had put an end to his patience. Such was the upshot, and she had brought it about!

She had imagined that she was waiting for destiny, but in fact she had been making destiny all the time, with her steely glances at Louis and her acrid, uncompromising tongue!... And did those other men really admire her? How, for instance, could Thomas Batchgrew admire her, seeing that he had suspected her of lies and concealment about the robbery? If it was on account of supposed lies and concealment that he admired her, then she rejected Thomas Batchgrew's admiration....

The self-accuser and the self-depreciator in her grew so strong that Louis' conduct soon became unexceptionable—save for a minor point concerning a theft of some five hundred pounds odd from an old lady. And as for herself, she, Rachel, was an over-righteous prig, an interfering person, a blundering fool of a woman, a cruel-hearted creature. And Louis was just a poor, polite martyr who had had the misfortune to pick up certain bank-notes that were not his.

Then the tide of judgment would sweep back, and Rachel was the innocent, righteous martyr again, and Louis the villain. But not for long.

She cried passionately within her brain: "I must have him. I must get hold of him. I *must!*"

But when the brief fury of longing was exhausted she would ask: "How can I get hold of him? Where is he?" Then more forcibly: "What am I to do first? Yes, what ought I to do? What is wisest? He little guesses that he is killing me. If he had guessed, he wouldn't have done it. But nothing will kill me! I am as strong as a horse. I shall live for ages. There's the worst of it all!... And it's no use asking what I ought to do, either, because nothing, nothing, nothing would induce me to run after him, even if I knew where to run to! I would die first. I would live for a hundred years in torture first. That's positive."

The hands of the clock, instead of moving slowly, seemed to progress at a prodigious rate. Mrs. Tams came in—

"Shall I lay mester's supper, ma'am?"

The idea of laying supper for the master had naturally not occurred to Rachel.

"Yes, please."

When the supper was laid upon one half of the table, the sight of it almost persuaded Rachel that Louis would be bound to come—as though the waiting supper must mysteriously magnetize him out of the world beyond into the intimacy of the parlour.

And she thought, as she strove for the hundredth time to recall the phrases of the letter—

"'Perfectly satisfactory explanation!' suppose he *has* got a perfectly satisfactory explanation! He must have. He must have. If only he has, everything would be all right. I'd apologize. I'd almost go on my knees to him.... And he was so ill all the time, too!... But he's gone. It's too late now for the explanation. Still, as soon as I hear from him, I shall write and ask him for it."

And in her mind she began to compose a wondrous letter to him—a letter that should preserve her own dignity while salving his, a letter that should overwhelm him with esteem for her.

She rang the bell. "Don't sit up, Mrs. Tams."

And when she had satisfied herself that Mrs. Tams with unwilling obedience had retired upstairs, she began to walk madly about the parlour (which had an appearance at once very strange and distressingly familiar), and to whisper plaintively, and raging, and plaintively again: "I must get him back. I cannot bear this. It is too much for me. I *must* get him back. It's all my fault!" and then dropped on the Chesterfield in a collapse, moaning: "No. It's no use now."

And then she fancied that she heard the gate creak, and a latch-key fumbling into the keyhole of the front door. And one part of her brain said on behalf of the rest: "I am mad. I am delirious."

It was a fact that Louis had caused to be manufactured for his own use a new latch-key. But it was impossible that this latch-key should now be in the keyhole. She was delirious. And then she unmistakably heard the front door open. Her heart jumped with the most afflicting violence. She was ready to fall on to the carpet, but seemed to be suspended in the air. When she recognized Louis' footsteps in the lobby tears burst from her eyes in an impetuous torrent.

CHAPTER XVII
IN THE MONASTERY

I

When Mrs. Tams brought in his early cup of tea that Easter Saturday afternoon, Louis had no project whatever in his head, and he was excessively, exasperatingly bored. A quarter of an hour earlier he had finished reading the novel which had been mitigating the worst tedium of his shamed convalescence, and the state of his mind was not improved by the fact that in his opinion the author of the novel had failed to fulfil clear promises—had, in fact, abused his trust. On the other hand, he felt very appreciably stronger, and his self-esteem was heightened by the complete correctness of his toilet. On that morning he had dressed himself with art and care for the first time since the accident. He enjoyed a little dandyism; dandified, he was a better man; the "fall" of a pair of trousers over the knee, the gloss of white wristbands, just showing beneath the new cloth of a well-cut sleeve—these phenomena not only pleased him but gave him confidence. And herein was the sole bright spot of his universe when Mrs. Tams entered.

He was rather curt with Mrs. Tams because she was two minutes late; for two endless minutes he had been cultivating the resentment of a man neglected and forgotten by every one of those whose business in life it is to succour, humour, and soothe him.

Mrs. Tams comprehended his mood with precision, and instantly. She hovered round him like a hen, indeed like a whole flock of hens, and when he savagely rebuffed her she developed from a flock of hens into a flight of angels.

"Missis said as I was to tell you as she'd gone to see Mr. Julian Maldon, sir," said Mrs. Tams, in the way of general gossip.

Louis made no sign.

"Her didna say how soon her'd be back. I was for going out, sir, but I'll stop in, sir, and willing—"

"What time are you supposed to go out?" Louis demanded, in a tone less inimical than his countenance.

"By rights, now, sir," said Mrs. Tams, looking backward through the open door at the lobby clock.

"Well," Louis remarked with liveliness, "if you aren't outside this house in one minute, in sixty seconds, I shall put you out, neck and crop."

Mrs. Tams smiled. His amiability was returning, he had done her the honour to tease her. She departed, all her "things" being ready in the kitchen. Even before she had gone Louis went quickly upstairs, having drunk less than half a cup of tea, and with extraordinary eagerness plunged into the bedroom and unlocked his private drawer. He both hoped and feared that the money which he had bestowed there after Julian's historic visit would have vanished. It had vanished.

The shock was unpleasant, but the discovery itself had a pleasant side, because it justified the theory which had sprung complete into his mind when he learnt where Rachel had gone, and also because it denuded Rachel of all reasonable claim to consideration. He had said to himself: "She has gone off to return half of that money to Julian—that's what it is. And she's capable of returning all of it to him!" ... And she had done so. And she had not consulted him, Louis. He, then, was a nobody—zero in the house! She had deliberately filched the money from him, and to accomplish her purpose she had abstracted his keys, which he had left in his pocket. She must have stolen the notes several days before, perhaps a week before, when he was really seriously ill. She had used the keys and restored them to his pocket. Astounding baseness!

He murmured: "This finishes it. This really does finish it."

He was immensely righteous as he stood alone in the bedroom in front of the rifled drawer. He was more than righteous—he was a martyr. He had done absolutely nothing that was wrong. He had not stolen money; he had not meant to steal; the more he examined his conduct, the more he was convinced that it had been throughout unexceptionable, whereas the conduct of Rachel ...! At every point she had sinned. It was she, not he, who had burnt Mrs. Maldon's hoard. Was it not monstrous that a woman should be so careless as to light a fire without noticing that a bundle of notes lay on the top of the coal? Besides, what affair was it of hers, anyway? It concerned himself, Mrs. Maldon, and Julian, alone. But she must needs interfere. She had not a penny to bless herself with, but he had magnanimously married her; and his reward was her inexcusable interference in his private business.

His accident was due solely to his benevolence for her. If he had not been wheeling a bicycle procured for her, and on his way to buy her a new bicycle, the accident would never have occurred. But had she shown any gratitude? None. It was true that he had vaguely authorized her to return half of the money replaced by the contrite Julian; but no date for doing so had been fixed, and assuredly she had no pretext whatever for dealing with all of it. That she should go to Julian Maldon with either the half or the whole of the money without previously informing him and obtaining the ratification of his permission was simply scandalous. And that she should sneakingly search his pockets for keys, commit a burglary in his drawer, and sneakingly put the keys back was outrageous, infamous, utterly intolerable.

He said, "I'll teach you a lesson, my lady, once for all."

Then he went downstairs. The kitchen was empty; Mrs. Tams had gone. But between the kitchen and the parlour he changed his course, and ran upstairs again to the drawer, which he pulled wide open. At the back of it there ought to have been an envelope containing twenty pounds in notes, balance of an advance payment from old Batchgrew. The envelope was there with its contents. Rachel had left the envelope. "Good of her!" he ejaculated with sarcasm. He put the money in his pocket-book, and descended to finish his tea, which he drank up excitedly.

A dubious scheme was hypnotizing him. He was a man well acquainted with the hypnotism of dubious schemes. He knew all the symptoms. He fought against the magic influence, and then, as always, yielded himself deliberately and voluptuously to it. He would go away. He would not wait; he would go at once, in a moment. She deserved as much, if not more. He knew not where he should go; a thousand reasons against going assailed him; but he would go. He must go. He could no longer stand, even for a single hour, her harshness, her air of moral superiority, her adamantine obstinacy. He missed terribly her candid worship of him, to which he had grown accustomed and which had become nearly a necessity of his existence. He could not live with an eternal critic; the prospect was totally inconceivable. He wanted love, and he wanted admiring love, and without it marriage was meaningless to him, a mere imprisonment.

So he would go. He could not and would not pack; to pack would distress him and bore him; he would go as he was. He could buy what he needed.

The shops—his kind of shops—were closed, and would remain closed until Tuesday. Nevertheless, he would go. He could buy the indispensable at Faulkner's establishment on the platform at Knype railway-station, conveniently opposite the Five Towns Hotel. He had determined to go to the Five Towns Hotel that night. He had no immediate resources beyond the twenty pounds, but he would telegraph to Batchgrew, who ad not yet transferred to him the inheritance, to pay money into his bank early on Tuesday; if he were compelled to draw a cheque he would cross it, and then it could not possibly be presented before Wednesday morning.

At all costs he would go. His face was still plastered; but he would go, and he would go far, no matter where! The chief thing was to go. The world was calling him. The magic of the dubious scheme held him fast. And in all other respects he was free—free as impulse. He would go. He was not yet quite recovered, not quite strong.... Yes, he was all right; he was very strong! And he would go.

He put on his hat and his spring overcoat. Then he thought of the propriety of leaving a letter behind him—not for Rachel's sake, but to insist on his own dignity and to spoil hers. He wrote the letter, read it through with satisfaction, and quitted the house, shutting the door cheerfully, but with a trembling hand. Lest he might meet Rachel on her way home he went up the lane instead of down, and, finding himself near the station, took a train to Knype—travelling first class. The glorious estate of a bachelor was his once more.

II

The Five Towns Hotel stood theoretically in the borough of Hanbridge, but in fact it was in neither Hanbridge nor Knype, but "opposite Knype station," on the quiet side of Knype station, far away from any urban traffic; the gross roar of the electric trams running between Knype and Hanbridge could not be heard from the great portico of the hotel. It is true that the hotel primarily existed on its proximity to the railway centre of the Five Towns. But it had outgrown its historic origin, and would have moderately flourished even had the North Staffordshire railway been annihilated. By its sober grandeur and its excellent cooking it had taken its place as the first hotel in the district. It had actually no rival. Heroic, sublime efforts had been made in the centre of Hanbridge to overthrow the pre-eminence of the Five Towns Hotel. The forlorn result of one of these efforts—so immense was it!—had been bought by the municipality and turned into a Town Hall—

supreme instance of the Five Towns' habit of "making things do!" No effort succeeded. Men would still travel from the ends of the Five Towns to the bar, the billiard-rooms, the banqueting-halls of the Five Towns Hotel, where every public or semi-public ceremonial that included conviviality was obliged to happen if it truly respected itself.

The Five Towns Hotel had made fortunes, and still made them. It was large and imposing and sombre. The architect, who knew his business, had designed staircases, corridors, and accidental alcoves on the scale of a palace; so that privacy amid publicity could always be found within its walls. It was superficially old-fashioned, and in reality modern. It had a genuine chef, with sub-chefs, good waiters whose sole weakness was linguistic, and an apartment of carven oak with a vast counterfeit eye that looked down on you from the ceiling. It was ready for anything—a reception to celebrate the nuptials of a maid, a lunch to a Cabinet Minister with an axe to grind in the district, or a sale by auction of house-property with wine *ad libitum* to encourage bids.

But its chief social use was perhaps as a retreat for men who were tired of a world inhabited by two sexes. Sundry of the great hotels of Britain have forgotten this ancient function, and are as full of frills, laces, colour, and soft giggles as a London restaurant, so that in Manchester, Liverpool, and Glasgow a man in these days has no safe retreat except the gloominess of a provincial club. The Five Towns Hotel has held fast to old tradition in this respect. Ladies were certainly now and then to be seen there, for it was a hotel and as such enjoyed much custom. But in the main it resembled a monastery. Men breathed with a new freedom as they entered it. Commandments reigned there, and their authority was enforced; but they were not precisely the tables of Moses. The enormous pretence which men practise for the true benefit of women was abandoned in the Five Towns Hotel. Domestic sultans who never joked in the drawing-room would crack with laughter in the Five Towns Hotel, and make others crack, too. Old men would meet young men on equal terms, and feel rather pleased at their own ability to do so. And young men shed their youth there, displaying the huge stock of wisdom and sharp cynicism which by hard work they had acquired in an incredibly short time. Indeed, the hotel was a wonderful institution, and a source of satisfaction to half a county.

III

It was almost as one returned from the dead that Louis Fores entered the Five Towns Hotel on Easter Saturday afternoon, for in his celibate prime he had been a habitué of the place. He had a thrill; and he knew that he would be noticed, were it only as the hero and victim of a street accident; a few remaining plasters still drew attention to his recent history. At the same time, the thrill which affected him was not entirely pleasurable, for he was frightened by what he had done: by the letter written to Rachel, by his abandonment of her, and also by the prospect of what he meant to do. The resulting situation would certainly be scandalous in a high degree, and tongues would dwell on the extreme brevity of the period of marriage. The scandal would resound mightily. And Louis hated scandal, and had always had a genuine desire for respectability.... Then he reassured himself. "Pooh! What do I care?" Besides, it was not his fault. He was utterly blameless; Rachel alone was the sinner. She had brought disaster upon herself. On the previous Saturday he had given her fair warning by getting up out of bed in his weakness and leaving the house—more from instinct than from any set plan. But she would not take a hint. She would not learn. Very good! The thought of his inheritance and of his freedom uplifted him till he became nearly a god.

Owing to the Easter holidays the hotel was less bright and worldly than usual. Moreover, Saturday was never one of its brilliant days of the week. In the twilight of a subsidiary lounge, illuminated by one early electric spark, a waiter stood alone amid great basket-chairs and wicker-tables. Louis knew the waiter, as did every man-about-town; but Louis imagined that he knew him better than most; the waiter gave a similar impression to all impressionable young men.

"How do you do, Krupp!" Louis greeted him, with kind familiarity.

"Good afternoon, sir."

It was perhaps the hazard of his name that had given the waiter a singular prestige in the district. Krupp is a great and an unforgettable name, wherever you go. And also it offers people a chance to be jocose with facility. A hundred habitué's had made the same joke to Krupp about Krupp's name, and each had supposed himself to be humorous in an original manner. Krupp received the jocularities with the enigmatic good-fellow air with which he received everything. None knew whether Krupp admired or disdained, loved or hated, the Five Towns and the English character. He was a foreigner from some vague frontier of Switzerland, possessing no language of his own but a patois, and speaking other languages less than perfectly. He had been a figure in the Five Towns Hotel for over twenty years. He was an efficient waiter; yet he had never risen on the staff, and was still just the lounge or billiard-room waiter that he had always been—and apparently content with Destiny.

Louis asked brusquely, as one who had no time to waste, "Will Faulkner's be open?"

Krupp bent down and glanced through an interstice of a partition at a clock in the corridor.

"Yes, sir," said Krupp with calm certainty.

Louis, pleased, thought, "This man is a fine waiter." Somehow Krupp made it seem as if by the force of his will he had forced Faulkner's to be open—in order to oblige Mr. Fores.

"Because," said Louis casually, "I've no luggage, not a rag, and I want to buy a few things, and no other place'll be open."

"Yes, sir," said Krupp, mysterious and quite incurious. He did not even ask, "Do you wish a room, sir?"

"Heard about my accident, I suppose?" Louis went on, a little surprised that Krupp should make no sympathetic reference to his plasters.

Krupp became instantly sympathetic, yet keeping his customary reserve.

"Yes, sir. And I am pleased to see you are recovered," he said, with the faint, indefinable foreign accent and the lack of idiom which combined to deprive his remarks of any human quality.

"Well," said Louis, not quite prepared to admit that the affair had gone so smoothly as Krupp appeared to imply, "I can tell you I've had a pretty bad time. I really ought not to be here now, but—" He stopped.

"Strange it should happen to you, sir. A gentleman who was in here the other day said that in his opinion you were one of the cleverest cyclists in the Five Towns."

Louis naturally inquired, "Who was that?"

"I could not say, sir. Not one of our regular customers, sir," with a touch of mild depreciation. "A dark gentleman, with a beard, a little lame, I fancy." As Krupp had invented the gentleman and his opinion to meet the occasion, he was right in depriving him of the rank of a regular customer.

"Oh!" murmured Louis. "By the way, has Mr. Gibbs come yet?"

"Mr. Gibbs, sir?"

"Yes, an American. I have an appointment with him this afternoon. If he comes in while I am over at Faulkner's just tell him, will you? I think he's stopping at the Majestic."

The Majestic being the latest rival hotel at Hanbridge, Krupp raised his eyebrows in a peculiar way and nodded his head.

Just as Krupp had invented a gentleman, so now Louis was inventing one. Neither Krupp nor Louis guessed the inventive act of the other. Krupp's act was a caprice, a piece of embroidery, charming and unnecessary. But Louis was inventing with serious intent, for he had to make his presence at the Five Towns Hotel on Easter Saturday seem natural and inevitable.

"And also I want the Cunard list of sailings, and the White Star, too. There's a Cunard boat from Liverpool on Monday, isn't there?"

"I don't *think* so, sir," said Krupp, "but I'll see."

"I understood from Mr. Gibbs there was. And I'm going to Liverpool by that early train to-morrow."

"Sunday, sir?"

"Yes, I must be in Liverpool to-morrow night."

Louis went across to the station to Faulkner's. He considered that he was doing very well. And after all, why not go to America—not on Monday, for he was quite aware that no boat left on Monday—but in a few days, after he had received the whole sum that Thomas Batchgrew held for him. He could quite plausibly depart on urgent business connected with new capitalistic projects. He could quite plausibly remain in America as long as convenient. America beckoned to him. He remembered all the appetizing accounts that he had ever heard from American commercial travellers of Broadway and Fifth Avenue—incredible streets. In America he might treble, quadruple, his already vast capital. The romance of the idea intoxicated him.

IV

When he got back from Faulkner's with a parcel (which he threw to the cloak-room attendant to keep) he felt startlingly hungry, and, despite the early hour, he ordered a steak in the grill-room; and not a steak merely, but all the accoutrements of a steak, with beverages to match. And to be on the safe side he paid for the meal at once, with a cheque for ten pounds, receiving the change in gold and silver, and thus increasing his available cash to about thirty pounds. Then in the lounge, with Cuban cigar-smoke in his eyes, and Krupp discoursing to him of all conceivable Atlantic liners, he wrote a letter to Thomas Batchgrew and marked it "Very urgent"—which was simple prudence on his part, for he had drawn a cheque for ten pounds on a non-existent bank-balance. At last, as Mr. Gibbs had not arrived, he said he should stroll up to the Majestic. He had not yet engaged a room; he seemed to hesitate before that decisive act....

Then it was that, in the corridor immediately outside the lounge, he encountered Jim Horrocleave. The look in Jim Horrocleave's ferocious eye shocked him. Louis had almost forgotten his employer, and the sudden spectacle of him was disconcerting.

"Hello, Fores!" said Horrocleave very sardonically, with no other greeting. "I thought ye were too ill to move." No word of sympathy in the matter of the accident! Simply the tone of an employer somehow aggrieved!

"I'm out to-day for the first time. Had to come down here on a matter—"

Horrocleave spoke lower, and even more sardonically. "I hear ye're off to America."

Louis looked through the fretted partition at the figure of Krupp alone in the lounge. And Horrocleave also looked at Krupp. And Krupp looked back with his enigmatic gaze, perhaps scornful, perhaps indifferent, perhaps secretly appreciative—but in any case profoundly foreign and aloof and sinister.

"Well—" Louis began at a disadvantage. "Who says I'm off to America?"

Horrocleave advanced his chin and clenched a fist.

"Don't you go!" said he. "If ye did, ye might be brought back by the scruff o' the neck. You mark my words and come down to the works to-morrow morning—*to-morrow*, ye understand!" He was breathing quickly. Then a malicious grin seemed to pass over his face as his glance rested for an instant on Louis' plasters. The next instant he walked away, and Louis heard him at the cloak-room counter barking the one word, "Mackintosh."

Louis understood, only too completely. During his absence from the works Horrocleave had amused himself by critically examining the old petty-cash book. That was all, and it was enough. Good-bye to romance, to adventure, to the freedom of the larger world! The one course to pursue was to return home, to deny (as was easy) that the notion of going to America had ever occurred to him, or even the notion of putting up at the hotel, and with such dignity as he could assume to restore to Horrocleave the total sum abstracted. With care and luck he might yet save his reputation. It was impossible that Horrocleave should prosecute. And what was seventy odd pounds, after all? He was master of thousands.

If he could but have walked straight out of the hotel! But he could not. His dignity, the most precious of all his possessions, had to be maintained. Possibly Krupp had overheard the conversation, or divined its nature. He strolled back into the lounge.

"A benedictine," he ordered casually, and, neatly pulling up his trousers at the knee, sank into a basket-chair and crossed his legs, while blowing forth much smoke.

"Yes, sir."

When Krupp brought the tiny glass, Louis paid for it without looking at him, and gave a good tip. Ah! He would have liked to peer into Krupp's inmost mind and know exactly how Krupp had been discussing him with Jim Horrocleave. He would have liked to tell Krupp in cutting tones that waiters had no right to chatter to one customer about another. And then he would have liked to destroy Krupp. But he could not. His godlike dignity would not permit him to show by even the slightest gesture that he had been inconvenienced. The next moment he perceived that Providence had been watching over him. If he had gone to America unknown to Horrocleave, Horrocleave might indeed have proved seriously awkward.... Extradition— was there such a word, and such a thing? He finished the benedictine, went to the cloak-room and obtained his hat, coat, stick, and parcel; and the hovering Krupp helped him with his overcoat; and as Destiny cast him out of the dear retreat which a little earlier he had entered with such pleasurable anticipations, he was followed down the corridor by the aloof, disinterested gaze of the Swiss whose enigma no Staffordshire man had ever penetrated.

CHAPTER XVIII
MRS. TAMS'S STRANGE BEHAVIOUR

I

In the house at Bycars, where he arrived tardily after circuitous wanderings, Louis first of all dropped the parcel from Faulkner's into the oak chest, raising and lowering the lid without any noise. Once, in the train in Bleakridge tunnel, he had almost thrown the parcel out of the carriage on to the line, as though it were in some subtle way a piece of evidence against him; but, aided by his vanity, he had resisted the impulse. Why, indeed, should he be afraid of a parcel of linen? Had he not the right to buy linen when and how he chose? Then he removed his hat and coat, hung them carefully in their proper place, smoothed his hair, and walked straight into the parlour. He had a considerable gift of behaving as though nothing out of the ordinary had happened when the contrary was the case. Nobody could have guessed from his features that he was calculating and recalculating the chances of immediate imprisonment, and that each successive calculation disagreed with the previous one; at one moment the chances were less than one in a hundred, less than one in a million; at another they increased and multiplied themselves into tragic certainty.

When Rachel heard him in the lobby her sudden tears were tears of joy and deliverance. She did not try to restrain them. As she stole back to her chair she ignored all her reasonings against him, and lived only in the fact that he had returned. And she was triumphant. She thought: "Now that he is in the house, he is mine. I have him. He cannot escape me. In a caress I shall cancel all the past since his accident. So long as I can hold him I don't care." Her soul dissolved in softness towards him; even the body seemed to melt also, till, instead of being a strong, sturdy girl, she was a living tentacular endearment and naught else.

But when, with disconcerting quickness, he came into the room, she hardened again in spite of herself. She simply could not display her feelings. Upbringing, habit, environment were too much for her, and spontaneity was checked. Had she been alone with a dog she would have spent herself passionately on the dog, imaginatively transforming the dog into Louis; but the sight of Louis in person congealed her, so that she became a hard mass with just a tiny core of fire somewhere within.

"Why cannot I jump up and fall on his neck?" she asked herself angrily. But she could not.

She controlled her tears, and began to argue mentally whether Louis had come home because he could not keep away from her, or for base purposes of his own. She was conscious of a desire to greet him sarcastically with the remark, "So you've come back, after all!" It was a wilful, insensate desire; but there it was. She shut her lips on it, not without difficulty.

"I've kept some supper for you," she said, with averted head. She wanted to make her voice kind, but it would not obey her. It was neither kind nor unkind. There were tears in it, however.

They did not look at each other.

"Why did you keep supper for me?" he mumbled.

"I thought you might find you weren't well enough to travel," she answered thoughtfully, with her face still bent over the work which she was spoiling with every clumsy, feverish stitch.

This surprising and ingenious untruth came from her without the slightest effort. It seemed to invent itself.

"Well," said Louis, "I don't happen to want any supper." His accent was slightly but definitely inimical. He perceived that he had an advantage, and he decided to press it.

Rachel also perceived this, and she thought resentfully: "How cruel he is! How mean he is!" She hated and loved him simultaneously. She foresaw that peace must be preceded by the horrors of war, and she was discouraged. Though determined that he should not escape from the room unreconciled, she was ready to inflict dreadful injuries on him, as he on her. They now regarded each other askance, furtively, as dire enemies.

Louis, being deficient in common sense, thought of nothing but immediate victory. He well knew that, in case of trouble with Jim Horrocleave, he might be forced to humble himself before his wife, and that present arrogance would only intensify future difficulties. Also, he had easily divined that the woman opposite to him was a softer Rachel than the one he had left, and very ready for pacific compromise. Nevertheless, in his polite, patient way, he would persist in keeping the attitude of an ill-used saint with a most clear grievance. And more than this, he wanted to appear absolutely consistent, even in coming home again. Could he have recalled the precise terms of his letter, he would have contrived to interpret them so as to include the possibility of his return that night. He fully intended to be the perfect male.

Drawing his cigarette-case and match-box from his hip pocket, by means of the silver cable which attached them to his person, he carefully lit a cigarette and rose to put the spent match in the fire. While at the hearth he looked at his plastered face in the glass, critically and dispassionately, as though he had nothing else in the world to do. Then his eye caught some bits of paper in the fender—fragments of his letter which Rachel had cast into the fire and on to the hearth. He stooped, picked up one white piece, gazed at it, dropped it, picked up another, gazed at it, dropped it fastidiously.

"Hm!" he said faintly.

Then he stood again at his full height and blew smoke profusely about the mantelpiece. He was very close to Rachel, and above her. He could see the top of her bent, mysterious head; he could see all the changing curves of her breast as she breathed. He knew intimately her frock, the rings on her hand, the buckle on her shoe. He knew the whole feel of the room—the buzz of the gas, the peculiarities of the wall-paper, the thick curtain over the door to his right, the folds of the table-cloth. And in his infelicity and in his resentment against Rachel he savoured it all not without pleasure. The mere inviolable solitude with this young, strange, provocative woman in the night beyond the town stimulated him into a sort of zest of living.

There was a small sound from the young woman; her breathing was checked; she had choked down a dry sob. This signal, so faint and so dramatic in the stillness of the parlour, at once intimidated and encouraged him.

"What have you done with that money?" he asked, in a cold voice.

"What money?" Rachel replied, low, without raising her head. Her hand had ceased to move the needle.

"You know what money."

"I took it to Julian, of course."

"Why did you take it to Julian?"

"We agreed I should, last week—you yourself said so—don't you remember?" Her tones acquired some confidence.

"No, I don't remember. I remember something was said about letting him have half of it. Did you give him half or all of it?"

"I gave him all of it."

"I like that! I like that!" Louis remarked sarcastically. "I like your nerve. You do it on the sly. You don't say a word to me; and not content with that, you give him all of it. Why didn't you tell me? Why didn't you ask me for the money?"

Rachel offered no answer.

Louis proceeded with more vivacity. "And did he take it?"

"I made him."

"What? All of it? What reason did you give? How did you explain things?"

"I told him you'd had the rest of the money, of course, so it was all right. It wouldn't have been fair to him if some one hadn't told him."

Louis now seriously convinced himself that his grievance was tremendous, absolutely unexampled in the whole history of marriage.

"Well," said he, with high, gloomy dignity, "it may interest you to know that I didn't have the rest of the money.... If I'd had it, what do you suppose I've done with it?... Over five hundred pounds, indeed!"

"Then what—?"

"I don't think I want any of your 'Then what's.' You wouldn't listen before, so why should you be told now? However, I expect I must teach you a lesson—though it's too late."

Rachel did not move. She heard him say that he had discovered the bank-notes at night, under the chair on the landing. "I took charge of them. I collared them, for the time being," he said. "I happened to be counting them when you knocked at my bedroom door. I admit I was rather taken aback. I didn't want you to see the notes. I didn't see any reason why you should know anything about my aunt's carelessness. You must remember you were only a paid employee then. I was close to the fireplace. I just scrunched them up in my hand and dropped them behind the fire-screen. Of course I meant to pick them up again instantly you'd gone. Well, you didn't go. You seemed as if you wouldn't go. I had to run for the doctor. There was no help for it. Even then I never dreamt you intended to light the fire in that room. It never occurred to me for a second.... And I should have thought anybody lighting a fire couldn't have helped seeing a thing like a ball of bank-notes on the top of the grate. I should have thought so. But it seems I was wrong. When I got back of course the whole blooming thing was up the chimney. Well, there you are! What was I to do? I ask you that."

He paused. Rachel sobbed.

"Of course," he continued, with savage quietude, "you may say I might have forced you to listen to me this last week. I might. But why should I? Why should I beg and pray? If you didn't know the whole story a week ago, is it my fault? I'm not one to ask twice. I can't go on my knees and beg to be listened to. Some fellows could perhaps, but not me!"

Rachel was overwhelmed. The discovery that it was she herself, Pharisaical and unyielding, who had been immediately responsible for the disappearance of the bank-notes almost dazed her. And simultaneously the rehabilitation of her idol drowned her in bliss. She was so glad to be at fault, so ravished at being able to respect him again, that the very ecstasy of existing seemed likely to put an end to her existence. Her physical sensations were such as she might have experienced if her heart had swiftly sunk away out of her bosom and left an empty space there that gasped. She glanced up at Louis.

"I'm so sorry!" she breathed.

Louis did not move, nor did his features relax in the slightest.

With one hand raised in appeal, surrender, abandonment and the other on the arm of her chair, and her work slipping to the floor, she half rose towards him.

"You can't tell how sorry I am!" she murmured. Her eyes were liquid. "Louis!"

"And well you may be, if you'll excuse me saying so!" answered Louis frigidly.

He was confirmed in his illusory but tremendous grievance. The fundamental lack of generosity in him was exposed. Inexperienced though he was in women, he saw in Rachel then, just as if he had been twenty years older, the woman who lightly imagines that the past can be wiped out with a soft tone, an endearment, a tear, a touching appeal. He would not let her off so easily. She had horribly lacerated his dignity for a week—he could recall every single hurt—and he was not going to allow himself to recover in a minute. His dignity required a gradual convalescence. He was utterly unaffected by her wistful charm.

Rachel moved her head somewhat towards his, and then hesitated. The set hardness of his face was incredible to her. Her head began to swim. She thought, "I shall really die if this continues."

"Louis—don't!" she besought him plaintively.

He walked deliberately away and nervously played with an "ornament" on the sideboard.

"And let me tell you another thing," said he slowly. "If you think I came back to-night because I couldn't do without you, you're mistaken. I'm going out again at once."

She said to herself, "He has killed me!" The room circled round her, gathering speed, and Louis with it. The emptiness in her bosom was intolerable.

II

Louis saw her face turning paler and paler, till it was, really, almost as white as the table-cloth. She fell back into the chair, her arms limp and lifeless.

"Confound the girl!" he thought. "She's going to faint now! What an infernal nuisance!"

Compunction, instead of softening him, made him angry with himself. He felt awkward, at a loss, furious.

"Mrs. Tams!" he called out, and hurried from the room. "Mrs. Tams!" As he went out he was rather startled to find that the door had not been quite closed.

In the lobby he called again, "Mrs. Tams!"

The kitchen gas showed a speck of blue. He had not noticed it when he came into the house: the kitchen door must have been shut, then. He looked up the stairs. He could discern that the door of Mrs. Tams's bedroom, at the top, was open, and that there was no light in the room. Puzzled, he rushed to the kitchen, and snatched at his hat as he went, sticking it anyhow on his head.

"Eh, mester, what ever's amiss?"

With these alarmed words Mrs. Tams appeared suddenly from behind the kitchen door; she seemed a little out of breath, as far as Louis could hear; he could not see her very well. The thought flashed through his mind. "She's been listening at doors."

"Oh! There you are," he said, with an effort at ordinariness of demeanour. "Just go in to Mrs. Fores, will you? Something's the matter with her. It's nothing, but I have to go out."

Mrs. Tams answered, trembling: "Nay, mester, I'm none going to interfere. I go into no parlour."

"But I tell you she's fainting."

"Ye'd happen better look after her yerself, Mr. Louis," said Mrs. Tams in a queer voice.

"But don't you understand I've got to go out?"

He was astounded and most seriously disconcerted by Mrs. Tams's very singular behaviour.

"If ye'll excuse me being so bold, sir," said Mrs. Tams, "ye ought for be right well ashamed o' yeself. And that I'll say with my dying breath."

She dropped on to the hard Windsor chair, and, lifting her apron, began to whimper.

Louis could feel himself blushing.

"It seems to me you'd better look out for a fresh situation," he remarked curtly, as he turned to leave the kitchen.

"Happen I had, mester," Mrs. Tams agreed sadly; and then with fire: "But I go into no parlour. You get back to her, mester. Going out again at this time o' night, and missis as her is! If you stop where a husband ought for be, her'll soon mend, I warrant."

He went back, cursing all women, because he had no alternative but to go back. He dared not do otherwise.... It was only a swoon. But was it only a swoon? Suppose ...! He was afraid of public opinion; he was afraid of Mrs. Tams's opinion. Mrs. Tams had pierced him. He went back, dashing his hat on to the oak chest.

III

Rachel was lying on the hearth-rug, one arm stretched nonchalantly over the fender and the hand close to the fire. Her face was whiter than any face he had ever seen, living or dead. He shook; the inanimate figure with the disarranged clothes and hair, prone and deserted there in the solitude of the warm, familiar room, struck terror into him. He bent down; he knelt down and drew the arm away from the fire. He knew not in the least what was the proper thing to do; and naturally the first impulse of his ignorance was to raise her body from the ground. But she was so heavy, so appallingly inert, that, fortunately, he could not do so, and he let her head subside again.

Then he remembered that the proper thing to do in these cases was to loosen the clothes round the neck; but he could not loosen her bodice because it was fastened behind and the hooks were so difficult. He jumped to the window and opened it. The blind curved inward like a sail under the cold entering breeze. When he returned to Rachel he thought he noticed the faintest pinky flush in her cheeks. And suddenly she gave a deep sigh. He knelt again. There was something about the line of her waist that, without any warning, seemed to him ineffably tender, wistful, girlish, seductive. Her whole figure began to exert the same charm over him. Even her frock, which nevertheless was not even her second best, took on a quality that in its simplicity bewitched him. He recalled her wonderful gesture as she lighted his cigarette on the night when he first saw her in her kitchen; and his memory of it thrilled him.... Rachel opened her eyes and sighed deeply once more. He fanned her with a handkerchief drawn from his sleeve.

"Louis!" she murmured in a tired baby's voice, after a few moments.

He thought: "It's a good thing I didn't go out, and I'm glad Mrs. Tarns isn't here blundering about."

"You're better?" he said mildly.

She raised her arms and clasped him, dragging him to her with a force that was amazing under the circumstances. They kissed; their faces were merged for a long time. Then she pushed him a little away, and, guarding his shoulders with her hands, examined his face, and smiled pathetically.

"Call me Louise," she whispered.

"Silly little thing! Shall I get you some water?"

"Call me Louise!"

"Louise!"

CHAPTER XIX
RACHEL AND MR. HORROCLEAVE

I

The next morning, Sunday, Rachel had a fancy to superintend in person the boiling of Louis' breakfast egg. For a week past Louis had not been having his usual breakfast, but on this morning the ideal life was recommencing in loveliest perfection for Rachel. The usual breakfast was to be resumed; and she remembered that in the past the sacred egg had seldom, if ever, been done to a turn by Mrs. Tams. Mrs. Tams, indeed, could not divide a minute into halves, and was apt to regard a preference for a certain consistency in a boiled egg as merely finicking and negligible. To Mrs. Tams a fresh egg was a fresh egg, and there was no more to be said.

Rachel entered the kitchen like a radiance. She was dressed with special care, rather too obviously so, in order that she might be worthy to walk by Louis' side to church. She was going with him to church gladly, because he had rented the pew and she desired to please him by an alert gladness in subscribing to his wishes; it was not enough for her just to do what he wanted. Her eyes glittered above the darkened lower lids; her gaze was self-conscious and yet bold; a faint languor showed beneath her happy energy. But there was no sign that on the previous evening she had been indisposed.

Mrs. Tams was respectfully maternal, but preoccupied. She fetched the egg for Rachel, and Rachel, having deposited it in a cooking-spoon, held it over the small black saucepan of incontestably boiling water until the hand of the clock precisely covered a minute mark, whereupon she deftly slipped the egg into the saucepan; the water ceased to boil for a few seconds and then bubbled up again. And amid the heavenly frizzling of bacon and the odour of her own special coffee Rachel stood sternly watching the clock while Mrs. Tams rattled plates and did the last deeds before serving the meal. Then Mrs. Tarns paused and said—

"I don't hardly like to tell ye, ma'm—I didn't hardly like to tell ye last night when ye were worried like—no, and I dunna like now like, but its like as if what must be—I must give ye notice to leave. I canna stop here no longer."

Rachel turned to her, protesting—

"Now, Mrs. Tams, what *are* you talking about? I thought you were perfectly happy here."

"So I am, mum. Nobody could wish for a better place. I'm sure I've no fault to find. But it's like as if what must be."

"But what's the matter?"

"Well, ma'am, it's Emmy." (Emmy was Mrs. Tams's daughter and the mother of her favourite grandchild.) "Emmy and all on' em seem to think it'll be better all round if I don't take a regular situation, so as I can be more free for 'em, and they'll all look after me i' my old age. I s'll get my old house back, and be among 'em all. There's so many on 'em."

Every sentence contained a lie. And the aged creature went on lying to the same pattern until she had created quite a web of convincing detail—more than enough to persuade her mistress that she was in earnest, foolishly in earnest, that she didn't know on which side her bread was buttered, and that the poorer classes in general had no common sense.

"You're all alike," said the wise Rachel.

"I'm very sorry, ma'm."

"And what am I to do? It's very annoying for me, you know. I thought you were a permanency."

"Yes, ma'am."

"I should like to give your daughters and daughters-in-law a piece of my mind.... Good heavens! Give me that cooking-spoon, quick!"

She nipped the egg out of the saucepan; it was already several seconds overdone.

"It isn't as if I could keep you on as a charwoman," said Rachel. "I must have some one all the time, and I couldn't do with a charwoman as well."

"No, ma'am! It's like as if what must be."

"Well, I hope you'll think it over. I must say I didn't expect this from you, Mrs. Tams."

Mrs. Tams put her lips together and bent obstinately over a tray.

Rachel said to herself: "Oh, she really means to leave! I can see that. She's made up her mind.... I shall never trust any servant again—never!"

She was perhaps a little hurt (for she considered that she had much benefited Mrs. Tams), and a little perturbed for the future. But in her heart she did not care. She would not have cared if the house had fallen in, or if her native land had been invaded and enslaved by a foreign army. She was at peace with Louis. He was hers. She felt that her lien on him was strengthened.

II

The breakfast steaming and odorous on the table, and Rachel all tingling in front of her tray, awaited the descent of the master of the house. The Sunday morning post, placed in its proper position by Mrs. Tams, consisted of a letter and a post-card. Rachel stretched her arm across the table to examine them. The former had a legal aspect. It was a foolscap envelope addressed to Mrs. Maldon. Rachel opened it. A typewritten circular within respectfully pointed out to Mrs. Maldon that if she had only followed the writers' advice, given gratis a few weeks earlier, she would have made one hundred and twenty-five pounds net profit by spending thirty-five pounds in the purchase of an option on Canadian Pacific Railway shares. The statement was supported by the official figures of the Stock Exchange, which none could question. "Can you afford to neglect such advice in future?" the writers asked Mrs. Maldon, and went on to suggest that she should send them forty-five pounds to buy an option on "Shells," which were guaranteed to rise nine points in less than a month.

Mystified, half sceptical, and half credulous, Rachel reflected casually that the world was full of strange phenomena. She wondered what "Shells" were, and why the writers should keep on writing to a woman who had been dead for ages. She carefully burnt both the circular and the envelope.

And then she looked at the post-card, which was addressed to "Louis Fores, Esq." As it was a post-card, she was entitled to read it. She read: "Shall expect you at the works in the morning at ten. Jas. Horrocleave." She thought it rather harsh and oppressive on the part of Mr. Horrocleave to expect Louis to attend at the works on Bank Holiday—and so soon after his illness, too! How did Mr. Horrocleave know that Louis was sufficiently recovered to be able to go to the works at all?

Louis came, rubbing his hands, which for an instant he warmed at the fire. He was elegantly dressed. The mere sight of him somehow thrilled

Rachel. His deportment, his politeness, his charming good-nature were as striking as ever. The one or two stripes (flesh-coloured now, not whitish) on his face were not too obvious, and, indeed, rather increased the interest of his features. The horrible week was forgotten, erased from history, though Rachel would recollect that even at the worst crisis of it Louis had scarcely once failed in politeness of speech. It was she who had been impolite—not once, but often. Louis had never raged. She was contrite, and her penitence intensified her desire to please, to solace, to obey. When she realized that it was she who had burnt that enormous sum in bank-notes, she went cold in the spine.

Not that she cared twopence for the enormous sum, really, now that concord was established! No, her little flutters of honest remorse were constantly disappearing in the immense exultant joy of being alive and of contemplating her idol. Louis sat down. She smiled at him. He smiled back. But in his exquisite demeanour there was a faint reserve of melancholy which persisted. She had not yet that morning been able to put it to flight; she counted, however, on doing so very soon, and in the meantime it did not daunt her. After all, was it not natural?

She began—

"I say, what do you think? Mrs. Tams has given me notice."

She pretended to be aggrieved and to be worried, but essential joy shone through these absurd masks. Moreover, she found a certain naïve satisfaction in being a mistress with cares, a mistress to whom "notice" had to be given, and who would have to make serious inquiry into the character of future candidates for her employment.

Louis raised his eyebrows.

"Don't you think it's a shame?"

"Oh," said he cautiously, "you'll get somebody else as good, *and* better. What's she leaving for?"

Rachel repeated Mrs. Tams's rigmarole.

"Ah!" murmured Louis.

He was rather sorry for Mrs. Tams. His good-nature was active enough this morning. But he was glad that she had taken the initiative. And he was content that she should go. After the scene of the previous night, their relations could not again have been exactly what the relations between master and servant ought to be. And further, "you never knew what women wouldn't tell one another," even mistress and maid, maid and mistress. Yes, he preferred that she should leave. He admired her and regretted the hardship on the old woman—and that was an end of it! What could he do to ease her? The only thing to do would be to tell her privately that so far as he was concerned she might stay. But he had no intention of doing aught so foolish. It was strange, but he was entirely unconscious of any obligation to her for the immense service she had rendered him. His conclusion was that some people have to be martyrs. And in this he was deeply right.

Rachel, misreading his expression, thought that he did not wish to be bothered with household details. She recalled some gratuitous advice half humorously offered to her by a middle-aged lady at her reception, "Never talk servants to your men." She had thought, at the time, "I shall talk everything with *my* husband." But she considered that she was wiser now.

"By the way," she said in a new tone, "there's a post-card for you. I've read it. Couldn't help."

Louis read the post-card. He paled, and Rachel noticed his pallor. The fact was that in his mind he had simply shelved, and shelved again, the threat of James Horrocleave. He had sincerely desired to tell a large portion of the truth to Rachel, taking advantage of her soft mood; but he could not; he could not force his mouth to open on the subject. In some hours he had quite forgotten the danger—he was capable of such feats—then it reasserted itself and he gazed on it fascinated and helpless. When Rachel, to please him and prove her subjugation, had suggested that they should go to church—"for the Easter morning service"—he had concurred, knowing, nevertheless, that he dared not fail to meet Horrocleave at the works. On the whole, though it gave him a shock, he was relieved that Horrocleave had sent the post-card and that Rachel had seen it. But he still was quite unable to decide what to do.

"It's a nice thing, him asking you to go to the works on a Bank Holiday like that!" Rachel remarked.

Louis answered: "It's not to-morrow he wants me. It's to-day."

"Sunday!" she exclaimed.

"Yes. I met him for a second yesterday afternoon, and he told me then. This was just a reminder. He must have sent it off last night. A good thing he did send it, though. I'd quite forgotten."

"But what is it? What does he want you to go on Sunday for?"

Louis shrugged his shoulders, as if to intimate that nothing that Horrocleave did ought to surprise anybody.

"Then what about church?"

Louis replied on the spur of the moment—

"You go there by yourself. I'll meet you there. I can easily be there by eleven."

"But I don't know the pew."

"They'll show you your pew all right, never fear."

"I shall wait for you in the churchyard."

"Very well. So long as it isn't raining."

She kissed him fervently when he departed.

Long before it was time to leave for church she had a practical and beautiful idea—one of those ideas that occur to young women in love. Instead of waiting for Louis in the churchyard she would call for him at the works, which was not fifty yards off the direct route to St. Luke's. By this means she would save herself from the possibility of inconvenience within the precincts of the church, and she would also prevent the conscienceless Mr. Horrocleave from keeping Louis in the office all the morning. She wondered that the idea had not occurred to Louis, who was very gifted in such matters as the arrangement of rendezvous.

She started in good time because she wanted to walk without hurry, and to ponder. The morning, though imperfect and sunless, had in it some quality of the spring, which the buoyant youth of Rachel instantly discovered and tasted in triumph. Moreover, the spirit of a festival was abroad, and visible in the costume and faces of passers-by; and it was the first festival of the year. Rachel responded to it eagerly, mingling her happiness with the general exultation. She was intensely, unreasonably happy. She knew that she was unreasonably happy; and she did not mind.

When she turned into Friendly Street the big black double gates of the works were shut, but in one of them a little door stood ajar. She pushed it, stooped, and entered the twilight of the archway. The office door was shut. She walked uncertain up the archway into the yard, and through a dirty window on her left she could dimly discern a man gesticulating. She decided that he must be Horrocleave. She hesitated, and then, slightly confused, thought, "Perhaps I'd better go back to the archway and knock at the office door."

III

In the inner office, among art-lustre ware, ink-stained wood, dusty papers, and dirt, Jim Horrocleave banged down a petty-cash book on to Louis' desk. His hat was at the back of his head, and his eyes blazed at Louis, who stood somewhat limply, with a hesitant, foolish, faint smile on his face.

"That's enough!" said Horrocleave fiercely. "I haven't had patience to go all through it. But that's enough. I needn't tell ye I suspected ye last year, but ye put me off. And I was too busy to take the trouble to go into it. However, I've had a fair chance while you've been away." He gave a sneering laugh. "I'll tell ye what put me on to ye again, if you've a mind to know. The weekly expenses went down as soon as ye thought I had suspicions. Ye weren't clever enough to keep 'em up. Well, what have ye got to say for yeself, seeing ye are on yer way to America?"

"I never meant to go to America," said Louis. "Why should I go to America?"

"Ask me another. Then ye confess?"

"I don't," said Louis.

"Oh! Ye don't!" Horrocleave sat down and put his hands on his outstretched knees.

"There may be mistakes in the petty-cash book. I don't say there aren't. Any one who keeps a petty-cash book stands to lose. If he's too busy at the moment to enter up a payment, he may forget it—and there you are! He's out of pocket. Of course," Louis added, with a certain loftiness, "as you're making a fuss about it I'll pay up for anything that's wrong ... whatever the sum is. If you make it out to be a hundred pounds I'll pay up."

Horrocleave growled: "Oh, so ye'll pay up, will ye? And suppose I won't let ye pay up? What shall ye do then?"

Louis, now quite convinced that Horrocleave was only bullying retorted, calmly:

"It's I that ought to ask you that question."

The accuser was exasperated.

"A couple o' years in quod will be about your mark, I'm thinking," he said.

Whereupon Louis was suddenly inspired to answer:

"Yes. And supposing I was to begin to talk about illicit commissions?"

Horrocleave jumped up with such ferocious violence that Louis drew back, startled. The recent Act of Parliament, making a crime of secret commissions to customers' employees, had been a blow to the trade in art-lustre ware, and it was no secret in the inner office that Horrocleave, resenting its interference with the natural course of business, had more than once discreetly flouted it, and thus technically transgressed the criminal law. Horrocleave used to defend and justify himself by the use of that word "technical." Louis' polite and unpremeditated threat enraged him to an extreme degree. He was the savage infuriate. He cared for no consequences, even consequences to himself. He hated Louis because Louis was spick and span, and quiet, and because Louis had been palmed off on him by Louis' unscrupulous respectable relatives as an honest man.

"Now thou'st done for thyself!" he cried, in the dialect. "Thou'st done for thyself! And I'll have thee by the heels for embezzlement, and blackmail as well." He waved his arms. "May God strike me if I give thee any quarter after that! I'll—"

He stopped with open mouth, disturbed by the perception of a highly strange phenomenon beyond the window. He looked and saw Rachel in the yard. For a moment he thought that Louis had planned to use his wife as a shield in the affair if the worst should come to the worst. But Rachel's appearance simultaneously showed him that he was wrong. She was the very mirror of happy confidence. And she seemed so young, and so obviously just married; and so girlish and so womanish at the same time; and her frock was so fresh, and her hat so pert against the heavy disorder of the yard, and her eyes were unconsciously so wistful—that Horrocleave caught his breath. He contrasted Rachel with Mrs. Horrocleave, her complete antithesis, and at once felt very sorry for himself and very scornful of Mrs. Horrocleave, and melting with worshipful sympathy for Rachel.

"Yer wife's in the yard," he whispered in a different tone.

"My wife!" Louis was gravely alarmed; all his manner altered.

"Hast told her anything of this?"

"I should think I hadn't."

"Ye must pay me, and I'll give ye notice to leave," said Horrocleave, quickly, in a queer, quiet voice. The wrath was driven out of him. The mere apparition of Rachel had saved her husband.

A silence.

Rachel had disappeared. Then there was a distant tapping. Neither of the men spoke nor moved. They could hear the outer door open and light footfalls in the outer office.

"Anybody here?" It was Rachel's voice, timid.

"Come in, come in!" Horrocleave roared.

She entered, blushing, excusing herself, glancing from one to the other, and by her spotless Easter finery emphasizing the squalor of the den.

In a few minutes Horrocleave was saying to Rachel, rather apologetically—

"Louis and I are going to part company, Mrs. Fores. I can't keep him on. His wages are too high for me. It won't run to it. Th' truth is, I'm going to chuck this art business. It doesn't pay. Art, as they call it, 's no good in th' pottery trade."

Rachel said, "So that's what you wanted to see him about on a Sunday morning, is it, Mr. Horrocleave?"

She was a little hurt at the slight on her husband, but the wife in her was persuaded that the loss would be Mr. Horrocleave's. She foresaw that Louis would now want to use his capital in some commercial undertaking of his own; and she was afraid of the prospect. Still, it had to be faced, and she would face it. He would probably do well as his own master. During a whole horrible week her judgment on him had been unjustly severe, and she did not mean to fall into the same sin again. She thought with respect of his artistic gifts, which she was too inartistic to appreciate. Yes, the chances were that he would succeed admirably.

She walked him off to church, giving Horrocleave a perfunctory good-bye. And as, shoulder to shoulder, they descended towards St. Luke's, she looked sideways at Louis and fed her passion stealthily with the sight. True, even in those moments, she had heart enough left to think of others besides.

She hoped that John's Ernest would find a suitable mate. She remembered that she had Julian's curtains to attend to. She continued to think kindly of Thomas Batchgrew, and she chid herself for having thought of him in her distant inexperienced youth, of six months earlier, as *that man*. And, regretting that Mrs. Tams—at her age, too!—could be so foolish, she determined to look after Mrs. Tams also, if need should arise. But these solicitudes were mere downy trifles floating on the surface of her profound absorption in Louis. And in the depths of that absorption she felt secure, and her courage laughed at the menace of life (though the notion of braving a church full of people did intimidate the bride). Yet she judged Louis realistically and not sentimentally. She was not conspicuously blind to any aspect of his character; nor had the tremendous revulsion of the previous night transformed him into another and a more heavenly being for her. She admitted frankly to herself that he was not blameless in the dark affair of the bank-notes. She would not deny that in some ways he was untrustworthy, and might be capable of acts of which the consequences were usually terrible. His irresponsibility was notorious. And, being impulsive herself, she had no mercy for his impulsiveness. As for his commonsense, was not her burning of the circular addressed to Mrs. Maldon a sufficient commentary on it?

She was well aware that Louis' sins of omission and commission might violently shock people of a certain temperament—people of her own temperament in particular. These people, however, would fail to see the other side of Louis. If she herself had merely heard of Louis, instead of knowing him, she would probably have set him down as undesirable. But she knew him. His good qualities seemed to her to overwhelm the others. His charm, his elegance, his affectionateness, his nice speech, his courtesy, his quick wit, his worldliness—she really considered it extraordinary that a plain, blunt girl, such as she, should have had the luck to please him. It was indeed almost miraculous.

If he had faults—and he had—she preferred them (proudly and passionately) to the faults of scores of other women's husbands. He was not a brute, nor even a boor nor a savage—thousands of savages ranged free and terror-striking in the Five Towns. Even when vexed and furious he could control himself. It was possible to share his daily life and see him in all his social moods without being humiliated. He was not a clodhopper; watch him from the bow-window of a morning as he walked down the street! He did not drink; he was not a beast. He was not mean. He might scatter money, but he was not mean. In fact, except that one sinister streak in his nature, she could detect no fault. There was danger in that streak.... Well, there was danger in every man. She would accept it; she would watch it. Had she not long since reconciled herself to the prospect of an everlasting vigil?

She did not care what any one said, and she did not care! He was the man she wanted; the whole rest of the world was nothing in comparison to him. He was irresistible. She had wanted him, and she would always want him, as he was. She had won him and she would keep him, as he was, whatever the future might hold. The past was the past; the opening chapter of her marriage was definitely finished and its drama done. She was ready for the future. One tragedy alone could overthrow her—Louis' death. She simply could not and would not conceive existence without him. She would face anything but that.... Besides, he was not *really* untrustworthy—only weak! She faltered and recovered. "He's mine and I wouldn't have him altered for the world. I don't want him perfect. If anything goes wrong, well, let it go wrong! I'm his wife. I'm his!" And as, slightly raising her confident chin in the street, she thus undertook to pay the price of love, there was something divine about Rachel's face.